Christopher Hinz

REFRACTION

**ANGRY
ROBOT**

ANGRY ROBOT
An imprint of Watkins Media Ltd

Unit 11, Shepperton House
89 Shepperton Road
London N1 3DF
UK

NOV - '21

angryrobotbooks.com
twitter.com/angryrobotbooks

An Angry Robot paperback original, 2020

Copyright © Christopher Hinz 2020

Cover by Kieryn Tyler
Edited by Robin Triggs and Paul Simpson
Set in Meridien

ISBN 978 0 85766 865 3
Ebook ISBN 978 0 85766 866 0

Printed and bound in the United Kingdom by TJ International.

9 8 7 6 5 4 3 2 1

To the stout of heart who face daily challenges: the shackles of disenfranchisement, the viral and the vitriolic.

PART 1
THE KIDS

ONE

Most days Henry Carpousis worried about something. Recurring anxieties included losing his job, getting mugged or contracting a flesh-eating disease. But, thirteen hundred miles from home on this warm April afternoon, he had a new concern.

Running into a killer grizzly.

The bears were active in this part of Montana's Rockies according to a local they'd encountered at a convenience store.

"Wouldn't head into back country without a rifle," the man had warned. "You'll be sorry sons of bitches if you meet a grizzly havin' a bad hair day."

Their guide, Greg Mahoney, insisted they carry no firearms. A retro hippie with ponytailed hair and bandanna, he got all weirded out if you even mentioned guns.

"Almost there," Greg said, checking coordinates on his GPS app. He pointed up the slope of the dry ravine they were traversing toward a clump of eighty-foot evergreens. "It should be just past those trees."

Thank God. Henry was winded by the exertion. He was fifty-five years old and more than a few pounds overweight. His friend Loren Childs, the third member of their group, also boasted a middle-aged gut. Greg was half their ages and in peak condition. He was one of those stalwart types, flush with wilderness savvy: just what city-breeds like Henry and Loren needed on such a trek. Still, Henry wished Greg had brought a rifle.

They'd hiked miles from the campsite, far from help should trouble arise. Cell phone reception was nonexistent. Henry's only weapon was bear spray. Back home in Milwaukee, he'd rigged his can of deterrent to a belt holster and spent hours practicing quick-draws.

Loren bubbled with excitement. "Oh, man, can you believe it! We're finally going to see 'em!"

"Just hope we can get close enough," Henry said, trying to concentrate on their quarry, the sole reason for risking a vacation week in grizzly-infested mountains.

Greg selected the least intimidating path up the ravine. Even so, it was a steep climb: nearly forty-five degrees in spots. Henry was soon breathing hard and worrying he'd miss a foothold, tumble to the bottom and suffer a broken back.

But he reached the top without incident and acknowledged a sense of conquest. The feeling didn't last. The weathered sign nailed to a wiry pine ignited fresh concerns.

RESTRICTED AREA WARNING
DEPARTMENT OF DEFENSE TRANSPORT CORRIDOR
NO TRESPASSING

Smaller lettering listed sanctions facing violators, including arrest and prosecution under an array of federal statutes.

"Maybe we should turn back."

Loren rolled his eyes, accustomed to Henry's apprehensions.

"Don't worry," Greg said. "Tau Nine-One is eight miles away. They won't have electronic surveillance this far out. The sign is just meant to scare you."

Henry grimaced. *It's doing its job.*

Greg led them into prohibited territory. They emerged from the trees onto a ridge overlooking a narrow valley.

"Stay low," Greg warned, ducking behind a line of bushes flanking the edge. Henry and Loren followed suit.

They were a couple hundred feet above the railroad that

meandered along the valley floor. The single track emerged from a natural tunnel of Douglas firs and deciduous trees to their left and vaulted a wide stream on a rock-ballasted truss bridge, its angular framework pockmarked with rust. After crossing the stream, the track swept into a tight S-curve to avoid a series of rocky outcroppings then vanished back into dense forest.

"Fantastic view," Loren whispered.

They'd chosen the location by studying Google Earth and US Geological Survey maps. What looked good from a distance often proved disappointing when actually on-site, but in this instance they'd nailed it.

Loren set up his tripod and still camera and Henry did the same with his trusty Samsung camcorder. Still, he couldn't allay the fear that they were too close.

"What if someone spots us from the train?"

"Stop being a wuss," Loren snapped. "We're gonna nail some great shots. ROM will go crazy!"

ROM was Railmasters of Milwaukee, their hometown club. Like many long-time members, Henry and Loren ventured far from their urban enclave in search of classic trains.

Greg fluffed his backpack into a pillow and stretched out on the dry ground. "Siesta time for me, trainspotters. Wake me when the choo-choo shows."

Henry didn't like the term *trainspotters*, which was often used to make fun of railfans. It was a bit unsettling being out here with someone not involved in the hobby. But Greg, a trucker whose route included the brewery where Henry and Loren worked, had made it clear that pristine Montana wilderness was the attraction, not documenting old locomotives.

And Greg had proved invaluable. Henry and Loren originally had intended to contact the Department of Defense for permission to document the train. Greg had dissuaded them, warning that not only would such a request be denied, it could trigger a Homeland Security investigation.

Tau Nine-One was a top-secret installation. Greg had even

tapped some military acquaintances for info but had learned little about the facility.

The winding sixteen-mile track connected Tau Nine-One with the small town of Churchton Summit to the south. The line was a surviving branch of a defunct carrier, the Milwaukee Road, built to reach early twentieth century gold and silver mines. Following the Milwaukee Road's abandonment in 1977, the DOD had purchased the severed right-of-way and a set of vintage locomotives and passenger coaches.

Henry was hungry. Even though he'd read that grizzlies could smell food up to eighteen miles away, he took a chance and opened a bag of peanuts.

An hour passed. Greg popped awake and got to his feet as the unmistakable growl of a vintage diesel engine echoed through the woods. The sound emanated from their left. The train was coming from Tau Nine-One as expected, on its late-afternoon southward trek ferrying workers back to Churchton Summit. It ran two daily round trips seven days a week: an early morning run to the complex, usually in darkness, and this one.

Henry double-checked the image in the Samsung's viewfinder, adjusted the shotgun mike and hit the record button. He would shoot a panorama, documenting the train as it emerged from the trees and crossed the bridge. Loren would nail close-up stills with his zoom. Tomorrow they would get additional shots from public property near Churchton Summit's enclosed, run-through passenger station. At next month's ROM meeting they would have all the ingredients for a dynamite presentation.

The roar of 1,500 horsepower diesel engines increased. Henry's excitement grew, until he caught a flash of movement beyond the bridge. His first thought was that it was a grizzly. But a closer look identified it as a different sort of animal.

A man, his camouflage attire blending him into the foliage. He held some sort of electronic device. If he was a railfan, he was certainly audacious. Henry never would have risked getting that close, even to record locomotive sounds.

The man turned and stared straight up at them. Henry froze, heart pounding, certain they'd been spotted. Abruptly, the man sprinted toward the bridge pier on the north side of the stream and ducked out of sight under the span.

The train slithering from the trees captured Henry's attention. The back-to-back locomotives with streamlined contours were gorgeous: vintage F7s built by the EMD division of General Motors, circa 1949. Tapering noses gave them a regal look, an effect softened by their drab color, army brown. Two men, an engineer and conductor, were visible in the cab of the lead diesel. The second loco was a slave unit, unoccupied. Their flanks were devoid of lettering except for DODX beneath the cab windows, a common reporting mark for military trains.

The locos pulled four passenger coaches in a similar shade of brown. Although the coaches were vintage pre-World War Two heavyweights with turtleback roofs, their windows had been retrofitted with modern shaded glass. It was impossible to see inside.

The locos slowed as they passed over the stream and entered the tight S-curve. And then the train was gone, again enveloped by wilderness. Henry left the camcorder running to capture the retreating whine of the F7s. He was pleased. They'd gotten what they'd come for.

"You're trespassin'. This is restricted property."

The three of them whirled. A man wearing a backpack stood in the trees behind them, garbed in camo like the earlier watcher. A holstered pistol hung from his belt. Tall and lean, he had a pale complexion, short-cropped red hair and a thin mustache. He sounded Scottish, or at least the version of Scottish that Henry had grown up hearing on TV. But there was another accent in there as well, maybe something Eastern European.

He wore a faint smile. Henry had the impression he was trying to contain amusement at having startled them.

"We were just shooting the train," Henry babbled. "We're from Railmasters of Milwaukee."

"Sorry to hear that, mate. You carryin' firearms?"

Henry vigorously shook his head. "No sir, absolutely not!"

The man whipped out the pistol and pointed it at them. "You'll be comin' with me." He gestured toward the woods, motioning for them to walk in front.

"What about our cameras?" Loren asked.

"They'll be confiscated."

Greg stood his ground. "Confiscated by whom?"

"Special Security Service."

"I'd like to see some ID."

"Shut up and move your asses."

Greg took the lead, followed by Henry, Loren, and their captor. Henry felt sick. They were going to be arrested. Even if he evaded prison, he'd have a criminal record. The brewery would fire him. Without steady income, he'd go bankrupt, lose his apartment, and end up living in the gutter.

Greg's boot snared a vine. As he leaned over to untangle himself, Henry realized he'd faked the mishap in order to slip a hunting knife from an ankle sheath. Greg pocketed the knife and whispered in Henry's ear. "This guy's not right. There is no Special Security Service. Only US Marines guard Tau Nine-One. We may have to take him down."

Henry's dread reached new heights. *Take him down! Oh, God, this isn't happening!*

"No talkin'," the man barked. "Keep movin'."

They reached the top of the steep ravine. The man ordered them to turn around at the edge. He spoke into a small mike on the lapel of his jacket. Henry noticed he wore an ear bud. Considering the area's lack of reception, it must be a radio rather than a phone.

"Kokay, we've got a little problem. My location, on the double."

The man studied each of their faces before settling his attention on Henry. "OK, video man. You going to tell me what you chaps are really doing out here? And no rubbish about watchin' trains."

"But it's the truth," Henry said. "I swear, that's the only reason we're here! Honest, we didn't mean to trespass."

Loren nodded vigorously. The man turned his attention to Greg. "You don't look the part, mate. Not an anorak?"

"Anorak?"

"Railway nerd." The smile radiated no warmth.

"He's our guide," Loren said.

Henry struggled to remain calm and not give in to escalating fear. Loren looked more indignant than upset, probably concerned about their cameras being confiscated. Whatever Greg was feeling, he hid it well. His attention remained riveted on their captor.

A second man, the one referred to as Kokay, emerged from the trees. He was the figure who'd ducked under the bridge. Dark-skinned and with the build of a linebacker, he had several electronic devices hanging from his belt. Henry had no idea what their function was.

Kokay scowled. "Hell of a mess, Nobe. Whadda we do now?"

The newcomer had a deep Southern drawl. The left side of his face didn't move when he spoke, as if some of the muscles were paralyzed.

"The Clerk will decide," Nobe said. "Watch 'em."

Kokay drew his sidearm. Nobe retreated a few paces into the forest and got back on the radio. Henry couldn't make out what he was saying.

Nobe finished the call and returned. "The Clerk's gonna send a shadow."

Kokay gazed uneasily into the surrounding woods, troubled by the impending arrival of the shadow. Whatever *that* was.

Henry made another attempt at convincing their captors of innocent intentions. But Nobe wagged his finger, warning him to be silent. He clamped his mouth shut and waited.

A few minutes later, the space between Nobe and Kokay darkened. A strange figure took shape, hovering several inches above the ground. It appeared to be a man in jeans and a pullover sweater. His face was hidden by what appeared to be a cheap version of a *King Kong* Halloween mask.

Henry squinted, trying to wrap his head around what he was

seeing. The ape-faced figure was partially translucent. Bits and pieces of the forested background occasionally became visible through his body. Was it some newfangled kind of hologram, a 3D image transmitted from a distant location?

Nobe spoke to the mysterious figure over the radio. "Trainspotters. Wrong place at the wrong time."

Henry could see the man's lips moving under the mask. Although he heard nothing, it was apparent the figure was responding through Nobe's ear bud. Hearing only one side of the conversation elevated Henry's fear.

"I agree... Uh-huh, not a problem, we're far enough from Tau... Consider it done."

The ominous dialogue ended. Nobe turned to Kokay and gestured to the electronic gear on his belt.

"Get what you need?"

Kokay nodded.

"Take off. Encrypt everything and upload the data."

Kokay gave a wary glance at the spectral figure before sprinting into the trees. Nobe returned his attention to the three of them.

"Well now, mates. We need a volunteer to get things off on the right foot. Any takers?"

"Takers for what?" Loren demanded, planting hands on hips and glaring at Nobe. Henry had seen such behavior by his friend in the past. You could only push Loren so far before he became blustery and indignant.

Nobe smiled. Then he lunged forward and landed a brutal kick to Loren's midsection.

One moment, Henry's friend was by his side. An instant later he was flying backward off the ravine.

Loren frantically pirouetted his arms as he fell. Twenty feet down, his head slammed a rock with sickening force. A series of violent somersaults followed. He landed face up amid thickets at the bottom. It was obvious from the way Loren's neck was twisted that he was dead.

Henry felt faint, unable to process such madness. He wanted to sit down, wanted to eat something, wanted to ask why the world had stopped making sense. But he was too frightened to speak. His vocal cords refused to shape words.

Greg whipped out his knife and fell into a defensive crouch. Nobe aimed his pistol between Greg's eyes.

"Not too smart. Drop it."

"Rot in hell."

Henry's attention was drawn back to the figure, which was becoming increasingly translucent. In seconds it was gone.

Greg kept his attention on Nobe, who seemed amused. Removing his backpack, Nobe tossed it and his gun on the ground behind him. He unsheathed a combat knife.

"Like your style, mate. Let's see what ya got."

Greg lunged, aiming for Nobe's belly. But Nobe moved like a wildcat, twisting sideways and gliding effortlessly from Greg's path.

Henry watched in mute terror as the combatants warily circled one another. He knew he should be doing something, helping Greg somehow, maybe trying to reach Nobe's discarded gun, maybe just running away from this insanity. But his fear was overwhelming. Muscles refused to obey.

Nobe dodged another slash from Greg's blade. In a blur of motion, he caught Greg's extended forearm and wrenched his knife hand backward.

Greg released a muffled scream. The knife slipped from his fingers. He leaned over to snatch it from the ground with his other hand. But before he could recover the weapon, Nobe grabbed him from behind in a choke hold and violently twisted.

Greg's eyes widened with shock as his neck snapped. His lips parted, as if trying to shape words. No sounds emerged. A shudder coursed through him. He crumpled to the dirt at the edge of the ravine.

Nobe stuck a boot under Greg's midsection and shoved the body down the slope. Greg rolled and tumbled to the bottom, landing a few yards away from Loren.

Henry felt disembodied, as if he was another person, as if the horror and madness of these events were happening to someone else.

Nobe retrieved and holstered his pistol. It was just the two of them now, alone at the edge. His captor offered an apologetic smile.

"Sorry about this. Way it's gotta be."

Henry knew he was going to die. But at that moment of recognition, some latent survival instinct took control of his frozen limbs.

He pivoted and leaped off the edge, began running down the wall of the ravine. Surprisingly, he managed to stay on his feet for the first dozen or so strides. But then gravity and his out-of-control acceleration exceeded any capacity for remaining upright.

He fell forward. His boot caught a rock. He tumbled down the last half of the hill with the fury of a dislodged boulder.

He came to a bone-jarring stop against something warm and soft. A hundred pains tore through him. He knew he must be covered in bruises from head to toe. But, amazingly, no bones seemed broken.

He staggered upright, saw that his right palm was covered in blood. The blood had come from Loren, whose body he'd plowed into. His friend had served to cushion his fall.

Henry didn't pause to consider his good fortune. Dashing for the trees on the other side of the ravine, he whipped his head back to the top. Nobe remained at the edge, calmly gazing down. But he hadn't drawn his gun and was making no move to pursue.

Why isn't he coming after me?

Loud crunching noises erupted from Henry's right. It sounded like heavy footsteps on dry underbrush. He whirled. In one jarring instant he knew the answer to his question.

Seven hundred pounds of grizzly towered over him. Somehow, Henry maintained enough presence of mind to whip the can of repellent from his belt.

He never got the chance to depress the trigger. A four-inch claw raked his shoulder, knocking the bear spray from his grasp. He screamed as chocolate fur stinking of moldy earth enveloped him. The last thing Henry saw before the world went dark was a giant paw descending toward his face.

TWO

His world is green. He is its prisoner.

Everything shimmers with verdant hues: limes and olives; mosses, hollies and teals; other green tints too obscure to merit names.

The bars of his cell gleam emerald. They terminate overhead in a railing of jade. Above the railing, two men and a woman gaze down upon him like omnipotent gods, their faces blurred by a green haze the color of late summer grass.

A female voice – resolute, commanding – emanates from somewhere beyond the three figures. The words seem familiar. Their meaning is cryptic.

"Singularity beguiles, transcend the illusion."

Aiden Manchester snapped awake from the green dream to the wailing shrieks of a child. Rolling out of bed, he bolted into the second-floor hallway and dashed to the front of the house. Taking steps two at a time, he raced up to the third floor.

Leah's door was open. He rushed in, flipped on the overhead light. His seven year-old niece was awake and upright in bed, her tiny hands pasted across her chest, her elfin face twisted into a rictus of fear.

"It's all right, honey," he said, peeling back a bedsheet patterned with Disney princesses to sit beside her. "Just a nightmare."

She wrapped Aiden in a bear hug and buried her face against

his chest. He stroked her curly blond hair and whispered soothing words until her little body began to relax.

"You'll be OK now. It's over."

She released him and turned to gaze out the dormer window. The golden light of daybreak backlit the gauze curtains. A Mickey Mouse wall clock with ridiculously large hands indicated 6:05.

"Want to go back to sleep?" Aiden asked, stifling a yawn and hoping for an affirmative response. He'd gotten to bed late after polishing off the better part of a six-pack of Yuengling. The beer, along with a forgettable cable movie, had served to power down his consciousness. A few more hours under the covers before rebooting would be nice.

"I want to get up," Leah said.

"Up it is then. I'll go down and start breakfast."

"Can I have waffles?"

"You had waffles yesterday. Sure you don't want cereal?"

She gave him *the look*, that blend of vulnerability and longing that melted away resistance. The look was so potent that it could get through to Aiden even on those occasions when he was nearly passed out drunk.

"OK, but if you turn into a giant waffle, don't blame me."

He ruffled her hair and extended his arm for their customary fist bump. Returning to his room, he slipped jeans over his boxers and trotted down the back staircase to the kitchen below.

An unpleasant surprise awaited him. Overnight, a chunkie had manifested. The brown mass had touched down on the countertop next to the oven. Worse, it had made landfall right atop his sister's new four-slot, Cuisinart toaster. She'd bought the appliance only last week.

"Shit," he muttered. "Shit, shit, *shit*!"

The toaster was ruined. The gelatinous glob had flowed down into the slots. Separating a chunkie from the inner mechanism would be a time-consuming task, likely requiring complete disassembly.

And that presumed the mass remained malleable enough to

attempt cleanup. Chunkies hardened fast from exposure to air. To scrape out every squishy bit, Aiden would have had to discover the manifestation within an hour or so of arrival. Considering that chunkies always made landfall while he slept, this one was probably too far gone.

Probing with a fingernail confirmed his guess. Rock solid. Cleanup would require hammer, a chisel, and sixteen-grit sandpaper.

His first thought was to replace the toaster before his sister got home from her night shift at the hospital. But that was less than two hours away. Nearby stores didn't open this early. And Aiden's sandy hair likely would turn gray before Amazon drones offered ultra-express deliveries to small towns like Birdsboro, Pennsylvania.

Which meant Darlene was going to bitch up a storm. His sister knew about his chunkies, of course, had come to accept the weird ability of her only sibling. But that wouldn't stop her from reaming him a new asshole. These days she was touchy as hell, on his case about being always out of work and never far from a six-pack.

He returned his attention to the manifestation. At inception, it would have had typical dimensions. Like all chunkies, it would have materialized in midair as a gelatinous brown sphere the size of a child's soccer ball. Snared by gravity, it would have dropped instantly. Had the chunkie landed on a flat surface, it would have spread into a thick pancake.

That hadn't happened here, the toaster preventing such a perfect configuration. The bits that hadn't fallen into the slots drooped over the sides. The impression was that the appliance had puked up its innards.

Aiden was nearly thirty and had been manifesting chunkies in his sleep since age twelve – the onset of puberty and a scant five months before his parents' untimely deaths in a car accident. During the short period Dad was still around, they'd set up video cameras and hooked Aiden up to an EEG monitor to try figuring out what was happening neurologically when a chunkie appeared.

Dad was no doctor, but he'd confirmed that Aiden was the cause. The EEG exhibited unusual spikes when a manifestation appeared, always during Aiden's deepest stage 4 sleep.

But they'd never been able to figure out what those spikes meant. Even today, Aiden had no idea what chunkies were or where they came from, or why he had such a freakish ability. All they'd confirmed was that a chunkie originated no farther away from him than about ten feet in any direction.

Fortunately, none had ever formed directly overhead and landed on him. But, having lived with Darlene on and off in various houses and apartments, they'd always made sure their bedrooms weren't too close. When Aiden had been fired from his last job and forced to give up his apartment, Darlene insisted he take the back room over the kitchen. It was as much of a separation as her old house could handle.

He peeled open a trash bag and eased the messy toaster into it, using moist paper towels to avoid touching the manifestation. A few bits of it might still be gooey. He'd once tried picking up a fresh chunkie and spent hours scraping the glue-like mass from his hands. The stuff adhered to flesh like Post-it notes from hell.

He twist-tied the bag and set it by the back door. About the only good thing about chunkies was that he knew someone who would buy them. Cash was tight since that idiot supervisor at Hardware Haven fired him just for taking a quick nap behind the shipping dock.

"Uncle Aiden, what's that?"

He whipped around, startled by Leah's voice. She stood in the doorway in pink pajamas clutching her favorite stuffed animal, Grumpy Cat.

"What's what?" he asked, stepping in front of the bag in a futile attempt to hide it.

"The trash doesn't go out until Monday night and it's only Thursday."

He loved Leah madly but didn't like that she was already picking up some of her mother's fastidious and rigid ways. What seven year-old was concerned about what day the goddamn trash was put out?

"I'm just getting rid of some smelly stuff," he lied.

"Mommy uses the small white bags for the smelly stuff."

That's not how Uncle Aiden does things, he wanted to retort, but held his tongue.

Leah hopped onto her seat at the table. Her gaze went to the countertop, expecting to see her waffles about to pop. She frowned when she realized the appliance was gone.

"Where's the toaster?"

"Broken. Sorry, kiddo, but no frozen waffles today. How about I mix up a batch of fresh pancakes?"

"OK." She brightened into a smile, for the moment forgetting about missing toasters and proper methods of trash disposal.

He fixed breakfast. Leah poured an ungodly amount of syrup on her pancakes but he didn't chide her the way her mother would have. *Let the kid be a kid,* he'd said to his sister in a similar situation last week, which had caused Darlene to go ballistic and pin him to the mats with one of her patented lectures about approved childrearing methods. He wouldn't step into that takedown again.

Watching Leah eat brought up a new concern. This was at least the third nightmare his niece had suffered since Aiden moved in. Darlene said they'd been happening regularly over the past year.

He recalled having nightmares at Leah's age. They'd ended around the time the manifestations began and seemed to have no connection to chunkies or his more benign green dreams, the latter plaguing him as far back as he could remember. Although nightmares might be typical of childhood, gooey brown messes and recurring fantasies of being in a verdant prison cell weren't. And then there was the cryptic message from that female voice that always ended his green dreams.

Singularity beguiles, transcend the illusion.

He'd puzzled for years over those five words. They seemed endowed with significance at the moment of utterance. Yet the phrase regressed to caricature in the light of day, no more meaningful than a New Age bumper sticker.

Darlene believed the words represented Aiden's subconscious expressing his true desires.

"It's pretty obvious," she'd explained in that annoying "big sister knows best" tone. "Singularity beguiles. That part means you're too much of a loner and afraid to make a real commitment to a woman and start a family. The illusion you need to transcend is that life doesn't have to be the cavalier way you live it."

As much as he resented Darlene's armchair psychology, her analysis might not be total crap. Still, he had a hunch the words bore a deeper meaning, one that didn't lend itself to such simple interpretation.

His thoughts returned to Leah. Was his niece on a similar trajectory? Would her nightmares end only to be replaced by weird manifestations? Would chunkies become a curse on her as they were on him?

Aiden needed to talk to someone about the possibility. He knew just the person, the same man willing to buy his chunkie. A trip to Washington, DC could serve as a twofer. As an added bonus, it would get Darlene off his back for a day.

THREE

Aiden walked Leah to the school bus stop. After seeing her aboard, he sprinted down the pavement. He was serious about his daily run and tried not to let bad weather or getting wasted the previous night interfere. Today was a pristine May morning, the sky a fierce blue, the temperature and humidity mild. Besides, he hadn't downed enough beers to get close to a hangover.

He passed vintage clapboard-sided homes similar to his sister's and crossed the railroad spur that accessed a nearby quarry. The run felt good. It provided a temporary reprieve from dwelling on chunkies and green dreams, not to mention finding a new job.

He'd been looking. But anything that paid decent wages was hard to find. Birdsboro and the surrounding region were rust-belt casualties, most good manufacturing gigs long gone. And getting axed from one-too-many crappy jobs hadn't exactly shined up his resume.

His lack of a college degree made any type of work higher up the food chain unlikely. He'd left college his freshman year after being berated one too many times by his roommates for leaving "gross-looking piles of shit" near his bed. A confrontation over the issue ended with Aiden punching a dorm proctor in the face, which prompted the school to "request" that he seek an education elsewhere. At the time, dropping out hadn't seemed a big loss. He'd primarily been majoring in non-degree electives, such as beer pong, MMO gaming, and massively indiscriminate sexual couplings.

Darlene was home when he returned. Still in her nurse's uniform, she was marching through the kitchen, putting away groceries from two heaping cloth bags. Seven years his senior, she'd lost her youthful slimness but remained an attractive brunette. At least when she wasn't scowling.

She gestured to the trash bag. "My new toaster, huh?"

"Sorry. I'll buy you another one."

"I hope Leah didn't see it happen?"

"No. We're good."

"We're not good, Aiden. We're barely OK."

He figured her mood wasn't likely to improve so he went for broke. He told her about Leah's latest nightmare and his concern that his niece might be carrying the same weird genes that afflicted Aiden.

Darlene shook her head. "Not possible."

"Why not? Just because you don't make chunkies doesn't mean your daughter won't someday get the curse? If it's genetic, something carried by Mom or Dad, it could have skipped over you and gone straight to the next generation."

"She'll be fine. You're worried over nothing."

"There's no way for you to know that." He paused, took a deep breath and plunged into the heart of the matter. "I'd like to take Leah to see Dr Jarek. He might be able to run some tests."

She stopped stacking canned goods in a cabinet. Her lips twisted into a scowl. "Not a chance."

"C'mon, sis. Let's at least talk about it without losing your cool."

"I am *not* losing my cool," she said, slamming a can of soup onto the countertop. Realizing what she'd done, she forced calm.

"Look, Aiden, I appreciate having you around to babysit when I have to work. But you can't hold a job. You drink too much. The women you bring home throw up in my house."

"Gimme a break. That was one time."

"No, two times. She threw up again on the porch as she was leaving."

"She had a stomach bug."

"What she had was too many tequila shots." Darlene sighed. "Look, I get it. You're a great-looking guy and most women think you're hot. But you're also smarter than you give yourself credit for, smart enough to know that these endless one-nighters won't ever bring you real satisfaction."

"And you know goddamn well why they're one-nighters!" Aiden wasn't about to risk a woman he'd just had sex with waking up covered in chunkie crap. "Besides, every woman I hook up with can't be as picture-perfect as Darlene Manchester."

"Screw you!"

They glared at one another. Darlene shook her head in exasperation. When the battle recommenced, she tried keeping her tone civil.

"Look, I know this chunkie business has always been a pain in the butt. But you'll be thirty years old in two months. At some point you have to realistically focus on making something out of your life. You have to accept the chunkies as a mild handicap and move on."

Mild handicap? Aiden had to restrain himself from launching another attack.

"Start looking at things on the bright side," his sister continued. "It's not happening nearly as often, right?"

She was right about the frequency of the manifestations. They'd lessened considerably over the years. These days they only occurred about once a month. As a teen, Aiden had suffered a chunkie nearly every night. Back then, fear that he'd manifest one in his sleep had kept him from the kind of regular activities that his school friends enjoyed, such as sleepovers and overnight camping trips.

Despite his parents' and sister's attempts to convince him that the manifestations weren't that big a deal, the reality felt different. He'd always been deeply embarrassed by them. The shame was probably akin to what a chronic bedwetter experienced. Although considering the composition of chunkies, an analogy to another bodily function was more apt.

Darlene droned on. "You can't stay unfocused forever, aimlessly wandering through life."

"Guess I'm just a screw-up and a loser," he countered, smothering the words in sarcasm. Chunkies had trapped him in a lifelong prison of sorts. Maybe that was the true meaning of being behind bars in the green dream.

He tried to repress his bitterness and get the conversation back on track. "Just stop fixating on me for a moment, OK? Think about what might be best for Leah."

"Fine. But I've never liked this Dr Jarek."

"You've never met him."

"Maybe so, but I think it's a waste of your time getting involved with weird psychic research, or whatever the hell he does. Besides, he's not a pediatrician."

"The Doc has legit medical credentials. Maybe he'll have some ideas that could help Leah or at least recommend someone who could."

"Her nightmares are nothing to worry about. A lot of kids have them. It's only been a little over a year since Tony passed. She still misses him."

A shadow touched Darlene's face at the mention of her husband. Tony, an Army staff sergeant, had been killed in Afghanistan.

"Anyway, it's not a big deal. It's just a stage Leah's going through."

"But what if it becomes a big deal later on? I know you don't like to think about this, but what if Leah starts having chunkies? And what if it's something that can be caught and corrected at a young age, maybe with medication."

"My daughter is *not* going on any weird medications."

Aiden shook his head in frustration. "You're not being objective about this."

"Trust me, Leah won't inherit your problem."

"How can you possibly know that?"

Darlene hesitated. She seemed about to say something when the phone rang.

It was the landline. Aiden thought paying for hardwired phone service when you owned a cell phone was a waste of money. But Darlene believed it was important to have a backup in case the cell network went down. The woman was prepared for everything short of Armageddon.

He was nearest the receiver and picked up.

"Hello, Manchester residence."

"Aiden Manchester?"

The caller was male. He didn't recognize the voice.

"Speaking."

"Mr Manchester, I don't know if you remember me. My name is George Dorminy."

The name didn't register. He waited for the man to continue.

"My wife and I bought your place up in Exeter."

The memory returned. Aiden had met the couple more than fifteen years ago, in those harrowing weeks following the tragedy. After burying their parents, Darlene had sold the New Hampshire farmhouse where they'd grown up to the Dorminys, who'd been nearing retirement age. His sister, his legal guardian until he came of age, had moved them to Pennsylvania so she could attend nursing school.

"George and Irene, right," Aiden said.

"Yes. How have you been getting along?"

"Fine. Living with my sister temporarily." He glanced at Darlene. She was watching him closely, intrigued by the conversation.

"Darlene is here. Would you like to talk to her?"

"Actually, it's you I was trying to reach. We've been remodeling the back part of the cellar in your old house. Making more room for my train layout, which, for better or worse, is growing larger than government debt."

A faint chuckle sounded through the receiver. Aiden waited impatiently for Dorminy to get to the point.

"Anyway, last week the workmen found a secret compartment in the wall behind that old coal furnace. Hidden inside was a small safe. It has a very unusual lock. A note was found atop the safe, a note addressed to you from your father. It says that the safe is yours and that you possess the key to opening it."

Aiden's interest notched upward. He imagined newfound wealth, perhaps a family treasure concealed decades ago. But what sort of key was his father referring to?

"I'm sorry it took a while to get hold of you. Irene and I aren't too computer savvy. We don't know much about using the Internet to track people down. I gave your name to our grandson and he found this phone number. Southeastern Pennsylvania, right?"

"Birdsboro. Can you ship the safe down here?" Aiden asked. "Naturally, I'd pay the freight charges."

There was hesitation at the other end of the line. Aiden wondered if George Dorminy expected a reward. Or maybe he was simply curious and wanted to see the safe opened in his presence.

But Dorminy had an altogether different concern.

"I don't think that would be such a good idea. You see, there's more to the note. It says the safe is booby-trapped and that any attempt to open it by someone other than you will, and I quote, 'result in the triggering of a tamper-proof self-destruct mechanism.' After I read that, I decided it was best not to jar it around too much."

Aiden smiled. His father had been an engineer and dedicated home tinkerer, and was certainly capable of designing such a protective device. But Dad also possessed a sharp sense of humor and was a big fan of James Bond-style intrigue.

In all likelihood, the booby trap warning was simply a way to discourage potential thieves. And even if the safe was rigged, his father never would have designed it to pose a danger to anyone.

"You want me to come up there."

"I think that would be best."

Aiden promised to call back as soon as he'd made travel arrangements.

"Oh, one more thing," Dorminy said. "The last line of the note says, and again I quote, 'The contents of this safe will change your life.'"

FOUR

Aiden left Friday morning for New Hampshire. He'd offered to wait another day until the weekend so the three of them could make the trip together, but Darlene insisted he needed to do this alone. There'd been something odd in her tone, something hinting that she knew more about the mysterious safe than she was letting on.

Aiden had flown a few times in his life but had never felt comfortable in planes. He imagined drifting off to sleep and manifesting a chunkie, which would get caught in some piece of vital control wiring above or below the passenger cabin, sending the plane into a death spiral. Whenever possible he avoided flying.

He didn't want to drive all the way either, which left Amtrak the best option. He drove his old Chevy Malibu to Philadelphia and caught the early morning Acela Express from 30th Street Station, paying for first-class travel with his credit card. Whatever the safe contained certainly would offset the expense. His plan was to take care of business with the Dorminys, stay in a motel overnight and catch a morning train back to Philly.

The express eased into Boston's South Station shortly before noon. An hour or so later, a rented Hyundai Sonata brought him to the southeast corner of New Hampshire.

He lowered the window, felt a dash of surprisingly cool air against his face. Even though it was May, the weather up here tended to cling to the past, hanging onto wintery chills longer than Pennsylvania.

Childhood memories flooded back as he cruised into the small town of Exeter and onto Water Street. He recognized stores he'd haunted as a youngster, some unchanged since he'd last been here. Driving past the circular bandstand near the center of town triggered thoughts of Mom. She'd been a big supporter of the brass band that performed there and had dragged Aiden along to more than a few concerts.

He continued north, out of town. It took twenty minutes to reach the tree-shaded driveway that curved into his former home.

The old stone farmhouse occupied a small tract shielded on three sides by forest. Decades past, it had been a working farm. Most of the original acreage had been sold off well before his parents had moved here when he was a baby.

He parked beside a vintage Chrysler Imperial and headed up the flagstone path to the familiar white door. Another memory skated into view. He was maybe seven or eight, helping a teenaged Darlene shovel the driveway after a massive snowfall. Suddenly, the two of them had been attacked by Dad, who pelted them from his latest workshop invention, a toy rifle that machine-gunned tiny snowballs. The memory of the impromptu battle, including a counterassault organized by Darlene, remained as warm as that day had been cold.

George Dorminy opened the door on the first ring. He'd aged considerably since their last encounter and walked with a cane. Tall and slim, he had thinning white hair. But his handshake remained firm and his demeanor gracious.

"Irene and I are just sitting down to lunch. We insist you join us."

The kitchen had been remodeled. Gray marble had replaced his parents' old Formica countertops. Irene Dorminy, short, plump and beaming with pleasure, ushered him to the table and doled out clam chowder and sandwiches.

Aiden was hungry and dug in. The three of them chatted amicably while they ate. The Dorminys oohed and aahed as he displayed wallet photos of Darlene and Leah.

"I guess you're anxious to see the safe," George Dorminy said, downing a trio of pills with his last gulp of water. Balancing himself with the cane, he walked toward the door to the backyard. Aiden was surprised their destination wasn't the basement.

"That business about the self-destruct mechanism was a bit worrisome," he explained. "I had our grandson carry the safe out to the shed. He was extremely careful not to jar it, just in case."

Aiden followed him along the brick path bisecting the neatly trimmed lawn. Irene called out to them from the door.

"Try not to blow yourselves up."

The shed was new. Made of cedar boards with a shingled roof and nestled against the tree line, it fit the property's rustic tone. A pair of windows flanked the door, providing enough natural light to reveal a small lawn tractor, gardening tools, and filled trash bags.

The safe squatted atop an old wooden desk in the corner. Aiden pulled out the matching chair and sat down. Dorminy perched on a stool behind him.

"Actually, I wasn't too worried about us blowing up," Dorminy said with a chuckle. "Putting it out here was mainly for Irene's peace of mind."

The safe was about fifteen inches high and eight inches deep. It looked to be made of burnished steel. Dorminy had described the lock after Aiden had called back with the details of his arrival. The man was certainly right about its unusual nature.

The mechanism protruding from the door consisted of a pair of old-time rotary phone dials, the upper one black, the lower one red. The original door handle had been removed and its opening plugged. Aiden knew at a glance that the modifications were his father's handiwork.

He withdrew the dusty note from the envelope atop the safe. It was typewritten except for his father's signature in ink. The note contained nothing of relevance that Dorminy hadn't already mentioned. In addition to the self-destruct warning, it spelled out his name and said he possessed the key to opening the safe.

The final sentence, that the contents would change his life, reignited fantasies he'd been having about discovering a long-lost family treasure and leaving here a wealthy man.

Amid those flashes of wishful thinking, however, he'd given serious thought as to how he was going to open the safe. The rotary dials suggested that the key was an alphanumeric code, a series of numbers and letters that needed to be dialed into one or both of the finger wheels.

Aiden had come up with a list of possibilities during the train ride. Although it seemed unlikely, he tried the obvious one first, their old home phone number. He dialed the ten digits into the black dial, then into the red one, and then alternated the number between the two dials. None of the attempts met with success.

Next he tried birthdays and other dates germane to the Manchester clan. After exhausting those entries, as well as the local zip code, the license plate of Dad's favorite Chevy and Aiden's sixth-grade locker combination, he switched to letters. He rotated the finger wheels to spell out the names of people, places and things that had been important in the lives of his family.

A half hour of futile efforts followed. Dorminy called it quits after fifteen minutes and excused himself to work on his model trains. The old man asked Aiden to give a holler if a solution presented itself.

None did. Another half hour went by. Aiden's fingers were beginning to tire from the constant dialing and he was getting frustrated. He needed a break.

He headed out into the yard. It was a beautiful afternoon. The sun felt good on his skin as he strolled through the short grass, trying not to think about numbers and letters and codes, trying to let his mind drift free in the hope that some fresh line of attack would slip into consciousness.

A black walnut tree at the western edge of the yard snared his attention, bringing forth another spate of childhood memories. He had often played in that tree, venturing out onto one of the horizontal limbs in imitation of a high-wire performer. Mom had caught him a few times, yelling for him to get down before he broke his neck.

The recollection jarred his mind onto a fresh tangent. Maybe the secret to unlocking the safe was some special word or phrase that his father or mother had uttered around the house. He doubted Mom's warning was a candidate. But there were certainly other possibilities, comments unique to the family.

"Blackie Redstone!"

He knew the instant the words popped from his mouth he'd found the key. It was so obvious he was surprised he hadn't thought of it sooner.

He raced back into the shed. The top rotary dial was *black*, the bottom one *red* – clear evidence to support his conclusion. But the primary clue was the nature of that faux-name and what it signified within family lore.

FIVE

Aiden had been passionate about rocketry as a kid. He played spaceflight simulator games and built models of NASA launch vehicles, some with motors. With Dad's help he'd sent the rockets aloft from a field near their home. The thrill of those launches had been amplified by fantasizing that he was aboard the spaceship, piloting the craft into the unknown.

One summer, in the pre-chunkie era, Dad had taken him on a memorable camping trip upstate. They'd stopped in Warren, a town even smaller than Exeter, whose claim to fame was a seventy-foot-high Redstone rocket in the village green.

The Redstone was America's first large ballistic missile. Warren's had been donated to the town in the name of a longtime New Hampshire senator. It served to honor another Granite Stater, Alan Shepard, who in 1961 boarded a capsule atop a Redstone ascent vehicle and became the first American in space.

That missile became engraved in Aiden's memory for what had occurred the day of their visit. A local daredevil – a man with obvious mental health issues – had somehow lassoed the conical apex of the Redstone and climbed to the top. Aiden and Dad had witnessed numerous attempts by the police, the man's family, and a psychologist to talk him down. All had failed. Finally, two burly firemen had wrestled the man onto the extended ladder of their fire truck and whisked him away to some unknown fate.

The man's nickname had been Blackie. From that day on, Dad

had adopted the phrase "Blackie Redstone" as a gentle means of castigating Aiden for behavior he deemed wild or foolish.

"Don't pull a Blackie Redstone," his father would utter. "Always think smart. That's the only way to stay ahead of your troubles."

To outsiders, a connection between the safe and his father's use of the "Blackie Redstone" phrase might have seemed tenuous. But to those who knew Dad well enough to have experienced his agile mind and offbeat sense of humor, the conclusion was inescapable.

Aiden dialed 2-5-2-2-5-4-3 into the upper black dial to spell out "Blackie" and 7-3-3-7-8-6-6-3 into the lower red one for "Redstone." No sooner had he entered the final digit than a sharp click sounded. It was followed by an alarming hiss of air rushing into the safe as the door opened a crack.

He gripped the door's edge and gingerly drew it all the way open. An odd contraption occupied the safe's cavity. It was attached by a series of thin steel shafts to the inside of the door, with the shafts entering holes drilled through the metal to connect to the rotary dials.

A pair of glass test tubes, each half filled with an amber liquid, hung from the bottom of the contraption. A small gyroscope was attached to the test tubes, which were hinged to a complex mechanism of levers and gears that reminded Aiden of the innards of an analog wristwatch.

Glued to the floor of the safe was a plastic tray. In the bottom of the tray was a sealed white envelope. Printed on the envelope were the words *Aiden Manchester: For Your Eyes Only.*

Aiden studied the contraption before touching it, concerned that his father might have incorporated some unusual bit of trickery. But, after a time, he felt he had discerned its basic operation.

The yellowish liquid must be an acid corrosive to paper. Should the safe be opened by any means other than dialing "Blackie Redstone," the mechanism would flip the test tubes 180 degrees, pouring the acid into the tray and destroying the envelope and its contents. The gyroscope served to keep the test tubes upright in case someone jarred the safe or turned it upside down.

No batteries were in view. The contraption appeared to be entirely mechanical in nature. That made sense. Batteries would go dead after a few years.

The hiss of air when the door opened suggested the safe had contained a partial vacuum. Dad must have created the vacuum before sealing the safe. A very slight change in air pressure, such as from a drill penetrating the walls, would have caused the envelope to receive an acid bath. Dialing the proper code had been the only way to neutralize the fail-safe mechanism.

Aiden marveled at the design. His father's main field of expertise had been electronics systems. But his non-circuitry inventions, such as this contraption and the snowball rifle, had always made the deeper impression. Sadness touched him as he thought back to those hours he'd spent down in the basement workshop with Dad, watching him bring one of his unconventional devices to life.

Of course, it would have been much simpler to keep the contents of the envelope in a safe deposit box. But simple had never been Dad's style.

Aiden withdrew the envelope but hesitated before opening it. The "Blackie Redstone" moniker's symbolic meaning resonated. Was the very act of opening the safe an example of wild and foolish behavior?

The contents of this safe will change your life.

He suspected that his father had been conflicted. The envelope contained something important Dad wanted him to have. Yet it also contained something wild, something that might better be left untouched. Still, his father would have known that Aiden had no real choice. What mere mortal could resist such temptation?

Still envisioning a waiting fortune – maybe details for accessing a secret bank account – he broke the seal. Inside was a four-page handwritten letter in his father's elegant cursive. The date indicated it was written when Aiden was twelve, only a few months before his parents died.

Aiden began reading. Before he got to the second page, his

hands were shaking. It felt as if a giant claw had grabbed hold of his guts and was applying relentless pressure.

By the time he reached at the end of the letter, he felt numb. The notion that the contents of the safe would change his life was the grossest understatement.

His entire world had just been ripped apart.

SIX

"Aiden, are you all right?"

George Dorminy gazed worriedly at him from the shed's doorway. Aiden, still in a daze, didn't know how long he'd been standing there.

"I'm fine."

"You finally got it open. What was the secret key?"

Aiden wanted him to leave. He wanted to be left alone to process the letter's monumental impact. Obviously, that wasn't going to happen.

He forced a smile and gave Dorminy a quick explanation of "Blackie Redstone" and the safe's self-destruct mechanism. The old man nodded and gazed at the letter clamped in Aiden's hand.

"No secret treasure," he said, trying to relax his tense body through sheer force of will, trying not to show the devastating emotions churning through him. "Just some personal stuff."

"Well, either way, Irene and I would like to invite you to stay for supper."

The last thing Aiden wanted to do was hang around and make small talk with the Dorminys. He politely declined, saying he needed to catch a train back to Philly. His original plan of staying overnight in a motel was history. He just wanted to go home.

Home. The word caught in his throat, its meaning forever altered by the letter.

Dorminy insisted on showing Aiden the basement and the

hollow cavity in the wall where the safe had been concealed. It was a clever hiding place, not readily accessible until the old coal furnace had been hauled away. The removal of the furnace, an unused relic even when Aiden lived here, had disclosed a section of false wall covered by wooden slats painted the same shade of ivory as the surrounding cement.

"I know you're eager to get on the road," Dorminy said. "But before you go, I'd really like you to see my pride and joy."

The old man drew aside a green drape that separated the front of the basement from the furnace area and stepped across the threshold. Aiden followed reluctantly, hoping the tour would be short.

Dorminy's HO-scale model railroad was spectacular. Butting up against three walls, with a peninsula jutting out into the center, the miniature empire was richly detailed. A single track studded with sidings and branch lines wound its way along portions of the Squamscott River and through replicas of New England towns, forests and mountains. The track terminated at a large freight yard in an urban area representing Concord, New Hampshire.

"It's part of the Boston & Maine rail system in the mid-1950s," Dorminy said, removing a device resembling a TV remote control from a hook and pushing some buttons. A set of maroon and yellow diesels pulling boxcars and gondolas crawled out of the freight yard and began its journey to the other end of the layout. Authentic sounds – growling engines and multi-chime horns – emanated from the locomotives.

"Like to try it?" Dorminy asked, offering him the throttle.

"No thanks."

Aiden feigned interest as the train threaded its way across the layout. All the while, he couldn't help dwelling on the act of fate that had brought him here. Had George Dorminy not desired to extend his layout by adding a branch line to be constructed where the furnace stood, Aiden never would have learned that his life had been built upon an unconscionable lie.

SEVEN

After removing the test tubes of acid and making arrangements with Dorminy to ship the safe to Philly, Aiden drove back to Boston. The letter was another matter. It was tucked securely in the vest pocket of his jacket.

He called Darlene from the train station to say he was returning a day earlier than planned. He told her about the safe but not about the letter, divulging only that he'd discovered no hidden riches. She sensed from his tone that something was wrong.

"Everything's fine," he lied, struggling to contain his anger. Now wasn't the time and place to unleash it. "I'll tell you everything when I'm back."

He hung up before she could respond.

My dearest son: There is no good way to reveal the things your mother and I kept hidden from you.

The opening words of his father's letter surged back into awareness. For the third time since the train departed Boston, Aiden slipped the pages from the envelope and read on.

I can only guess what your reaction will be. Hurt, anger, fear, and perhaps other emotions I can't fathom. In any event, your mother and I made a vow to one another that we would not reveal these things until you turned twenty-one. We felt that by that age, you'd

*have acquired a maturity that would allow the rigors of your mind
to temper the turbulence that likely would tear at your heart.*

*We intended to sit down with you and unveil these secrets face
to face. This letter is the backup plan. I can only assume that since
you're reading it, your mother and I have died or are in some way
incapacitated, and that the location of the safe was passed on to
Darlene, and ultimately to you, through our estate attorney.*

Aiden paused, wondering again why his sister hadn't removed
the safe prior to selling the house. Had there been some sort of
mixup? Had Darlene never learned about the safe?

Those details would become clear soon enough, when he
confronted his sister.

He continued reading.

*I've always considered myself a reasonably courageous man, but
your reaction to all this was not something I was eager to face. But
these are things you deserve to know. For better or worse, they are
your heritage.*

*Your birth date is correct as far as we know, but not much
else related to the first eighteen months of your life. You are
not our biological child. You were not born in that Allentown,
Pennsylvania, hospital, but in a clinic in Helena, Montana, to a
poor itinerant woman who died giving birth.*

*We never knew your real mother's name, only that she
apparently had no close relatives who might be willing to take care
of a newborn, and that she had to make some really hard choices
to get by. If she even knew the identity of the father – your father –
she took it with her to the grave.*

*You were eighteen months old when your mother and I adopted
you. Had the circumstances of your early life not been so unusual,
we would have revealed your true origins earlier. Maintaining this
secret was partly for your own protection.*

*As you know, I spent most of my professional life as an engineer
for Innovative Electrodyne Corp., working originally in IEC's*

Allentown office. What I never revealed is that your mother, sister and I moved out west for several years. For part of that time I was with a design team sent to work at a top-secret military research facility in the wilds of Montana. It was known as Tau Nine-One.

IEC had won a Defense Department contract for the design, testing and installation of a state-of-the-art electronic sensor net for safeguarding the installation. But I never knew much about what went on at Tau Nine-One. My security clearance only permitted involvement with peripheral elements.

What I do know is that one of their projects, rumored to be the most secret of them all, involved seven orphaned babies. It was an experiment of some sort, ostensibly done under the strictest medical guidelines, and with the babies subjected to nothing harmful. The children were roughly the same age, all born within a few months of one another.

The experiment ended abruptly when they were eighteen months old. It was rumored that ethical considerations surfaced in Washington – better late than never – and the project terminated. The seven orphans were put up for adoption.

You were one of those babies. That's how your mother and I were afforded the opportunity to become your parents. We'd always wanted another child, but after Darlene's birth, your mother could no longer conceive.

After my work at Tau Nine-One and at some other West Coast job sites, we returned to Pennsylvania. Shortly after coming back, I accepted a transfer to IEC's New Hampshire office and we moved north.

Because of the unusual nature of how we came to adopt you, your mother and I made the decision to pass you off as our natural offspring. Since we didn't have many close living relatives and hadn't seen most of our friends back east in years, the fiction held up. We soon had reason to be glad we'd taken this step.

Although the experiment on the babies supposedly was finished, I learned that you were being discreetly monitored, presumably by Tau Nine-One researchers. Someone was secretly accessing your medical records from our family physician, as well as your test scores, grades, and behavioral profiles from elementary school. The monitoring went on for a number of years. As far as I could ascertain, it ceased when you were about ten.

We thought that was the end of it. But then you turned twelve and your weird ability appeared. Your mother and I became quite frightened by those manifestations, not so much by the chunkies themselves but by the fact that, in all likelihood, they somehow were related to what had been done to you at Tau Nine-One. Although we have no proof this, it seems reasonable to assume a connection.

We feared that if the government learned what you could do, they'd take you away from us. We couldn't bear the thought of that, which is the main reason we encouraged you to keep the manifestations to yourself and never talk about them with anyone outside the family, and why we kept up the fiction that you were our natural child.

Once you get past the initial shock of these revelations, you may find yourself wanting to delve into your past. If you do, please be extremely careful. The people who run Tau Nine-One belong to a very secretive part of our government. Making direct inquiries likely would uncover little information and could draw unwanted attention.

Your mother and I never felt responsible for what was done to you in the first eighteen months of your life. That was beyond our control. But we are responsible for everything that happened afterwards, including hiding these truths from you for so long.

But please know that when we first set eyes on you, smiling and giggling in a playpen, we fell instantly in love. In all these years that love has never wavered. You brought us a joy that made our lives more meaningful than we ever could have dreamed. We can only hope and pray that you'll remember the good times you had with us and find a way to get through all this.

Love,

Dad

Aiden returned the letter to his pocket and gazed through the Acela's spacious window. The train was cruising through the seaside town of New London, Connecticut, home to a naval base. The conning tower of a docked submarine was visible in the distance. He had a hunch the sub was preparing to head out to sea, maybe for a descent into uncharted depths.

EIGHT

Leah was on a sleepover at a friend's house when Aiden returned late Friday evening. That was just as well. There was no good reason for a seven year-old to be in the house for the screaming match about to ensue.

"How'd it go?" Darlene asked. She was in her pajamas, nestled on the living room sofa reading a nursing magazine.

"Fuck you."

All the venom he'd accumulated during the return train ride poured into those words.

"What happened?" Her voice was softer than usual. It was good to hear her not sounding all haughty and superior for once.

"You're going to play innocent with me, huh?"

"Aiden, please just tell me."

He threw the letter in her lap. She began reading. He grabbed a beer from the fridge and paced back and forth in front of her.

She finished and gazed up at him with sad eyes. "I'm sorry you had to learn this way."

"So you admit you knew."

"About Tau Nine-One, about you being adopted, yeah. Dad and Mom swore me to secrecy. They said they weren't going to tell you until you were an adult. But I swear to you, I didn't know anything about this letter or the safe."

"What about the estate attorney? He never told you?"

"Mr Devereux was an old man. I think he was suffering from

mild dementia. He died a couple months after Mom and Dad. Somehow, the existence of the safe and the letter must have slipped through the cracks."

"OK, I'll buy that. But why the hell didn't *you* tell me I was a goddamn orphan?"

"Oh, God. Aiden I wanted to! So many times. But you always seemed to have so many other problems in your life. I thought that learning all this would make things even worse for you."

She got up from the sofa and moved toward him. She spread her arms, intending to envelop him in a hug.

"Keep the hell away from me!"

A hurt look crossed her face. Aiden didn't care. Her voice fell to a whisper. "What are you going to do?"

"I'm going to find out more about this Tau Nine-One. I figure Dr Jarek is a good place to start."

"You think he knows about the experiment?"

"If something was done to me and those other babies that caused us to develop weird psychic powers, he might have been in the loop."

Darlene nodded. "What about your birth mother?"

"What about her?"

"Are you going to try to find out more about her?"

"What's the point? She's been dead three decades."

"You could have distant relatives living out there in Montana."

"If I do they don't mean shit to me!"

Darlene pinned her gaze to him. He knew she wanted him to keep talking, let his anger out so they could get past it. It was his sister's tried-and-true way of dealing with him.

But Aiden didn't bite. He headed for the door.

"Where are you going?"

"Out for a drink. And tomorrow morning, I'm driving down to DC."

He opened the front door. An instant before he stepped outside and slammed it shut, he yelled back:

"And I'm not replacing your goddamn toaster!"

NINE

U-OPS had no public face and few people knew of the agency's existence. Passersby to the upscale Georgetown row home assumed the brass sign – *Dr Abelicus Jarek* – signified a traditional psychiatric practice.

Jarek did hold a PsyD among a slate of advanced degrees. But he had no patients. His so-called practice was a cover for the comings and goings of researchers and volunteers engaged in secret, government-sponsored psychic experiments in a basement lab. Aiden had been down there for sleep tests wearing headgear studded with EEG sensors and other oddities.

Although it was a Saturday, Jarek had agreed to a morning meeting after Aiden insisted it was an emergency. He'd downed a lot of beer the previous night in a futile attempt to hatchet the letter's turmoil yet still managed to get on the road early, before Darlene awoke. He was still too pissed to deal with her.

He found a parking space a block away, threw the trash bag with the chunkie-infused toaster over his shoulder and rang the bell. Abel Jarek, sixty-something and portly, opened the door. Stylish the man wasn't. He was garbed in a rumpled sports jacket and jeans a couple sizes too large.

Jarek led him through the reception area to his office, where the psychiatrist charade was operating full throttle. The framed degrees were from top-tier universities and the bookshelves were crammed with medical texts. Aiden settled into the sofa.

Jarek took the armchair and gestured to the bag.

"I presume that's your latest manifestation."

"Uh-huh, two nights ago. As a bonus, you get a free toaster."

Jarek looked at him quizzically. Aiden explained.

"Other than the touchdown, was there anything else unusual about it?"

"Pretty much the same as the others."

He wished there had been something different, something good for a change. Instead of chunkies, maybe a bundle of cash in large denominations. He'd fantasized about such things since his teens. If he had to have a psychic power, why couldn't it have been something useful? The ability to predict the future or do Jedi mind tricks would have been cool. Instead, he'd been given the inglorious and embarrassing ability to create sticky, shit-colored blobs in his sleep.

"I'll have a full analysis done to be sure it's the same as previous manifestations."

The chemical makeup of chunkies was as unusual as their appearances. They were composed of small amounts of various elements and compounds; nearly a third of the periodic table was represented. Among the exclusions were the naturally radioactive and synthetic elements. Although the fundamental building blocks of life were present, chunkies betrayed no evidence of ever having been alive.

"About my fee," Aiden said. "How about four hundred this time?"

"Three hundred per manifestation has been our agreement."

"Inflation." He put on his best pleading face. "I really need it."

Jarek sighed. "All right. Just this once."

The Doc had money to burn and had paid generously since their first encounter. Aiden had answered an innocuous website ad, one of U-OPS' clandestine efforts at trawling for individuals with authentic psychic abilities. The researchers, in addition to studying his chunkies, had subjected Aiden to tests and procedures aimed at having him create manifestations while conscious. That hadn't happened. The best he'd done was make one in his sleep last year, during an all-nighter in the lab. Despite needing the money, of late he'd grown tired of being a guinea pig and had been avoiding further testing.

"So, Aiden, you claim this is an emergency? Did something else of a psychic nature occur?"

"The thing is, my niece has been having these nightmares. She had one the same night I made this chunkie."

He had to remind himself that Leah wasn't really his niece, not by blood anyway. Nor was Darlene his real sister. He still found it difficult to get a handle on that new reality.

"And you think there's a connection?"

Aiden shrugged, waiting for Jarek to go on.

"I'm afraid I have little familiarity with children's nightmares. And I've never encountered evidence to suggest a genetic basis for psychic powers. There's simply no data to indicate it runs in families. Therefore, I strongly doubt she inherited your manifestational ability."

"So you never worked with kids," Aiden probed, observing Jarek closely.

"No."

"How about babies? Ever work with them?"

Jarek frowned. "Aiden, I'm afraid you're losing me. And I fail to see how any of this constitutes an emergency."

He decided it was time to dispense with the small talk and get to the real reason he was here.

"What about Tau Nine-One? They experimented with babies and psychic powers, didn't they?"

Jarek raised his eyebrows. "Where did you hear about that place?"

"Came across it somewhere. What do you know about the experiment?"

"Very little. My understanding is that it ended decades ago."

"Yeah, when the babies were eighteen months old." Aiden paused. "And it's no coincidence I happen to be twenty-nine."

Jarek's surprise was palpable. "You believe you were one of those babies? A quiver kid?"

"A what?"

Jarek hesitated. "I shouldn't be talking about this. Technically, I could be in violation of national security documents bearing my signature."

"I won't tell if you don't. C'mon, Doc, what's a quiver kid?"

"I don't know."

Aiden scowled.

"I'm telling the truth. Those babies were referred to as quiver kids but I never knew details of the experiment, nor the rationale for that nomenclature."

"So tell me what you do know."

"First answer a question. What makes you think you're one of them?"

Aiden brought him up to speed on the events of the past few days, including sharing the main points of his father's letter. When he finished, Jarek wore a deep frown.

"I had no idea. You were the right age, of course. But U-OPS did a thorough background check and there was no indication you were adopted. There was nothing to connect you with that place."

"My parents kept a lid on it."

Jarek got up and retrieved a water bottle from a mini-fridge beneath the credenza. "Would you like one?"

"No thanks. What about Tau Nine-One?"

"In its current configuration it's been around since 1991. That's how it got its name. Tau is the nineteenth letter of the Greek alphabet. Ergo, Tau Nine-One.

"The site was originally an early-twentieth-century mining camp with a railroad line built to service it. Gold and silver had been discovered, but the veins played out quickly and the mining camp went bust.

"In the early 1950s it was taken over by the government and reconstituted as a support facility for the Pinetree Line, a joint US-

Canadian initiative. Pinetree was one of the first early warning systems to guard against an ICBM sneak attack by the Soviets. A series of radar stations were constructed farther north, around the Canadian border.

"The site's function as part of Pinetree didn't last long, however. It was shut down by the late Fifties. A few years later, the DOD retasked it into a storage depot for extra ordnance: artillery shells, grenades, what have you. But in the late Eighties, environmental groups learned about the explosives and campaigned to have them removed. The DOD eventually gave in and removed the ordnance. They were in the process of mothballing the facility when something happened."

Jarek sat down and took a hearty swig of water before continuing.

"Naturally, the site had been classified since the Pinetree years. But in 1991 it acquired its new name and disappeared from regular military and Congressional oversight." He paused. "It entered the shadow realm."

"And you have no idea why?"

Jarek shook his head. Aiden believed him.

"What about the other quiver kids? My father's letter said there were seven of us."

"All born around the same time, a year or so after Tau Nine-One's inception. However, yours is the first evidence I've heard to suggest that the experiment was related to psychic abilities."

"Do you know the identities of the others?"

"No."

"Why did the experiment end?"

"Same reason your father mentioned in his letter. Some higher-ups at the Pentagon or White House got wind of it." Jarek's face darkened. "Illicit human experimentation, I'm sorry to say, occurred far too often throughout the Cold War years and even after. I suspect the powers-that-be were mortified by the possibility of a public relations disaster if word leaked out."

Aiden could envision the headlines: *Pentagon Conducting Secret*

Tests on Helpless Babies. The outrage would have been potent, maybe enough to bring down an administration.

"I found some information online," Aiden said. "Tau Nine-One is run by DARPA, the Defense Advanced Research Projects Agency. A website that tracks secret government programs claims they work on advanced chemical warfare. But another site says its real purpose is to build the next generation of robotic combat systems."

"It's possible neither of those is true. A black facility like that might employ an aggressive disinformation campaign, leak false clues to cover up its real function. The tactic is quite common."

"Another strange thing. There aren't any roads leading there, and only a few fire trails in the general area. Access is either by helicopter or by a private train that shuttles workers to and from the nearest town."

"That alone should indicate its level of secrecy."

"So if a former guinea pig shows up on their front stoop, you don't think they'd welcome him back?"

Jarek's frown implied that Aiden was insane for even suggesting such an idea.

"Don't worry, I'm not going to storm the ramparts. But one way or another, I'm going to find out what was done to me in that place. Can you help? Make some inquiries?"

Jarek squirmed in his chair. "I'm sorry, Aiden. I can't. It would only serve to put me under the microscope and invite unwanted scrutiny."

"Afraid that the guys in the black SUVs will haul you away for a waterboarding vacation?"

"That's not quite how it works. But if I were to be investigated, U-OPS could suffer political fallout. Tau, Area 51, various cyberwarfare efforts, other highly classified programs – we all compete for funding. There are constant behind-the-scenes power plays to gain larger shares of the black ops budget. U-OPS is a tiny player and we've already undergone steep cuts. I can't risk further economic vulnerability."

"OK, so how about just pointing me in the right direction? I'll keep your name out of it. No one would ever know."

Jarek warmed to the idea and scribbled a name, phone number and Baltimore address on a note and handed it to Aiden.

"A friend and former colleague. I don't believe he was involved directly in the quiver kids experiment. But he was definitely at Tau Nine-One during that period. He might be willing to talk. Off the record, of course."

"Naturally."

"By the way, have you given any more thought to our last discussion? The current research downstairs is quite exciting. I'd love to have you involved again."

Jarek's desire to have Aiden back within the U-OPS fold was the reason he'd been given the colleague's name, as well as the higher fee for the chunkie. The Doc wanted reciprocation.

"Sorry, but I can't be a lab rat for you right now."

Jarek looked disappointed. Aiden threw him a bone.

"But after I get this Tau Nine-One business figured out we can talk some more."

"Fair enough."

Jarek ushered him to the receptionist's office. He peeled $400 in twenties from a lockbox in the desk and handed it to Aiden. At the front door, he had a final warning.

"Be careful. What your father said in that letter is correct. Tau Nine-One is dangerous territory."

"I'll watch my ass. Oh, and have fun with the new chunkie. Just don't try making toast."

TEN

Aiden called the number Jarek had provided when he was back in the car and on his way out of Georgetown. A woman answered. She said her husband was at Towson University in suburban Baltimore and gave him that number. After ping-ponging through an automated phone tree, Aiden reached his quarry.

Dr Edward Marsdale had retired from the university but remained a professor emeritus in the geosciences department, where he specialized in stratigraphy, the study of rock strata. He still maintained an office on campus.

Aiden kept the reason for his call vague, saying only that he was a friend of Abel Jarek and that he'd like to discuss a science project. He thought that was fuzzy enough to get him through the front door.

Marsdale was agreeable. He'd finish his work at the university by four pm and would meet Aiden at a small café near the campus. Aiden arrived at Towson early and killed time in a parking lot doing more online research from his phone. But he found no new information on Tau Nine-One.

At the café, he took an outside table amid a handful of young couples. He spent the next ten minutes nursing an iced coffee and observing pedestrians and bicyclists in the outdoor shopping plaza across the street. They appeared to be mainly college students.

A tall, sprightly man in a light jacket and jeans strode toward the café. Thinning gray hair peeked out from under the edges of a Towson Tigers football cap. He spotted Aiden and broke into a warm smile.

"Mr Manchester?"

Aiden rose and shook the extended hand.

"Ed Marsdale. Sorry I was a bit delayed."

"No problem."

Marsdale sat down across from him.

"Thanks for seeing me on such short notice," Aiden said, still trying to come up with an inoffensive way to dispense with the fiction of wanting to meet about some innocent science project.

"My pleasure. Abel's an old friend. We met as undergrads at Princeton although I was two years ahead. How do you know him?"

"We've been associated for the past several years."

"Associated? That's rather vague."

Aiden hesitated, debating whether to mention U-OPS. He had no idea how much, if anything, Marsdale knew about the secret agency.

"The two of us worked together on a project."

The professor chuckled. "I'm guessing you're talking about what goes on in that basement lab of his in Georgetown."

"You know about that?"

"I know *nothing*. I can neither confirm nor deny the existence of any such laboratory."

The abrupt shift to a serious tone left Aiden momentarily confused on how to respond.

Marsdale released a hearty laugh. "I'm pulling your chain. Honestly, I don't know what Abel does, only that much of it's classified."

Aiden felt guilty for lying about his reason for being here. Marsdale had a warm and open demeanor. He decided to drop all pretense.

"Listen, Professor, I have to tell you something that—"

"Call me Ed."

"Ed, there is no science project. I mean, there is in a way, but I kind of got you here under false pretenses."

Before Marsdale could respond, a waitress appeared. The professor ordered a small salad and bottled water. Aiden, who'd skipped lunch, opted for a chicken sandwich and fries.

"Well, now," Marsdale said after the waitress left. "So what is this about?"

"The Doc said you might be able to help me with another matter."

"And that would be?"

"Tau Nine-One."

Marsdale's face underwent a subtle change. Candor gave way to guardedness.

"What exactly has Abel been telling you?"

"Not much. Just that you were there."

"More than twenty years ago. And my work remains classified."

"Understood. I was just hoping you could give me a little background on the place. Nothing that would violate a security oath."

"Let me guess. You're writing a book or an article. Or planning a documentary on America's secret military installations."

"I'm a quiver kid."

Marsdale's eyes widened.

"I'm trying to find out what was done to me, how and why I was experimented on."

For a moment, Aiden had the feeling that Marsdale was going to get up and leave. But the retired geoscientist settled back in his seat with a wry nod.

"Over the years, I've found myself wondering what happened to the seven of you. For a time, my wife and I had even considered being one of the adoptive parents. But she got pregnant and that put the kibosh on the idea."

"All of us found homes?"

"As far as I know, although I wasn't privy to the details of the adoptions. All I know is that the people in charge wanted the babies to be raised in emotionally stable environments by caregivers with high IQs."

Aiden nodded. That criterion certainly fit Byron and Alice Manchester.

"Do you happen to know your color?" Marsdale asked.

"My color?"

"You weren't given traditional names. Instead, each of you was designated by a specific hue. I thought then, as I do now, that the idea of color-coding babies was demented. Of course, I suppose the same might be said for the whole experiment."

"Green," Aiden whispered slowly. "That was my color."

Another piece fell into place. He told Marsdale about his recurring dream.

"Sounds like you might be re-experiencing facets of early memories. Feeling that you're in a prison cell, the bars rising above you, those three giant faces above peering down at you. Maybe you're an infant in a crib."

Aiden was astonished. The idea made perfect sense. He was surprised it hadn't occurred to him earlier and said so.

"You could have been too close to the problem to see the obvious answer," Marsdale offered.

"Are memories from such an early age even possible?"

"That sort of thing might be more up Abel's alley. But some theorists believe that with the right stimulus, individuals can recollect primal sensations and images from very far back, even pre-birth."

"If I'm reliving actual memories, why is everything green?"

"Perhaps because Green was your name, the word that your infant mind heard uttered numerous times. Later in childhood, when you developed sufficient mental acuity and came to understand the more general meaning of the word green, your subconscious made a connection, fused those two things together. When you dream, that fusion becomes prominent. Your early name, Green, becomes synonymous with the color green." Marsdale allowed a faint smile. "Just a theory, you understand."

It sounded plausible to Aiden. "The dream always ends with

a woman's voice that says, 'Singularity beguiles, transcend the illusion.' Does that phrase mean anything to you?"

Marsdale shook his head.

"Do you remember me as a baby?"

"I do. The seven of you were mostly sequestered in a special area but the researchers apparently wanted at least some degree of normal socialization. The five or six nannies who cared for you around the clock occasionally brought you into the cafeteria or other public areas." Marsdale smiled with the recollection. "Many of us got a kick out of watching seven curious babies crawling and toddling around."

"And what was being done to us when we weren't being socialized?"

If Marsdale sensed the bitterness in Aiden's words, he didn't show it.

"I don't know what the experiment was about, just that it supposedly was considered groundbreaking. But I have no idea of its purpose. We were told repeatedly that you weren't being harmed, that the research was totally innocuous."

"And you have no idea what they did to us?"

"The rumor was it involved some sort of infusions given during your first weeks of life."

"What does that mean? They injected us with something?"

"Honestly, I don't know. *Infusion* was the only term I ever heard. It was never made clear what that entailed."

Aiden believed him. Still, he suspected the professor knew more than he was letting on. This time, Aiden made no attempt to constrain his rancor.

"So, you simply accepted the word of these Tau Nine-One researchers that everything was harmless. You had no trouble with the idea of seven orphaned babies being experimented on in a secret military facility. All just fun and games, huh?"

Marsdale sighed. "Did I have doubts? Of course I did. I wouldn't be human if I didn't. I know this will sound like an excuse, like I'm trying to let myself off the hook in terms of taking any responsibility for what happened out there. But I had no input or control over the experiment."

"Maybe so. But you could have gone public, told the world what Tau Nine-One was doing."

"Not as easy as it sounds. There can be severe repercussions for whistleblowers, particularly when you're dealing with top-secret government programs. Frankly, I had no desire to go to jail or be forced to seek asylum in another country. But let me ask you a question. Do you believe that what was done to you caused you harm or has had injurious effects on your life?"

Marsdale seemed reasonably honest. But talking about chunkies wasn't in Aiden's game plan. He shifted the conversation.

"What about the other quiver kids? You have no idea what happened to them?"

"I don't."

"What were their names? Their color names."

"Blue, Red and White were the other boys. The three girls were Gold, Magenta and Cyan."

"Why name us after those colors?"

Marsdale shrugged. "No deep mystery. One of the researchers apparently spotted a TV color-bar test pattern and suggested using the seven colors on the top row. His idea received a final tweak – someone figured gold sounded better than yellow. The thinking was that once the babies were adopted, their parents would give them regular names.

"Oh, I just remembered something. White never received the infusions. He was referred to as the anomaly because he arrived later, when the others were about nine months old. We heard through the grapevine that he'd been added as a control for the experiment, someone not impacted by the phenomenon being studied."

"A phenomenon you remain completely in the dark about," Aiden said, his tone reflecting disbelief.

Marsdale paused as the waitress arrived with their food. Aiden chomped into his sandwich with a vengeance. He sensed the professor watching him closely.

"I guess I'd be angry too if someone did experiments on me as a child," Marsdale said.

"Who says I'm angry?" Aiden snapped.

The words came out garbled. His mouth was so stuffed that he sprayed bits of food onto the table. He forced himself to calm down.

"Yeah, OK, I'm pissed. It's not just the experiment itself. Until yesterday, I didn't even know I was adopted."

Aiden provided a quick version of recent events, leaving out any mention of the manifestations. When he finished, Marsdale offered a sympathetic nod.

"I'm sorry. That's a lot to deal with."

"Yeah. What about the other kids? Was there anything about them that could help me track them down?"

"Not really. You were just a bunch of little babies."

Marsdale read Aiden's skepticism and reconsidered.

"Six of you were Caucasian. Blue was either a light-skinned African-American or Latino. Magenta, she was the liveliest, the most curious of the seven. Gold was the opposite, she didn't seem to learn as quickly as the rest of you. Red was a bit bigger and bolder than the others. Cyan always seemed a bit shy, kept to herself. White seemed to keep apart from the others too, but in his case it didn't seem due to shyness. Maybe it had something to do with not being part of the original group. Blue and Green – Blue and *you* – tended to scrap. It was as if the two of you had conflicting personalities."

None of that seemed helpful in finding them. Aiden pressed on.

"What else can you tell me about Tau Nine-One?"

"Not much."

"Can you at least tell me who was in charge back then?"

"Colonel Royce Jenkins was the ranking military officer. A real martinet and, frankly, a rather unpleasant man. He took ill. Pancreatic cancer, I believe they said it was. He died right around the time the experiment was ending.

"There were more than a hundred civilian and government

scientists and technicians working under him, as well as the Marine guards and support personnel. Although many of us socialized, it was drummed into everyone to keep their mouths shut and not discuss our work."

"Can you give me the names of the other top people?"

"As far as I'm aware, the others are still alive. So I'm afraid my answer must be no."

"How about some titles at least?"

Marsdale hesitated then gave a slight nod. "There was a Director of Research, the man with overall responsibility for the scientific contingent. And there was the Project Director, the woman directly in charge of the quiver kids experiment. Along with Colonel Jenkins, the three of them pretty much ran things."

Two men and a woman. Aiden wondered if they were the three blurred faces staring down at him in his green dream.

"Byron Manchester was my father. He was with IEC, an engineering firm. Did you know him?"

"We could have run into one another. But the name doesn't ring a bell."

"Why were we called quiver kids?"

"I'm not sure."

Aiden knew from the way Marsdale averted his eyes he was lying.

"Surely something like that can't matter after so many years."

"One would think. However, even after all this time, I still get occasional visits from federal agents who want to know if anyone has approached me seeking information about my work at Tau. I'm acquainted with other scientists involved with classified government research. None of them receives such a level of follow-up."

Aiden suspected part of the reason for the ongoing interest was to keep a lid on the experiment's illicit nature. Even after all this time, the fact that babies had been used in a secret military experiment would still spark public outrage toward those responsible.

"Sounds like someone's trying to cover their asses."

Marsdale nodded. "I imagine that WikiLeaks and other groups that publish classified information are a constant source of worry to those with oversight of Tau."

"Next time these spooks show up for a chat, tell them I tortured you for information. Tell them I made you reveal everything. That should let you off the hook."

Marsdale gave a half-hearted laugh and pushed his unfinished salad to the side.

"I really should be going."

Aiden couldn't resist some final probing.

"Why a geologist specializing in stratigraphy? What could that possibly have to do with experimenting on babies?"

"I never said there was a connection."

"But there was, wasn't there?"

Marsdale glanced around before answering, as if making sure there were no eavesdroppers.

"Yes, there's a connection. Aiden, I'm sorry, but I just can't tell you anything else. And I trust you'll keep our little meeting confidential."

"What meeting?"

Aiden scribbled his phone number and e-mail address on a scrap of napkin and extended it to Marsdale.

"Just in case you think of anything else that might help."

Marsdale pocketed the note and stood up. He reached for his wallet but Aiden waved him off.

"I got this. I appreciate you taking the time."

They shook hands.

"Good luck, Aiden. I truly hope you find what you seek."

ELEVEN

Aiden spotted the craggy-faced man as he pulled into a Holiday Inn on the outskirts of Baltimore. The man was getting out of a 1990s-vintage SUV, a dark blue Ford Bronco parked a few spaces away.

He was short but powerfully built, and dressed in black pants and a zipped jacket. His cratered face suggested a bad case of childhood acne. Close-cropped brown hair was graying at the edges; he looked to be in his early fifties. He reminded Aiden of some movie version of a stone-cold mob enforcer.

The man caught him staring and leaned back into the Bronco to withdraw a laptop. Opening it on the hood, he hunched over the computer as if studying something. Aiden had a sense he was only pretending, that he realized he'd been spotted and was trying to deflect suspicion.

Keeping the man in his peripheral vision, Aiden retrieved a travel bag from the Chevy. Maybe he was being paranoid. It could be just a coincidence he'd noticed the man earlier, near the café where he'd met Marsdale. At the time, Aiden hadn't given it a second thought. Just another face in the crowd, albeit one with distinctive features. But now, crossing paths half an hour later and miles away…

Is he following me?

Both Dad's letter and Dr Jarek had hinted of the dangers of looking into Tau Nine-One's activities. And Marsdale claimed he was still being visited by the feds decades after he'd left the facility. It seemed a distinct possibility that the craggy-face man had gotten wind of Aiden's investigations. But how?

Was his phone bugged? Had someone planted a listening device in Jarek's office?

He drew a deep breath to settle growing unease and strolled into the motel lobby. The craggy-faced man didn't follow. Aiden asked the desk clerk for a top-floor room facing the front parking lot so he could keep an eye on the man's Bronco, then added an unusual request.

"I'd also like to rent the room directly below it."

The desk clerk, an older black man with a mustache, gave him a long hard look. Aiden provided an excuse for the expensive request he'd come up with years ago.

"Sometimes late at night I walk around the room and bounce a rubber ball off the floor. It relaxes me. But I wouldn't want to disturb any guests staying below."

"Of course," the clerk said, accessing his computer. He was probably used to weird requests. And if the motel was getting paid double, who was he to care?

If a chunkie should manifest tonight, it would land in Aiden's room, on the roof above or in the empty room below. He'd clean up any mess inside and not worry about a roof touchdown.

He put the transaction on his credit card. Five minutes later he was in the top-floor room. He edged aside the drapes and peered down at the parking lot seven stories below.

The Bronco was gone. The craggy-faced man might have realized that his cover was blown. But if indeed he'd been following Aiden, then it was likely someone else had taken over the surveillance. From here on out he'd have to stay extra sharp, keep an eye out for tails.

He hadn't intended the Baltimore excursion to be an overnighter. But, after meeting with Marsdale, he was tired and needed to rest. He'd feel better after a good night's sleep before making the two-hour drive back to Birdsboro.

His phone rang. Caller ID revealed it was Darlene. She'd called several times throughout the day, leaving messages asking her to please call him back so they could talk. He wasn't in the mood. As before, he let her call go through to voicemail. He didn't bother listening to it.

He sat by the window and kept an eye on the parking lot while reviewing what he'd learned so far. The experiment at Tau Nine-One had something to do with Marsdale's area of expertise, stratigraphy. Six babies, nicknamed quiver kids, had been given some sort of infusions, while the seventh – the anomaly, White – was believed to have served as the control for the experiment. The infants were referred to by colors instead of being given regular names. For their adoptions, they were required to be raised in emotionally stable homes by parents with high IQs.

Of course, the child-rearing mandate could be simply common sense. After all, the researchers wouldn't have sought the opposite scenario, looked to have the babies raised by emotionally unstable idiots.

Still, Aiden had a hunch those requirements meant something more. His parents had been well adjusted, which probably had something to do with them being older than typical couples, closer to mid-forties by the time of his adoption.

Both had been highly intelligent. Dad was a brilliant engineer. Mom, although mainly a stay-at-home parent, had once taught college courses in contemporary pop music. In fact, his parents had met as teens at a famed 1965 Beatles concert at Shea Stadium in New York. Despite his new feelings about his family, a smile came over Aiden as he recalled growing up bathed in the sounds of *Sgt Pepper's Lonely Hearts Club Band* and *The White Album*.

Most intriguing was Marsdale's revelation that the experiment had been considered groundbreaking. What had the researchers hoped to achieve? Were they trying to develop children with some kind of bizarre psychic abilities? Somewhere in the world today, were there other men and women who also manifested chunkies?

Dad's letter had mentioned that Aiden had been secretly monitored, that someone had accessed his medical and school records throughout his early childhood. It followed that the other quiver kids also would have been subjected to such discreet inquiries.

He stifled a yawn. Last night he'd slept fitfully, his mind endlessly processing the impact of his father's letter. He grabbed the base of the bed and dragged it to the middle of the room to get it as far as possible from the adjoining rooms in case he spouted a chunkie. Slipping off his Reeboks, he flopped across the bed. Normally he didn't like going to sleep when it was still light out. But a brief nap might clear his head, help him figure out his next move.

TWELVE

Aiden snapped awake. Something was wrong.

It was night. The room was deep in shadow. The only illumination came from locator LEDs on the wall switches and a sliver at the window where two closed drapes didn't quite overlap. The bedside clock read 12:38am.

He gazed at the drapes, momentarily puzzled. And then he remembered. When he'd lain down, the drapes had been open.

A chill coursed through him. He wrenched himself upright in bed.

A figure lunged toward him from the bathroom door. A man's hand clamped across his mouth, preventing him from crying out. The man's other arm encircled his neck and yanked him off the bed.

He clawed frantically at the arms. It was no use. The man was incredibly strong. He couldn't break free.

A second man strode toward him, stopped within the narrow shaft of light coming through the slightly parted drapes. He was tall, with short-cropped red hair and a bushy mustache. He wore a dark suit and tie.

The redheaded man withdrew a small cylinder from an inside vest pocket. It had a long thin neck, like a nasal spray. Coming forward, he grabbed a fistful of Aiden's hair to hold his head in place and jammed the nozzle into Aiden's left nostril.

With his mouth covered, Aiden had no choice but to draw a

deep breath. The inhalant from the cylinder blasted into his head. It burned like crazy. A flaming spike, rammed straight into his brain.

His eyes watered. A wave of dizziness washed over him. Muscles felt suddenly weak.

He began to lose focus. The last thing he saw before drifting into darkness was the smirk on the face of the redheaded man.

THIRTEEN

Aiden awoke. He was lying on his back. At first, he thought grogginess and weakened muscles were the reason he couldn't move. Then he realized his immobility was due to a more ominous reason.

A wide leather strap held his arms tightly against his torso. Similar straps around his ankles, thighs, and chest pinned him to an old workbench. Illumination was dim: a single low-wattage bulb looped over a wooden rafter. Its power cord ran to a car battery on the floor, suggesting the absence of a working electric service.

Fighting panic, Aiden whipped his head around. He was in a deserted two-bay service garage. The brick walls were crumbling. Detritus littered the floor. A set of grimy wheel ramps flanked an inspection pit for working on the underside of vehicles. The garage probably had seen its heyday before the era of pneumatic lifts.

The wall farthest from him had two windows. Most of the panes were shattered, the others layered in dirt. It was pitch black outside.

The front vehicle door and an inset pedestrian door were closed. He craned his neck to see what was behind him. Nothing but old tires stacked atop a trio of rusting oil drums. Beyond that was a back door. It too was shut.

"Help!" he yelled, surprised how weak his voice sounded. Drawing a deep breath, he tried again.

"Help! If anyone can hear me, I'm being held prisoner! Call the police!"

The front pedestrian door opened. The redheaded man ambled in, trailed by Aiden's other assailant, a barrel-chested brute whose chin looked to have been crafted with a straightedge.

"Who are you! What the hell do you want! Cut me loose, goddammit!"

The pair approached the foot of the bench. The redheaded man smiled. Flat Chin betrayed no emotion.

Aiden bellowed for help with all the strength he could muster. His shouts reverberated through the garage.

His captors didn't react. He stopped hollering.

"Very good, mate," the redheaded man said. "Strong lungs. Yell some more if you like. Get it out of your system."

He sounded Scottish, but with the accent overlaid with another one that defied identification. His certainty was unnerving. Aiden's worst fears were confirmed. Wherever they were, it was far from civilization. His shouts wouldn't be heard.

The redheaded man withdrew a satellite phone from his jacket and punched numbers into the keypad.

"It's Nobe," he said when someone at the other end answered. "Our boy's awake."

Nobe. Aiden mouthed the name, committing it to memory. If he got out of this, it could be a clue to help the police track down...

The thought vaporized, overwhelmed by terror.

If he got out of this.

There was a possibility that wouldn't happen, that he would die tonight, strapped to this bench.

Panic gurgled up. He clenched his fists, fought off the fear. If he was to have any chance of surviving, he had to hold it together.

Nobe continued with the call. "Yeah, he's fine... just normal stress adjustin' to his new digs."

Aiden didn't sense deference in Nobe's tone. Yet he had a hunch the person on the other end was the one in charge.

"Uh-huh, got it. See you then."

Nobe hung up and nodded to Flat Chin. "Farlin, roll up his sleeves."

Farlin obediently peeled back Aiden's shirt to the elbows. Nobe withdrew an eight-inch pewter cylinder from an inside jacket pocket. It resembled a narrow-profile flashlight. He flicked a switch, igniting a three-inch needle of blue-white flame at one end.

"This is London," Nobe said, touching the tip of the flame to a patch of bare skin a few inches above Aiden's wrist.

Aiden winced in pain at the touch of the hot needle. Nobe withdrew the cylinder. Aiden stared in horror at the result, a wicked red blister the diameter of a cigarette.

Nobe aimed the needle at a fresh target three inches higher on Aiden's forearm. "And this is Liverpool," he said, creating another ugly burn. "Now, what's say we link these wee little cities of the mighty British Empire."

Aiden had no time to contemplate the disdain expressed in those last three words. Nobe ran the fiery needle up his arm, incinerating the length of skin between the two burns. Curls of smoke wafted up from sizzling flesh. Aiden screamed in mad agony. The pain was unbearable.

Nobe leaned over Aiden's chest and inched the flame toward his other arm. Aiden felt his whole body tensing in expectation of fresh agony.

"How about we go stateside, mate? What say we bring together New York and Boston?"

FOURTEEN

Even through Aiden's shrieks, some analytic portion of his brain recognized that Nobe had skills as a torturer. The man created just enough pain to keep him screaming, but not so much that it took him past a threshold into what would have been blissful unconsciousness.

Although Nobe smiled throughout the ordeal, Aiden didn't get the sense the man was experiencing heightened pleasure. Nobe seemed too professional, too detached to be deemed a sadist. His smile didn't reveal an emotional state. It was simply a mask, meant to cloak a deadened soul.

When the torture finally ended, when Nobe killed the switch and sucked the hot needle back into its cylinder, Aiden's forearms each bore three parallel gashes. It looked liked he'd been raked by a pair of fiery claws.

Lost in an afterglow of throbbing pain, he could only lie there in torment as the minutes passed. The men had asked no questions, demanded no information. The reason for the torture remained a mystery. A part of Aiden wanted to ask why they were doing this. Conversation might help wrench his thoughts away from the agony of his sizzled flesh.

He held back. They probably wouldn't have answered his questions anyway. But fear was a more fundamental reason for keeping quiet. He didn't want to upset the status quo. Engaging the men in discussion could lead to a reappearance of the fiery needle.

A muffled whirring sound came from overhead, drew closer. A helicopter was approaching. Aiden heard it touch down nearby.

The back door creaked open. He twisted around, caught a glimpse of a tall man in an overcoat before the newcomer slipped behind the tires and oil drums.

The man's voice was deep and self-assured. "Aiden Manchester, quiver kid extraordinaire. Naturally, the *extraordinaire* part is merely a guess. But by the time we're through here, I can assure you, I'll know your parameters."

"Who are you?" Aiden whispered.

"Who am I?" The man chuckled. "Let's pretend it is Christmas and go with a color of the season. Why don't you call me Red."

"You're a Tau Nine-One baby."

The man clapped his hands in a mocking manner. "Outstanding! And do you happen to know your own color?"

Aiden saw no reason to lie. "Green. That's the color I dream about."

"I, alas, do not suffer such simplistic dreams. Nevertheless, I'm pleased to make your acquaintance, Green. I'm truly honored that we can finally meet."

Echoes of sincerity seemed to reverberate from the man's flamboyant style of speech. Considering Aiden's predicament, the notion was jarring.

"Green, I am greatly relieved you're not of that dimwitted species, *Moronosaurus rex*. Now Blue, there was a most ignorant creature. Of course, Blue had spent much of his pathetic existence incinerating brain cells with illicit drugs and God knows what else. I trust you're intelligent enough not to waste time attempting to penetrate the realm beyond the beasts."

Aiden didn't understand the remark. He sensed it was rhetorical and required no response. Red rambled on.

"So, to business then. Let's talk about shadows."

"Shadows?"

"Really? Must the two of us play cat-and-mouse games? Waste everybody's time with a drawn-out Q-and-A? It's getting close to dawn and I have a busy day ahead. Why don't we cut to the chase."

"The chase?"

"That's right. Pedal to the metal! Balls out! Show and tell!"

"I don't know what you're talking about."

An exaggerated sigh emanated from behind the barrels. "If you want to do this the hard way, we can oblige. But please be aware of the consequences. Nobe and Farlin have already given you a sampling. I'd hoped those burns would have put you in the right frame of mind. At the very least, they should cue you as to the seriousness of our intentions."

A shudder ran through Aiden. His ravaged arms still hurt. But it wasn't close to the level of agony he'd experienced while the torture was being inflicted.

He struggled to make sense of it all, comprehend what they expected of him. It was clear he had to say something. If not, the burning needle would return.

"You want to know about my psychic abilities?"

"Excellent! I knew you'd come around. Please continue."

Aiden babbled out his history, explained about his manifestations. He included the latest one, though he didn't mention anything about his sister or niece. No way could he risk putting them in peril.

When he finished, Red gave a dismissive chuckle.

"Oh, Green, you're priceless. I could almost begin to buy this nonsense."

"I swear to you, it's the truth."

"Not even one little old shadow to your credit?"

"I swear I don't know what you're talking about."

Nobe took a menacing step toward him with the needle.

"What possible reason would I have to lie?" Aiden blurted out.

Red went quiet for a long moment, as if weighing Aiden's response. When he spoke again, his voice carried an air of resignation.

"As my dearly demented and departed father used to say, 'Never underestimate the unconscious nature of your average citizen.' Still, we must be certain. Would you gentlemen be so kind as to cut off Green's right forefinger."

Nobe ignited the flame. Farlin gripped Aiden's wrist with one hand and bent the forefinger away from the palm with his other hand. Like a surgeon undertaking a delicate operation, Nobe inched the blue-white needle toward the finger's joint.

Numbing terror rippled through Aiden. He tried yanking his hand away, but the bindings and Farlin's iron grip made movement impossible. His head pounded.

"Goddamn it, tell me what you want! Just tell me! I'll cooperate, I swear!"

The flame eased closer. It was less than an inch away. Aiden could feel its heat.

He closed his eyes and gritted his teeth. His head was pounding. It felt as if his brain was going to explode.

But the pain of the needle severing his finger never came. He opened his eyes.

Red was standing over him. He was an imposing figure, at least six feet tall and movie-star handsome. Smooth blond hair was combed straight back. Pale blue eyes studied Aiden's panic with glacial calm.

"No need to prolong this," Red said to his men. "If Mr Manchester had something to tell or show us, he'd have revealed it by now."

Nobe turned off the flame and retracted the cylinder. Farlin, disappointed, released Aiden's finger.

Aiden felt his tightened muscles unwind. His plight hadn't changed. But for the moment, another round of unbearable torment had been averted.

"Nobe, you'll fly back with me," Red ordered. "Tarantian is a go for Wednesday. We'll rendezvous at the cabin that morning for final prep."

"Zero hour?" Farlin asked.

"Late afternoon. Figure on somewhere around 1700, give or take."

Nobe frowned. "I'm telling you again, the op should happen after dark with NVGs."

"The timing can't be helped. Deal with it."

Red returned his attention to Aiden. "I must admit I'm feeling rather invigorated. Do you ever get that warm and tingly sensation when things seem to be going exactly the way you want them to?"

Aiden didn't answer. Red's expression changed to faux sympathy. "But I suppose it's in poor taste for me to be gloating at a time like this. After all, as good as I feel, your world at the moment is rather… well, let's just say you don't have much to be optimistic about."

He turned to Farlin. "You'll take care of cleanup."

Farlin nodded. Red turned and walked away without another word. Nobe followed. Aiden heard the back door open and the two men exit. A few moments later came the sounds of the helicopter taking off.

A new wave of terror washed over Aiden. *You'll take care of cleanup.*

Farlin exited through the front door. Aiden heard a vehicle trunk opening and closing. Farlin returned with two five-gallon plastic containers. Unscrewing the caps, he poured a clear liquid from the first container in a circle around the bench on which Aiden was strapped. The garage's musty odor was overwhelmed by the rich stink of gasoline.

"Oh, Jesus!" Aiden screamed. "Don't do this! Please!"

He may as well have pleaded with a rock. Farlin was going to burn down the garage and everything in it.

I'm going to die.

As the fumes wafted through the garage, the man who was about to terminate the existence of Aiden Manchester backed toward the door with the second gas can, spilling a liquid trail to serve as a fuse. Stopping just inside the door, Farlin lowered the can and drew a matchbook from his pocket.

FIFTEEN

Farlin tore off a match. He made a move to draw it across the striking surface but froze at the last instant. A cold smile came over him. Unlike Red and Nobe with their professional iciness, Farlin enjoyed cruelty.

The second time, Farlin didn't hesitate. The match lit. He held the glittering spike aloft until the flame stabilized.

A figure holding a closed laptop in two hands lunged into the garage behind Farlin. The figure swung the laptop at the side of Farlin's head.

Keyboard met sadist with an explosive crack. Farlin stumbled forward. The lit match flew from his fingers. The flame puffed out before it touched the gas-soaked floor.

The force of the blow would have dropped a normal man. But Farlin recovered fast, whipped a handgun from under his jacket.

Aiden recognized the attacker. It was the craggy-faced man from the motel.

The attacker swung the laptop again, slammed it down across Farlin's wrist. The blow dislodged the gun. The weapon clattered across the floor, slid to the edge of the inspection pit.

Farlin lowered his head and charged. The craggy-faced man raised the laptop for strike three. But he wasn't quick enough.

His opponent slammed into his midsection. The laptop took flight. It splattered across the floor, shedding plastic.

Farlin got a choking grip around his opponent's neck. Aiden's hopes sank. His potential savior looked badly outmatched. Farlin was taller and beefier, and a good quarter century younger.

But there was a quality on the face of the craggy-faced man, a smoldering intensity that suggested defeat wasn't in his nature. He grabbed hold of Farlin's wrist, the one that had taken the blow from the laptop, and squeezed. Farlin grunted in pain and released his stranglehold.

That was all the craggy-faced man needed. He twisted free and spun away.

The combatants warily circled one another. Farlin glanced toward the gun at the edge of the pit. But the craggy-faced man was closer. However, he made no attempt to retrieve the weapon. Instead, he took a step away from the gun, as if taunting Farlin to go for it.

Farlin took the bait and scrambled toward the gun. The craggy-faced man waited. Just as Farlin retrieved the weapon, he danced forward. Spinning like a shot-putter, he lifted his right leg.

His boot caught his enemy's left temple. Stunned, Farlin dropped the gun into the inspection pit and collapsed to his knees. The craggy-faced man grabbed Farlin's head and slammed it down against the wheel ramp. A sickening crack of flesh and bone meeting hardened steel echoed through the garage.

The craggy-faced man repeated the brutal action five more times. When he lifted Farlin's head it was soaked in blood, the nose smashed, the eyes jellied.

The craggy-faced man rifled Farlin's pockets and lifted two wallets. He transferred car keys and a phone to his own jacket then went through one of the wallets. Finding nothing of interest, he cast it aside.

Shoving Farlin into the inspection pit, he glared down at his vanquished foe before turning to Aiden.

"Pretty rough time, huh," he said, unstrapping Aiden from the bench. "Well, hang in there. I'll have you out of here in a jiffy."

The voice was mild, the tone paternal. Aiden had a difficulty connecting the calm words with the explosion of violence he'd just witnessed.

"Who are you?"

The craggy-faced man undid the last strap and helped him off the bench, being careful not to touch Aiden's burned forearms. Aiden, wobbly from the ordeal, immediately fell to his knees.

"Deke Keats," the man said, helping him to his feet.

The name meant nothing to Aiden. A burly arm swept across his back, supported him until they reached the front door. By then, he was able to stand on his own.

Keats retrieved the broken laptop and Farlin's matchbook. Striking a match, he set the whole book aflame and hurled it onto the liquid fuse.

The garage interior exploded into flames as Deke Keats, savior extraordinaire, hustled Aiden out the door.

SIXTEEN

In the murky darkness, Keats used the procured keys to start Farlin's SUV, a Cadillac Escalade. Aiden eased himself into the passenger seat and gazed back at the garage.

His torture chamber squatted under pristine night skies amid forested hills. By the time Keats wheeled them onto the adjacent two-lane road, tongues of flame were licking through the roof.

The road looked long-abandoned. Headlights revealed trees and underbrush encroaching onto the shoulders. Weeds sprouted from cracks in the macadam. Potholes were ubiquitous. Keats drove slow to dodge the worst of them. Even so, the Escalade bottomed out several times.

The bouncy ride agitated Aiden's burns. On top of the renewed pain came the realization of how narrowly he'd escaped death. A shudder went through him. He gripped the dashboard to stop his hands from shaking.

Keats took note. "That's normal post-traumatic reaction. It'll pass. But we need to get those arms looked at."

Aiden had a thousand questions. But the one demanding priority concerned Keats' savagery when taking down Farlin.

"Think he was still alive after you...?"

"Doubt it. In any case, he's a crispy critter by now."

"I know what he tried to do to me so don't take this wrong. But the way you pounded his head into that wheel ramp..."

"Yeah, got carried away. Shouldn't have gone full-tilt on his ass.

Might have squeezed some intel out of him before he croaked."

"That's not exactly what I meant."

Keats shrugged. "Humanity's like a sports team, not everybody makes the cut." The pockmarked face morphed into a scowl. "What's the matter, don't approve of having your butt saved?"

Aiden hesitated, confused by his own feelings. "Better him than me."

"Damn straight. And whatever guilt you're feeling, you should know that Rufus Farlin was walking scum. He took part in at least two massacres of non-combatants that included the rape and torture of women and children. Trust me, Mother Nature's waking up in a better mood this morning knowing Farlin's no longer pissing on her garden."

Ahead of them, a faint tinge of purplish light above a mountain range signaled dawn.

"Where are we?"

"West Virginia, about a hundred miles from Baltimore. This road and everything on it was bypassed by a new highway decades ago. Do you remember how they snatched you?"

Aiden related what he could recall of the attack at the motel.

"Sounds like they knocked you out with that aerosol. Probably a psychogenic anesthetic. Numbs the brain but leaves the body awake. You would have looked drunk. They probably kept their faces averted from the security cameras and walked you right out of the motel without arousing suspicion."

"Why bring me all the way out here?"

"Privacy. I doubt if there's an occupied building within miles. Fits their MO."

"They've done this before?"

"At least once. Victim was tortured in a similar way then burned alive."

"Jesus."

"Jesus doesn't run within a thousand klicks of this crowd."

Keats removed a hand from the wheel and turned on Farlin's phone. He scowled.

"Shit! Triggered a memory wipe. Personal data is gone, including address book and call history. Careful bastards."

He turned off the phone, dug out the battery and SIM card. One at a time, he hurled the three pieces out the window and into the woods.

"How come you were following me?" Aiden asked.

"I wasn't."

"But I saw you at the motel. And earlier at that cafe near Towson University."

"*I* was trailing Farlin. *He* was following you. They must have picked up your trail recently. I spotted Farlin spying on your meeting with that prof. My bad that you spotted me at the motel. I was trying to avoid pulling into a space too close to Farlin and ended up parking near your ride."

"So who are you? Some kind of federal agent?"

"Not exactly."

Keats turned off the road. Dodging small trees, he plowed the Escalade through thick foliage. A hundred feet in they came upon his Bronco. It was hidden behind the crumbling stone foundation of what appeared to be a small derelict factory.

He wiped down the Escalade's steering wheel and dashboard with a handkerchief.

"Clean anything you touched," he instructed, handing the rag to Aiden. "Don't want to leave fingerprints. No time to do a full DNA scrub so this'll have to do."

Outside the car, Keats cleaned off the door handles. He squatted at the rear bumper and from beneath it, retrieved an object the size of a hearing-aid battery.

"Tracker," he explained, as they transferred to the Bronco. "Planted it after I found Farlin. Unfortunately, I made the mistake of falling asleep back at the motel. Didn't think they'd try kidnapping you in the middle of the night. Lucky I downed a beer before hitting the sack."

"A beer?"

"Woke up to take a piss. Checked the tracking software on my laptop and saw that Farlin's car was already miles away. After I realized they'd taken you, I followed the signal. Hid the Bronco and crept up to the garage. Just before I got here I heard a 'copter take off." Keats grimaced. "That was Nobe, wasn't it?"

Aiden nodded.

"Anyway, heard your screams and came a-runnin'. Didn't have time to find a proper weapon, like a two-by-four." Keats gestured to the busted laptop. "So much for my tracking software."

They drove back onto the abandoned road. Keats stopped long enough to sweep away their tire tracks with a leafy branch and cover the spot where they'd entered the woods with fallen branches and clumps of foliage. When he finished, there was no evidence to indicate the passage of vehicles.

"With any luck, it'll be a while before the police find the Escalade. And getting an ID on the body might take some time. Did Farlin happen to say anything about meeting up with Nobe?"

"I think something big is happening Wednesday. Farlin was supposed to rendezvous with them at some cabin that morning."

"They happen to say where this cabin is?"

Aiden's throat was parched. "Got anything to drink?"

Keats gestured to the back seat. Aiden retrieved a well-worn backpack and plopped it on his lap. The contents included a change of clothing, first-aid kit, flashlight, water bottle and wallet. He took two hearty gulps from the bottle.

"The cabin?" Keats pressed.

"I don't think they said. Just that the rendezvous was for some sort of op that's going to happen that day at around 1700 hours. It had an odd name... Tarantian, that's it."

"Doesn't ring a bell. Anything else?"

Aiden swallowed more water. "Nobe wanted the op to happen after dark. And then he mentioned some acronym I'd never heard before."

"NVGs?"

"Yeah, I think so."

"Night vision goggles." Keats went quiet for a time, mulling things over. "OK, whatever this op is, once Farlin's a no-show they'll assume you're still alive. Ideally, that gives us three days before they realize he's missing."

"Three days to do what?"

Keats steered onto the shoulder to dodge a massive pothole. He didn't answer Aiden's question but instead asked for a recounting of the exact events that had occurred in the garage.

Aiden related the story but left out significant parts, including his weird psychic ability and the reason for the torture, as well as the fact that he and Red were quiver kids. He wasn't ready to spill everything to Keats, not until he knew a hell of a lot more about his mysterious rescuer.

At the end of the story, Keats frowned, as if sensing that Aiden hadn't told all. But he didn't press the issue.

"Pour some water on those burns. And pop a couple acetaminophen tabs from the first-aid kit. They'll help with the pain."

Aiden rifled through the kit and swallowed two pills with another hearty gulp from the bottle. He winced as he trickled the liquid onto his arms. The parallel gashes had lost their sharp definition, were now ragged and ugly. The skin was peeling in spots.

Replacing the kit in the backpack he glanced at the wallet. Unable to resist, he flipped it open to reveal a photo of a much younger Keats and a lithe pale-skinned woman. They were sitting together on a beach, building a massive sandcastle. Judging by the steep, white-capped waves breaking behind them and gloomy skies overhead, a storm was coming. But the couple looked happy, oblivious to the weather.

He flipped to the next wallet page, which showed a different woman, older and with short auburn hair and a generous smile. Flanking her were a teenage boy and girl. Opposite the picture was a contemporary photo ID of one Decimus Dionysius Keats, a federal employee. The card had been issued by the GAO.

"You work for the General Accounting Office?"

Keats glared. "Didn't your parents ever teach you not to snoop through other people's belongings?"

"You're an *accountant*?"

"Analyst with the GAO's Defense Capabilities and Management team. Part of my job is studying DOD operation of military facilities with an eye toward improving business practices." Pride crept into his voice. "Every week, we save taxpayers millions of dollars."

"And just for kicks, you rescue kidnap victims and kill bad guys."

"Good to see your sense of humor's intact. Some people who survive trauma take a long time to joke about it. Others never do."

"Decimus Dionysius Keats," Aiden murmured, committing the clunker to memory. "Unusual name."

"Shit happens. Mother taught Ancient Greek and Latin. Oh, and speaking of wallets, here's yours."

Keats handed Aiden the second wallet taken from Farlin. Aiden checked it. His money and various cards and IDs seemed intact. He shoved the wallet in his back pocket but bumped his burned left arm as he did so. He winced with an explosion of fresh pain.

The worst of the agony passed. Aiden realized how tired he was. He leaned the seat back and tried closing his eyes. But there was still too much adrenaline flowing for slumber to take hold.

"What happens when they find out I'm still alive?" he asked.

"Next time, they'll make sure the job's done right. But look on the bright side. They probably won't torture you again. I'm sure they already got what they needed."

Keats paused, as if waiting for Aiden to take the hint and come clean about the reason for the torture and what really had gone on in the garage. But he remained silent.

His rescuer shrugged. "Anyway, next time it'll likely be a quick execution."

"Lucky me."

SEVENTEEN

By the time the abandoned road intersected a highway, the crimson glory of a new dawn painted eastern skies. Traffic was light but Keats waited until no vehicles were visible in either direction before guiding the Bronco around a weathered barricade. They bounced across a shallow drainage ditch and accelerated onto the four-laner, heading west.

"Where are we going?" Aiden asked. "Not back to Baltimore?"

"Bad idea. Nobe may have left one of his men at the motel to see if anyone comes asking about you."

"So the nearest police station, then."

"Bad idea number two."

Aiden didn't object. No matter how crazy things were, no matter how much pain he was in, he didn't want to involve the authorities either. Considering that he wasn't prepared to tell Keats the entire truth, he certainly wasn't ready to unload to a bunch of cops. But beyond that there was a reason more profound: a persistent and inexplicable urge to continue his quest no matter what the cost.

"What about my car? My phone, clothing and the rest of my stuff is back there?"

"Consider them lost. How much cash do you have?"

Aiden eased a hand into his back pocket for the wallet, winced as his burned forearm rubbed the material.

"About $600." It was pretty much all he had to his name and included the money from Jarek. He'd withdrawn nearly everything from his bank account for the New Hampshire trip, and the motel had nearly maxed out his credit card.

"That should hold you for a little while."

"I need to call my sister. Do you have a phone?"

"You don't want to call or text anyone. I'm not sure how long Farlin was on your tail, but it's possible they bugged your sister's phone as well as yours. If so, letting them know you're still alive could put her in danger."

The thought of Darlene and Leah under threat sent a stab of worry through Aiden. But if Keats was right, it was best to avoid any contact, at least for the time being.

"So where are we going?" he repeated.

"Got an old buddy living in Virginia, about an hour's drive. He can look at those arms."

Despite the pills, the pain wasn't lessening. Aiden didn't relish waiting that long. "Might be a hospital closer."

"Doctors will ask about those burns and possibly call the police. Even if you make up some bullshit story and they buy it, once Farlin's body is found you'll become a suspect. Then you'll have cops on your ass as well as mercs."

"That's what Farlin was? A mercenary?"

"Yeah. He worked for Nobe." Keats again grimaced at the name. "Noa Bruno Novakovic. Born to a well-to-do Croatian family who moved to Scotland after the father was accused of war crimes. Nobe joined the army, worked his way into the SAS – British special forces. They booted him for excessive brutality. He was a PSC for a while – private security contractor. Then he went rogue, put together a gang of like-minded killers. They've been linked to the Russian drug trade, assassinations in Colombia, tribal massacres in Nigeria and South Sudan, you name it. If it's nasty you want, they're top of the game."

Keats reached into the glove compartment and withdrew a manila envelope. He handed it to Aiden. Inside were autopsy photos of a naked man whose face and upper body were badly scorched. One photo showed a closeup of the forearms, which had escaped the worst of the fire. A pattern of burns similar to Aiden's was faintly visible.

In contrast to the grisly images was a photo of him in better days, probably a high school graduation picture. Rodrick O. Tyler, age twenty-nine at the time of his death, was the only child of British husband-and-wife orthodontists. His olive skin tone suggested either a Latino or African-American heritage.

"He was my age," Aiden whispered.

Keats raised an eyebrow. "That mean something to you?"

Aiden responded with a noncommittal shrug. He still wasn't ready to tell all. But if his interrogator back at the garage had been truthful – and Aiden had no reason to suspect Red had lied – the dead man was the quiver kid known as Blue.

"You sure you didn't know him?"

Aiden shook his head. "Where did this happen?"

"Scotland Yard found him three weeks ago in an abandoned, burned-out apartment building in London. They suspect arson. Rodrick Tyler was a long-time addict. Heroin, fentanyl, whatever he could get his hands on. The cops figured he crossed some drug gang and it was a revenge killing. Of course, you and I know different."

Keats again waited expectantly for him to divulge more. Aiden changed the subject.

"Why burn the bodies?"

"Good way to eliminate evidence of a crime. Besides, it was one of Farlin's special delights. Those civilian massacres I mentioned? His weapon of choice was a flamethrower."

"So what's your connection to all this?"

"I'm trying to track down Nobe's employer, the person behind it all. From what you've told me, this man Red sounds like a prime candidate. Did your captors ever mention someone called 'the Clerk'?"

"No. Who's that?"

"Not sure. Just a name I came across."

"Are you really a GAO analyst?"

"I am, but I'm on a leave of absence." Keats hesitated. "Let's just say I have a night job."

"Working for whom?"

"Can't say."

Aiden stuffed the photos back in the envelope and returned it to the glove compartment. An immense tiredness rose up from deep inside. He felt his eyes drifting shut.

"I think... I need... to sleep."

He leaned back. Before consciousness dissolved, he perceived a blurred image of a room filled with six cribs, three on a side. The cribs were empty but the room echoed to the sound of crying babies.

EIGHTEEN

The trailer park looked clean and tidy. Preschoolers romped in a playlot under the watchful eyes of two obese young women in shorts and halter-tops. A group of older kids with bats and gloves ambled toward an adjacent field for an early Sunday game.

Aiden awoke and stretched to wipe away the vestiges of sleep. The movement brought stabs of pain in both arms. The nap had eased his fatigue but had done little to relieve his burns.

Keats parked the Bronco in front of a well-maintained trailer with a fenced-in vegetable garden. A one-legged man sat on the stoop reading a newspaper. He was in his forties and had ruddy skin, long sideburns, and a receding hairline. His attire consisted of a Baltimore Ravens sweatshirt and tie-dyed shorts.

His left leg was missing from mid-thigh down. In its place was a crude prosthesis, obviously homemade. A series of anodized rods were held together with an ungainly collection of hinges, ratchets and ball joints. The foot was a flat aluminum plate with a decorative clump of sneaker glued to the top. A tiny American flag decal marked the spot where a big toe should have been.

Keats and the man greeted one another with smiles then a bear hug that could have crushed diamond.

"Rory Tablone, Aiden Manchester," Keats introduced. "Aiden's had a little accident."

Rory held open the screen door and ushered them into the trailer. The funky prosthesis worked well; his limp was barely noticeable. But there was a *click-clack* noise whenever he bent at the knee.

They sat at the kitchen table. Rory gripped Aiden's wrists, studied the scorch marks. "Somebody don't much like your ass, huh? Hope you got payback."

Aiden didn't reply. Rory turned to Keats.

"Pretty decent clinic a few miles down the road. I know one of the docs."

"Rather not."

"You flying under the radar here, Deke?"

"Yeah. Can you help?"

Rory disappeared through a draped partition into the bedroom. He returned with a medical kit and bandages. Motioning for Aiden to stretch out his arms, he probed at the wounds with surgical scissors. Aiden tried to keep still but flinched each time he was touched.

"Mostly second-degree burns. If they were third degree, it actually might not hurt as much. Underlying nerves would be gone."

"You're a doctor?"

Rory chuckled. "How many docs you know who live in trailer parks? No, I was squad medic way back when."

He dabbed at the wounds with a cool wet cloth and trimmed loose pieces of skin. Aiden clenched his fists against the pain and looked away. He found himself gazing down at the prosthesis. Rory took notice.

"Don't see one of these everyday, huh? Want to guess where I lost the original?"

"Iraq? Afghanistan?"

"Interstate 81," Rory said with a wry grin. "Did a couple tours, including some unconventional ops, and hardly got scratched. Then came home on leave and crashed my Harley into an eighteen-wheeler."

Aiden guessed that "unconventional ops" referred to special forces missions. Keats and Rory must have served together in one of the elite units.

"The VA fitted me with an artificial limb but I didn't take to the sucker. Used it as a template to make this one." He turned to Keats. "How's family?"

"Fine."

"Alexandra?"

"Hanging in there," Keats mumbled, quickly changing the subject. "What about you? How's Cindy?"

"Marriage is one wicked-ass seesaw, never know who's going to have the upper hand." Rory grinned. "But hey, at the end of the day it all balances out."

"Sorry I couldn't make the wedding."

"No sweat. Toothpick and Bling showed their ugly mugs, so the old gang was represented."

The small talk continued as Rory cleaned the burns. Aiden learned that Deke Keats had a wife, Tonya, and two children, and that they lived in a northern Virginia suburb within commuting distance of DC. The son was in middle school and the daughter was doing well as a freshman at the University of Delaware. They were obviously the ones Aiden had seen in Keats' wallet.

It wasn't clear who Alexandra was. But Keats definitely didn't want to talk about her. He chopped off several more inquiries before Rory finally got the message. Aiden had a hunch she was the lithe woman from the other photo, the one building the sandcastle with him on the beach.

Rory finished by coating Aiden's burned skin with silver sulfadiazine, an antibiotic cream. He dressed the wounds with strips of gauze and secured them with tape.

"That's about all I can do for you. I'll give you some extra bandages and cream. Change the dressing and recoat the wounds at least once a day. Don't break the blisters. And these should help with the pain."

He handed Aiden a pillbox with two dozen ivory tablets.

"What are they?"

"Basement baddies." At the look on Aiden's face, he explained. "Homemade shit, a variant of oxy. They can be addictive little suckers so don't get carried away. Pop one only when the pain gets real bad."

Rory stood up.

"For burns like these, infection's your main worry. If you get swelling, redness or a lot of pus, don't listen to Captain America here." He playfully booted Keats in the shin with his metal foot. "Hightail your ass straight to the nearest emergency room."

Rory went to the bedroom, returned shortly with jeans, a long-sleeved plaid shirt and fresh underwear and socks. He handed the clothes to Aiden. "We look about the same size."

"Thanks. I really appreciate this." He reached for his wallet. "I can pay you–"

"Forget it. I owe Deke big time. Because of him, I'm still suckin' air." Rory's face buckled into a clumsy smile, as if embarrassed by the revelation. "But hey, it all works out in the long run. Karmic balance, circle of life, pay it forward. Shit like that."

"Since you're in such a munificent mood," Keats said, "I need a couple more favors."

"Shoot."

"Something to eat. An hour or so alone with Aiden. Oh, and I don't think anybody's going to come asking about us, but in case they do–"

"You were never here," Rory finished. "Got toast, cereal and breakfast bars, not much else. Cindy's hitting the supermarket on her way home from work this afternoon."

"That'll do fine."

Rory headed for the door. "I'll be at the McDonald's down the road if you need me. You gonna be gone before I get back?"

"Expect so."

"Deke, if you need an extra hand on this one…"

"This is some bad shit. You don't want a piece of it."

"Offer stands."

Keats nodded. Rory left the trailer. Through the screen door, the *click-clack* of his artificial knee faded into the distance.

NINETEEN

Aiden was famished. After changing into the new clothes, he drowned cereal in milk and trucked the bowl to the bedroom. Keats sat at a compact desk using Rory's laptop to search for Tarantian. Aiden perched on the bed within viewing distance and attacked breakfast.

The search engine revealed Tarantian to be a geosciences term used in stratigraphy. It referred to a recent stage of the geological time scale, from roughly twelve thousand to one hundred and twenty-six thousand years ago, a period characterized by the appearance and recession of glaciers, the global spread of humans and the extinction of many animals, such as mammoths and saber-toothed tigers. It seemed obvious to Aiden that the term somehow related to whatever Marsdale had been working on at Tau Nine-One.

Keats picked up on something about his reaction. "Mean anything to you?"

Aiden shook his head.

"I'll check with my sources in DC, see if Tarantian is a known code name. Might be some DOD or CIA op that Nobe tapped into."

"Is that who sent you after Nobe and Farlin?" Aiden asked. "The Pentagon or the CIA?"

Keats turned off the computer. "You look like you're feeling better."

"Yeah, pain's not nearly as bad. Rory's pill definitely helped. And the food."

"Good. Then it's time to come clean. For starters, I want to know why they snatched you. And I want to know everything that happened in that garage."

"Information's a two-way street."

"Fair enough. You first." Keats folded his arms in a stern pose and waited.

Aiden gobbled the rest of his cereal while considering options. Despite Keats having saved his life, he still didn't fully trust the man. And if he started talking about chunkies, Keats might well think he was a nutjob. Yet Aiden also knew he needed help, and that his life could depend on it. A leap of faith was required.

He told Keats everything that had occurred in the past few days starting with his father's letter. He talked about his manifestations, his adoption, his recurring green dream that signified his color name, and Tau Nine-One. He described the encounter with Marsdale and what the professor had revealed about the quiver kids experiment and its possible connection to the field of geology. He ended his revelations with the details of Red's interrogation in the garage.

When he finished, Keats gave a thoughtful nod. "So this Red seems to believe you have some other kind of psychic power, something more than just making these chunkies. And you figure that's why they tortured you?"

"Yeah. He was trying to force me into telling him or showing him what I could do."

"I never believed in psychic stuff. Thought it was bullshit. In fact, not too long ago I would have taken you for a genuine whack job. But my thinking on the subject has evolved.

"Last month there was a deadly incident near Tau Nine-One. Three men – two railfans and their guide – were out hiking. They were trying to get pictures of the train that shuttles workers back and forth. The hikers ended up in the wrong place at the wrong time. They ran into Nobe and his right-hand man, an electronics expert named Kokay. Another nasty piece of work."

Keats swiveled toward the bedroom window, his attention drawn by movement at the neighboring trailer. Two children were playing hide-and-seek. The boy jumped out from behind a recycling container and swung around a washline pole, startling the girl.

"Nobe murdered the guide and one of the railfans. The second railfan, Henry Carpousis, was trying to escape when he had a close encounter with a grizzly.

"The hikers' bodies landed at the bottom of a ravine. Henry Carpousis was mauled and bleeding bad so Nobe left him there. Probably figured that by the time a search party found him, he'd be dead, and that the searchers would assume the hikers had run into the bear at the top of the ravine and fallen to their deaths. It's a story that likely would have held up to routine scrutiny.

"But leaving Henry Carpousis alive turned out to be a mistake on Nobe's part. It took three days, but this badly injured, mild-mannered railfan managed to crawl his way out of that wilderness." Keats shook his head. "Lots of guys I know couldn't have done what he did. Happens to some folks when they're pushed to the brink. Hidden courage and strength awakens, and they turn into real meat-eating SOBs."

"I don't recall hearing about any of this on the news."

"The incident was hushed up in the name of national security. Henry Carpousis was persuaded to lie about what really happened. Standard operating procedure. Keep black sites like Tau Nine-One as far from media scrutiny as possible.

"But here's where it gets weird. Henry Carpousis ran into more than just Nobe, Kokay and a pissed-off grizzly."

Keats told Aiden about the ghostly projection, the figure with the *King Kong* mask that may have been some new kind of hologram.

"Nobe referred to it as a shadow. That mean anything to you?"

"Red mentioned the word. But that's the first time I heard it, at least in that context. Could this Henry Carpousis have been hallucinating?"

"That's what the military interrogators concluded. Three days alone in the wilderness, badly injured, can mess up your head, jumble fantasy and reality. But I have some contacts at the DOD, and one of them slipped me the video of Henry's debriefing. He might have misinterpreted what he was seeing but my gut tells me it was real."

Aiden added Keats's fresh information to what, over the past few days, was a relentlessly expanding mystery. The only thing that seemed clear was that Tau Nine-One was at the center of it all.

"So what were Nobe and Kokay doing near Tau in the first place?" Aiden asked. "I'm guessing they weren't taking pictures of old trains."

"Best guess by the debriefers was that it was a recon mission, maybe to gauge Tau Nine-One's defenses. They theorized that the mercs were following the tracks toward the facility. Kokay was carrying instruments of some sort. It's possible his gear was being used to locate Tau Nine-One's outer-perimeter sensor net."

"They were looking for a way in?"

Keats nodded. "That's the theory. Still, there are some big holes in it. First, it's hard to imagine they could actually penetrate that place. It's well protected. State-of-the-art sensors, satellite sweeps, not to mention a detachment of Marines. But whatever Nobe and Kokay were up to, it was important enough to risk the murder of those hikers to keep it under wraps."

"Do you have any idea what goes on there?"

"Over the years a few files crossed my desk at GAO. Tau is under DARPA's purview. Much of the research involves metamaterials engineering. They develop advanced battlefield materials to protect soldiers and equipment."

"But that's just smoke and mirrors."

"No, it's genuine. But there's something else there, a project above my clearance level. It's a SAP – a Special Access Program – and one of the blackest ones I've ever come across. Even its budget is classified. It doesn't show up in GAO files except as a code number."

"Tau's big secret," Aiden murmured. "Any chance your Washington connections can get us through the door?"

"Forget it. And since the incident with the hikers, security's been tightened even more."

Aiden began pacing the small bedroom. "We need to figure out why Red is killing quiver kids. That's got to be the key to everything that's happened. Which means we have to find the other four. Gold, Magenta, Cyan and White."

"You're presuming they're still alive. Red may have gotten to them already."

"I don't think so. When he talked about Blue, this Rodrick Tyler, I had the sense he was bragging. I think if he'd killed the others he'd have enjoyed telling me about it."

Keats warmed to the idea of tracking down the other quiver kids. "If we could locate just one of them, we could set a trap for Red and Nobe."

"Sounds like a plan. But first, you need to tell me who you work for."

"That's classified."

"I think you mean not officially sanctioned. I'm guessing that explains why you were the only one coming to rescue me. After what happened to those hikers, I'd have thought there'd be a major investigation underway."

"There is. Homeland Security and DOD have agents out questioning anyone with past or present links to Tau Nine-One."

"But that's not your job, is it?"

Keats turned back to the window. The children had left the neighboring yard. A pit bull was now tied to the washline pole. It looked mean and hungry.

"No," he said quietly. "Not my job."

"This whole mess could end with Red and Nobe captured and put on trial," Aiden said. "But I'm guessing not everyone in our government would want such a public spectacle, even decades later. If word of the quiver kids experiment ever leaked out..."

Keats didn't answer. He didn't have to. Aiden's darkest suspicions seemed to be confirmed. Keats wasn't like those other government agents. He hadn't been dispatched to bring Red and his cronies to justice.

He'd been sent to kill them.

PART 2
THE CLERK

TWENTY

Michael de Clerkin gazed out the west windows of his Century City penthouse office. It was an early Sunday afternoon in the Los Angeles basin and the skies were clear, an inversion layer having swept the smog out to sea. Beyond the buildings and freeways visible from his fortieth-floor perch he glimpsed a swath of Pacific Ocean.

At the moment, the sea was tranquil. But should some cataclysmic offshore event occur, such as the fracturing of a suboceanic fault line, that serenity would vanish in an instant. A monstrous tidal wave would crash ashore, possibly killing millions.

Michael liked the sea, liked its latent strength. He and the sea were similar in that respect. At the moment, he too was serene. But that could change the instant he donned a shadow and utilized its special power. And, if Wednesday's long-gestating events went according to plan, that power would undergo a spectacular expansion.

The thought was so pleasant it turned him on. He beeped the desk phone for Trish, his newest executive assistant.

The door opened. Trish Belmont peeked around the edge. Her reticence brought to mind a nervous child entering an adult sanctum.

She was petite with short blond curls. A loose pantsuit from some knock-off designer veiled attractive curves. Michael was intrigued by her combination of camouflaged sexuality and natural beauty. Even after a few years out of some no-name Midwestern religious college, Trish remained less worldly than his previous assistants, most of whom had been unabashed social climbers eager to become the first Mrs de Clerkin. Although all of them ultimately had surrendered to his sexual demands, none had come close to getting their claws into his fortune.

A short career as his executive assistant at Krame-Tee Corp was a given. His last one had left after threatening Michael with a lawsuit. The aggravating incident had occurred at an arts fundraiser sponsored by the company.

The assistant had contradicted him in public, in front of a US senator and some business associates no less. Later in the limousine, he'd lectured her to the point of tears, then driven the lesson home with a kidney punch. His fist barely knocked the wind out of her but she'd quit the next day. As in previous incidents, his promise of a generous out-of-court settlement with an ironclad nondisclosure agreement was enough to buy her silence, keep her from getting all self-righteous and trying to out him with that hashtag-me-too bullshit.

"Sir?" Trish asked. She stood awkwardly on the other side of his desk, waiting for a response.

Michael drank in her beauty, aware he was making her anxious but enjoying making her wait. When it looked like she couldn't stand another moment without peeing her pants, he smiled and handed her a sheaf of pages fresh from his printer.

"Revisions in maternity leave and daycare policy," he explained. "More generous benefits. Keeps us competitive with what other companies are offering. Not to mention it's the right thing to do."

Michael could care less. His legal department had requested the changes to align corporate policy with the latest changes in way-too-liberal California law. Normally, one of his VPs handled such things. Michael had only bothered making a printout to convince Trish he was a caring person.

Besides, he liked paperwork, liked the feel of cellulose pulp. Paper was something real. Computerized data propelled the twenty-first century economy, yet gazing at a screen wasn't the same as holding a printout. It was the difference between a window and a door, between a thing you merely looked through and a thing you could actually touch.

A window and a door. He was struck by the analogy to his own power. Today he was a window, able to transmit a shadow of himself – essentially a live hologram – to practically anywhere on the planet. Yet he couldn't physically interact with a destination environment, only observe.

In three days, however, years of effort would be rewarded when Tarantian reached fruition. Once he had the prize in hand, perhaps he would become a door, able to transmit not just a mere shadow but his entire physical being. That alone could make him the most potent and extraordinary human on the face of the Earth. But it might represent only a start. There was no telling what fantastic abilities would cluster to him.

He'd felt for a long time now that he was in possession of a great latent power. That power was just waiting for the right impetus to burst free, to bloom.

It's my destiny.

He grinned, pleased by the thought. Trish, not comprehending the reason for his expression, reacted with a tentative smile.

Naïve yet sexy. Such sheltered women were few and far between. Seduction took extra effort with girls like Trish, who wore their decency like a cloak of armor. But Michael trusted his persuasive abilities. Eventually, she'd come around.

And if Wednesday went well, Michael could be on his way to a state mirroring divinity. Gods, by definition, transcended the petty rules of society. Gods implemented their own agendas. Perhaps then he'd no longer bother with seduction games. Perhaps he'd simply fuck women like Trish when and where he pleased.

"Have Legal vet the policy," he instructed. "Oh, and thanks again for coming in on a Sunday. I hope I didn't spoil your weekend."

"Not at all, sir."

She turned to leave but was startled by a man standing in the doorway.

Michael scowled. "It's all right, Trish. I know this gentleman."

Nobe wore uncharacteristic attire: a gray suit with a gaudy chartreuse tie. He grinned lecherously at Trish as she slipped nervously past him and closed the door behind her.

"What are you doing here?" Michael demanded.

Nobe settled his lanky frame in the office's four-thousand-dollar Eames lounger and propped his feet on the coffee table. "That doll doesn't look your type. Too wholesome."

"I asked what you're doing here."

He and Nobe had flown in from West Virginia this morning on the corporate jet after taking care of business with Green in that garage. By now, the merc should have been boarding a commercial flight to Montana to make final preparations for Tarantian.

Nobe squirmed in the chair, trying to get comfortable. There was something fastidious in his movements, a trait that worked to his advantage. Opponents often underestimated him, not realizing until too late just what sort of deadly predator they faced.

"Well?" Michael was losing patience. Nobe's attitude could be tiresome.

"Well what, mate? Can't stop by for a friendly visit to the Clerk?"

Michael restrained his annoyance. He didn't care for the nickname the mercs had given him. Nobe was the only one bold enough to use it to his face, however. He had to admit, the man was fearless. Even when Michael had created a shadow in his presence for the first time, Nobe hadn't been intimidated. An imperious self-confidence seemed to immunize him against normal human reactions.

Nobe finally got to the point. "Kokay and I needed to finish some business downtown. Had to see a man about a grenade launcher."

"I thought you'd already purchased all the equipment."

"Never hurts to pack a spare RPG. I'll send you the bill."

Michael grimaced. "Yes, do that."

Nobe got up and ambled to a shelf by the window. He picked up a drone toy displayed there, a bat-like monster with a quartet of claws. It was from a product line manufactured by a Krame-Tee subsidiary in Taiwan.

He activated the controller. A faint whirring filled the office as coaxial rotors lifted the bat monster off the shelf.

"Having fun?" Michael asked.

"Always. Have you heard from Farlin?"

"No, why?"

"I've been trying to call him. Can't get through."

"I had trouble with my own phone in that wilderness."

Nobe had selected an excellent location for the interrogation and disposal of Green. But such isolated regions did have drawbacks. For Wednesday, they'd be equipped with satellite phones, obviating such concerns. Although Nobe had used a sat to call Michael during the incident with the railfans, he was wary of their overuse. Even though the sats were encrypted, they tended to be scanned more diligently by NSA snoops.

"Farlin wouldn't be hanging around out there," Nobe said, hovering the drone so close to the window that its plastic rotors chattered against the glass. "He should be hundreds of miles away by now."

"Maybe he's out of range of a cell tower."

"Maybe."

"The fire was discovered?"

"Local cops found a burned body. No ID yet."

"Doesn't sound like we have a problem. Farlin was only supposed to check in if something went wrong."

Michael knew from experience that when it came to missions, Nobe was a perfectionist. Anything out of the ordinary caused him to fret, and he'd fretted up a storm after that unexpected encounter with the railfans. It was a good trait for someone in his profession.

"You could have told me all this over the phone," Michael said.

"I could have. But there's something else. An itsy bitsy little matter. Thought it best to broach it in person."

"If this is about money, let me point out that you and your men are already being paid an obscenely large fee."

"It's not about the money."

"What then?"

Nobe grinned as he guided the drone to a gentle landing on the shelf. "I found your long-lost princess."

"Magenta," Michael whispered. A faint tremble of excitement coursed through him.

"Her name is Jessica Von Dohren. Lives near North Platte, Nebraska."

"How'd you locate her?"

"One of my sources came through."

Michael nodded. The merc had a network of governmental and military contacts rivaling his own. That was impressive, considering Krame-Tee was a major defense contractor with deep roots into Washington.

"We could fly out there this evening," Nobe suggested. "She lives all by her lonesome, a ranch house in the middle of nowhere. Won't even have to set up a snatch. We can do her in the comfort of her own bedroom."

Nobe bared his teeth. Michael suspected he entertained his own fantasies for the female quiver kid once the interrogation was complete. Nobe had admired the photo Michael had snapped of Magenta when the two of them had met briefly a decade ago. She'd been drop-dead gorgeous back then. It was doubtful the passage of years had dimmed such extraordinary beauty.

Michael found it odd but comforting that after years of searching, he'd located three quiver kids in the space of a month. First Blue, then Green. And now Magenta. There was no reason to go after White, who hadn't received an infusion. That left only the other two girls, Gold and Cyan, in the wind. And the way Michael's luck was going, he fully expected to locate and eliminate those two in the near future.

Maybe it wasn't luck. Maybe fate was aligning itself with him in recognition of his soon-to-be remarkable abilities. Perhaps ultra-intelligent beings like himself, who grasped the nuances of power and knew how to groom themselves to wield it, had a direct impact – a godlike impact – upon destiny itself.

He drummed his fingers on the desk, debating options. A trip to the Midwest would consume a good chunk of time. He had a dinner meeting this evening and afterwards intended to do a final review of Tarantian, make sure no details of the assault plan had been overlooked. Still, he could complete that work on the jet.

Although it was doubtful Magenta had advanced any farther than the others, Michael wanted to confront her face to face. Only then would he be able to gauge whether she had significant abilities and posed a threat.

He hadn't done that with the first quiver kid. Instead he'd sent a shadow to that abandoned London apartment building for Blue's interrogation. Rodrick Tyler had been a hopeless addict. Even after Nobe had employed the hot needle to put him in the proper frame of mind, the man had provided little useful information. He'd admitted that his adopted parents had revealed to him that he was the quiver kid known as Blue and, like Michael and Aiden Manchester, he'd begun to experience manifestations when puberty kicked in.

But he hadn't gone on to develop his abilities. Instead, he'd apparently become fixated on some crazy urge to, in his own words, "penetrate the realm beyond the beasts." The desire likely was the byproduct of a drug-addled brain. Still, perhaps there was something more to it than Michael's shadow-self had been able to perceive.

However potent a shadow, it produced a kind of distancing effect between user and the environment he entered. It was indeed a window but a window that could be blurred, not in a visual sense but in Michael's ability to accurately discern the more subtle emotional states during a transmission. That's why he'd decided to confront Green and the rest of the quiver kids in person.

"Do you have Magenta under surveillance?" he asked.

Nobe shook his head. "But I can have Vesely and Rosen onsite by evening."

"Do it." Michael hesitated. "Are you sure this won't compromise preparations for–"

"Relax, Tarantian is set. No need for any of us to be in Montana this soon."

"All right. We'll pay Magenta a visit. Meet me tonight at the airport. Ten-thirty sharp."

Nobe slithered from his chair and ambled toward the exit.

"And please ask my assistant to step back in."

Nobe opened the door and gestured to Trish. As she entered, the merc made a leering face behind her back and mouthed the words *too wholesome*.

TWENTY-ONE

Aiden lobbied for a second crack at Dr Marsdale. But Keats believed that even if the retired professor could be persuaded to divulge more about Tau Nine-One, it wouldn't help them find the other four quiver kids. Instead, Keats got on the phone and chartered a turboprop to fly them from the nearest airport to Sioux Falls, South Dakota, to see a man named Chef. He refused to say why.

Before arranging for the flight, Keats had made three other calls from Rory's trailer. Aiden had been asked to step into the kitchen so Keats could have privacy in the bedroom. However, the walls were thin. By cupping his ear, Aiden was able to garner a few snippets.

The first call was to someone who went by the name, or codename, of Icy Ned. Keats divulged what he knew about Tau Nine-One and the quiver kids, and asked Icy Ned to look into the matter and forward what he learned to Chef.

The second call was to Chef himself. But Aiden missed most of that conversation because of Rory's refrigerator, which had a bad compressor. The unit had come on, and the rattling noise made eavesdropping impossible.

The fridge shut down in time for Keats' final call, to his wife Tonya. They'd argued. She wanted Keats to come home. He said he couldn't until his work was completed. The name Alexandra again surfaced. Aiden gathered that Alexandra was institutionalized because of some psychological malady. Keats wanted Tonya to visit Alexandra while he was gone, but Tonya apparently wasn't keen on the idea.

After Keats had finished the calls, Aiden asked to borrow his phone.

"I need to get hold of my sister, tell her I'm OK."

"Bad idea. Like I said, the mercs might be tapping her phones."

"You called your wife."

Keats glared at Aiden's admission that he'd been eavesdropping. "No one knows I'm connected to any of this. My phone's safe. Can't say the same for your sister's."

"I thought of a way around that. Darlene has a neighbor who sometimes babysits my niece. She's a retired cop so she'll be cool. I'll get her to deliver my message to Darlene face to face."

"There's still a risk."

"I'm not asking."

He extended his hand. Keats grudgingly surrendered the phone. "Make it quick. We need to catch that flight."

The neighbor was naturally curious when Aiden outlined his odd request. But she was savvy enough not to ask too many questions after he stressed how vital it was to keep things confidential. He passed along the message, doing his best to make it sound reassuring.

Since the harrowing events of the previous night, he'd come to regret storming out on Darlene in a rage. Although he was still mad at her for keeping the truth from him, he didn't want her needlessly worrying. The neighbor promised to talk to his sister right away and tell her that Aiden was fine but would be traveling for a few days and be incommunicado.

They departed for the airport. The drive gave Aiden time to think, which also helped keep his mind off his burned arms. Rory's homemade pills helped. But the pain was still there, like a constant background noise.

There was plenty to occupy his thoughts. Unfortunately, little of it was encouraging. On this beautiful Sunday morning he should have been back in Birdsboro, maybe taking Leah to the playground or firing up his old Xbox. Instead, he was in the company of a government assassin, on the run from ruthless mercenaries who wanted him dead.

He repressed a shudder as the memory of his torture resurfaced. The terror of those moments with Nobe's flesh-burning needle likely would haunt the rest of his days.

They pulled into a garage near the airport's main terminal. Keats parked the Bronco and turned to him.

"From here on out, things are liable to go from bad to worse. So you have a choice. Board the plane with me, or take my car and head out on your own. If you choose to go on the run you'll need to lay low, stay off the grid as long as possible. Avoid main roads and urban areas where you're more likely to be scanned by municipal camera pods or retail security cams. Don't use plastic. Pay cash for everything and stretch your dollars. They might have to last you a while."

"Doesn't sound like much of a choice."

"It's not. But I need you to be clear about something. I'm taking down Red, Nobe and the whole lot of them. Best case scenario, we locate another quiver kid and use him or her to set a trap. But if that doesn't pan out, I might have to go with Plan B."

Aiden understood. "Use *me* as bait."

"Once they know you're still alive, we can draw them in." Keats paused. "I like you, Aiden. I really do. If things go south, I'd probably even shed a tear at your funeral."

"If things go south, I'm guessing we'll be in matching caskets."

Despite his brazen words, Aiden acknowledged a temptation to take the safer course, go underground until this mess was over. Yet he also recognized a feeling that had been growing since setting eyes on his father's letter. It was the sense of being caught up in forces beyond his control, being swept toward some unknown destiny. He was on a journey, one that was connected in some mysterious way to the nature of quiver – whatever the hell *that* was. He had the eerie sense that it was a journey he'd been on his entire life.

He opened the door and hopped from the Bronco.

"C'mon, Keats, we're wasting time. We've got a plane to catch."

TWENTY-TWO

Their Cessna landed at Sioux Falls Regional Airport by midafternoon Sunday. For once, Aiden wasn't bothered by flying and the fear that he might fall asleep and manifest a chunkie and cause the plane to go into a tailspin. His peculiar brand of aerophobia was no match for recent near-death memories of pain and flame.

They left the terminal on foot and headed south through an industrial area. A winding two-mile walk brought them to a memorial park. Aiden waited on a bench along a flag-laden circular concourse while Keats approached a man standing beneath a tree.

Chef was basketball tall, at least six-foot-four, with ruddy skin and a ponytail harnessing black hair streaked with white. He looked a bit younger than Keats, and of Native American descent. Wearing an ivory business suit, he watched Keats' approach from behind designer sunglasses.

Aiden was too far away to make out what they were saying. The conversation was brief. Chef lit a fat cigar, put a small object in Keats' palm and walked off into the trees.

Keats returned and led them to the parking lot. Aiden probed for information.

"Chef another old Army buddy?"

"Uh-huh."

"Pretty good cook?"

"Couldn't barbecue a decent steak to save his life. He originally got tagged with the name Chief, which he hated – thought it was racist. Punched out a couple SEALs at Fort Bragg who called him that. The incident pissed off some JSOC general who had a bad case of the PCs. The general ordered all concerned to give Chief a new handle. The letter 'i' got the boot."

The object Chef had given Keats turned out to be a set of keys for another old Ford Bronco, this one a gaudy shade of orange. Keats got behind the wheel and retrieved a briefcase from under the seat. Inside were a Glock semiautomatic pistol in a paddle holster, four fifteen-round magazines and a sheathed combat knife.

"We came all the way to Sioux Falls just for weapons and OJ's favorite ride?"

Keats gave the dashboard an affectionate slap. "Don't be insulting Broncos. They're liable to get pissed and throw you. As for the gun and knife, I used to have a laptop for whacking people but it got busted."

"How come you didn't have a gun back at the garage?"

"I've been flying a lot. The TSA being what it is, best not to leave a sidearms contrail. If we have to fly again, I'll ditch the Glock and make other arrangements."

Aiden imagined a string of associates spanning the country, each ready to provide Keats with guns and vintage Broncos.

The bottom of the briefcase contained a manila envelope.

"Intel from Icy Ned," Keats explained, breaking the seal to withdraw a sheet of paper. It was biographical sketch of one Maurice A. Pinsey.

He was a 79-year-old retired widower living in Iowa. Pinsey was choir director at his Lutheran church as well as fundraising coordinator for the church's building fund. A long-time volunteer for the United Way, he helped the local senior citizens council serve meals to the homebound. On top of that, he took care of a handicapped daughter.

"Sounds like genuine salt of the earth," Aiden said. "What does Pinsey have to do with us?"

Keats accessed a phone app and took a photo of the printout

with the camera. Onscreen, the app transformed the words into a morphing jumble of letters and numbers.

"Encrypted data," Keats said. "Icy Ned wrote a program that encodes hidden information into the structure of innocuous sentences. My app has the cipher that unlocks the code."

Aiden wanted to know more about the mysterious Icy Ned. But he suspected any inquiries would be rebuffed.

The screen's digital metamorphosis ended, revealing the secret part of the message.

Dr Maurice Pinsey, a biologist by training, is a former Director of Research at Tau Nine-One. He was there during the quiver kids experiment.

Aiden could barely contain his excitement as Keats flipped the paper over, revealing a satellite map of a small subdivision near Storm Lake, Iowa. A house at the end of a cul-de-sac was circled by a red marker pen. Scrawled at the bottom of the page was the address. Keats programmed it into his phone's GPS app.

"Lucky break. Only about a three-hour drive."

Aiden fastened his seatbelt. "What are we waiting for?"

TWENTY-THREE

The subdivision appeared to be a product of the suburban construction boom of the 1950s. Maurice Pinsey's two-story home had steep roofs and twin dormer windows. The walls were clad in vinyl siding, the windows cloaked by heavy drapes. A Jeep Grand Cherokee, sparkling from a recent wash, squatted in the driveway.

Keats parked at the curb. It was nearing the supper hour. The cul-de-sac was free of pedestrians and moving vehicles.

"Think the house is being watched?" Aiden asked.

"I doubt it. Someone of Pinsey's importance would have been interviewed as part of the investigation into the killing of those railfans. But considering his age and his bio, it's hard to imagine there'd be a reason for extended surveillance."

Keats had changed into a wrinkle-free suit and tie from his travel bag. He looked presentably official. Aiden, in Rory's jeans and plaid shirt, felt like a slob by comparison.

But Keats had a plan, a deception to squeeze information out of Maurice Pinsey. He would pretend to be a federal agent and would do the talking. Aiden would keep his mouth shut and, ideally, be mistaken for a silent partner whose grungy attire suggested undercover work.

A middle-aged Black woman with generous hips opened the door. A crucifix hung from her gold necklace. She wore a heavy kitchen smock with overlapping stains.

"We're here to see Maurice Pinsey," Keats announced, flashing his ID card for the General Accounting Office faster than she could read it.

She led them into the living room, a shrine to gloom with dark woodwork and smoky wallpaper. Ornamental bookcases seemed like relics from the Victorian era. There was no TV. A pair of high-backed wooden chairs flanked a credenza. Faint sunlight spilling from the edges of heavy drapes provided the only illumination.

The bookcases were crammed, and alphabetized by author. Aiden noted numerous novels, including collections of Faulkner and Hemingway.

The woman had a thick Creole accent. "Mr Pinsey's in the back yard painting the railing. I'll fetch him."

As she disappeared down the hallway, footsteps emanated from upstairs. A young woman bounded down the staircase with the enthusiasm of a third-grader at the end of a school day. She took the last four steps in a single leap and landed with a deliberately loud thump. Her voice, high-pitched and squeaky, bubbled with excitement.

"Do you like *The Dick Van Dyke Show*? I have the first season on DVD!"

She was short and pencil-thin, and couldn't have weighed more than ninety pounds. Pale skin suggested she didn't get outdoors much. Her yellow pajamas were imprinted with stars and rocketships.

"I have my own TV," she bragged. "It's in my room. Wanna see?"

It was difficult to estimate her age. Deep-set hazel eyes and a thinning hairline suggested she could be a contemporary of Keats. Yet her skin retained the tautness of a younger woman. Her demeanor and goofy entrance left no doubt she was Maurice Pinsey's handicapped daughter.

She strode toward Aiden with an absurdly happy smile, not stopping until their faces were barely three inches apart.

"We could go to my room and watch the episode where Rob and Laura dance this new dance, the twizzle. It was filmed January 9th, 1962, but didn't air until February 28th, 1962. Wanna see?"

"No thanks." Aiden forced a smile as he backed away from the severe violation of his comfort zone.

"Daddy promised to buy me season two for my birthday."

"Lucky you."

"Watching old black and white TV shows is the best. Color ruins everything."

"Bobbie!"

Startled, she whirled toward the booming male voice. Her expression mirrored that of a schoolgirl caught doing something naughty.

Maurice Pinsey entered the living room, trailed by the woman. The elder Pinsey was garbed in paint-splattered coveralls. He was nearly as thin as his daughter but taller, nearly six feet. His face was framed by a silvery pompadour and neatly trimmed beard.

Pinsey's voice softened at the sight of Bobbie's panic. "Honey, please go upstairs."

"Daddy, are you mad at me?" She looked ready to cry.

"Of course not. But I need you to go back to your room for a while so I can talk to these men in private. Will you do that for me?"

"Daddy, I need to go to the bubble room first."

"All right. Shaleah will take you."

The woman took Bobbie's hand and escorted her up the staircase.

"Shaleah, hurry!" Bobbie urged, trying to scamper ahead of her. "I gotta go real bad!"

They disappeared from view. Aiden guessed that the bubble room was her childish name for the bathroom.

Keats flashed his ID card from across the room, hoping Pinsey wouldn't bother with a closer look. The tactic worked. Pinsey ignored the ID and launched into a rant.

"I don't care who the hell you are or what spy agency you're from! This is the second time in the past month that you people have invaded my home, and that's twice too many! Can't you get it through your thick skulls that I'm retired from government service."

"Sorry," Keats offered, adopting the sheepish expression of a dutybound bureaucrat. "But we need to talk a bit more about Tau Nine-One."

"I told the other agents everything I could remember."

"I'm afraid some important details may have been overlooked."

"Why the reason for this sudden interest?"

"You know we can't get into that. I'm sure the other investigators also informed you that this matter remains classified."

"Fine. Then I have nothing further to say. You gentlemen need to leave."

Keats hesitated, uncertain how to respond. Aiden chimed in. "I suppose we could mention last month's incident."

Keats went with the flow. "All right. First, understand that what I'm about to tell you remains classified."

Pinsey gave an exaggerated sigh.

"There were some hikers killed near the Tau Nine-One perimeter. The men responsible may have been attempting an infiltration. That's why the recent interest."

"This is important, Dr Pinsey," Aiden added. "We'd really appreciate your cooperation."

"Fine, let's just get it over with."

He motioned them toward the sofa and turned on the chandelier. The dark room seemed even bleaker under its faint incandescent lighting.

"Bobbie is sensitive to sunlight. That's why we keep the drapes closed," Pinsey explained, settling into one of the high-backed chairs. "What are your questions?"

"We'd like you to tell us everything you know about Tau Nine-One," Keats said.

"We'll be here all night."

"The short version. We're especially interested in information pertaining to the quiver kids."

Pinsey darkened. "You know I can't talk about that, not even with you."

Keats countered with a knowing smile. "Naturally we don't

expect you to violate any deep secrets. However, we've been running into roadblocks regarding the general background on the babies who received the infusions. Frankly, we need help. As the highest ranking scientist at Tau Nine-One back then, you could possess information that might seem innocuous, but prove valuable to our investigation."

Aiden had to hand it to Keats, he was smooth. And Pinsey looked impressed that he knew even that much about the experiment. Still, their host wasn't ready to ante up.

"Sorry. I can't help you."

"This is a matter of urgent national security."

"The answer is no. I won't talk about the quiver kids."

Keats clearly wasn't expecting to be chopped off at the knees. But it was obvious that Pinsey intended being even more guarded on the issue than Marsdale. Aiden decided it was time to scrap their original plan and go for a gut punch.

"Enough bullshit," he snapped, glaring furiously at the older man.

His anger wasn't all artifice. He was through being stonewalled. They needed to know – *he* needed to know – the details of Tau Nine-One's most clandestine experiment.

"Listen very carefully, Dr. The quiver kid you once knew as Red is hunting down and killing his old crib mates. He caught Blue and burned him alive. Last night, Green barely escaped the same fate. Bottom line, we need answers before more of them die."

Pinsey's shock was palpable. "Red is murdering the others?"

"After torturing them."

"Dear God!"

Pinsey slumped into the chair and squeezed his eyes shut, as if trying to blot out the impact of Aiden's words. But finally, his resolve stiffened.

"All right. I'll tell you what I know."

With a strange faraway look, Maurice Pinsey launched into a story more bizarre than anything Aiden could have imagined.

TWENTY-FOUR

"The year 1991 was more momentous than the average citizen realized," Pinsey said. "The Gulf War began with air strikes against Iraq and the Cold War technically ended with the dissolution of the Soviet Union. But behind the scenes, it was also the year of an incredible discovery.

"Deep in the Montana Rockies, an old man was panning for gold in a mountain stream near a remote ordnance depot in the process of being mothballed. The old man suffered from a neurological disorder that caused tremors in his limbs, sometimes violent ones. One of these tremors caused him to stumble and land on his knees in the water.

"It was a fortuitous fall. Submerged in front of him was a smooth glassy stone partially embedded in sedimentary rock. He chipped the stone out of the rock and was surprised to find it perfectly spherical, about the size of a tennis ball. It was also unnaturally light, a fraction of the weight of a real tennis ball. Because his tremors had led to the discovery, he named it *quiver*.

"He sold the quiver stone to a science teacher living in Churchton Summit, the nearest town, for seventy-five dollars. The teacher showed it to a friend, an army captain coordinating the depot's closure. That's how the discovery fell into the hands of the government.

"The old man and the teacher were given generous payoffs to buy their silence, and a research team was dispatched to the site.

They retrieved the slab of rock in which it had been embedded and located the underground source of the stream. A cataclysmic flood in the distant past had broken off the slab and carried it to the surface. Dating of the rock strata revealed that the stone had been trapped in the rock for seventy thousand years."

"Midpoint of the Tarantian stage," Aiden interjected, giving Keats a knowing look. That had to be the basis for Red's codeword for whatever was to happen Wednesday. It also explained Marsdale's involvement. The discovery of the stone in seventy thousand year-old rock would have called for the expertise of a geologist specializing in stratigraphy.

Pinsey went on. "The former ordnance depot was taken over by a contingent from DARPA and renamed Tau Nine-One. Under DARPA's auspices, many classified research initiatives have taken place there. But Tau's main purpose was to study quiver.

"The stone yielded a number of extraordinary discoveries. It was composed of an ultra-lightweight substance with no Earthly parallel. At the subatomic level it was even more mysterious, defying the tenets of quantum theory, seemingly neither mass nor energy but some bizarre state in between. Some researchers theorized it was a sample of long-sought-after dark matter. Others believed it was the product of some fantastic manufacturing process."

Keats raised an eyebrow. "We're talking ETs here?"

"An extraterrestrial intelligence is one theory among many put forth. When I was still at Tau, the only thing most scientists agreed on was that quiver was not of this world. Possibly it arrived on Earth within a meteorite or some other vessel that disintegrated in our atmosphere seventy millennia ago. But even that's just a guess. How it arrived and whether its arrival was accidental or deliberate has never been established."

"If it was sent here, for what purpose?" Aiden asked.

"The answer to that question might well earn someone a Nobel Prize if quiver was ever made public. I can't attest to current research. But judging from my experience in those early years, I doubt it will surrender its mysteries. In some respects, the more quiver was studied, the less it was understood."

"So what's your theory?" Aiden wondered.

"I've come to a simple but profound conclusion. We're not meant to know."

Pinsey grew silent, lost in thought.

"Why aren't we meant to know?" Aiden prodded.

"Having accepted Jesus Christ as my savior, I now realize there are questions in this life that have no answers. Some things must be accepted purely on faith."

In light of what had been done to Aiden as a child, the answer sounded smug. His father had cited a famous quote originally about politics but later referenced to religion: that it was the last refuge of a scoundrel. Dad had a special disdain for people like Pinsey, who rationalized their foul deeds by cloaking them in the sanctuary of the church.

"And what about the quiver kids?" Aiden demanded, fighting another onrush of anger. "How do they figure into all this? How does your faith jibe with experimenting on babies?"

"It doesn't. We were overcome by false pride, one of mankind's greatest sins. Not a day goes by that I don't look back on our foolish conceit, for not questioning the ethics of that experiment. Believe it or not, our intentions were noble. They arose from what was, and likely still is, quiver's most amazing quality."

TWENTY-FIVE

From upstairs came the faint echo of voices. Pinsey cocked his head toward the sound, straining to hear. When he continued his tale, his voice bore resignation and regret. Aiden also had the impression of a man glad to get something off his chest.

"As one of the numerous research initiatives, quiver was brought into contact with various test mammals, up to an hour of direct skin exposure at a time. The tests were meant to ascertain if it had any effect on them. Nothing was apparent, at least not when the animals were more than about a month old. But something amazing occurred when they were very young. Infantile test subjects who came into physical contact with quiver, even for as little as ten seconds, displayed an immediate escalation of intelligence. Mice and hamsters grew up learning to navigate mazes faster. Rhesus monkeys demonstrated increased problem-solving capabilities. As these subjects were tracked, the intellectual advantages appeared to be permanent.

"We could never figure out what quiver did to cause such neurological changes. There were no indications it was being absorbed through the skin and entering the bloodstream. Necropsies revealed nothing. Yet some sort of osmosis clearly had taken place with these young test subjects.

"The potential was astounding. If quiver could likewise increase intelligence in humans, we might put an end to mental handicaps. Individuals with already high intellects perhaps could be elevated to genius level. From the military's standpoint, raising the IQ of the average soldier might create an army capable of outwitting its enemies. Other researchers dreamed of an even grander notion, giving an IQ boost to the entire planet, enabling humanity to overcome its petty ignorances, and work together toward global harmony."

Pinsey barked a cynical laugh. "The hubris! As if we mortals could take the place of God in heaven."

"So you tested quiver on human babies," Aiden said.

"Not at first. Initially, we used adult volunteers, hoping that there would be a similar effect. But there was no discernible escalation of intelligence. That mirrored what occurred when test animals more than a month old were given the infusions. The IQ boost was only triggered in mammals with a high degree of cerebral plasticity, specifically when the neocortex – the part of brain most associated with abstract thought and problem solving – remained in the early stages of development. So we took the next logical step."

"Who exactly is *we*?" Aiden asked.

"The three of us in charge. Myself, Colonel Jenkins and the project director, Dr Ana Cho."

Aiden recalled his green dream, the three giants peering down into what Marsdale had suggested was his crib. Two men and a woman. He was more certain than ever of his earlier hunch. They were the trio from Tau Nine-One.

Pinsey went on. "We knew that obtaining official approval for such an experiment was doubtful. So we initiated it on our own."

Keats looked surprised. "You kept Washington in the dark?"

"Not exactly. Many higher-ups at the Pentagon knew what we were doing or learned about it shortly after the experiment began. In private, they supported our efforts. And Colonel Jenkins was skilled at averting excessive oversight.

"As the three of us were setting up the experiment, we debated how many human infants to include. We mutually arrived at the same number: six." Pinsey frowned. "The symbolism didn't become clear to me until years later."

"What symbolism?" Aiden asked.

"I'll get to that in a moment. Six newborn orphans were found, three boys and three girls. They were given infusions, a fancy way of saying they were brought into skin contact with quiver so that the osmosis could occur. We reasoned that the experiment was harmless and had no downside. If successful, the babies would grow up smarter and thus have a better chance of overcoming the social deficits of beginning their lives as orphans. They would be nurtured in a supportive environment, given the best medical care available. When the time came for them to leave Tau, everything possible would be done to place them in good homes.

"But things didn't go as planned. In the eighteen months or so that the babies remained in our care, no measurable improvements in mental acuity were detected beyond statistical norms. We wondered if the IQ boost might require more time to reveal itself in human subjects.

"But then someone at the White House learned of the experiment and, fearing a public outcry, demanded we terminate. We were ordered to put the babies up for adoption immediately, ahead of our schedule. Our original plan had been to keep them at Tau until they were at least three years old, until they learned to talk and maybe could relate anything unusual they were experiencing.

"Still, we held out hope for a delayed reaction. Only adoptive homes where one or both parents were highly intelligent were considered. It was felt that any intellectual gains due to the infusions would be amplified by being around smart, creative people."

"And you continued tracking their progress from afar," Aiden concluded.

Pinsey vehemently shook his head. "Absolutely not. We desired to do so, of course. But the powers-that-be were too appalled by what we'd done. The three of us were reprimanded, our careers impacted. Colonel Jenkins, as the one ultimately in charge, took the brunt of Washington's displeasure. He received a dishonorable discharge, posthumously. I later heard that his family suffered great hardship from the loss of his military pension."

Pinsey went quiet for a time, submerged in a well of sorrow and regret. A part of Aiden felt as if he should have sympathy for the old man. But he didn't.

"What about the adoptions?" he demanded.

"Washington was paranoid about the possibility that the children could be tracked down and the illicit nature of what we'd done revealed to the world. Under the threat of worse sanctions – imprisonment for treason was mentioned – the three of us were instructed to do the adoptions on our own, then destroy all files related to the placements as well as to the experiment itself."

"Considering how you deceived Washington," Aiden argued, "why would they trust you to do all that on your own?"

"Politics 101," Keats said. "You want to make sure that someone else does your dirty work. Keep your own hands clean. Attempting direct oversight risks leaving a paper trail that could come back to haunt them."

Pinsey nodded. "We were ordered to have no further contact with the children and never reveal the details of the experiment."

Aiden believed him. Yet according to his father, someone had been secretly accessing his medical and school records early on.

Pinsey continued. "By the time of the adoptions, Colonel Jenkins was near death from pancreatic cancer. The legwork fell to Dr Cho and I."

Shaleah came down the stairs and entered the living room. Pinsey gazed at her with concern. "Is Bobbie all right?"

"The girl is fine. She got herself too excited and made a little mess. She's gone to bed. I'm gonna clean things up."

Shaleah retreated to the hall closet for a bucket and cleanser. Pinsey watched her return upstairs.

"My live-in housekeeper. My wife passed away a few years ago. Things were rough for a while, trying to take care of Bobbie on my own. Shaleah's been a godsend."

Aiden recaptured the old man's attention. "You must have

some idea what quiver did to those babies, how it changed them?"

Pinsey sighed. "We remained in the dark. Neurologically, there were no alterations in brain functioning, at least none that were measurable. But as it turned out, there were... side effects."

The old man retrieved an envelope from the credenza and handed it to Aiden. It was addressed to Pinsey. The return address was a post office box in North Platte, Nebraska.

"This was sent to me three years ago."

Aiden opened the envelope. The letter was handwritten in a beautiful cursive script. The stylish presentation contrasted sharply with the writer's bitter tone.

Keats leaned over Aiden's shoulder to read along.

Dr Pinsey,

I've learned you were one of the assholes in charge of Tau Nine-One back in the good old days, when experimentation on helpless infants was in vogue. I want you to know how your nasty science project screwed up my life.

The letter went on to describe how the infusion of quiver caused the writer to suffer *random manifestations of organic gelatinous matter.*

That sounded like Aiden's experiences with one exception. The writer's manifestations apparently were alive when they appeared.

When I was old enough to understand what had been done to me, I vowed to find every one of you Tau bastards and mess up your lives like you messed up mine. Lucky for you my hormones aren't in such a rage these days. Still, every time I suffer a manifestation, I feel like a freak.

I've never believed in life after death but I hope I'm wrong. I hope there's a hell and you and the rest of your Tau Nine-One bloodsuckers will be plunging straight into it. So, in conclusion...

Die soon, you motherfucker!

The letter was unsigned. Aiden handed it back to Pinsey. He

resisted an urge to tell the old man that he pretty much agreed with the writer's sentiments.

"Do you know which quiver kid penned this?" Keats asked.

"Not at first. I wrote back, admitted how awful I felt about what we'd done. I never got a response. Even though Dr Cho and I were ordered to destroy all the adoption files, between us we'd directly arranged for the seven placements, and this turned out to be one of mine. I was able to do some online follow-up and determine that a quiver kid I'd originally placed with a couple in New Jersey ended up moving to Nebraska."

Pinsey returned the letter to the credenza. When he spoke again, his words were tinged with sadness.

"Magenta. She was a beautiful child. Very bright, very playful. Even at infancy, she was somehow more gregarious than the others. We were supposed to refer to the babies only by their color names. But in Magenta's case, some people at Tau defied that edict. They called her Princess."

Pinsey's eyes misted over. He turned away, dabbed the moisture with a handkerchief. Aiden drew him from his reverie by asking him to explain the earlier comment about symbolism.

"Isn't it obvious? The three of us mutually agreed that we should use six babies for the experiment."

"I don't follow."

"Three of us – six babies. In other words, three sixes. In the book of Revelation, 666 represents the number of the beast, the Antichrist."

Aiden glanced at Keats, who looked equally surprised by Pinsey's bizarre conclusion. Aiden tried to shoot down the religious interpretation with a simple fact.

"But the experiment didn't involve six babies. There was a seventh one. White, the one they called the anomaly."

Pinsey's features underwent a subtle change. Until now, his expressions had suggested sadness and guilt. But a more disturbing emotion now took hold, one Aiden recognized from his experience in that West Virginia garage.

Fear.

Pinsey withdrew a wooden cross from the pocket of his coveralls and clutched it tightly. Whatever unsettling emotions Aiden's words had triggered, the old man's faith was serving as an antidote. Lowering his head, he murmured a short prayer. Aiden caught a few words. It sounded as if he was asking God's forgiveness.

"What is it that scares you?" Aiden demanded. "Is there something about White you're not telling us?"

Pinsey took a deep breath to steady himself and met their gazes. He seemed to have regained his poise.

"White was referred to as the anomaly because he served as the control for the experiment. He came to us much later, when the babies were about nine months old. He never received an infusion."

"We know all that. You didn't answer my question. Why does talking about White scare you?"

"It doesn't. You've misunderstood."

"I don't think so. How does White figure into your 666 symbolism?"

"He doesn't."

"I don't believe you."

Pinsey's face hardened. "It's clear neither of you share my faith. Further discussion on the subject is pointless."

Considering how open Pinsey had been about the experiment, his sudden stonewalling seemed curious. Aiden found himself wondering why the old man had revealed so much to them in the first place. Why abandon years of secrecy and divulge Tau Nine-One's secrets to total strangers?

Clearly, he was consumed by guilt. It was possible he'd been on the cusp of confessing his sins for a long time and had just needed the right impetus to come clean. Yet his outpouring had begun right after Aiden had revealed that Red was torturing and killing quiver kids.

Comprehension hit like a firestorm. Woven into Pinsey's

disclosures was an even deeper secret, something he'd been fighting not to divulge.

Aiden lunged from the sofa and raced up the staircase, ignoring Pinsey's entreaties to stop. He reached the second-floor landing just as Shaleah emerged from a room. The housekeeper slammed the door behind her and blocked the entrance.

"Is that the bubble room?" Aiden demanded.

Shaleah shook her head. He knew she was lying.

Pinsey and Keats appeared behind him. The old man was furious.

"You have no right to go traipsing through my home!"

"I know what you've been hiding all these years. Your daughter is a quiver kid. That's why you revealed Tau Nine-One's secrets to us. You're afraid Bobbie could be Red's next victim."

Pinsey's anger melted away. Sadness took hold.

"Which one is she?" Keats asked.

The old man shook his head, unwilling to answer.

Aiden pressed on. "We know it's not Magenta. So it has to be either Gold or Cyan." He recalled what Marsdale had said about one of the babies being a slow learner. "She's Gold, isn't she?"

Pinsey gave a resigned nod and turned to Shaleah.

"It's all right. Open the door. Let them see."

TWENTY-SIX

They entered the bubble room, a small windowless space devoid of furnishings. A discolored paintball helmet hung from a nail hook. The checkerboard linoleum floor, plain gray walls and ceiling were smeared by long-hardened chunkies in various shades of brown. One spot on the left wall remained soft, the stain glistening under the bluish light of an inset fluorescent lamp. Bits of the latest chunkie dripped from it at a glacial pace.

"Your daughter calls them bubbles," Aiden concluded, moving closer to examine Bobbie's most recent manifestation. "You've trained her to come in here when the urge strikes her."

Pinsey gave a weak nod. "They usually manifest directly in front of her and shoot away from her body to splatter. I once used a radar gun to gauge the velocity. Close to 75 miles per hour."

"Sometimes there's backspray," Shaleah said, gesturing to her stained smock, then pointing to the paintball helmet. "I wear that to protect my face."

"How often does Bobbie make a bubble?" Aiden asked.

"These days, only a few times a month. She's learned to recognize the subtle signs that one is imminent. Heightened emotional states are often the trigger. I suspect your presence excited her. Usually, she's able to make it up here in time."

"Did quiver cause her handicaps?" Keats asked.

"No, she was diagnosed with likely developmental issues at birth. That's one of the reasons she was chosen for the experiment.

129

It was hoped that quiver's IQ boost could work on someone with such deficits, perhaps enable her to lead a more normal life.

"That wasn't to be, of course. But Bobbie's handicaps didn't stop my late wife Gloria and I from falling in love with her. Gloria was one of the nannies who cared for the babies. When they were put up for adoption, we jumped at the chance."

"Did you mention anything about your daughter when you wrote back to Magenta?" Keats asked.

"Only that I had a child with a disability."

"When did Bobbie's manifestations begin?"

"The first one happened just shy of her sixteenth birthday."

Aiden had been twelve when his chunkies had started. The onset of puberty likely had been the trigger. Given Bobbie's developmental issues, it was possible she'd hit puberty later.

"Any idea what this crap's made of?" Keats asked, gesturing to the walls.

"A mixture of common elements and compounds bound in a polyepoxide material."

"Epoxy."

Pinsey nodded. "That accounts for their initial stickiness."

"Are Bobbie's alive like Magenta says hers are?" Aiden asked.

"Not as far as I've been able to tell. If they are, they terminate upon impact. However, close to one-third of the periodic table is represented, including the CHNOPS sextet."

"The what?"

"Carbon, hydrogen, nitrogen, oxygen, phosphorus, sulfur. The elemental ingredients for life."

That was similar to what Dr Jarek had discovered about Aiden's chunkies.

"Who else knows about Bobbie?" he asked.

"Only Shaleah."

Keats questioned Pinsey about the other adoptions. "We need to know where all of them were placed."

"As I said, Dr Cho and I divided the process between us. She took care of four adoptions. I only have details on the three I handled."

"Your daughter, Magenta and...?"

"Blue."

Aiden flashed disappointment. Blue had been tortured and slain in London. He'd been hoping for information on Red or one of the others still unaccounted for.

Pinsey read their frustration. "Although Dr Cho and I didn't officially communicate about the adoptions, I once overheard her mention that Red had been placed with a wealthy California industrialist."

"Got a name?" Aiden asked.

"Sorry. But is there anything else you can tell me about him? About Red?"

"Other than that he's a murderous psychopath?"

Pinsey looked ill. "Do you think he'll come after Bobbie?"

"If he finds out about her, I'm afraid so."

"Stay alert," Keats suggested. "Watch for strangers in the neighborhood. Come up with an emergency escape plan and put together a go-bag. Anybody raises the hackles on the back of your neck, get your daughter and your housekeeper away from here fast. The three of you go somewhere where you're not known."

Aiden agreed with the advice although he doubted it could protect Gold against Red and his ruthless mercs. But perhaps Bobbie's handicaps would serve to keep her safe. It seemed logical that Red was only interested in eliminating quiver kids who posed some unknown threat to him, and it was hard to imagine Bobbie falling into that camp. Then again, Blue had been a hardcore drug addict. That hadn't stopped Red from killing him.

Aiden provided Pinsey with descriptions of Red and Nobe. Keats did the same for Kokay, the electronics expert who'd been with Nobe during the railfans incident.

The old man led them back down to the living room. But Aiden hesitated at the top of the stairs.

"I need to see Bobbie again. Alone."

Pinsey wasn't pleased. "She's probably asleep. She's often tired and naps after a bubble."

"I still need to see her."

"Why?"

Aiden decided it was time to come clean about his identity. "I'm a quiver kid."

The old man froze. When he found his voice, it was spiked with fear.

"Which one?" he whispered. "Which one are you?"

Aiden considered lying and saying he was White just to see Pinsey's reaction. Would the old man raise his cross like a shield? Maybe douse Aiden with holy water in the manner of a priest confronting a vampire?

He didn't have the heart for such cruel deceit. "I'm Green."

Pinsey looked relieved.

"I gather that you also suffer the manifestations?"

Aiden nodded. "A bit different but same basic concept." He headed down the hall before Pinsey could mount further objections.

The room at the end was Bobbie's, her name printed on the door in block letters. It was unlikely Gold had any useful information. Still, Aiden knew he had to try.

The door was ajar. He entered.

Plain white walls were decorated with various posters, including several of rockets and NASA space vehicles. A mobile of the International Space Station hung above the single bed. The room reminded Aiden of his own childhood passion. Did Bobbie Pinsey also fantasize about piloting spacecraft into the unknown?

She was awake. She sat at a small desk with her back to Aiden, intently writing in a loose-leaf notebook.

"Hi Bobbie. What are you up to?"

She whirled and brightened into a smile. "I listed the first season of *The Dick Van Dyke Show*. See! I put a checkmark for each time I watch an episode. Some of them I've seen ten times or more!"

Aiden leaned over the desk, pretended to study the notebook. "Looks like you crushed it."

Bobbie frowned and examined the notebook's spine. "No, it's not crushed at all."

"Never mind," Aiden said, gesturing to the poster-clad walls. "I used to like rockets a lot too. At one time I thought about being an astronaut and piloting spaceships."

"Don't you think about it anymore?"

"Not so much."

"I wouldn't want to fly in spaceships. I'd be scared."

"Yeah, me too probably. But listen, Bobbie, I'm curious about something. Do you ever write in your notebook about your bubbles?"

Bobbie frowned. "Daddy says I'm not supposed to."

"Do you ever dream about them?"

"Uh-uh."

"What about other kinds of dreams? Like, for instance, did you ever have a dream that maybe had a certain color in it? Like maybe the color gold?"

Bobbie looked puzzled for a moment then burst into giggles. "That would be funny!"

"Yeah, I suppose it would be."

She jumped up from the desk and did a back flop onto the bed.

"I'm going to try it!"

"Try what?"

"I'm going to go to sleep and try to dream about the color gold!"

She folded her hands across her chest and squeezed her eyes shut, as if willing herself into slumber.

Aiden headed for the door. Bobbie obviously could be of no help. Still, with what they'd learned from Pinsey there was a ton of new information to process, along with a plethora of new questions.

What exactly was quiver? What had it done to them and for what purpose? Why did he, Bobbie and Magenta – and probably Red and the rest of the original six as well – possess somewhat different manifesting abilities? And what was it about White that so terrified Tau's Nine-One's former director of research?

No answers were apparent. But Maurice Pinsey certainly knew more than he was letting on, particularly about the seventh quiver kid.

Aiden reached the hallway. He was about to shut Bobbie's door behind him when she spoke.

"Singularity beguiles, transcend the illusion."

Aiden spun around. Bobbie's eyes remained closed, her mummy-like posture suggesting deep sleep. Yet her tone was more self-assured, more adult-sounding than the utterances marking her waking life. Equally stunning was that Bobbie's altered voice was the same one that spoke to Aiden in his green dreams. But he had the impression the words didn't originate with Bobbie. Someone – or *something* – was speaking through her.

"Bobbie, what did you say?"

She stirred but didn't open her eyes.

"Bobbie!"

She popped awake, grinning madly. Leaping out of bed, she rushed back to the desk.

"I made a mistake! I watched 'The Twizzle' episode twelve times, not eleven!"

"What was that you said when you had your eyes shut?"

Bobbie shrugged and put a new checkmark next to "The Twizzle" in the notebook. Aiden repeated his question but she just frowned. She seemed to have no recollection of having uttered the words.

Deep in thought, Aiden returned to the living room. Pinsey was scowling.

"I hope you didn't upset my daughter."

"She's fine. But she said something strange. 'Singularity beguiles, transcend the illusion.' Do you know what that means?"

"Bobbie often says odd things. Probably something she picked up from that TV show she's obsessed with."

Aiden was pretty sure the words didn't come from a sixty-year-old sitcom. "Did Bobbie ever utter that phrase before?"

"Not that I recall."

Keats looked eager to get on the road, no doubt to track down Magenta. But Aiden knew there was more to be learned here.

"You need to tell us about White."

This time, Pinsey maintained iron control of his emotions. "There's nothing else to tell."

"I think there is."

The old man led them to the door to evade further grilling. Aiden wasn't about to cut him slack.

"You need to talk to us. What is it about White that–"

"I have work to finish. You have to leave."

It was clear they'd hit a brick wall. When it came to White, Pinsey's fear was too strong. Aiden switched topics.

"So where can we find this Ana Cho?"

"As I just explained to your partner, I've had no contact with Dr Cho in decades. I don't know where she lives, or even if she's still alive." He frowned. "You're the investigators. You should know her whereabouts."

"Anything at all you can tell us about her?"

"Very little."

Aiden made no move to leave. Pinsey sighed, knowing he needed to divulge more.

"Back then Dr Cho was single and lived alone. No family or friends outside of Tau, at least none I ever met. She was young, still in her twenties. Quite brilliant, obviously. Twin doctorates in neuroscience and child psychology. That's all I know."

Pinsey swept open the front door. The three of them stepped outside. Across the street, the western sun had fallen low in the sky, silhouetting rooftops against amber light.

Keats gave Pinsey his phone number. "Call if anything happens."

"Or if there's anything else you need to tell us," Aiden added.

Pinsey gave a swift nod and retreated into the house. Aiden doubted they'd hear from him.

They got in the Bronco, and Keats broached the idea of using Gold as bait to snare Red and the mercs.

"If Magenta doesn't pan out, Bobbie Pinsey could be our best shot."

"No way," Aiden said. "We can't put someone with those kind

of handicaps in harm's way. Besides, I thought using me as bait was Plan B."

Keats shrugged. "That'll work too." He changed the subject. "How come you didn't ask Pinsey about your birth mother?"

"You heard him. He didn't handle my adoption."

"He didn't handle Red's either but he had a smidgen of background on it."

"My parents are Byron and Alice Manchester. They died when I was twelve."

Keats sensed the sudden hardening of his tone and dropped the line of questioning.

As they wove their way out of the subdivision, Aiden accessed Google Maps on Keats' phone. The quickest route to North Platte, Nebraska, was about four hundred miles.

It was vital they reach Magenta. That was a helluva lot more important than wasting time on genealogical nonsense. Trying to learn more about some long-dead woman who'd just happened to have given birth to Aiden was an exercise in futility. He didn't even want to think about it anymore.

But now that Keats had raised it, he couldn't help himself. He recalled the paragraph from his father's letter that referred to his biological mother.

She had to make some really hard choices to get by.

Added to that statement was that his birth mother apparently hadn't known who had gotten her pregnant. Aiden had been trying not to think about those facts even though they'd popped into his head more than a few times.

He suspected that his father had left unsaid a fundamental truth, having wanted to spare Aiden an additional wallop in what was already a document overloaded with gut punches.

A bitter laugh escaped him. Keats glanced over but remained silent.

Thanks, Dad, but your ploy didn't work.

It seemed more than likely that his biological mother was a prostitute.

TWENTY-SEVEN

They got on Interstate 80 and headed south. Keats made another call to Icy Ned and gave him Magenta's post office box address. The mysterious confederate worked his magic. Twenty minutes later, Keats received a coded text message that he decrypted using his app.

The box was rented by one Jessica Von Dohren. Icy Ned included the geographic coordinates of her isolated home as well as a bio.

She'd been adopted by Elizabeth Von Dohren, a Princeton cultural anthropologist who'd married a Tau Nine-One researcher. Elizabeth ended up divorcing the researcher and raising Jessica on her own. When her daughter was eleven, she gave up her tenured position, relocated to Nebraska and opened an agricultural supply business. She'd died of natural causes three years ago.

"Cultural anthropologist to agricultural businesswoman," Keats mused. "Pretty radical change."

Aiden had a hunch what had prompted Elizabeth Von Dohren's striking transition. Age eleven likely had been when Jessica began experiencing the manifestations. Like other parents of quiver kids, Elizabeth would have feared that her daughter's ability would attract Tau Nine-One's interest and had opted for an isolated existence to protect her.

Keats surpassed the speed limit on their way to North Platte. He seemed to have innate radar for knowing when to slow down, usually moments before a statie's cruiser appeared on I-80's darkening flanks. Even with a quick stop for fuel and sandwiches, they made the trip in five-and-a-half hours.

It was nearly eleven o'clock at night when they passed a huge Union Pacific railyard and exited the interstate. A short drive brought them to a narrow road bisecting farmlands and accessing properties outside of town. The last turnoff was Jessica Von Dohren's driveway.

Keats ignored a series of *No Trespassing* and *Keep Out* signs and headed in. They drove a good half-mile on the driveway's crunchy gravel. A final bend around a shrub-caked hill brought them to a modest, two-story house with clapboard siding. An old Dodge pickup was parked in front. Keats turned the Bronco around to face the lane and killed the headlights.

The silhouette of a TV antenna rose beside the chimney. Other than a rectangle of amber light seeping from a curtained upstairs window, the place was dark. There was just enough starlight to guide them toward the front porch. It was so quiet their footsteps on the gravel made them sound like a pair of city-stomping Godzillas.

At the side of the house, chicken wire enclosed what appeared to be a small cemetery with seven tombstones. Upon closer inspection, Aiden realized the squat monoliths weren't grave markers. They were porcelain toilet tanks without the bowls. What he'd taken for a cemetery was actually a weird garden. The lids had been removed and the tanks served as planters for tomato vines and a variety of flowers.

They reached the front porch. Curtains were drawn. Keats stepped to the side of the door and unholstered the Glock.

"Is that necessary?" Aiden whispered.

"Judging by Pinsey's letter and those driveway signs, I'm guessing our girl might not be the most congenial type."

Aiden peeled back the screen door and banged three times with the horseshoe knocker. The sound reverberated in the darkness, loud and ominous.

There was no response. He waited a few moments then smacked out another triplet. Still nothing.

He was about to try again when the door whipped open, revealing a silhouette cloaked in shadows. The barrel of a shotgun slithered from the portal and pressed into Aiden's belly. Alarmed, he took a step back.

"What do you want?" The voice was deep and raspy, but decidedly feminine.

"Easy, girl," Aiden whispered, raising his hands.

"Don't call me girl."

"Sorry. We're not here to make trouble."

"That so? Then why is *we* holding a pistol?"

She motioned toward Keats, now in a two-handed shooter's stance.

"Nice shotgun," Keats offered, his voice calm. "Remington twelve-gauge autoloader. Four-round mag?"

"Only need one to blow a hole in your buddy."

"I'm guessing you don't want to do that any more than I want to put a bullet through your skull. How about we both stand down."

"How about you tell me what the hell you want."

"You're Jessica Von Dohren?" Aiden asked.

"And if I am?"

"Then you're also Magenta. We were babies together at Tau Nine-One. I'm Green."

She lowered the shotgun, stepped from the shadows and uttered the words "Basic Instinct." Her command tripped an audio sensor, activating the porch lights.

Jessica Von Dohren was far from the ogre her aggressive intro might have suggested. Despite frumpy attire – tattered sweater and jeans – she was beautiful, fashion model tall with generous curves. Wavy blond hair cascaded to her shoulders. Aquamarine eyes regarded Aiden with cool detachment.

"Call me Jessie," she said, cradling the shotgun under her arm and motioning them inside.

TWENTY-EIGHT

"Fatal Attraction."

Jessie's command tripped another sensor. Downstairs lights came on, revealing a rustic living room with a ceiling corralled by thick beams. A coffee table cut from a tree slab seemed to be growing out of the floorboards. A grandfather clock guarded the staircase leading to the second floor.

Matching sofas angled to face an old TV built into a cabinet. A vintage Norelco radio the size of a microwave squatted on a buffet table. Entertainment technology appeared to have been stopped dead in its tracks many product generations ago.

Jessie hung the shotgun over the fireplace and motioned them to sit. Aiden and Keats selected one sofa. She perched on the farthest armrest of the other one as if they bore some dread disease.

Considering her greeting, Aiden didn't mind the separation. The phrases she'd used to trigger the lights, "Basic Instinct" and "Fatal Attraction," were the names of movies featuring murderous female villains.

"Nice house," Aiden began. "Live here long?"

"You came all the way out here for small talk? What do you want?"

"Any strangers snooping around lately?" Keats asked.

"You mean except you? Not really."

"Most people don't greet you with shotguns."

"Story got passed around town that I like to walk through the

140

house bare-assed. I do – fucking sue me. Then some asshole I dated for two nanoseconds decides to make it a thing on social media. So now, adolescent boys come out here at night on a dare and peek through my windows. Think I'm going to put on a show for 'em." She gave a derisive snort. "Jerkoffs. Used to yell at them to get lost. But the Remington gets the point across faster."

"The quiver kids are in danger," Aiden said.

He reviewed his own history, dovetailed it into a brief account of recent events. Keats interjected various details, including the murder of the railfans. Jessie remained calm throughout the account although she seemed to listen more intently when Keats mentioned the holographic figure glimpsed by Henry Carpousis. But when Aiden related his capture and torture by Red, she muttered "Fuck" and jumped off the sofa. By the time he'd finished with highlights of their visit to Maurice Pinsey, she was pacing back and forth in a frenzy.

"Pinsey! The bastard mentioned having a disabled kid when he wrote back. But I never imagined it was Gold. Trying to gain my sympathy, I figured."

"What do you know about Red?" Keats asked.

"I met him once. I'd just turned eighteen. It was an age when I really burned with curiosity about my past. My father had been a researcher at Tau. Although he worked on other projects, he'd managed to learn a few things about the experiment."

"Your dad still around?" Keats asked.

"Yeah, but he was never really in my life. He and Mom divorced when I was pretty young. Get Christmas and birthday cards from him, that's about it." A flicker of pain touched her face.

"Anyway, through some old connection of Dad's, Mom learned the identity of the family who'd adopted Red. The de Clerkins of California." Jessie unleashed another snort. "They named their little bundle of joy Michael."

Michael de Clerkin. Aiden connected the name to the face of the man who'd ordered his kidnapping, torture and attempted murder.

"He was living in LA. I flew out there on my own without telling Mom. I called him up, told him I was a quiver kid. We met in this upscale restaurant.

"He was charming, at least at first. He asked about my life, bombarded me with compliments. But I played it close to the chest, didn't tell him where I lived or even my real name. I wanted to get to know him better first." She paused. "Lucky for me I was cautious.

"After dinner we went to his condo. He had his own place. Very swank. He was trying to get me into bed. Frankly, I was considering it. He was pretty sexy. But I started picking up red flags. There was something creepy about him, something I couldn't put my finger on. After he snapped a photo of me without asking if it was cool, I got pissed.

"I told him I had to leave. That's when the *real* Michael de Clerkin showed up. He got pushy as hell, didn't want me to go. Then he started ranting about how powerful us quiver kids were and about how he was personally destined to become a god. It was the most megalomaniacal crap I'd ever heard.

"By then, I just wanted out of there. He cooled it with the god talk and begged me to stay for one last drink. I said OK but I was suspicious. Good that I was. I caught him slipping something into my rum and coke. For sure, some kind of roofie." She scowled. "The bastard was planning to rape me.

"Anyway, I bolted out the door as fast as I could. Caught a taxi to the airport and took the next flight home."

"You never told him about your manifestations?" Aiden wondered.

"No. But looking back on it, I realized he'd been asking subtle questions that suggested he knew something about them. I'm pretty sure he was experiencing the manifestations too. We were both trying to learn about each other without revealing our own secrets."

"Did either of you mention anything about your medical and school records being secretly accessed?"

"Michael never said anything. And I don't think my records were looked at. Mom was wary of Tau Nine-One doing secret follow-ups. I don't think she'd have missed something like that. Yours were accessed?"

"According to my father, yeah. Did you ever dream about your color?"

"No."

Michael de Clerkin and Bobbie Pinsey hadn't experienced color-themed dreams either. That and their records not being accessed seemed to indicate that Aiden was different from the other quiver kids in some fundamental way. Then again, with a sample size of four he might be jumping to conclusions.

Jessie ambled toward the kitchen. "You guys want a beer?"

They nodded. She returned with three open bottles of Heineken.

"So what do you think Michael's up to?" Aiden wondered. "Why come after the rest of us? If he is planning an assault on Tau Nine-One, why? Vengeance for what they did to him?"

Jessie shook her head. "I don't think he'd care about that. At least not in the way I used to care about such things. If I had to guess, I'd say he's trying to…"

She paused. Her face erupted with insight.

"He's going after the quiver! He wants a second infusion!"

"For what purpose? Quiver's only supposed to work on babies."

"Yeah, but we're different. We've already been exposed to it. I've had this increasing urge to touch quiver again. It's just a feeling but I think it means something. I believe a second infusion might be like getting a booster shot, that it would open up a whole new frontier for me."

"A frontier?" Keats asked.

"New psychic abilities."

Aiden mentioned the phrase from his green dream, *Singularity beguiles, transcend the illusion*, and how Bobbie Pinsey had uttered it in her sleep. But the revelations drew a blank stare from Jessie.

"Why do you think Michael's trying to eliminate the others?" Keats asked.

"Probably because we're the only ones who could truly threaten him."

"Threaten him how?"

"He's trying to become a god. And gods, by their very nature, don't tolerate competition."

TWENTY-NINE

Michael's dinner meeting was a waste of time. The two software geeks looking for an angel investor for their new company must have thought he had a sucker target on his back. Their facts were shaky and their data slim; their proposal reeked of desperation. Numerous venture capital firms had already turned them down.

Still, it was a relaxing meal at a prestigious restaurant. Since they were picking up the tab, Michael upped the bill by requesting a $1,200 bottle of Pinot Noir and secretly enjoyed their struggle not to look appalled as the waitress handed them the check. He especially liked how their upbeat faces collapsed into disappointment when he announced, "No sale, gentlemen."

He waited outside the restaurant for JoJo to bring the limo around. It was only a little after 9:30pm, and his scheduled departure for North Platte from Santa Monica Airport wasn't until 10:50. He considered calling one of his regular hookers and doing her in the limo.

He decided against it. There really wasn't that much extra time and he didn't want to have to make it a rush-fuck. Besides, remaining celibate for the next few days and concentrating on reviewing every aspect of Wednesday's assault made more sense. Tarantian was too important. This likely would be his last opportunity to subject the plan to microscopic scrutiny. Abstinence was a small price to pay for the divine power he might soon achieve.

The limo pulled up to the curb. JoJo got out and held the back door open.

Michael's chauffeur-bodyguard didn't look all that imposing. She was short and chubby, and had a puffy face likely to develop jowls in a decade or so. But the former Marine could kick ass. Michael had once sat in the limo at the end of a dark alley and watched her put on an enjoyable show. JoJo had taken a baseball bat to a pair of drunks who'd had the audacity to piss on the lawn of one of his West Hollywood apartment buildings.

JoJo headed west toward Pico Boulevard. It was a short ride to the airport.

"I have some business," Michael instructed. "Don't bother me unless it's urgent."

"Yes sir."

She raised the opaque window, isolating him in the back seat. He opened his encrypted laptop, keyed in the security code and brought up the seventeen-page breakdown of sequential events that would bring Tarantian to fruition.

Nobe would have considered him anal for wanting to go over the assault yet again. They'd already vetted each detail, worked out countless variations to deal with every contingency. Still, there was always the chance of an unanticipated event throwing a monkey wrench into the plan.

Such an event had occurred only last month. Who could have guessed those railfans would turn up at the same time Nobe and Kokay were doing their recon? Even though the trio was also trespassing and likely wouldn't have reported the incident, the stakes were too high to risk letting them live.

Nobe originally was going to bury the bodies. In that wilderness they might not have been found for a long time, if ever. But the grizzly attack gave him a better idea. It made more sense to leave the bodies in the open to be found quickly rather than risk search parties scouring the region for months and possibly interfering with Tarantian. Unfortunately, a survivor crawled out of there, prompting a full-blown investigation.

Michael seethed when he thought back to Nobe's mistake. But there hadn't been anything to be done about it other than taking the merc to task. Nobe had countered his criticism with a shrug and a pointed reference to the classic fuck-up excuse, "shit happens."

Thankfully, according to Michael's DOD contacts, the investigators misinterpreted what Nobe and Kokay were doing in that wilderness. And they remained oblivious to Michael's secret weapon: his insider at Tau Nine-One. The young woman he'd recruited more than a year ago was a key part of the plan.

The insider had reported heightened vigilance since the railfans incident but nothing likely to upset Tarantian's timetable. An extension of Tau's sensor net was in the works but had to go through the Pentagon's complex procurement process and wouldn't be installed for months. By then, the insider would have carried out her part of the bargain, for which the balance of her five million dollars in compensation would be placed in an offshore account.

Michael's phone beeped. It was Nobe.

"Rosen called. He and Vesely have been watching the house. Two men showed up. There was some kind of confrontation with Princess at the front door. She had a shotgun and one of the men had a pistol. Rosen couldn't hear what was being said. Everyone eventually cooled off and went inside."

Michael frowned. "Federal agents?"

"Vehicle doesn't look like government issue. An old Ford Bronco. Rosen's running the plates."

"Did they get a look at these men?"

"Wrong angle for the NVGs. Couldn't see their faces. Might just be a couple of her mates who showed up unannounced and surprised her."

The drawing of guns didn't sound like a misunderstanding among old friends. Michael couldn't afford to leave the matter unresolved.

"We need to know what they're doing there."

"I'll have Rosen and Vesely secure the house."

"Make sure Princess and her guests don't make any emergency phone calls."

"Not a problem. The house is in a dead zone for cell coverage. Rosen had to hike half a mile to reach me. They'll cut the land line before they go in."

"What if they have sat phones?"

"Rosen and Vesely will hit hard and fast. No one will have a chance to make any calls."

Michael thought carefully. Capturing Magenta was one thing but taking out her visitors, who just might be federal agents, could have repercussions for Wednesday. Still, the need to know their identities and what they were doing there trumped such considerations.

"Make sure your men understand we need all three alive."

"Want them to do a little prep on Princess, put her in a cooperative mood?"

"No."

The word came out sharper than Michael intended. Unlike the interrogations he'd conducted with Blue and Green, he didn't want Magenta sullied.

Ten years ago, she'd snuck out of his LA condo before he could pry any useful info out of her. He'd been equally frustrated about not getting her into bed. She'd been one of the few women over the years who'd escaped his charms.

To hell with celibacy. Tonight, after the interrogation, he intended to remedy that.

THIRTY

Jessie had grown quiet since mentioning Michael's desire to become a god. The house mirrored her quiescence. The only sound was the ticking grandfather clock.

Aiden broke the silence. "You OK?"

She snapped out of her reverie and put down her beer. "I've been trying to decide if I want to show you."

"Show us what?"

She came to a decision and opened a squeaky door under the staircase. Wooden steps led to the basement. She motioned to them to follow her down the rickety staircase.

The basement was unfinished, with an undulating floor of packed dirt and three walls of whitewashed concrete. The fourth wall facing the rear of the house was composed of unpainted wooden slats. Rafter-mounted fluorescent lights revealed a small fridge, a sink and a washer-dryer set. A short flight of steps at the front of the basement ascended to an outside storm door.

Seven toilet bowls were lined up in the center of the basement. The bowls were without their tanks, which explained the unusual planters in Jessie's garden. The original plastic or ceramic lids on the bowls had been replaced with slabs of clear Plexiglas.

Jessie led them down toilet row. The inner surfaces of the first three bowls were antiseptically clean. But half-submerged in the fourth bowl, sloshing in a thick broth, was a gelatinous brown clump. It resembled one of Aiden's chunkies.

Except it was alive.

"One of my little children," she said without apparent sarcasm. "I manifested this morning. Want to pet it?"

"I'm good," Aiden said, adding what happened when he touched a fresh chunkie.

"Yeah, mine are sticky too. But once they're in the broth they're not nearly as bad."

"You get the urge and one of these appears?" Keats asked.

"Yeah. A kind of energy builds up inside me. It's hard to explain. But that energy, it's got to be released. Or else I start feeling all kinds of crazy."

Jessie, and presumably Red, had a degree of conscious control over their manifestations. Aiden was impressed by what they could do. But also a bit jealous.

"They started when I hit puberty," she said. "Mom helped me recognize when I was in a certain mental state, when the energy was present. It has to do with my emotions, my mood. When I was a teen, sex was a big trigger. Just fantasizing about a new boyfriend could manifest one. I call 'em droppers, by the way.

"First time I was with a guy, we were on a mattress in the back of his pickup. At a moment of intense passion, I splattered a dropper across his rear cab window." She barked a laugh. "Fortunately, he was too preoccupied to notice."

Aiden sensed that he and Jessie were alike in one respect. Because of their abilities, both of them likely had soured on having good intimate relationships.

"Eventually I learned to control the energy, direct it. These days I can bring it on at will, sometimes as often as once a day. Naturally, Mom and I kept things under wraps. She was worried those Tau Nine-One assholes would drag me away for more experiments."

Aiden moved to the fifth toilet bowl. This dropper had begun to sprout nodules.

"Are they some sort of embryos?"

"Of a sort. That one's from two days ago." She gestured to the sixth bowl. "And this little bugger is five days old."

The dropper in bowl six had at least a dozen nodules. Several had grown into five-inch tentacles that thrashed violently in the liquid, making *thwapping* sounds as they smacked the underside of the plexiglass lid.

Jessie moved to the final bowl. This manifestation was similar to the previous one but wasn't moving. The tentacles hung limply.

"Is it dead?" Aiden asked.

"Close to it. Once they're about a week old, that's what happens. I've tried removing them from the bowls, putting them in different types of solutions. So far, nothing's worked.

"When I was younger, I used to dream of finding a cure, putting an end to the manifestations. It took me a long time to come to terms with the fact that I was probably never going to be free of them. Finally I decided to start my own little science project.

"My droppers sound like they're similar to Gold's in that they shoot away from my body. Had lots of splatter jobs in the early days. After some trial and error I figured out how to incubate them. The broth is an isotonic saline solution enriched with minerals, similar to the amniotic fluid found in the womb. I mix up batches from off-the-shelf chemicals and nutrients. When I feel the urge to manifest, I come down here. I've learned to direct a dropper's trajectory and control release velocity. As long as I'm close to a bowl I can make them land softly in the broth."

She led them toward the rear wall, the one made of boards. Aiden hadn't noticed from farther away but there were seams outlining a rough-hewn door. Jessie slid her fingers under the edge and swung it open. The light spilling in revealed a furnace and an oil tank. A ground-level window high on the wall had been spray-painted over.

The corner opposite the furnace was piled almost to the ceiling with dead manifestations. They gave off an unpleasant odor, like rotting fruit.

"I didn't know what to do with them," Jessie said. "I tried burying them out back but they kill the plant life. Some kind of natural herbicide, I'm guessing. But when this place fills up I'll have to find another means of disposal."

"Ever have them examined by a lab?" Keats wondered.

"Never found anyone I'd trust enough to do it on the sly. Couldn't risk some asshole blogger putting it out there and making me public spectacle number one."

"Do you think Michael's manifestations are similar to yours?" Aiden asked.

"I don't know. But I'll bet anything he's also been cultivating them. From what you've told me, either his abilities are far more advanced than mine or fundamentally different. Those shadows of his, transmitting a kind of hologram of himself to distant locations. Wow, that is some amazing shit. I've never even imagined something like that..."

She trailed off. Her face blossomed confusion.

"What's wrong?" Aiden asked.

"I don't know. I feel kind of... funny."

Jessie moved unsteadily toward the door. She was losing control of her muscles. Aiden was certain of the diagnosis because the same thing was happening to him.

A wave of dizziness swept over him. He tried to reach out to the wall for support but never made it. He dropped to his knees.

"Something's wrong," he whispered. A distant part of his brain realized just how inane that conclusion sounded.

Keats wrapped his arms around a furnace pipe, struggling to stay upright. Jessie sat on the floor shaking her head, trying to fight grogginess. The last thing Aiden saw before unconsciousness took him was the huge pile of dead manifestations.

THIRTY-ONE

For the second time in less than twenty-four hours, awakening brought terror. Aiden slithered from a dreamless sleep to realize he was once again a prisoner.

He was slumped on a sofa in Jessie's living room. His ankles were tightly secured with plastic flex cuffs and his wrists were bound in front of him the same way. Keats, similarly restrained and still unconscious, was sprawled in a chair closer to the front door. Jessie sat stiffly upright on the second sofa, also bound. She was staring at the TV. The set wasn't on.

The house was silent. There was no sign of their captors.

Aiden realized Jessie wasn't looking at the screen. Atop the TV cabinet was a pair of night vision goggles as well as the contents of their pockets. Wallets and keys. Keats' knife and gun.

"Jessie," he whispered. "You OK?"

She turned to him. He saw the fear in her eyes. He gestured toward the TV.

"I'm going to try to get the Glock." He might be able to fire it even with his wrists bound.

But when he tried to squirm off the sofa, he realized there was another obstacle. He couldn't move his feet more than a few inches. He leaned forward and looked down. A longer flex cuff was looped around the one binding his ankles. It was fastened to a fat screw eye that had been twisted into the floorboards.

Keats and Jessie were afflicted with similar hobbles. They weren't going anywhere.

Footsteps sounded on the stairs. A man trotted down from the second floor. He looked to be in his thirties. Long brown hair streamed out the back of a Texas Longhorns football cap. His dark windbreaker was unzipped, revealing a holstered pistol.

Seeing that Aiden and Jessie were awake, he hollered up the steps.

"Hey, Rosen. Guess who's up?"

The second man joined him. Rosen wore a similar windbreaker, the bulge of a holstered gun visible beneath it. With thinning brown hair and wire-rimmed glasses, he reminded Aiden of an unpleasant elementary-school teacher he'd endured, a man who seemed to have no love of children.

Rosen had found Jessie's wallet upstairs. He removed the driver's license and compared the ID photo with an image on his phone.

"Definitely her. We need to call it in. Hike out to where you can get a signal."

"Christ, why bother. They'll be here in an hour or so."

"It's the way the Clerk wants it, Vesely. And I went last time."

Vesely snatched the keys to the Bronco from atop the cabinet.

"No," Rosen said. "On foot. Leave their vehicles where they're parked. Get our car and drive it back here."

"What the hell does it matter?"

"It matters," Rosen said, punctuating his words with a glare.

Vesely grimaced but put down the keys. He planted himself in front of Jessie, stared down at her with a lecherous expression. She averted his gaze.

"Goddamn, you are one hot bitch." He turned to Rosen. "Why don't we do her?"

"The Clerk says she's not to be touched."

"Who's going to know?"

"Nobe will. Want to deal with that shit?"

Vesely clearly didn't. Muttering under his breath he headed for the door. But he stopped at Keats' chair and kicked the unconscious man in the ankle.

Keats' eyes snapped open. He glared up at his tormentor.

"Thought you were awake. The gas doesn't have that long an effect." Vesely grinned at Rosen. "Old fart thinks he can play games, pretend to be out of it."

Vesely grabbed the cuffed wrists to prevent Keats from moving his arms and squeezed his neck.

"Like to play games, you acne-faced prick? Well, Mr Decimus Dionysius Keats, real soon we'll be doing a number on your ass. Whadda ya say to that?"

Keats said nothing. His eyes, hard and unyielding, never left his captor's face. Sneering, Vesely released him and stomped out the door.

Aiden's spirits sank lower as he digested their predicament. Nobe was on his way here with the Clerk, aka Michael de Clerkin, aka Red. Painful interrogations would be on their agenda. Aiden and Keats would be asked about the garage and about Farlin. Jessie would be quizzed about her manifestations. And after Red was satisfied with their responses…

He tried to repress a shudder, failed. This time, more care would be taken. This time, the mercs would make sure their executions occurred without any hitches.

Jessie had turned pale, aware of what awaited them. Judging by Vesely's lewd outburst, things might go even worse for her.

The situation seemed hopeless. The three of them were in the middle of nowhere, bound hand and foot, guarded by two ruthless mercenaries. There was no way out.

He turned his attention to Keats. No trace of fear marred his features. That fortitude helped Aiden to recover his own.

We're not going to die. We're going to get out of this.

But how?

Rosen strolled into the kitchen. Aiden heard the refrigerator open. The instant the merc was out of view, Keats tried yanking the screw eye from the floor by jerking his legs back and forth.

It wouldn't budge. He switched to a new strategy. Gripping the metal loop with his fingers, he attempted to unscrew it from the floorboard. Aiden mimicked his effort.

It was no use. The screw eyes had been driven deep into the grain, probably with a drill to make a starter hole. Their shackled wrists prevented gaining enough leverage to twist them out.

"That's the spirit," Rosen said, grinning at them from the kitchen portal, a bottle of Heineken in his hand. "FYI, though. First one who gets loose, I shoot out a kneecap."

They gave up the effort. Aiden knew there was little chance of undoing the screw eyes anyway, not without some kind of tool.

But they had to do something. Any hope of escape would end the moment Vesely returned. Against a single merc they had a chance, however slim.

Rosen returned to the kitchen. The sound of cabinets opening suggested he was hunting for a snack.

The thought of eating gave Aiden an idea. It was outrageous and unlikely to work. But considering their predicament…

He caught Jessie's attention. Keeping his voice at a whisper, he conveyed his desperate plan.

THIRTY-TWO

Rosen returned, nibbling crackers between swigs of Heineken. Jessie wasted no time.

"I'm thirsty," she said, indicating across the room.

The end table held her unfinished beer. Rosen shook his head.

"No booze."

They don't want her to feel relaxed, Aiden realized. Alcohol prior to tortuous interrogation could defeat its purpose.

"How about water?" Jessie said. "There are bottles in the fridge. Please. I'm so parched I'm losing my voice."

She cleared her throat with a convincing cough. It was a nice touch.

For a moment, Aiden thought Rosen wasn't going to oblige and that his plan was DOA. But the merc retreated to the kitchen and returned with a twelve-ounce bottle.

"Catch."

He lowered his arm, preparing to toss the water from across the room. Aiden's hopes sank. Rosen probably needed to be closer.

Don't catch it, Jessie! Let it fall. Make him hand it you.

Rosen threw the bottle. Jessie's natural instincts skewered the plan – she made a perfect grab. Aiden sensed from her expression that she realized the error the instant she made it.

But she adapted, kept the plan alive. Pretending to be unable to twist off the cap with her fettered hands, she extended the bottle toward Rosen.

"Please?"

The childlike tremor in her voice was flawless. Aiden couldn't tell whether it was authentic or an act.

The merc took the bait. She handed him the bottle. As Rosen unscrewed the cap, Jessie closed her eyes. Their faces were less than three feet apart when she manifested the dropper.

The brown mass formed in front of her face and flew away from her like a fastball. It splattered across the lower part of Rosen's head, just below his eye line, enshrouding nose, mouth and upper neck.

The merc staggered backwards, struggling to breathe through blocked orifices. His chest heaved as lungs tried to suck air past the obstruction. But that made things worse. Globs of the manifestation were drawn into his mouth and nose. His fingers clawed frantically at the sticky mass, trying to dislodge it.

Nodules sprouted from the dropper's surface, instantly grew into five-inch snaking tentacles. Two of the tentacles curled around Rosen's palms and tightened. Two more gripped his fingers and yanked the digits violently backward, snapping the bones. The merc's eyes bulged with pain.

Rosen's frantic efforts to rip the dropper from his face pushed even more of the mass into his throat. What they could see of his expression morphed into panic. He lunged across the room like a madman, twisting and jerking. A flailing arm sent the vintage radio crashing to the floor.

His air ran out. He crumbled, landed face down by the TV. Shudders coursed through him as bodily functions shut down. Aiden didn't know how much Rosen knew about the manifestations. But there was a fair chance he had no idea what was killing him.

His movements ended. Stillness took the room. Keats returned his attention to the screw eye binding him to the floor. Grunting, he twisted and pried at it.

Aiden looked at Jessie. She was gazing at Rosen with a stunned expression.

"Jessie, do you have any tools?"

"I didn't think I could do it," she whispered. "I only made my last dropper this morning. I've never been able to create more than one a day. And the tentacles, they were instantaneous this time."

"Tools," Aiden repeated with more urgency.

"Something is different in me," she said, faint excitement in her voice. "Something's changed."

"Cut the crap!" Keats hollered. "We don't have much time. That end-table drawer beside you, can you reach it?"

Jessie snapped out of her reverie. She was close enough to swing her bound hands up to the drawer.

"Screwdriver, scissors, anything we can use to free ourselves."

"This is all there is," she said, holding up a thick pen.

"It'll have to do," Keats said. "Aiden is closer, chuck it to him."

Jessie flipped the pen to Aiden. He caught it and slipped it through the screw eye at his feet. Although plastic, the pen was wide around the middle. He hoped it wouldn't break.

The effort was awkward with his bound wrists. But finally, the screw eye began to turn. He was a few twists away from dislodging it from the wood when they heard an approaching vehicle.

"Hurry!" Keats urged.

Aiden twisted the pen as fast as he could. The screw finally popped from the floor.

The vehicle stopped out front. Its engine shut off.

Aiden threw the pen to Keats and lunged from the sofa. Bunny-hopping around Rosen's body, he reached the TV cabinet and picked up the Glock.

"Aim for the center of his torso," Keats calmly instructed. "Squeeze the trigger. It's a semiautomatic. After you fire the first shot, take a breath, retarget and squeeze again. Keep on firing until he's down and not moving."

Outside, a porch floorboard creaked.

Aiden couldn't adopt a proper shooter's stance with his ankles hobbled by the flex cuff. He leaned against the cabinet for balance and took aim at the door. He hoped the adrenalin coursing through him would stop his arms from shaking long enough to get off a clean shot.

The door opened. Vesely took a half step inside, froze at the sight of Rosen lying dead in front of the TV.

Aiden fired.

And missed.

The shot went wide, impacted the door jamb inches from Vesely's side. The merc's arm dove beneath his jacket.

Aiden was too wired to follow Keats' instructions to the letter. He didn't take a breath between shots. But he did allow himself an instant to take better aim.

He squeezed the trigger. The second bullet tore through Vesely's shoulder as the merc was drawing his gun. Vesely's fingers splayed open. His pistol clattered to the floor. Before Aiden could get off a third round, his target lunged back out the door.

"After him!" Keats hollered. "We can't let him get away!"

Aiden hobbled out onto the porch. Vesely was already at the back of his vehicle, a dark-colored SUV. He was unwrapping a blanket that held something long and cylindrical.

A rifle.

Aiden leaned against the porch post for support. This time, he was able to take careful aim. He fired.

Vesely jerked to the side and dropped the rifle. He collapsed face down in the gravel.

Aiden couldn't tell if the merc was dead. But he wasn't about to risk hopping down the steps and hobbling out there in the dark to find out. Seeing no signs of movement, he returned to the house.

Keats had freed himself from the floor with the pen. He was on his knees in front of an open closet, rooting through a toolbox.

"You get him?"

"I think so."

Keats procured wire cutters, chopped through his wrist and ankle cuffs. He severed Aiden's bindings and slipped Rosen's gun from its holster. He was about to free Jessie when they heard the sound of an engine starting.

Throwing Aiden a reproachful look, Keats snatched the Bronco's keys and dashed outside. Vesely was driving away. Keats leaped into the Bronco and raced after him.

Aiden returned to the living room and cut Jessie's flex cuffs. She didn't say anything, just stared at him with that vaguely excited look.

"You OK?" he asked.

She nodded and retreated upstairs. Aiden went back onto the porch. There was no sign of either vehicle. But if the wrong one returned...

Headlights appeared in the distance, interrupting his thoughts. Worst-case scenario, the merc was returning instead of Keats.

Vesely's rifle lay where he'd dropped it. Aiden snatched it and dashed to the vegetable garden. He took up a defensive position behind a toilet tank and aimed the rifle at the fast-closing vehicle.

THIRTY-THREE

It was the Bronco. Aiden was relieved to see Keats behind the wheel. He stood up and waved.

"Where's Jessie?" Keats demanded as they entered the house.

"Right here."

She trotted down the steps. She'd cleaned up and changed into a fuchsia-colored blouse and black jeans.

"Is the other one…?"

"Worm meat. Aiden's second shot drilled him in the guts. Bled out before he reached the end of your property. But he made it past the dead zone. His phone was in his lap. Pretty sure he managed to make a call."

"To Red?" Aiden asked.

"Or Nobe. Either way, we have to assume the worst, that he told them what happened. We can't stay here."

"Why not wait for them and set up an ambush?" Aiden had no desire for more gunplay. But this might be their best opportunity to end it.

Keats shook his head. "Now that they presumably know the score, one of two things will happen. Either they won't come at all, in which case we'll sit around twiddling our thumbs. Or, they'll come in force. Nobe has a good number of mercs at his disposal. And they'll have serious firepower this time. I wouldn't make book on our odds of getting out of here alive."

He rifled through Rosen's pockets, relieved the merc of wallet and phone. Jessie hesitated at the bottom of the stairs.

"You don't want to stay here," Keats warned.

She nodded and raced up the steps. "I just need to pack a few things."

"Five minutes. We've got to move, put some distance between us and this house."

"I should have made sure Vesely was dead," Aiden said. "Then an ambush might have worked."

"Maybe, maybe not. Bottom line, you saved our butts. Don't tear yourself a new asshole doing the shoulda-coulda-woulda dance." Keats headed for the back door. "I want to check something outside. Gather up all the weapons and ammo and put it in the Bronco. Pack us some provisions, too. We're not making any restaurant stops until we're far away from here."

"Where are we going?"

"Wyoming."

Keats scurried out the door without further explanation. Aiden grabbed Jessie's shotgun and Vesely's rifle and shoved them under a blanket in the back of the Bronco. Returning to the kitchen, he slapped together some sliced cheese sandwiches and grabbed a box of crackers and a six-pack of water bottles. He met Jessie in the living room. She had a large handbag and a backpack slung over her shoulder.

"Hope you don't mind us raiding your pantry," he said.

"Not high on my list of concerns."

Keats returned. He was holding a small cylinder. Trailing from one end was a thin rubber hose.

"Found this attached to the outside of the basement window, the one that's painted over. They must have heard us down there. They used a muted drill to bore a tiny hole in the window frame. The cylinder held Copak-7, a fentanyl derivative. It's a relatively new knockout gas, fast and odorless."

Jessie opened her backpack and loaded the food and water Aiden had gathered. She gestured to Rosen's body.

"What about him?"

"No time to hide him and his friend and do a proper clean-up," Keats said. "If they are coming, we need to get far away from here fast."

They headed out to the Bronco. Jessie took the back seat. Aiden watched her turn around to gaze at her house as they drove away. Her expression seemed mournful, like someone who knew they were leaving home for good.

THIRTY-FOUR

Live imagery transmitted through Nobe's satellite phone wasn't top grade. The camera was an add-on and could handle only low-res video; the picture on Michael's phone screen was jittery and freezing. Still, the imperfections didn't lessen the disturbing impact of what he was seeing.

The video came from inside Jessica Von Dohren's home. Nobe slowly panned the camera across the living room. He paused for a closeup on Rosen's face. The hardened brown remnants of the manifestation caked over the merc's mouth and nose revealed how he'd been overcome.

"A shitty way to go," Nobe said over the headset, his voice devoid of humor.

Michael sat in the cabin of his private jet parked at North Platte Regional Airport. He'd changed his plans about driving to the Von Dohren house after Nobe had received the call from the dying Vesely. Michael decided it was more prudent to let the mercs handle the incident.

It wasn't clear who'd shot Vesely. He'd been found in his vehicle at the end of the driveway. But Rosen must have been Magenta's handiwork. Had Green possessed such an ability, he would have used it in the garage to stop his torture. Targeting a manifestation with that much precision indicated a high level of conscious control. And those strange tentacles... It was obvious Magenta's manifestations gave her a very different sort of power.

Michael realized he'd been operating under a false assumption, that the six of them were endowed with essentially the same ability. But considering how different Magenta's ability seemed from his own, it followed that the other quiver kids likely possessed unique skill sets as well. Blue, in his final moments jabbering about penetrating the realm beyond the beasts, might have been talking about an actual physical effect.

More worrisome at the moment was Green, Aiden Manchester. Vesely's call had provided the identities of Magenta's late-night visitors. Michael had been stunned to learn that Aiden had survived the fire. It also explained why they hadn't been able to get in touch with Farlin. Presumably, the merc's scorched remains were now in the hands of a West Virginia coroner.

And there was the third individual, the man who likely had engineered Green's rescue. Michael was still trying to learn more about Decimus Dionysius Keats. What was a GAO analyst doing in the company of a quiver kid?

Most disturbing of all was that Green and Magenta apparently had joined forces. Two or more quiver kids united against him had been something Michael had feared from the beginning.

And then there was the fact that Aiden had overheard them discussing Tarantian in that garage. By now, he and Princess would have put two and two together and concluded that Michael was after the quiver for a second infusion. They might already have warned Tau Nine-One about the impending assault.

A fit of rage overcame Michael. He pounded his fists on his chair's leather armrest. Mere days away from his ultimate ascendance to godhood and now this!

"Are you all right, sir?" JoJo asked, entering the cabin from the flight deck.

"I'm fine."

Michael buried his anger beneath a cold smile. It was something he'd learned to do as a child when forced to deal with the asinine demands of his adoptive parents.

JoJo slipped into a seat up front and opened a magazine, *Model*

Airplane News. His bodyguard-chauffeur flew drones as a hobby.

Michael would have to try contacting the insider. If Tau Nine-One had been alerted, she'd know. In that case, last-minute adjustments to the plan would need to be made.

His attention was drawn back to the phone imagery. Nobe had entered the basement. He panned the camera across the toilet bowls, revealing manifestations in various nascent forms. Princess' method for growing them was crude yet effective. At Michael's lab in his Montana chateau, medical-grade containment vessels costing twelve thousand dollars apiece were used to cultivate and keep his manifestations alive. He had to admit, Princess had done an impressive job on a pauper's budget.

Nobe broke his train of thought. "So, what's the plan, mate? Want us to pursue them?"

Michael checked his watch. It was nearly 3am. Several hours already had been lost over this incident.

"Forget it. They've got too much of a head start. Do you have explosives?"

"Some PBX, a few incendiaries."

"Set charges in the basement. Make sure the fire consumes everything, especially the manifestations. The bodies of your men and their vehicle need to burn as well."

"No problem."

Michael had another concern. Nobe had lost three mercs in the past twenty-four hours.

"Are we going to be undermanned for Wednesday?"

"I overbooked. You always anticipate battle losses. Nature of the brute."

Michael liked the symbolism of that last phrase. *Nature of the brute.* For the first time since landing in North Platte, he permitted himself a smile.

THIRTY-FIVE

Faint violet streaks colored the eastward horizon in the rearview mirror as they drove toward Wyoming. Dawn was approaching on this Monday morning, the start of a new workweek for millions. For Aiden, it signified the end of the most frightening weekend of his life.

He'd taken over the wheel to give a break to Keats, who slumbered in the back. Jessie was out too, curled into a fetal ball in the passenger seat.

Keats had provided directions to Casper, Wyoming. He'd said little else about their destination other than that it would provide temporary sanctuary. Presumably, it was the domicile of another old army buddy.

Aiden had snatched a few hours sleep earlier. He was still tired but beset by enough unsettling emotions to keep him alert. It was the same mix of feelings he'd experienced after leaving Rory's yesterday, a sense of being caught up in forces beyond his control, being swept toward some distant horizon where perhaps the strange abilities of the quiver kids somehow intersected.

He feared what awaited him on that horizon.

The pain from his burned arms had abated somewhat after popping another of Rory's pills. Or maybe he was simply getting used to it.

"Alexandra," Keats mumbled, stirring in the back. "Can't find it... can't find our painting..."

Aiden glanced in the mirror. Keats was in the throes of some painful dream.

"It's gone, Alexandra. It's gone…"

Keats bolted awake, awash in confusion. It took him a moment to realize where he was.

"You OK?" Aiden asked.

He recovered his poise. "How far yet?"

"Two or three hours."

"Want me to take the wheel?"

"I'm good."

"I was talking in my sleep?"

"Uh-huh. Something about Alexandra and a missing painting. Who is she?"

Keats gazed out at a passing field.

"A friend or relative? A lover?" Aiden had a hunch it was the latter.

He nursed a desire to know more about Keats. For better or worse, he was inextricably linked to this assassin who'd saved his life. The extraordinary nature of their relationship made him needy to learn who Decimus Dionysius Keats really was.

His entreaties drew only silence. Aiden gave up the effort. But a mile later, Keats surprised him.

"Alexandra was my first wife. We married young."

His words, hesitant at first, grew into a deluge.

"I'd just turned eighteen and enlisted. Alexandra was a year younger, still in high school. I'd never met anyone like her. She had this wild energy, a passion that she directed toward her art. She was a really good painter, did these incredibly lifelike oil portraits.

"Most of the time she painted from photographs. Only rarely did she use live models. You could understand why after seeing the results. When she painted a real person, everything was somehow different. The brush strokes, the colors, the composition." Keats shook his head. "The person came out looking scary or grotesque or deeply disturbed.

"Those pictures should have served as a warning to me. But I was young, madly in love. It wasn't until years later that I realized that when Alexandra painted a real person, she projected her own madness onto them.

"She started having these fits where she'd babble incoherently at some object. The kitchen sink, a lamp on the wall, a shoe. There was no accounting for what might set her off. The police arrested her at the mall one time for screaming obscenities at a water fountain.

"At first I blamed myself. I wasn't around enough and thought that might be making her nuts. By then I was involved with a Ranger battalion and later with more covert units. I was gone for long periods on missions. Later I wondered whether the two of us being so different had something to do with her illness. I was planning to be a career soldier and she was an artsy type. Not exactly a match made in heaven."

Aiden glanced over at Jessie. She remained curled up in the seat but her eyes were open. She was listening intently.

Keats went on. "Looking back on it, I suppose those things might have played a role. But they weren't the real reasons she lost her mind. Her first breakdown happened when I was overseas. By the time I got back, she was hospitalized and on anti-psychotic meds. She barely recognized me. The shrinks labeled it schizophrenia coupled with MDD – major depressive disorder. But one of the docs, probably the most honest of the bunch, said he didn't have a clue what was really going on with her.

"She was in and out of hospitals over the next several years. Somewhere around then I met Tonya and realized she was the one I wanted to spend the rest of my days with. But I couldn't just abandon Alexandra. When you're on a mission, everybody comes home. You don't leave your people behind.

"Alexandra's been institutionalized now for close to twenty years. I visit her pretty often. Sometimes Tonya comes along. Alexandra seems to like that."

He paused and hunched forward. Ahead of them to the west,

the dark heavens remained punctuated with a handful of stars, holdouts against the creeping dawn.

"Sometimes, rarely, Alexandra smiles and talks to Tonya about the flower garden outside her window or about the weather. But it's never more than surface chatter, never anything of substance. And she never mentions her art. She doesn't seem to remember that she was once a fine painter."

Keats hesitated. Aiden pressed for more.

"You said something about 'our painting.' About it being gone?"

"It's not gone. I have it at home. I'm not sure why I dreamed it was lost."

That last remark didn't ring true. Keats knew why the painting figured in his dream.

Jessie turned to him. "What's the painting of?"

"It's one she did from a photo. She captured the essence of the scene, the essence of us."

"The photo in your wallet," Aiden said. "The one of you and Alexandra on the beach."

Keats nodded. "A friend snapped it. We were vacationing at Cape May. At the time, we were still living in this cramped, one-bedroom apartment. We were building the sandcastle and making it huge, giving it all these extra rooms. Alexandra did the painting a few weeks later."

He clamped his mouth shut, as if that was the only way he could stem the outpouring of revelations. There was obviously more to the story, something beyond what seemed obvious, that Keats was still in love with his first wife. Aiden wondered how Tonya felt about that. But the tormented look on Keats' face made it clear that now wasn't the time to delve deeper.

THIRTY-SIX

They reached Natrona County, Wyoming, by 8am. The region was a mix of petroleum facilities and cattle and sheep ranches. Casper was about a half hour to the northwest.

Keats came alert, scanned the terrain ahead.

"There," he said, pointing to a gravel lane angling to the right.

A white post held a rickety mailbox. Fading paint spelled out the name: I.C. Nedelka. It took Aiden a moment to make the connection and realize this was the home of Icy Ned.

He made the turn, proceeded up a steep hill to the apex. The lane dead-ended at a small clearing in front of an L-shaped ranch house. The modest domicile squatted amid a forest dominated by Ponderosa pines. Off to the left was a separate three-bay garage.

The exterior of the house defied architectural conventions. One side was constructed with cinderblocks and creosoted logs, the other with white bricks and rough-hewn cedar siding. Three shades of asphalt shingles clad sections of roof that intersected at deranged angles. The highest roof had a trio of satellite dishes.

A petite woman wearing jeans and a sweater emerged from the house. Bangs of white hair framed a pixie face. Her skin was ruddy as leather. She greeted Keats with a smile and a hug.

"Mabeline, good to see you again. You're looking well."

"Ned told me you'd called. Had a hunch you'd be stopping by."

"How's he doing?"

"Good days mostly, a few bad ones here and there. He's on some new meds. They seem to help."

Keats introduced Aiden and Jessie. They fell in step with their host, followed her toward the entrance.

"I was so sorry when I heard..." Mabeline began.

Keats grimaced. "We don't need to talk about that right now."

She glanced back at Aiden and Jessie, nodded. Aiden wondered if she was referring to Alexandra. But then he realized that made no sense. Surely Mabeline would have known that Keats' first wife had been institutionalized for decades.

Mabeline ushered them into the house and down a hall to a paneled office. Shelves covered nearly every square inch of wall space. The shelves overflowed with books, magazines, maps and documents. Items that couldn't be contained were stacked on the floor. Several stacks reached almost to the ceiling.

Aiden scanned the collection. The subject matter was eclectic. Film noir, advanced metallurgy and baroque musical composition clamored for attention amid automotive journals, astrophysics texts and treatises on military history.

Books and papers covered the solitary desk as well, with only a small footprint reserved for a keyboard and large monitor. The wiring tunneled through a hole in the floor. Presumably, the guts of the computer were housed in the basement or another room.

"Well, look what just crawled out of the crapper," boomed a voice behind them.

A lump of a man in a motorized wheelchair swept into the office. He'd apparently reached a point in life where personal grooming was no longer a priority. Clumps of salt-and-pepper hair fell across the shoulders of a tattered denim shirt. A mustache drowned his upper lip. If he lowered his head, the scraggly beard would tickle his stomach.

Keats made the introductions. "This is Icy Ned. He taught strategy and tactics to half the special ops community."

The older man gave a dismissive grunt. "Icy Ned? Sounds like one of those gut-busting gins served in some Southeast Asian excuse for a bar. Can't even remember who saddled me with it." He went quiet for a moment, stared blankly at a bookcase. "Anyway, neither here nor there. Just plain Ned is fine."

"Ned's also got some amazing talents in the digital realm."

"And Deke Keats knows how to spread it on thick. He'll put so much grease on the nozzle you won't feel him tunneling across your demilitarized zone."

Keats grinned. He handed Ned the phones taken from Rosen and Vesely.

"I took out the batteries to disable tracking. Pretty sure they've got memory-wipe that'll activate when they're powered up. Anything you can do?"

"Probably need to punch in a code within a few seconds of turning them on. I've got an RF-proof room in the basement and know a few tricks. But don't get your hopes up."

Ned pocketed the phones and turned to Aiden with a lopsided squint. "Boy, you look like crap on a cracker. What the hell's Deke been doing, draggin' you through spiderholes?"

"It's been a long night," Aiden admitted. "We could use a few more hours of sleep."

"Mabeline!"

"Right here, hon," she said, stepping out from behind Keats.

"These kids need to clean up and bed down. See to it while Deke and I do some catchin' up."

Mabeline guided Aiden and Jessie to a tidy bedroom at the back of the house. She retrieved sheets from the closet and made up a futon roomy enough for two.

"Bathroom's there," she said, gesturing to an adjoining door. "Plenty of towels. Extra PJs in the bottom of the dresser."

Aiden hesitated. "Jessie and I aren't together like that."

"Sorry, this is the only extra bedroom. If one of you wants to sleep on the living room couch–"

"We're cool," Jessie said.

Mabeline departed, closing the door behind her.

"I'll sleep on the floor," Aiden offered.

"Bed's big enough.

"OK."

She headed for the bathroom. He heard the shower go on.

He'd wash later. Stripping to his underwear, he got under the covers. He was already drifting off when he felt Jessie slip in beside him. The warmth of her body felt good.

He mumbled "Good night," closed his eyes and was gone in an instant.

THIRTY-SEVEN

Jessie was dressed when Aiden awoke. She was perched on a settee by the window, peering through a gap in the curtains.

"What time is it?" he asked, swinging his legs out of bed.

"One o'clock."

He felt better, at least in terms of having gotten some decent rest. But his burned arms pulsated beneath the dressings. Time to pop another pill.

He leaned over her shoulder to see what she was looking at. A clump of forest. He caught a whiff of her perfume or body wash, a pleasant flowery aroma.

"I never killed anyone before," she said quietly.

"Me neither," he offered, laying a hand on her shoulder. "Not the easiest thing to do, is it?"

She turned to him. He expected a look of regret or sadness at having been forced into murdering another human being. But she wore a weird smile.

"I know I should feel bad about killing that prick. But I'm energized. It's like a runner's high. Is there such a thing as a killing high?"

"Don't know. Maybe."

His thoughts turned to the merc he'd shot, Vesely. There'd been no choice. He didn't feel bad, but he certainly wasn't juiced about it either.

Jessie got up from the window. Not for the first time, he noticed just how beautiful she was. A guy could lose himself in those aquamarine eyes. He imagined their lips touching, a prelude to cascading pleasures.

She sensed his interest, motioned to his bare arms. "Those dressings should be changed."

"I'll deal with it later."

"We'll deal with it now. C'mon."

She led him to the bathroom.

"I should take a shower first," he said.

"Good idea. You smell like something that's been living in a sewer."

"Thanks for the image."

"While you're getting wet here's something to remember me by."

She gripped his head and drew them together, planted her lips on his. The kiss was brief but frenzied.

He pulled away from her. There was something creepy in that kiss. It brought a feeling of revulsion. Fantasies he'd entertained only a moment ago were drained of carnal power.

"I could help you in the shower," she whispered.

"No thanks. I think I need a bit of alone time." His words sounded lame. *What's wrong with me?*

Jessie didn't try to mask her feelings. She looked annoyed, maybe even angry. Aiden retreated to the bathroom and closed the door. Had he encountered her before this weekend, they'd probably already be slipping and sliding under soap and spray. But now...

He stripped off everything but his bandages and entered the stall, being careful to keep his injured arms clear of the spray. The hot water was close to steaming. He tried to imagine Jessie in here with him. Maybe if he forced the fantasy it would spark interest.

It didn't. Instead, the more he thought about the two of them making love, the more unsettling the idea became.

THIRTY-EIGHT

Body odor vanquished, Aiden changed his own dressings and joined Jessie and Mabeline at the kitchen table. Despite the hour, Mabeline had laid out a generous variety of breakfast staples. He dove in, sampled everything. He was hungrier than he'd imagined. The scrambled eggs, bacon, sausage, wholewheat toast and silver-dollar pancakes went down with ease.

Ned wheeled himself to the table as Aiden and Jessie were finishing their coffee. He ate like a creature from the wild, hunched over his plate, his beard collecting scraps. At one point, he leaned back and allowed Mabeline to use an old toothbrush to comb out crumbs trapped in his facial growth.

"What's for dessert?" Ned growled, handing her his empty plate.

"No dessert till supper. Remember what the doctor said?"

His cheeks flared crimson. He slammed his fist on the table, startling Aiden and Jessie. "Goddamn it, woman! I'll be dead soon! A man needs his dessert."

"The pancake syrup was sweet, dear."

"Of course it was! Don't you think I know that?"

Mabeline, unruffled, carried his plate to the sink. Ned picked up his fork to spear more food. Confusion bloomed on the grizzled face when he realized the plate was gone. His eyes betrayed growing panic.

"Mabeline?" he whimpered, sounding like a lost child. "Mabeline, where are you?"

"Right here, hon. I'm right here." She hustled back to the table, gently massaged his shoulders. "You mustn't let yourself get too excited."

Ned came back from whatever dark place his mind had wandered into. He nodded to Aiden and Jessie. "Deke's in the study. Join us when you're done."

He pivoted the wheelchair and accelerated from the room. Mabeline offered an apologetic smile.

"I hope my husband didn't alarm you."

"Alzheimer's?" Jessie asked.

Mabeline nodded.

"I'm sorry."

"He's all right most of the time," Mabeline said, clearing more plates from the table. "He just hits a few speed bumps now and then."

Aiden knew that those speed bumps were destined to grow higher and more foreboding. The father of one of his high school friends had suffered from the early onset version of the disease.

They offered to help with the dishes. Mabeline shooed them away with a resolute smile.

"It's all right. I can handle things."

THIRTY-NINE

The door to the study was open. Keats and Ned were leaning over the desk, perusing a rumpled US Geological Survey map. Aiden and Jessie entered quietly.

"Don't see how they could do it," Keats was saying, his index finger tracing a path across the rolled-out map. Its frayed edges were pinned down by vintage lead soldiers depicting World War I American doughboys.

"You've got no roads, no landing strips. There's the railroad. But even if they could somehow get aboard the train, the late-day trip is going the wrong direction, taking the workers from Tau back to town. The track's severed from any main lines, so even if you had your own locomotive, no way you could get it there for an assault by rail. Which, by the way, is one nutbag idea."

"Certifiable," Ned agreed.

Aiden and Jessie flanked them at the desk. The map showed the region of western Montana encompassing Tau Nine-One and the town of Churchton Summit.

"What about railtrucks?" Aiden asked. "You know, those maintenance vehicles. Drive one right onto the tracks from a grade crossing."

Keats shook his head. "The only decent grade crossings are in town. You'd be seen. You could access the rails in the woods, I suppose. Still, I don't see the logic of it. Tau would spot you well before you reached the fence."

"Motorcycles or off-road vehicles?" Jessie proposed. "Or maybe just hike in?"

Ned ran his fingers through his beard, as if searching for crumbs that had eluded Mabeline's toothbrush. "You could use some of the fire trails in the area to maybe sneak a bit closer. But no matter how you're trying to get there, you're going to run into perimeter sensors out the wazoo. Cameras, motion detectors, infrared, the works. You'd have a shitstorm coming down on you before you could even think about breaching."

"How far do you think the sensor net extends?" Aiden asked.

"A couple klicks, with the density increasing the closer you get. Anywhere near that fence you won't be able to fart without raising an alarm. Even if you could somehow nullify the sensors, you'd be under counterassault once you got within visual range. Doesn't help that the attack's planned for broad daylight, without even the cover of darkness." Ned shook his head. "This whole thing makes as much sense as a polonium enema. This de Clerkin character must be crazy if he thinks he can pull this off."

"What about a lightning assault with choppers?" Keats proposed.

"The immediate perimeter will be a no-fly zone with radar coverage down to treetop level. Even if you come in hot and fast, the choppers would be targeted. RPGs for sure, maybe even a hidden, fixed-installation SAM. Odds are they shoot your birds out of the sky. And even if your choppers somehow make it as far as Tau's landing pad, how the hell does your assault force get penetration? Those Marines ain't gonna just let you walk in there, you know. And, for all practical purposes, they command the high ground."

"Good points," Keats admitted. "But for the sake of argument, let's say that Michael and the mercs have a viable assault plan. They've found a way to get past the guards and enter the facility."

"Then you have a whole new set of problems. If their goal is to steal this weird-ass quiver stone, you can bet it won't be left lying around. It'll be in a secured area, probably something equivalent to an MCL."

"What's that?" Aiden asked.

"Maximum containment laboratory."

"Basically, a hot lab," Keats added. "Even if quiver isn't considered a pathogen like Covid-19, or something even worse like smallpox or Ebola, its properties are bizarre enough that it makes sense they'll have a protocol for keeping it isolated. Airlocks, separate HVAC system, biosafety cabinets. Probably an armed guard or two."

Ned shook his head. "This ain't happening. Are you absolutely sure this op is for real?"

"Not a hundred percent," Keats admitted. "But there's good circumstantial evidence. Bring up that image again."

Ned worked the keyboard and the screen brightened into a satellite photo. Three long narrow buildings formed a triangular configuration. In the middle of the triangle was the core building, a circular structure. A trio of equidistant walkways connected the core with the outlying buildings. A chainlink fence with razor wire surrounded the complex.

"Tau Nine-One," Aiden murmured, awed to be getting his first close-up look of the mysterious facility that had placed such a burden on his life. He'd accessed some online maps earlier but they hadn't offered this level of detail. Figures were even visible standing inside the fence.

"I didn't think you could get such satellite views of classified facilities," Jessie said.

Ned grinned wickedly. "Ain't the only thing I'm not supposed to have access to. That's why I keep the computer guts in the basement. They're booby-trapped. Anyone but me tries to access 'em and bulk erasers activate, followed by a hydrochloric acid bath. The drives get fried. Total memory loss."

Ned frowned and stared into the distance, as if realizing how that last sentence reverberated with personal meaning. Being in the early stages of Alzheimer's meant that much of the time he would be fully aware of his terrible fate.

A small helipad with two helicopters was visible between two of the wing buildings.

"They're not gunships," Keats said. "Probably for flying the brass in and out."

"Still, nothing to stop the Marines from appropriating one in the event of a breach," Ned countered. "Hover fifty meters up and strafe yourself some merc ass."

The only breaks in the fence were a pair of gates that allowed the railroad line to enter and leave the grounds. The track to Churchton Summit emerged from the trees, tunneled through one of the long outlying buildings and emerged out the other side. After passing back through the fence, the track made a sweeping arc across a grassy expanse and rejoined the main line at a switch. The loop enabled the train to be readied for departure without the need for a turntable, wye or runaround track.

Ned continued. "That building is T-wing – named for the train, obviously. The other two are A-wing for administration and offices, and S-wing for sleepover staff and the Marine barracks. All experimentation is done in the core building, thirty feet below ground level. That's where the quiver's most likely kept."

"I don't see any electric lines," Jessie said. "Are they buried underground?"

"Not necessary. The installation is nuke-powered; there's a small modular reactor deep below the main building. Which means no opportunity for the attackers to gain an advantage by knocking out the power."

Aiden focused on the tracks. "The train stops inside the building. That's where the workers embark and disembark?"

"Uh-huh. Like a subway station. Not one you're likely to pass through at your leisure, though. Coming or going, you and your carry-on will have to pass through scanners."

"Can you pull up a view of where Nobe and Kokay encountered the railfans?" Aiden asked.

Ned worked the keyboard and a new image appeared. It was another aerial view but from a wider perspective. The track was visible sporadically through the thick canopy. But enough could be seen to discern a short tangent section coming from the direction of the complex. The track crossed a stream on a spindly truss-girder bridge and immediately entered a sharp S-curve to navigate a series of rock outcroppings.

"How far is the bridge from Tau?" Aiden asked.

"Thirteen klicks south, give or take."

"Eight miles," Keats translated. "Roughly halfway to Churchton Summit."

Aiden traced his finger along the straight section. "The train might be traveling at a reasonable speed until they reach the bridge. But it would have to really brake for those curves. Maybe slow down enough for the mercs to easily hop aboard?"

Comprehension dawned on Keats' face. "Son of a bitch! We've been looking at this backwards. They're not going to attack Tau."

"They're going to ambush the train," Aiden said.

"Which explains what Kokay was doing at the bridge that day. He must have had scanners and spectrum analyzers. They needed to nail down the frequencies used by the train crew and Marines."

Jessie looked puzzled.

"Signal suppression," Ned said. "They'll jam communications traffic to and from the train an instant before they hit it. Knock out phones, radios, microwave, the works. In fact, if they're smart they'll do more than that: hijack those frequencies and transmit false data. That way, no one back at Tau will even know the train's come under attack."

Keats nodded. "Buys them a little extra time."

"How much time?" Aiden wondered. "How long does it take the train to get from the bridge to Churchton Summit?"

"This ain't exactly high-speed rail," Ned said. "It's an old right-of-way with lots of twists and turns. A one-way trip, sixteen miles, takes a good thirty-five minutes. And the sharpest curves tend to be closer to town. I figure at least twenty minutes from the bridge."

"The night-shift workers will be waiting at the station to return," Keats said. "But you can figure another ten minutes or so before they get suspicious about the train being late and start making calls to Tau. That ideally gives the mercs a half-hour window for an intercept."

Ned looked skeptical. "Yeah, but you're forgetting the big picture. How the hell do they get the quiver onto the train?"

"Michael must have someone at Tau," Jessie said. "That's the only thing that makes sense. An insider who's going to smuggle it out for him."

"Even with that, they might need some kind of diversion at the facility for the theft to work," Keats said.

"But then why go to all the trouble of an ambush in the first place?" she wondered. "Why not just wait until the train gets to Churchton Summit and hand over the quiver."

"Higher risk," Ned said. "The setup in town is similar, an enclosed station with a turning loop. Even if your insider slips the contraband out of there without tripping any alerts, you'd want to get hold of the quiver ASAP."

Keats agreed. "In case Tau learns about the snatch too soon and alerts the station in town. In which case everybody on the train would end up getting searched. No, Aiden's right; midway is your best bet, a surprise assault. Out there in the sticks you've got the highest odds of getting away clean. And if there's a shootout in those mountains it'll likely be too far away to be heard at either of the end points. Besides, if the plan was to simply hand it over to someone in town, there'd be no need for the mercs in the first place."

"How many Marines do you think they'll have to deal with?" Aiden asked.

"Total detachment at Tau is a small platoon," Ned said. "Maybe thirty jarheads, split between day and night shifts. Figure a third of them being off-duty at any one time, so that's how many will be on the train. They probably ride together in the last car. That's ten highly trained men and women, all armed. And the engineer and conductor will likely be packing as well."

"But none of them will carry more than sidearms," Keats said. "Assault weapons would be kept onsite. And if the Marines are all in one car, Nobe probably has a plan for putting them out of commission."

"Makes sense. But here's something else to consider. If we could game this scenario, so could those folks at Tau. They ain't dummies, you know. They might already be staking out the bridge."

"I don't think so," Keats said. "The interrogators who questioned Henry Carpousis were convinced he was hallucinating when he was talking about the weird figure he claimed to have seen. They were equally certain Kokay was using his gear to detect the outer reaches of the sensor net. You know as well as I do that once an assumption is made, the group becomes strongly invested in it. They stop considering alternatives."

Ned gave a grudging nod. The four of them were silent for a moment, considering possibilities. Jessie summed things up.

"OK, we know Tarantian is happening late afternoon Wednesday and we know where. What now? Contact Tau Nine-One and warn them?"

Keats shook his head. Aiden knew what he was going to say before the words left his mouth.

"We go to Montana. We stop them."

"Who exactly is *we*?" Ned wondered.

"Yours truly," Keats said. "Aiden and Jessie if they're willing to risk it."

"Risk it? The three of you against Nobe and his mercs?"

"We'll have the tactical advantage. They won't know we're coming."

"General Custer probably said some shit like that before he ran into those Indians at Little Bighorn."

"It's a workable plan."

"It's a clusterfuck waiting to happen."

Keats stiffened. "This is going down. I need you onboard."

Ned sighed. "All right. But maybe this would be a good time to cash in your chips."

"No."

"It would at least give you a fighting chance."

"No."

Aiden didn't know what Ned meant about cashing in his chips and Keats didn't offer an explanation. But Aiden agreed with the older man. The idea of the three of them trying to stop Michael and the mercs on their own sounded insane.

He wondered again just who Keats was working for. It was unlikely his mysterious handlers had sent him on a suicide mission. Aiden tried to inject some rationality.

"Wouldn't it make more sense to warn those Marines at Tau Nine-One and have them set a trap for the mercs? A trap that could result in Michael and Nobe and the rest of them being killed or put out of commission?"

Keats shook his head.

"Trying to do this on your own is a big mistake," Aiden maintained.

"Maybe. But it's my call."

"I've got a stake in this too, Keats. More than you have, frankly. Quiver warped my life. Jessie's too."

"Then come with me. Maybe you'll find some answers."

The idea was tempting... and ludicrous. "No. We need to call someone at Tau, warn them."

"I'm not doing that."

"Then maybe I will."

Keats' voice fell to a menacing whisper. "That would be a serious mistake."

Aiden looked to Ned for support. But the older man remained silent.

"Keats is right," Jessie said. "We have to do this on our own."

Aiden turned to her in surprise.

"But not just to interrupt the assault," she continued. "If Michael's plan fails, he won't give up. He'll find another way to get the quiver. He's got to be stopped once and for all." She faced Keats. "Promise me that if we do this we go all the way."

"Count on it," Keats said grimly. "Michael de Clerkin is DMW."

Jessie looked perplexed. Ned translated.

"Dead Man Walking."

Aiden shook his head. They were all talking crazy. He wasn't surprised by Keats' attitude. But Jessie? Had killing that merc given her a taste for it, left her hungry to repeat the experience?

She left the room. He followed, caught up in the hallway.

"Keats' plan is nuts. Why are you supporting him?"

"Well, duh! Michael tried to kill us, remember?"

She turned away. He grabbed her shoulder. She spun toward him with a snarl.

"Let go of me!"

He withdrew. Her anger retreated.

"Look Aiden, we can't let Michael get hold of the quiver. That's the bottom line."

"Because he's trying to become a god."

"That's right."

Aiden suspected that Jessie's rationale wasn't that simple. Had he been able to overcome the strange revulsion to her touch and make love to her in the shower, would she still be considering such a course? Was part of her desire to do this insane thing – march into a firefight with impossibly bad odds – a result of misplaced emotions because Aiden had rejected her sexual advances?

Maybe he was giving himself too much credit. He'd only known Jessie for a day and she certainly came across as someone who wouldn't get that bent out of shape over a mild rejection. On the other hand, from his own experiences – including marathon fights with his sister – he knew that unexamined emotions could render both parties wildly irrational.

Jessie headed back to their bedroom. He stared after her. Maybe he was misreading the situation entirely and her eagerness for battle arose from a different motivation. He recalled what she'd said about Michael, back when Aiden and Keats had first arrived at her house.

Gods, by their very nature, don't tolerate competition.

As scary as Michael de Clerkin was, could Jessie have a similar agenda? Beneath their surfaces, did the quiver kids known as

Red and Magenta have more than a little in common? Did Jessie want to stop Michael from getting the quiver so she could have it for herself, use it to boost her own abilities? Could Aiden's subconscious recognition of that reality be the reason he'd been so creeped out by the thought of being intimate with her?

I'm overthinking this.

He hoped that was the case. Because, whether fighting a man yearning for godhood or fighting in the company of a woman with the same aspirations, the ultimate outcome couldn't be good.

FORTY

It was late afternoon when Aiden stepped outside Ned's hilltop home to prepare for departure. Mabeline had driven into town on some errands and they'd said their goodbyes earlier. Aiden had expressed concern to her about leaving Ned alone. But Mabeline said she often did so for short periods, and seemed confident he'd be all right.

Aiden had little choice but to go with Keats and Jessie. Staying here with the Nedelkas wasn't an enticing option. But he still had grave doubts about Keats' plan.

Ned had loaned them a ride, an old Ford F-150 with a crew cab. Keats said they couldn't take the chance that Michael had used his influence to inform the authorities to be on the lookout for the Bronco, or even if that wasn't the case, that someone else may have spotted them driving to or from Jessie's house and ID'd their vehicle. Once the dead mercs were discovered they'd become suspects.

Aiden doubted Keats' theory, especially the part about Michael using his influence to set the cops on them. More than likely, dangling the possibility was meant to provide extra incentive for Aiden to stay on the run and follow Keats' agenda: reach Tau and somehow stop Michael and the mercs.

"I don't use it anymore," Ned grumbled, gesturing to the truck. "Promised Mabeline my driving days are over. Goddamned whitecoats think I'll have an *episode* behind the wheel."

"Best to be safe," Jessie offered.

"Safe my ass. And this coming from a girl about to prance her merry behind into a shitstorm."

Jessie's response was a tight smile as she helped Keats transfer the weapons confiscated from the mercs into the pickup. They hid the guns under a pile of blankets behind the front seats.

"What are you packing?" Ned asked.

Keats opened his jacket to reveal the holstered Glock. "Plus what we lifted from those dead mercs: two more handguns and a rifle. And Jessie's 12-gauge. I think we're good."

Ned grunted. "That's not good; it's barely adequate. If you're hunting big game, you need serious firepower."

He pivoted his wheelchair toward the house, hollered, "Mabeline! Key to the armory, if you please!"

"She went to town," Aiden gently reminded him.

Ned darkened. Aiden thought he was going to throw another tantrum. But he muttered something about getting the key himself and motored toward the door.

"Want me to put the Bronco in the garage?" Keats called after him.

"Hell no. If things go belly up, I don't want any trace you were here. There's an old fire trail a quarter mile down my lane. Drive the Bronco into the woods and hide it off-road as far in as you can."

Keats nodded and got behind the wheel. Jessie offered to go with him. Aiden followed Ned into the house, watched him retrieve a key from a kitchen cabinet. As he propelled the wheelchair back into the hallway, Aiden stepped in front of him, blocking his path.

"You got a problem, son?" Ned challenged.

"Lots of them, actually. But right now what I need are some answers. We both know that Keats' plan is lunacy."

"Certifiable."

"So why's he going through with it?"

"Those assholes tried to kill him. Screw with a man like Deke Keats and you're askin' for a bullet bath."

"There's more to it than that. He was committed to going after Michael and Nobe from the beginning. I need to know who he's working for and why."

The hoary face regarded him with amused contempt. "Is that so? Well, I suggest you ask Deke."

"I'm asking you."

"What makes you think I know?"

Aiden sighed. "Really?"

"Even if I did know, not my business to say."

"That doesn't cut it."

Ned eased the wheelchair forward until the footrest bumped into Aiden's ankles. Aiden didn't budge.

"Keats implied he's on some kind of secret mission to stop Michael and the mercs. He's hinted that he wants to spare the government a messy public trial."

"Bingo."

"There's more to it than that. Who sent him?"

"Are you going to move aside? Or do I have to run your ass over?"

"Look, I've already had two bad encounters with these guys. I figure my chances of surviving a third one are slim to none. If I'm going to get killed in some battle out in the wilderness, don't you think I at least deserve to know why?"

Ned looked uncomfortable. Aiden was getting through to him, instilling some guilt. Aiden gripped the wheelchair's armrests, leaned in close until their faces were a foot apart.

"You were a soldier once. I'm guessing you wouldn't have put one of your own men in harm's way without at least making sure he understood the reason."

"A soldier does his duty, does what he's told."

"Yeah, but you still know I'm right. I deserve the truth."

Ned's body language betrayed his doubts. He was caught between maintaining Keats' secret or doing the honorable thing.

He shifted his chair into reverse and backed down the hallway. Aiden wondered if he was positioning himself for a high-speed attack, run over the stubborn human blocking his path.

"I deserve to know," Aiden insisted.

Ned's fingers drummed the armrests, rhythmic evidence of his indecision.

"All right," he said finally. "But this stays between you and me. Deke doesn't learn what I'm about to tell you."

Aiden nodded.

"A few months ago, his son came back east to visit his mother. Father and son had a bad falling out a long time ago. I'm guessing you've spent enough time with the man to know he can be one stubborn son of a bitch."

Aiden was confused. He recalled eavesdropping on the conversation in Rory's trailer. Keats' son was in middle school. "I thought the boy still lived at home with them in Virginia?"

"I'm not talking about Tonya and her boy. This is Deke's older son, the one he had with his first wife, Alexandra. The kid hated his dad and by association, the military and everything it stood for. He blamed Deke's dedication to the service for making his mom crazy.

"That wasn't the case. But that's how the kid saw it. Bottom line, the two of 'em got along like fused dynamite and a BIC lighter. You know about Alexandra, about her being institutionalized?"

"Uh-huh."

"Well, the boy comes to see his mom. He'd been living in the Midwest, didn't get east very often. It just so happened Deke was visiting Alexandra at the hospital the same day and they run into one another. Turns out to be the first time the family – mom, dad, son – are together in the same room in years.

"Lo and behold, Deke and the kid don't go for the jugulars. Maybe being in the presence of Alexandra, even if she is pretty much gone with the wind, makes 'em mind their ps and qs. They don't exactly kiss and make up but it's definitely the start of something. They leave the hospital, spend a few hours together, heal some old wounds. Things go well enough that they make plans to meet again."

Ned paused. His voice grew solemn. "Deke was planning to fly out to visit the boy last month. Couldn't wait for the kid to get back from his wilderness trip to Montana. In fact, Deke even helped him do a little background research on the area he'd be hiking through."

Aiden connected the rest of the dots. "Which happened to be near a certain government facility known as Tau Nine-One."

"Deke's son was one of the three hikers. Their guide. According to that survivor, Henry Carpousis, the kid went down fighting. Deke had taught him to handle himself but it didn't help. That bastard Nobe broke his neck and kicked his body down into a ravine.

"The kid hated guns, probably another way to prove he was different from his old man. Deke believes if he'd been armed he'd have stood a chance." Ned shook his head. "Doubtful. Not against a trained killer like Nobe."

Aiden recalled Keats' revelations about his first wife and his dream involving Alexandra's painting.

We were still living in this cramped, one-bedroom apartment. We were building the sandcastle and making it huge, giving it all these extra rooms.

Aiden understood the painting's deeper symbolism. The couple had been dreaming of their future together, dreaming of a home big enough to raise their baby son. Alexandra likely was in the early stages of pregnancy.

It's gone, Alexandra, Keats had muttered in his dream. *It's gone.*

Keats had been robbed of his future, and more than once. His wife's mental illness had put a strain on their relationship and caused feuds with his son. And just when he and the boy were on the verge of reconnecting, a chance encounter near Tau Nine-One had stolen his hopes.

"The kid's name was Greg Mahoney," Ned continued. "Used his mom's maiden name. Deke didn't have a problem with that, per se. But he was hoping that someday he'd make Greg proud enough to again call himself a Keats."

Aiden registered the larger truth. Deke Keats wasn't on any

secret mission sanctioned by some clandestine agency. No one had sent him after Michael and Nobe. His impetus had nothing to do with sparing the government public embarrassment. Instead, he was driven by one of the most primeval of human emotions: vengeance. He wanted to kill the men responsible for his son's death.

Ned glowered at him. "Happy now?"

"Almost. I need a favor."

"Betraying the confidence of a friend isn't favor enough?"

"I think I know what it took for you to do that. And I appreciate it. But this is important. I need you to track down a woman. Dr Ana Cho."

After leaving Pinsey's home, Aiden had used Keats' phone to search for the quiver kids' project director. But the name was common enough to generate an overabundance of hits. Without knowing more about her, no clear leads had been forthcoming. There was also the possibility Cho had married and changed her name.

Aiden provided Ned with the details. The old man looked annoyed but gave a grudging nod.

"Is that all? Maybe you also want me to yank out a couple teeth and give 'em to you as souvenirs? Or hop up from this goddamn chair and do some back flips for your entertainment?"

"If you're up for it, by all means. But I'll settle for Cho's current address."

FORTY-ONE

Ned's small armory was beneath the garage and accessed through a disguised hatch. Keats descended the short ladder and handed up a selection of weapons and ammo. Aiden and Jessie carried them to the truck and put them under the back seat with the other weapons.

Jessie looked enthused at the sight of the four Heckler & Koch UMP submachine guns with folding stocks and a pair of older M16 rifles outfitted with scopes. But for Aiden, the weapons, combined with what he'd learned about Keats' real motivations, filled him with an even greater sense of impending doom.

Ned hadn't yet attempted to pry data from the mercs' protected phones. He promised to work the problem after they left and get in touch if successful.

"That's it then," Keats said to the older man as they prepared to depart.

"I'd tell you to watch your asses," Ned grumbled. "But since you're determined to put them in places they don't belong, I'd be wasting my breath."

He handed Keats a phone. "It's a burner and encrypted. In case you want to call and have me talk you out of this nonsense."

The two men shook hands. Keats got behind the wheel of the F-150. Jessie hopped into the bench seat beside him, leaving Aiden the passenger-door side. Even before they reached the bottom of Ned's lane, Keats and Jessie were engaged in an animated conversation about the advantages of specific weapons for various tactical situations. She seemed to have a good handle on the subject.

"Where'd you learn this stuff?" Keats asked.

"My uncle, my mom's brother. Ex-Army. He lived with us for a while and had a serious gun collection. Took me hunting and taught me how to shoot."

Aiden knew enough about guns to get by but had little interest in the topic. Still, he acknowledged a tinge of jealousy. Jessie and Keats seemed to be bonding in a way that left him odd man out.

They reached the main road and headed north. Keats adhered strictly to the speed limit, wise considering what lay hidden behind them. Trying to explain to some statie who pulled them over why they were carrying a cache of automatic weapons would more than challenge their combined bullshitting skills.

As the crow flies, it was some four hundred miles to Jaffeburg. The small town was fifty miles west of Churchton Summit and Tau Nine-One. Ned had an old friend there, a retired navy captain who owned a hotel and restaurant. The man had agreed to put them up for the night, no questions asked. It was safer than the three of them having to show ID to check into some roadside motor lodge. For all they knew, a nationwide bulletin indeed had been issued for their arrests. Staying off the grid remained the safest course.

And if they somehow survived going up against Michael and the mercs, what then? No matter how events unfolded, they'd certainly be wanted for questioning. Engaging in a gun battle near a DOD black site no doubt carried a stiff prison term.

Aiden's burned arms were starting to bother him again. He popped another of Rory's pills and tried his best to get comfortable and settle in for the ride. But he couldn't shake those bad feelings. His mind kept cycling through a trio of unpleasant futures, one of which he seemed destined for.

I'll be dead, sent to prison or forced to go on the run the rest of my life.

Wading through those appalling prospects made him more depressed by the mile. Finally, he forced himself to squelch the negativity and focus on what lay at the heart of his entire predicament.

Quiver.

Everything that had happened to him, not just over these past few days but pretty much his entire life, was centered on that mysterious stone.

What was it? Were Maurice Pinsey and the Tau Nine-One researchers correct in their theory that the stone had been sent to Earth by some fantastic alien civilization seventy thousand years ago? If so, for what purpose? The reason had to involve something more profound than enabling a small group of human beings to experience various types of manifestations.

He recalled the words from his green dream, the words echoed by Bobbie Pinsey.

Singularity beguiles, transcend the illusion.

Who or what was behind that cryptic message? How and why did it apparently use Gold as its means of communication? More to the point, precisely what was the singularity beguiling Aiden and how was he supposed to transcend it?

The questions piled up. The only thing that seemed clear was something he'd acknowledged earlier. He was snared by forces beyond his control and was being propelled toward some unknown destiny. Although he didn't know where he was bound, he sensed his journey revolved around deciphering quiver's true nature. Yet he couldn't see how that could be accomplished by taking part in a battle with hopeless odds.

"Bathroom break," Jessie announced, ending a silence that had gripped the pickup for the past half hour. It was nearly nine o'clock. They'd been on the road four hours.

Keats turned into an all-night diner whose parking lot was dotted with eighteen-wheelers, pickups and a pack of brooding Harleys. Aiden didn't like the look of the place but the diner was serene, belying his apprehensions. The crowd was a mix of long-haul truckers at the counter and families tucked into booths. The motorcyclists, huddled around a large table in the back, turned out to be a group of middle-aged mill workers reliving their youth via a cross-country trek from Chicago to Seattle.

Jessie told Keats to order her coffee and a slice of lemon meringue pie, and headed for the lavatory. Keats grabbed a booth where he could keep an eye on the pickup. A waitress with a ruddy face and no-nonsense attitude took their order.

Keats' encrypted phone rang. He answered, listened for a moment. Disappointment marred his features.

"It's Ned," he said, handing the phone to Aiden. "He couldn't get anything out of the mercs' phones. He wants to talk to you."

The old soldier wasted no words on pleasantries.

"Ana Cho. Second generation Chinese-American. Divorced, one adult son. Kept her married name, Hilbertson. Lives in Portland, Oregon. I have a street address."

Aiden borrowed a pen from Keats and scrawled the address on a napkin.

"Learn anything else about her?" he asked.

"That's it. And don't go throwing my name around as a source. You have no idea where you got this information, right?"

"Absolutely. And thanks, I really appreciate–"

Ned hung up. Aiden returned the phone and pen to Keats, who looked skeptical.

"Waste of time trying to talk to this woman. Even if she knows something, stopping Michael and the rest of them is what's important."

"What's important to you."

Their food arrived a few minutes later. Jessie hadn't returned. Aiden munched on a burger and fries and fought an urge to tell Keats he knew the real reason he was going after Michael and the mercs. Considering the stakes, the truth should be out in the open. But the promise he'd made to Ned compelled him to hold his tongue.

Keats wolfed down a heaping plate of meatloaf and potatoes, and finished his coffee. Anxious to get back on the road, he kept glancing toward the bathroom. Finally, he flagged the waitress and asked if she'd check on Jessie for them. She returned a minute later looking annoyed.

"Your girl told me to mind my own business. Told me she'd be done when she was done and not a moment sooner." The waitress scowled. "She best not be doing drugs in there."

Aiden assured her such was not the case. The woman didn't look convinced and stared long and hard at Keats. Aiden had grown accustomed to his appearance. He'd forgotten just how much the man looked like some brutish heavy from a gangster flick.

The waitress left. They waited a while longer. Still no Jessie. Aiden volunteered to check on her.

A small corridor accessed a pair of unisex lavatories. He knocked on the first door.

"Jessie?"

There was no response. He twisted the knob. The door was locked. He knocked again.

"You OK in there?"

The lock clicked. The door opened a crack.

"Are you alone?" she whispered.

"Yeah."

She let him in and redid the lock. The bathroom was compact, just a corner sink, urinal and a stall with a swinging door. Jessie had a strange expression. He couldn't tell whether it signified bliss or constipation.

She gestured toward the stall. Aiden reached for the door handle, hesitated.

"Go ahead," she urged. "Take a look."

He swung the door open. The back wall above the toilet, just below the grating of a vent, was slimed with overlapping manifestations. Trails of brownish goo dripped slowly to the floor.

"Now stand back and watch this," she said.

Aiden moved from her path. Jessie backed away from the stall as far as possible in the cramped bathroom and closed her eyes.

A manifestation appeared in front of her face, instantly shot away from her as if launched from a cannon. The dropper smashed into the vent just above the slimed barrier with a *splat*.

Jessie beamed with excitement. "I had it all wrong! Those experiments I was doing in the basement, I was obsessed with growing the droppers, like maybe I expected them to blossom into some sort of alien flowers. But I was missing the whole point.

"Things started to become clear to me after I killed that merc. It took a while for it all to hit home, for it to coalesce in my head. But suddenly I'm in here doing my business and I *know*. I feel it to the core of my being!"

"Feel what?"

"My manifestations, they're *weapons!* Suddenly, there's this incredible energy inside me. I can create droppers within minutes of one another, rather than hours or days. I can send them shooting away from me like missiles. And those tentacles, they're optional, only appear as needed. You remember how they broke that merc's fingers, kept his hands from trying to get the dropper off his face? They're like an anti-tampering system so when my missiles hit their target, they can't be interfered with!"

Aiden kept his doubts to himself. Maybe she was right and her manifestations were weapons. But her enthusiasm reminded him of someone on a caffeine high. It left him feeling warier than ever of her

"Michael has a power and it's potent," she continued. "He can turn a manifestation into a shadow and project it, maybe anywhere in the world. But he can't do what I can do!"

Aiden's earlier suspicions returned. Did she want the quiver for herself, to give herself a second infusion?

Someone knocked hard on the door. The waitress.

"All right, enough's enough! I don't know care what the two of you are doing in there, you need to stop it and come out now."

"Be out in a sec," Jessie said.

A key snaked into the lock. Aiden shut the stall door to hide evidence of the manifestations.

The waitress barged in, scowling. Two beefy truckers stood in the hallway behind her, no doubt recruited as backup.

A *splash* came from inside the stall. The waitress shoved past Aiden and pushed open the door. Her scowl deepened as she gazed at the splattered wall.

"What the hell's this?"

A gelatinous clump bobbed in the bowl. Part of Jessie's last projectile had slipped from the vent's grating and took a fortuitous bounce off the toilet tank.

Aiden shrugged. "You got some kind of nasty leak in your air handling system. Better get it checked."

The waitress glared. But she obviously couldn't come up with a more rational explanation. Aiden and Jessie squeezed past her. The truckers stepped aside.

Thrilled by their escape, Jessie playfully rubbed Aiden's arm. Like before, he instinctively pulled away.

This time she took offense. "What's the matter, don't like a woman touching you? If you're gay just come out with it."

"It's not that. Those manifestations of yours kind of freaked me out."

Her expression indicated she knew he was lying.

Aiden remained confused over his reactions. At some fundamental level Jessie did actually repulse him.

Keats was at the checkout counter, paying their bill. Annoyed by the delay, he handed her a doggie bag.

"Your coffee and pie."

She explained what had happened as they headed for the parking lot. Keats wasn't impressed.

"You shouldn't have made a scene. That waitress will remember us."

"Shit happens."

"That supposed to be funny?"

"Lighten up, Keats. Besides, with what I can do now with my droppers, our odds of kicking some merc ass just got way better."

Aiden came to a decision as they reached the pickup.

"I'm not going with you. I need to talk to Ana Cho."

Keats scowled, as if Aiden was the crazy one. Jessie shrugged.

"We're better off without him."

Keats regarded him for a long moment, then nodded. "Do what you gotta do."

The two of them got in the pickup, with Jessie assuming the driving duties. As the taillights disappeared into the night, Aiden was left standing alone in the parking lot, wondering if he'd made the right decision.

FORTY-TWO

The chartered helicopter dropped Michael and Trish Belmont at his Montana chateau on Tuesday, an hour before dawn. It immediately lifted off for another assignment. Michael watched it soar out over the endless expanse of treetops under a star-blazing sky.

His executive assistant had been reluctant to make the trip. Back in LA she'd voiced her objections in that awkward yet endearing manner he found so intriguing.

"Sir, no disrespect meant, but it doesn't really sound like you'll have enough work available for me up there. It might be best if I stay here at the office."

Her real concerns were transparent. She'd probably chatted with other Krame-Tee employees – females, of course – who'd warned her that Michael was a letch of Presidential proportions. They would have advised her not to go on any overnight trips where they'd be alone, particularly at his chateau. In hushed whispers, they would have repeated the rumors about Maisey Latorsky, the attractive young woman who two years ago supposedly had gone missing on the way there.

Michael had been forced to adopt his most reassuring tone to persuade Trish her fears were unfounded. "This trip is important business. I won't even be at the chateau most of the time but I do need you close by. There may be some contract matters that need to be drafted in a hurry. And frankly, you deserve this. I'm still impressed with your excellent work on our acquisition of Janssen Software."

He'd finished his pitch with a lavish description of the chateau. "So Trish, even though this is by no means a vacation, you will be able to spend two days and a night in an absolutely gorgeous setting. Now honestly, are you really that adverse to a little adventure?"

"I suppose it would be OK," she'd said haltingly.

"Of course it will."

Of course, the real reason he'd brought her up here was to have her available for a post-Tau celebration. After he acquired the quiver, he deserved to reward himself. First he'd try a little wine and song to convince Trish to freely partake. If that didn't work he'd opt for his old reliable: a roofie fuck. The method had failed him only once, with Jessica Von Dohren.

He showed Trish her private upstairs bedroom and left her to unpack. He retreated onto the front wraparound porch and gazed across his vast property, some 150,000 acres of mostly pristine wilderness.

The wood-framed structure had been erected by an early-twentieth-century timber magnate as a vacation home. No expense had been spared. Granite for its foundation had been mined from a nearby quarry created especially for the purpose. Rooms and hallways on both floors featured elaborately carved mahogany imported from Brazil. His father had paid a premium price for the chateau and land.

As a boy, Michael had once quizzed the asshole on why he wanted a house in rugged terrain in the middle of nowhere. The question had come at a bad time, as many of Michael's questions invariably did. It had earned him a slap across the face and a warning not to bother a busy man.

After Michael inherited control of the business, he'd learned from the busy man's papers why he'd wanted the place and why he was touchy about it. The chateau was west of Helena and the state had been talking about a new highway through the region.

Funding had fallen through, however. Instead of prime commercial real estate, his father had been left with an expensive boondoggle in the middle of nowhere. No matter how successful in business, the prick couldn't stomach even the occasional failure.

Michael had considered selling the property. But after setting his sights on the quiver, he was glad he hadn't. It gave him a base of operations within reasonable flying distance from the cabin near Churchton Summit, where they'd rendezvous for the assault.

The chateau was built into the side of a hill, elevating the stilted porch twelve feet off the ground. The helipad was on a lower terrace, adjacent to a six-bay garage stocked with gas- and battery-powered cars and ATVs. A private road wound down the side of the mountain for a dozen miles before reaching a public road and, eventually, civilization.

Michael gazed out over the canopy. It was still dark but chirping birds nestled in the branches indicated dawn was imminent. The air was cool and dry. Forecasters predicted sunny days in the low-seventies the whole week.

Tomorrow's assault still had a green light. The insider had gotten back to Michael. A coded text message assured him that Tau Nine-One had received no fresh alerts. She'd contact him again if that status changed. But so far, it appeared that Princess and her cohorts hadn't warned Tau officials about what was coming.

That begged the question, what exactly were the three of them up to? It was unlikely they'd attempt to directly interfere with the assault. That fell somewhere between foolhardy and suicidal. The more probable scenario was that they were counting their blessings at having escaped death – twice in Green's case – and were lying low. Still, if Michael was wrong and they were indeed contemplating some sort of intervention...

A stiff breeze and a smacking sound interrupted his thoughts. The branch of a tree growing at the end of the porch whipped against the railing. Michael had given the chateau's caretakers, a local husband and wife, the week off. He'd have to take them to task for not keeping the closest trees properly trimmed. He wasn't paying them to be negligent.

The notion of negligence returned his thoughts to two years ago, to one of the few times in his life he'd been guilty of it. He and Maisey Latorsky had taken a leisurely drive up to the chateau for a getaway weekend.

Maisey had been the only woman in Michael's life who he'd felt really understood him, who really grasped his true nature. Even better, she'd loved him for it, loved the idea of being with a man hypercharged with such aggressive and dominant tendencies. She was masochistic at heart but it was more than just a sexual kink. She'd loved Michael for how he perceived the world, how he saw it as a great carcass to be picked over. She'd loved how he wasn't overly concerned with the thoughts and feelings of others, that he perceived such emotions as a form of weakness. Maisey had admired the very qualities in him that others saw as twisted and egocentric.

And he'd loved her back, the first woman he could honestly say that about. He'd even entertained thoughts of asking her to marry him. But allowing himself to be open to such emotions had proved to be a mistake, one he would never repeat. It had led to his negligent act that fateful weekend.

He'd left the hidden door to the basement lab unlocked. Maisey had wandered in while he was in the midst of one of his early experiments. Bad enough she'd seen his expensive containment vessels into which he directed his psychic creations: the gelatinous brown spheres that were the common legacy of the quiver kids. The spheres alone could have been explained away. But Maisey had happened to enter during his attempt to create a shadow. She'd screamed at the sight of his ghostly doppelganger floating above the floor.

Maybe if she hadn't reacted in such a panicked fashion, it would have been OK. Maybe if she'd been able to accept what she was seeing as easily as she accepted so many other aspects of Michael's personality, he wouldn't have felt threatened and lashed out.

But he couldn't change the past. He *had* felt threatened. He *had* lashed out. For the rest of his life, a part of him would regret his subsequent actions. Even as Maisey was trying to bring her screams under control, he'd come up behind her – the real him, not the shadow she was transfixed upon – and wrapped his arm around her neck.

He remembered telling himself as she struggled to break free that he shouldn't go through with it. But those were his weaker emotions speaking. By sidestepping such feelings, a trick he'd learned as a child from his brutal father and delusional nutcase of a mother, he'd found the strength to continue. With a wicked twist, he'd snapped her neck.

Michael leaned against the porch railing and stared down into the trees. Although a band of violet creased the eastern sky, it was still too dark to make out the old trail running behind the garage that accessed the quarry. That's where he'd carried Maisey Latorsky's lifeless body, digging a hole in the rubble and burying her deep. The last time he'd checked, a layer of damp moss covered her grave.

He'd reported her disappearance to the authorities in Helena and Los Angeles, claiming she was supposed to drive her own car up to Montana to meet him but had never arrived. The LA detectives who'd interviewed him suspected foul play, as did Maisey's parents. But they'd never been able to prove it, especially since before giving the report he'd had Nobe steal her car from her West Hollywood apartment and dispose of it.

Since Maisey's demise he'd installed more rigorous safeguards. A palm lock, retinal scanner and door sensors were linked to the chateau's security system and controlled via an app. Any attempt at illicit entry would prompt notification wherever he was.

Michael had been involved in other murders over the years. But Maisey remained the only person he'd killed with his own hands. He'd derived no pleasure from it. Still, there were times when he fantasized about the incident, reimagining it as a slow strangulation rather than a quick neck snap, his fingers choking the life not out of her, but out of his adoptive parents. *That* he would have enjoyed.

Unfortunately, he hadn't been afforded such a luxury. When arranging for his parents to be killed by sabotaging their Cessna, circumstances dictated that it look like an accident.

PART 3
THE SHROUD

FORTY-THREE

Aiden was saddlesore. He'd spent nearly twelve hours on the back of a Harley with only two quick stops for munchies and bathrooms. The ride would have been a trial for anyone who didn't ride motorcycles but road vibration accentuated the pain from his burned arms. He'd popped three of Rory's pills during the trek.

Skinny Hank, the moniker bestowed on his chauffeur by fellow bikers at the restaurant, got him to Portland by midmorning Tuesday. Aiden disembarked on a tree-shaded avenue in the city's Southeast section and paid the biker, who easily tipped the scales at three hundred pounds. Skinny Hank roared off to rejoin his brothers in leather two hundred dollars richer.

Ana Hilbertson's two-story detached house had vinyl siding and a porch with all-weather chairs. A driveway ascended to a two-car garage in back. Aiden climbed the steps and rang the bell. A man in jeans and sweatshirt holding a little boy opened the door. A startled look gave Aiden the impression he'd been recognized.

The man had a skinny frame and a ruddy complexion, as if he spent a lot of time outdoors. His gaunt face was outlined with a chin-strap beard. The boy, who looked about two, stared at Aiden with inquisitive blue eyes.

"I'm looking for Ana Hilbertson," Aiden said. "Is this the right house?"

"She's not home. Something I can help you with?"

"Know when she'll be back?"

"Ana is my mother. What's this about?"

"It's personal."

The man was around Aiden's age. A lack of Asian features suggested he'd been adopted. Was this White, the anomaly?

Aiden gestured to a porch chair. "Mind if I wait?"

"Best you come inside."

The front room had a funky, lived-in look that Aiden found appealing. A pair of armchairs with tan fabric fronted a leather sofa and recliner. Mismatched throw rugs were strewn across the floorboards like bandages. Expressionist prints in dinky frames dotted the walls. Aiden recognized three of the most colorful ones as Chagalls.

Weirdly out of place in the corner was a giant statue of an obese male clown. Made of ceramic material that was chipped and cracked, the figure was a good four feet wide and almost touched the ceiling. A hole in its belly was covered by a sheet of opaque fabric. An arrow pointed to the hole along with instructions.

TICKLE MY INNARDS, IF YOU DARE!

"It's from a 1920s carnival," the man explained. "The barker would put a slab of raw meat in the hole and dare people to reach in. Later, the raw meat was replaced by a generator that gave the victim a mild electric shock. Mom bought it at an auction."

"Cool conversation piece. Big, too."

The man lowered the boy, who scooted to a bookcase. The lower shelves were crammed with toys.

"I'm Grant," the man said. "That's my son, Lucas."

"Aiden."

Grant nodded as if he already knew the name.

Aiden flopped on an armchair, which was ridiculously comfortable compared to his previous butt support on the bike. He watched Lucas upend a shoebox of building bricks and start assembling them. The boy's combination of intense concentration and physical awkwardness reminded him of Leah at that age.

Grant revealed he was a software developer who worked at home and took care of Lucas. His wife was a bank manager. Aiden kept his side of the conversation nondescript, talked about the weather and Portland's laid-back reputation. Still, the more they spoke, the more convinced he was that Grant knew plenty about him.

They heard a car pull into the driveway. The front door opened and a gray-haired woman with Asian features entered the house, a heaping bag of groceries in her arms. She froze at the sight of Aiden but recovered fast and transitioned to a warm smile.

"Aiden Manchester. I'm glad we can finally meet."

FORTY-FOUR

Ana Cho, aka Ana Hilbertson, deposited the groceries in the kitchen and rejoined them in the front room. Aiden guessed she was in her late fifties or early sixties. She was slender and petite. Her wraparound skirt had a pattern of yellow daffodils.

She sat beside Grant on the sofa, folding her hands demurely in her lap. Lucas grew tired of playing and flopped across a portable daybed. He was asleep in seconds.

"What brings you to our home?" Ana Cho asked.

Aiden had intended to squeeze every dollop of information he could from Tau's former project director and keep his own life as cloaked as possible. But here in this room, face to face with Cho and her son, something prompted him to come clean.

He began with a history of his manifestations and recurring green dream, segued into an overview of the terrifying recent events starting with his father's letter. He stuck to the high points and avoided mentioning the abilities of the other quiver kids he'd encountered. As promised, he also left out any mention of Ned.

Grant's shock was palpable at hearing of the violence perpetrated by Michael. Ana Cho's reaction seemed closer to a weary sadness.

"I made a terrible mistake in allowing Red's adoption into that family," she said. "We weren't given a lot of time to do the placements and none of the prospective parents rung alarm bells. This was in the primordial days of internet search engines, so there was a limited amount of information to be gleaned in that manner. I employed private investigators but in Red's case they clearly didn't dig deep enough. Still, I should have done a better and more thorough job of vetting. Only much later did I learn what a dysfunctional home I'd consigned him to."

"Not your fault, Mom," Grant said, laying a hand on her shoulder. "Under the circumstances, you did the best you could."

"Not good enough, as it turned out. Blue apparently paid for my error with his life. And Michael may come here next."

Cho and Grant cast worried looks at the sleeping Lucas.

"You weren't easy to find," Aiden reassured them. "The person who tracked down your location has a special talent for locating people. And at least for now, I'm guessing Red is focused on stealing the quiver."

"Do you think Magenta and this soldier can stop him?" Grant asked.

"I don't know. But is Jessie right? Will Red become more powerful with another infusion?"

"For the test animals and the babies the IQ boost was a one-time event," Cho said. "Re-infusions were tried but there were no measurable changes. As for adult quiver kids?" She shrugged. "Uncharted territory."

Grant asked Aiden if he'd ever attempted to cultivate his own abilities like Red and Magenta.

"It was never an option." Aiden told them about the psychic research he'd been paid to do in Dr Jarek's Georgetown lab. "No matter how hard I tried, I could never consciously create a chunkie."

Cho was surprised. "They only come when you're asleep?"

He nodded and hazarded a guess. "You're the one who secretly kept tabs on the quiver kids, right?"

"Yes, for about a decade. I tracked the progress of you and the others whose adoptions I was responsible for: Green, Red and Cyan." She paused. "And White. My ex is a physician and he taught me how to game the medical bureaucracy to secure health records. Scholastic files were more of a challenge. It took some subterfuge to get the schools to release them."

"Why'd you stop tracking us?"

"After all that time there were no indications of an IQ boost. And privacy laws were becoming more restrictive. Actually, I never completely stopped. I've occasionally looked in on what the four of you were up to. None of you are overly active on social media but there's still information to be found online. I attended your high school graduation, Aiden. Discreetly of course, from the back of the auditorium. I happened to be visiting a friend in the area at the time."

Aiden faced Grant. "And what about you? You're one of us, right?"

"I am."

"I adopted Grant as a single mother," Cho said. "I bent the rule that the children were to be placed in traditional, two-parent households."

"Mom didn't marry until later," Grant added. "Dad never knew about the experiment. She kept that part of my life secret from everyone."

"So you're the anomaly, White," Aiden concluded.

Instead of confirming it, Grant and Cho exchanged a cryptic look.

"Maurice Pinsey was really that terrified of White?" Cho asked.

"Yeah, acted like White and Satan were BFFs. He was going on about the fact there were three experimenters and six babies, which he believed represented the number of the beast, 666."

Cho sighed. "Maurice always had strong religious beliefs. Unfortunately, he allowed those beliefs to overcome the rational skepticism every good scientist requires. We chose six babies simply because... well, it just seemed like the right number for the experiment."

"You didn't confirm that you're White," Aiden said, turning back to Grant. "Is that your color name?"

Another odd look passed between mother and son.

Aiden frowned. "OK, what's going on?"

"I promise we'll reveal everything," Cho said. "But please bear with us a moment. It's important. What else can you tell us about the others, about the precise nature of their powers?"

Aiden spoke of Michael de Clerkin's ability to transmit a hologram of himself to distant locations and about Bobbie Pinsey's manifestations, as well as her cryptic message that matched the words from Aiden's green dream. He revealed Jessie Von Dohren's growing ability to use her manifestations as weapons and his fear that she too might try to go after the quiver. He also mentioned what Michael had said about Rodrick Tyler, about Blue's desire to penetrate the realm beyond the beasts.

When he finished, Grant and Cho launched into a mystifying dialogue.

"Could the message that came through Gold refer to an initial step for safe entry into a cleaving?" Grant asked.

"Possibly," Cho said. "The Pinsey girl could be some sort of telepath, receiving information from within the shroud. Blue's talk of penetrating a realm beyond the beasts could be a similar reference."

"Red's ability to transmit himself... a means for traveling through the shroud? And Magenta's powers a defensive system for enabling safe passage?"

"Possibly. But we shouldn't jump to any conclusions."

"Conclusions about what?" Aiden demanded. "What the hell are you talking about?"

"I've suspected for a long time that the quiver kids represent six pieces of a jigsaw puzzle," Cho told him. "They fit together to achieve a common purpose."

"What purpose?"

Again, mother and son exchanged meaningful looks. Aiden's displeasure grew.

"Look, just tell me what you're not telling me, OK?"

"You've had a lot to deal with over these past few days," Cho said. "Learning you were adopted, that you're a quiver kid. Those encounters with Red and his mercenaries. But now I'm afraid you're going to have steel yourself for a shock far more profound."

She nodded to Grant, who continued. "I'm a quiver kid. But I'm not White. *I'm* Green. Mom thought it best to take the added precaution of hiding your real identity. The truth is, you're the seventh quiver kid, the anomaly. *You're* White."

"Believe it," Cho said, seeing the doubt playing across Aiden's face. "In your final months at Tau, I subjected you to an intense psychological campaign meant to indoctrinate you into thinking of yourself as Green instead of the color name you were commonly addressed by. When the two of us were alone, I called you Green. I brought you green toys and endlessly repeated that color to you. I read you stories filled with green imagery. I used sleep-learning, played low-volume tape recordings in your crib repeating the word green. I did everything in my power to saturate your young mind with that hue, and likewise make you forget your real color.

"And it worked. That color was successfully imprinted upon your infantile psyche, and to such an extent that you dreamed about it in later years. When you finally learned you were a quiver kid, you naturally assumed you were Green."

Aiden had no reason to doubt her. It also might explain why he was the only quiver kid of those he'd encountered to dream of a color.

"OK, so you brainwashed me into thinking of myself as Green. But what about my parents? Wouldn't they have known my real color?"

"Yes, but we encouraged the adoptive parents, at least the ones who'd had contact with the babies at Tau, never to use their color names. We wanted all of you to grow up with a clean slate, to have no conscious memories of a different identity in your earliest years. It was sensible advice and clearly your parents took it to heart. Not even your father's letter revealed the truth."

Aiden remained confused. "But why? Why go to all that trouble to change my color?"

"I was afraid of what Maurice and Colonel Jenkins might do.

Although the colonel was dying, I was concerned he may have passed on knowledge about an aspect of the experiment to his military associates. Jenkins was a rather cold and unpleasant man. I feared that his associates could be of a similar ilk." Cho grimaced. "People not overly concerned with morality and ethics."

Aiden cracked a bitter laugh. "*You're* talking about morality and ethics? Really?"

"Point taken. I'm aware that I bear responsibility for initiating the experiment. It boils down to a matter of degree. There were certain lines I wouldn't cross. Colonel Jenkins had few such qualms. He once suggested that we euthanize one of the babies in order to do a detailed autopsy, look for physiological changes that might only be detectable postmortem."

"Bastard," Grant muttered.

"And then there was Maurice, whose full-blown descent into supernatural beliefs was accelerated by White's arrival – *your* arrival. Pinsey grew increasingly tormented. I feared that his faith might someday compel him to hunt you down, possibly with harmful intentions in mind. Your earlier comment about him equating White with Satan isn't far from the mark. In his worldview, you came to represent something evil, something that needed to be destroyed.

"Changing your color identity wasn't an all-encompassing solution. It certainly would have done little to safeguard you should Maurice or Colonel Jenkins' associates attempt to track you down. Its main purpose wasn't so much protection from them as it was protection from yourself. I felt that if you ever unearthed what had occurred in your earliest years, it would be better for you to believe that you were one of the six, not the anomaly."

Cho laid a comforting hand on her son's shoulder. "Grant was always the real Green, of course. Since you'd already encountered or become aware of most of the other quiver kids, it was only logical for you to make the erroneous assumption that he was White."

Aiden shook his head, more confused than ever. "So Jenkins

saw me as a lab rat and Pinsey as the devil. But none of this makes any sense. White was supposed to be the control in the experiment. He wasn't infused with quiver. Yet I suffer from the manifestations like the others. Did I somehow acquire my ability by being around the other babies? Is that why I was called the anomaly?"

Cho and Grant stared at him. Aiden saw the flaw in his reasoning.

"But that can't be. I didn't have my first chunkie until I was twelve. So why would you call me the anomaly when I was only eighteen months old and still at Tau?" The answer came to him. "There was something else different about me, something apparent early on."

Cho asked Grant to get her laptop and he headed upstairs. While they waited for his return, she gazed at Aiden with the oddest expression, something between curiosity and sadness. It made him uneasy. He had a hunch that everything he'd learned over these past days was mere preamble to what was about to be revealed.

Grant returned with a MacBook. He spread it on the coffee table in front of Aiden and maneuvered the trackpad to open a file.

A video played. It was grainy, as if shot in low light by an older, analog camera. There was no audio. Point of view was from up high, probably from a ceiling mount. The lens was aimed down the length of a small nursery with curtained windows. There were six cribs, three on each side. The colors of the cribs matched their occupants. Boys were on the left, Blue, Green and Red. The girls – Gold, Magenta and Cyan – were on the right side of the central aisle.

"Surveillance video from more than a quarter century ago," Cho explained. "It was taken the day you arrived at Tau Nine-One."

The babies looked to be about nine months old. They were lying on their backs, asleep.

Suddenly they awakened, weirdly in unison. All six crawled to the foot of their cribs facing the aisle. Red, Magenta and Cyan were strong enough to pull themselves upright. The others remained on their bellies, staring through the bars.

Something was happening in the aisle. A ball of quivering energy formed about a foot above the floor. Resembling a miniature sun, it bathed the nursery in a surreal gray light.

The babies stared at the ball of energy. None of them seemed frightened or surprised. Aiden thought it was downright creepy the way the six of them were transfixed

The energy brightened for an instant, then disappeared as swiftly as it had arrived. Left in its wake on the floor was another baby, a boy, naked, squirming and crying heartily.

A door at the far end was flung open. A youthful Ana Cho rushed into the nursery. For a long moment, she gazed in stunned silence at the howling baby on the floor. Recovering her poise, she picked up the seventh quiver kid and cradled him in her arms.

Grant paused the video. He and his mother remained silent, waiting for Aiden to absorb the implications. For what seemed like minutes but was probably only a few seconds, Aiden could only gaze in disbelief at that final screen image of Cho holding him.

He finally found his voice. "I don't... understand. You're saying that I just... appeared?"

"Yes."

He shook his head, unwilling to believe. "No, this is some sort of trick. A special effect. The video was doctored."

"I assure you, such is not the case. This video documents exactly what happened in the nursery that morning. Your arrival at Tau had nothing to do with you serving as a control in the experiment. It was unplanned and unprecedented. Spontaneous generation of a fully formed human baby, age approximately nine months."

"That isn't possible."

"Analysis of both your mitochondrial DNA and nuclear DNA reveal that the standard twenty-three pairs of chromosomes residing in nearly every cell in the human body are proportionally present in the other six. In a very real sense, those babies are your biological parents. Genetically, you are the offspring of the six original quiver kids.

"Extensive tests proved that you were approximately the same age as the others. Physically, emotionally and mentally, you exhibited the typical features of a baby at that developmental stage. Strictly for your own future reference, we approximated and assigned you a birth date of nine months earlier."

"This is crazy. How could I just pop out of thin air?"

"A question I've puzzled over for decades. What meager evidence there is would seem to suggest you were formed by the combined nascent abilities of the other six. You are a sui generis creation."

Aiden's hands began to shake, probably a delayed reaction to the impact of the revelation. He locked his palms together in a futile effort to stop the shaking. Cho remained serene in the face of his agitation.

"If I wasn't born here, then where the hell did I come from?"

Cho shrugged. "Prior to the moment you appeared in that nursery it was as if you simply didn't exist. The first nine months of your life never happened."

Aiden stood up. He felt lightheaded. He gripped the chair arm for support.

"This is nuts. It makes no sense."

"I'm sorry, Aiden. I know this must be difficult to absorb."

Difficult? The word didn't come close to describing the turbulent feelings cascading through him.

"The truth of your arrival was known only to me, Dr Pinsey and Colonel Jenkins. The three of us conspired to keep it that way. We invented the story that you'd been brought to Tau to serve as the control for the experiment, and that you were born to a poor itinerant woman who died giving birth. We confiscated this video before anyone else could view it.

"Shortly thereafter, Pinsey began to go off the rails. He assigned increasingly religious interpretations to your appearance. Colonel Jenkins became lost in fantastic imaginings as well, although with more sinister goals in mind. He wondered if quiver might become a means for the spontaneous creation of soldiers who, because they lacked traditional parents, wouldn't require the civil rights and legal protections afforded the rest of the citizenry. He envisioned an army of such children, an army whose members could be isolated from earliest childhood and trained as perfect soldiers, unfettered by the niceties of a civilized upbringing."

Cho grimaced and shook her head. "Insanity. Jenkins and Pinsey, in their own distinctive ways, were both quite mad. That's why I put such effort into trying to hide your true identity."

My true identity. Aiden's mind raced. His thoughts became a jumble of ideas, all clustered around the notion that he wasn't really a human being. The story that he'd been born to a woman who died bringing him into the world, and who he'd assumed had likely been a prostitute, now seemed like a wonderfully desirable past. Better such a fable than the truth, that he'd never had a real mother and father.

Cho continued, her words a relentless attack on his very nature. "It would appear that whatever immeasurable changes the six experienced from the quiver infusions enabled them, perhaps through some unconscious gestalt process, to bring you into the world fully formed. It's possible your arrival was a primordial flexing of their combined powers. Such unintentionality could explain why the others experience manifestations that lead to the development of distinct abilities, whereas in your case such abilities appear to be stillborn."

"You're saying I'm a side effect?"

"I wouldn't necessarily put it in those terms."

But Aiden could tell that's what she believed. It was all too much to absorb. He'd come here looking for answers only to find them in the form of a wrecking ball slamming into his consciousness, reducing the pillars of his life to rubble.

He couldn't stay another moment in this house. He bolted for the front door, ignoring the shouts of Cho and Grant. Their voices melded into a droning roar, the sound of a mind seeking escape from itself.

FORTY-FIVE

Aiden sprinted down the pavement, oblivious to direction or destination. Zigzagging from street to street, he ignored strolling pedestrians. A pack of preteen girls lunged from his path, their eyes widening with alarm as he bolted past. Whether they saw pain or madness on his face, he couldn't have said.

The weather was comfortable, reminiscent of a morning run in Birdsboro this time of year. Aiden noticed neither the cloudless skies and cool breeze, nor the smattering of passing vehicles and occasional weaving bicyclist. The world had morphed into an unreal blur, a distorted reflection of his inner state. He felt unhinged. A lifetime's illusion that he was fundamentally like everyone else had been shattered.

I was never born. I never had real parents. I'm a freak.

Running usually provided a respite from his troubles. Today it brought no relief. But he had no choice but to keep going. Maybe running until he was overcome by exhaustion would result in a blessed fall into unconscious oblivion.

Feelings of being different had plagued him from the first time he'd manifested a chunkie. But Cho's revelation had ramped up those feelings to an unbearable level. He wanted a do-over, however desperately childish such a wish. He wanted to go back in time five days to that fateful call from George Dorminy.

I don't want the damn safe, he would have told Dorminy. *Drive it to the nearest river and drown it in the depths.*

The do-over fantasy ignited memories of his father. More than ever, he missed Dad, missed the man's comforting presence. Had Aiden asked his father how he should deal with such overwhelming torment, Dad would have put that keen engineering mind into overdrive, dug into a storehouse of sage advice and generated a solution.

Aiden abruptly recalled the letter's final paragraph, where Dad had talked about how he and Mom had fallen in love with Aiden the first time they'd seen him smiling and giggling in a playpen.

In all these years that love has never wavered. You brought us a joy that made our lives more meaningful than we ever could have dreamed. We can only hope and pray that you'll remember the good times you had with us and find a way to get through all this.

A red light fronted a busy intersection. Aiden halted his mad dash. Leaning over, he planted his hands on his thighs and gulped down fresh air. He'd been running without breathing properly, without pacing himself, without having a destination in mind. Dad would have considered such behavior wild and foolish and told him so.

Don't pull a Blackie Redstone. Always think smart. That's the only way to stay ahead of your troubles.

The memory of his father's presence and those words served to lift Aiden from the all-consuming funk. Despite Cho's revelations, the pillars of his life had not been destroyed. A foundation remained, strong and abiding, built deep into the bedrock of Byron and Alice Manchester's unconditional love.

He was a freak, yes, but he was a freak who'd been raised in a strong and supportive environment. His birth might have been swaddled in unreality but his upbringing was not. His parents had endowed him with the strength to face whatever challenges were thrown in his path.

He straightened. The breeze seemed sharper, the faint sounds of traffic on the intersecting avenues keener.

A car horn blared. He turned. A green Honda SUV nestled up

to the curb in front of him. Ana Cho's son was behind the wheel.

"Get in," Grant urged.

Despite freeing himself from those bleak thoughts, Aiden wasn't ready to return to their home.

"I'm not heading back to the house," Grant said. "Mom is brilliant and I love her. And there probably wasn't a good way to reveal the truth to you. But sometimes she can be insensitive, out of touch with how her words can hurt. And, for what it's worth, as fascinating as she finds the whole quiver kids experiment from a scientist's perspective, a part of her feels terrible about her role in it."

Aiden wasn't swayed. Nevertheless, common sense won out. Alone and dashing haphazardly through a strange city with a limited supply of cash didn't present a lot of options.

He hopped in the passenger seat. "Where are we going?"

"I have something to show you."

"I've had enough surprises for the day."

"This one you won't want to miss."

FORTY-SIX

They drove west. For a time, neither of them spoke. Aiden sensed that Grant was waiting for him to make the overture. He kept silent until they'd crossed the Willamette River into Portland's downtown.

"Do the other quiver kids or anyone else know the truth about me?"

Grant shook his head. "At least I don't think so. Maurice Pinsey could have told someone, maybe at his church. But Mom always doubted it. He was too frightened by the whole thing. And Colonel Jenkins wasn't the kind of man to share secrets. If he had, you can bet that Pentagon spooks would have been tracking the seven of us to this day. To the best of our knowledge, that didn't happen."

"What about your Mom? Could she have inadvertently leaked it to someone?"

"No. Like I said, not even my adoptive father knew."

Aiden found himself chuckling. The emotional release felt good.

"What's so funny?"

"That word, *father*. I just realized that as well as having an adoptive one, I have *you*."

"I suppose that's got to feel weird."

"FYI, I'm not going to start calling you Dad."

"Good. And technically, I'm only one-sixth of your parentage."

Aiden's amusement evaporated when he considered that his heredity also included Michael de Clerkin. And on the female

229

side there was Jessie. The physical revulsion he'd felt toward her when intimacy threatened now sort of made sense. Some innate part of him may have recognized that hooking up with one of his biological mothers was a genetic no-no. But for whatever reason, Jessie didn't experience the same reaction.

His thoughts wandered to the one quiver kid he knew nothing about. "What about Cyan? What's her story?"

"Her name is, or was, Meira Hirshfeld. Mom tracked her early on, same as she did with you and Michael. Meira was adopted by a couple from Washington State who'd established a chain of upscale restaurants.

"But when Meira was ten, her parents sold the business and moved them to British Columbia, to a small town north of Vancouver. Not long after that they pulled a disappearing act, went off the grid. Mom tracked them as far as Australia. One rumor has it that after Meira reached adulthood, she traveled to Thailand and became ordained as a Theravada Buddhist monk." Grant shrugged. "But we really have no idea whether that's true, or if she's even still alive."

"Age ten," Aiden mused. "Early puberty maybe, the start of the manifestations? Sounds like Meira's parents did something similar to Jessie's mother, moved away from civilization to protect her child."

"That's Mom's theory too."

Aiden had refrained from asking the obvious question: What ability did Grant possess? He had a hunch that Green – the *real* Green – was planning to reveal it soon.

"Mom mainly does freelance work these days, neuroscience consulting for tech companies. But no surprise, her real passion is trying to make sense of the quiver phenomenon and the seven of us. You showing up unexpected, and with what you've told us about the others, will keep her energized for months. Still, sometimes I think Maurice Pinsey was right. According to Mom, he used to say that the more quiver was studied, the less it was understood."

"He's still saying it."

"Quiver seems to have been engineered by some fantastic alien science and sent here by unknown means seventy thousand years ago. Beyond that, it's pretty much all guesswork. It's possible we don't even have the language or tools to comprehend quiver's fundamental nature. We can only explore the edges, pick at the outer layers."

"The IQ boost would seem to be a big part of it," Aiden said. "Maybe quiver is like those black monoliths in *2001: A Space Odyssey*. It's meant to push the human race into making some kind of quantum evolutionary leap."

"On the surface that sounds plausible. But Mom and I have come to doubt that raising mammalian intelligence is quiver's main purpose. She still has contacts at Tau Nine-One who tell her that the IQ boost remains the primary focus of their research. No more testing on human babies, obviously, but plenty of infusing all sorts of other infant mammals. They've even experimented on dolphins. But no manifestations have ever resulted from those test animals. That suggests only *Homo sapiens* can develop such abilities. A logical conclusion is that quiver is human-centric."

Aiden gazed ahead. They'd left Portland's urban core for a mountainous region northwest of the city. The hilly two-lane road curled through a forest of Douglas firs and big-leaf maples. Verdant treetops formed a wavering outline against a rich azure sky.

"We suspect that the IQ boost is merely an enticement," Grant said. "It makes us curious enough to want to experiment further with quiver. Looking at it another way, quiver is a delivery system for endowing an intelligent species with enhanced abilities. The manifestations and whatever they lead to are what's important, not the raised IQs. That's just a trick to get us to bring babies into contact with the quiver stone. And from what you've said about the others, it seems certain that our abilities come in six different forms."

Aiden recalled Cho saying that the quiver kids were part of a jigsaw puzzle, that they fit together to achieve a common purpose.

"But what's the ultimate objective?" he wondered. "Why would these presumed aliens go to all this trouble?"

Grant shrugged. "I suppose that's up to us to find out."

"Up to the six of you, maybe. It's pretty clear I'm odd man out. I don't have abilities like the rest of you." Aiden grimaced. "I'm just a side effect."

"Mom believes that but I'm not so sure. There are other scenarios to consider."

"Like what?"

"Like we're here," Grant said, turning into a gravel parking lot. It served as a transition point for exchanging rubber tires for rubber-soled boots. At the end of the lot, a trail snaked uphill through the trees.

"Ready for a little hike?" Grant asked.

Aiden looked doubtful.

"You can't beat nature as a tonic, especially when your day's gone to hell."

"Fine. Lead on."

Aiden followed him up the winding dirt path. They encountered a trio of hikers coming downhill. Beyond that, the trail was deserted.

The sound of cars on the road below grew muffled. Other than chirping birds, the woods grew silent as well. Stepping on twigs produced inordinately loud crackling.

The trail finally leveled off. Grant took a spur that angled to the left. The side trail was narrower and overgrown with tangled vines and protruding branches. Aiden had to walk far enough behind him to avoid being face-whipped by springy shoots he pushed aside.

The path grew even less hospitable, disappearing entirely in spots. Aiden tripped on a vine and almost fell. He was about to protest they'd gone far enough when they reached a small clearing. Four boulders were positioned evenly around its perimeter like makeshift seats. A ring of stones in the center marked an old campfire.

"Stumbled on this place a couple years ago," Grant said. "It's become my go-to rest stop."

The boulders were draped in moss and dead leaves. Grant swept debris off two of them and sat, motioning Aiden to the opposite boulder. They perched across from one another, the campfire stones between them.

Grant folded his hands in his lap and closed his eyes. A serene expression came over him, as if slipping into a meditative state. Aiden forced patience but soon felt antsy. Any sort of New Age, contemplate-your-navel activities had never been a strong suit.

"If you start in with chanting and mantras, I'm out of here," Aiden jokingly warned.

Grant's eyes remained shut. "I'm trying to get in the right mood so I can show you."

"Show me what?"

"This."

FORTY-SEVEN

Grant opened his eyes. A manifestation appeared in the air between them. It resembled one of Aiden's chunkies. But it didn't fall to earth. Fascinated, Aiden watched the levitating brown sphere grow larger until it was about four feet in diameter. The center became translucent then faded entirely, leaving a hole the size of a manhole cover. When the manifestation completed its transformation, it reminded Aiden of a giant chocolate donut.

"My manifestations began at puberty too," Grant said. "But I didn't figure out how to do this until a few years ago."

"Exactly what are you doing?"

"I call it a cleaving, I can only keep it stable for a few minutes. Imagine holding your breath. The longer you do it, the more you feel the need to exhale and suck down fresh air. So we don't have much time. I'd like to try a little experiment. I'd like you to stick your hand through the hole."

Aiden hesitated.

"No one's ever been harmed," Grant assured him. "Mom and I figured out a way to secretly give this test to hundreds of people."

Aiden recalled the giant ceramic clown in Ana Cho's living room. "The hole in its belly. You create one of these donuts, hide it behind the clown and entice people to tickle its innards."

"Exactly. What they're really doing is sticking their hand through a cleaving. Hidden cameras and test gear are set up to record any effects. But please, Aiden, save your questions for later. Like I said, I can't keep this intact for very long."

Aiden approached the hole. "My dad once said that when a lion willingly opens its mouth, that's not the best time to practice animal dentistry."

"You need to hurry."

"What do you expect to happen?"

"I have no idea." Grant sounded frustrated that Aiden wasn't being a good little volunteer. "That's the whole point. It's a test."

"Screw it," Aiden muttered, ramming his hand and forearm through the hole before he could think of more reasons not to.

The extended appendage disappeared. It seemed to have passed through an invisible barrier into some other realm or dimension. Startled, he withdrew the arm. He was relieved when it became visible again. More importantly, it seemed normal.

"Try it again," Grant whispered. His voice was strained, as if finding it increasingly difficult to maintain the cleaving.

Aiden complied. This time he kept the invisible arm inserted through the hole.

"Feel anything?" Grant asked.

"A slight drop in temperature. But that could be due to the breeze."

"There is no breeze."

Aiden raised his other hand, rotated the palm in search of air currents. "You're right. The breeze is only in there. Weird. What if I tried sticking my hand through from the other side of the hole?"

"There'd be no difference. Our tests indicated that cleavings are bidirectional."

Grant started to say something else. But Aiden's attention was snared by another voice, one he'd heard many times before.

"Singularity beguiles, transcend the illusion."

It was Bobbie Pinsey, or whoever or whatever was speaking through her. The words seemed louder and more resolute than in Bobbie's bedroom or in his green dreams.

"Do you know that phrase?" Aiden asked.

"What phrase?" Grant asked.

"You didn't hear it?"

"Hear what?"

Grant stared quizzically. Before Aiden could explain, the breeze wafting across his extended arm turned icy cold.

"Whoa! Suddenly feels like my hand's stuck in a freezer. But the rest of my body seems perfectly normal and–

"Oww!"

He yanked his arm from the hole. Something jagged, like coarse-grained sandpaper, had scraped the back of his hand. He examined it, expecting to see a brush burn. But it was unmarred.

The donut began to fade. In seconds it was gone. Grant hunched forward on the boulder, his brow covered in sweat.

"I'll be OK in a sec," he said, breathing hard. "Why'd you yank your hand out?"

"Something else was in there with me. It brushed against me." He acknowledged a tinge of fear as he imagined what it might have been. Something alive? Something monstrous?

"This happen to any of your other test subjects?" he asked

"No. Mom and I performed the experiment hundreds of times. Friends, relatives, acquaintances, neighborhood kids who wanted to tickle the clown's innards. But nothing unusual ever occurred. It was just as if they were sticking their hand through an open window." He paused. "You're the first to have any kind of reaction."

Aiden should question Grant and Cho's ethics for performing such a test on unsuspecting victims. But the effort would have been wasted. He was fast learning that *quiver kids* and *ethics* had no business sharing a sentence.

"Ever stick your own arm in there?" he challenged.

"Physically impossible," Grant said. "Ever try to bring together the like poles of a really powerful magnet? You can't do it. The poles repel one another. Same thing with me and a cleaving. The harder I try pushing through it, the harder it pushes back."

"And your mom?"

"Same as everyone else, no effect. But I've always sensed that there was something on the other side, that I'm opening a portal into another universe or dimension. You're the first person able to reach across to that place."

"And you call this other place the shroud." He recalled the word from Cho and Grant's cryptic conversation.

"The name popped into my head. It seemed appropriate."

Grant got up from the boulder. He looked recovered from his ordeal. "So that phrase you heard, it was the one from your dreams?"

"Yeah. Back at the house you and your mom said something about Gold's message being an initial step for safe entry into a cleaving, that she might be a telepath receiving information from within the shroud."

Grant nodded. "Part of a theory Mom and I have bandied about. Red's ability could have something to do with traveling through the shroud and Magenta's power some kind of defensive system to enable safe passage. Blue's ideas about penetrating a realm beyond the beasts could refer to whatever's on the other side too. Presumably, Cyan is somehow linked as well."

"Six pieces of a jigsaw puzzle," Aiden mused. The thought bubbled with hidden significance. But a connection remained elusive.

"Until today, it was just speculation," Grant said, his voice building with excitement. "An unprovable theory. But you've changed that."

Aiden knew where his thoughts were headed. He short-circuited the idea before Grant could utter it.

"Don't even think about asking me to climb through one of those holes."

Grant was undeterred. "Mom's theory about your birth being random, a side effect, could be wrong. For all we know, the rest of us were unconsciously compelled to create you because *you're* the only one who can truly cross over to the other side. At the very least, the fact that you successfully inserted your arm suggests a more comprehensive test is warranted."

"Forget it. I'm not going all Aldous Huxley and exploring your brave new world."

"At least think about it. It'll take a day or so for me to build up the strength to create another cleaving. You can stay with us until I'm ready."

Aiden admitted that Grant's idea made sense. Whatever existed on the other side of one of those holes could answer fundamental questions about quiver. But he was more than a bit creeped out by what had happened when that thing brushed his hand. Did some other form of life exist over there, something with malignant intentions?

If he remained in Portland, Grant and Cho would push him to enter a cleaving, maybe even attempt to trick him into doing it. He had to get away from them, that much was certain. But he wasn't left with a lot of good options. Return home to Birdsboro? Do what Keats had initially proposed, go into hiding and stay off the grid?

Neither was appealing. They would only postpone the inevitable. Sooner or later, Red would likely come after him again, possibly enhanced in some way from the stolen quiver and more powerful than ever. He couldn't chance putting Darlene and Leah in danger. And his lack of funds made wandering aimlessly a nonstarter.

The solution to his dilemma was obvious. A sane and rational part of him warned against it. But he saw no other choice.

"Michael has to be stopped from getting a second infusion," he said. *And if it comes down to it, Jessie too.*

Grant couldn't hide his disappointment. "You're going to Montana."

"Feel like a road trip?"

"I wouldn't be much help. I've never even fired a gun. And I have my family to consider." He paused. "I suppose that makes me a coward."

"No, I get it. I'd probably do the same in your shoes."

They hiked back toward the main trail.

"There's another reason I can't go with you," Grant said. "The truth is, over the past few years I've also had this increasing desire for another infusion of quiver. Sometimes the urge becomes almost overwhelming. It's as if quiver is some powerful drug and I'm in need of a fix. If I came along, you might have three quiver kids to contend with rather than just two."

Aiden wasn't surprised by the admission.

"I suspect it's common to all of us," Grant continued. "If Gold wasn't mentally impaired and Blue hadn't been an addict, they likely would had the compulsion too. Probably Cyan as well."

But not me. Aiden was the exception, the anomaly. Given the choice, he wanted nothing to do with quiver.

"Any buses out of Portland heading in the direction of Tau?"

Grant nodded. "But none that would get you real close."

"In that case, you got a spare vehicle I could borrow?"

"There you're in luck."

Aiden doubted that *luck* was the right word for it.

FORTY-EIGHT

Grant's loaner was an old Toyota, with emphasis on *old*. Its black paint was scratched and in spots devoid of polish. The doors creaked. The driver's seat was wretchedly uncomfortable. Aiden squirmed a lot during the long drive.

Ana Cho had been gone when they'd returned to the house, having taken Lucas to a playground. Aiden was glad for her absence. He wasn't in the mood for a further Q&A or a mother-son tag team trying to get him to leap into some alternate universe.

Grant had packed him a lunch, a chicken sandwich and apple. He'd wolfed those down in the first hour on the road and, during his first fuel stop, bought a Coke and a bag of chips. In the restroom he'd changed his dressings and popped another of Rory's pills.

The Toyota's radio was dead. Aiden was left alone with his thoughts. Fresh doubts nagged at him. It was unsettling to realize just how warped his motivation was for rejoining Keats and Jessie. Bottom line, battling mercenaries was preferable to staying in Portland and risking being persuaded to go donut-hole diving. He was sure that whatever was on the other side of a cleaving represented a whole different order of freakish and scary.

He reached Jaffeburg, Montana, just after sunset. His hope was to rendezvous with Keats and Jessie at the café owned by Ned's old friend, the former naval captain. If the pair had left already he'd have to figure out some other way to rejoin them. Whatever the case, he'd promised Grant he wouldn't drive the Toyota all the way to Churchton Summit and risk that someone associated with Tau would find the vehicle and trace its ownership. Later, when things calmed down, he'd return the car to Portland.

If he was still alive.

He repressed that latest glum thought as he cruised down the town's main drag. Jaffeburg straddled a dry river valley in the Northern Rockies pinched between high mountains. Storefronts were bathed in the yellowish glow of old-style streetlamps.

The three-story Moonsign Hotel was at the far edge of town, a century-old brick building in the Neoclassical Revival style. A squared-off roofline featured ornamental pilasters. The architecture reminded him of southeastern Pennsylvania.

He thought of Darlene and Leah. He'd call them tomorrow before heading into the wilderness. It might be their last chance to talk.

There was no sign of Ned's pickup as he turned into the hotel's parking lot. But Keats and Jessie could have parked elsewhere.

Aiden had been expecting a rough-and-tumble barroom atmosphere but the Moonsign had more of an upscale feel. Off to the side, a shadowy dining room radiated candlelight and low conversation. He was about to stroll toward it when he spotted a wizened stringbean of a man with a military-style crew cut behind the bar. Judging by his age, Aiden had a hunch he was Ned's friend.

Hopping onto a barstool, Aiden ordered a local craft beer.

"You the owner?" he asked.

"Eduardo Fernandez, at your service."

"I'm looking for Deke Keats."

There was the slightest hesitation. "Afraid I don't know the name."

It was possible Keats and Jessie hadn't arrived yet. But Aiden had a hunch they'd been here and had instructed Eduardo to keep it quiet.

"It's OK, I'm a friend. I was with Keats yesterday at Ned's place."

"Icy Ned? Ex-Marine?"

"Ex-Army."

"That old coot still doing three-mile runs every morning?"

"Not unless Mabeline's lifting him out of his wheelchair and sprinting with him on her shoulders. So enough with the trick questions, OK? Are they here or not?"

Eduardo gestured at the ceiling. "They booked a room. But they went out early this afternoon."

"Any idea where?"

"Nope. And you're not the only one asking. Four guys came in a while ago looking for 'em." Eduardo motioned to the dining room.

Aiden's guard went up. Had Michael and his mercs somehow tracked Keats and Jessie here?

He debated options. If the men indeed were mercs, it was unlikely they'd try anything in public. Then again, if the audacious Nobe was among them, that theory might be worth crap.

Aiden's beer arrived. He left a five-spot, grabbed the brew and walked boldly into the dining room before he could talk himself out of it.

"Hey Aiden!"

He spun toward the voice. Rory Tablone sat at a table tucked in the back corner, munching on a basket of chicken wings. Aiden recognized the biggest of his companions, ponytailed Chef, the man they'd rendezvoused with in Sioux Falls. The other two were strangers.

Rory snatched a chair from an adjacent table. Aiden squeezed in beside the one-legged medic.

"What are you doing here?" Aiden wondered.

"Eating."

Rory field-stripped a chicken wing with his teeth, wiped barbecue sauce from his lips and introduced Chef.

"We've met, sort of," Aiden said, extending his hand. The big Native American declined to shake, settling for a nod so as not to interrupt his assault on a heaping plate of spaghetti.

Rory motioned to the others. "These lowlife meateaters are Toothpick and Bling."

The monikers seemed fitting. Toothpick was a skinny Black man with oversized glasses and a prominent scar on the bridge of his nose. Bling, a squat, big-bellied Latino guy, had gold chains dangling from his neck and a matching earring. The pair looked around the same age as Rory and Chef.

"Come here often?" Aiden asked.

Rory broke into a lopsided grin. "Icy Ned called, told us about you and the girl. Said Deke was leading you into a category-five shitstorm but was too proud to ask for help."

"No surprise there," Toothpick grumbled.

"We flew into Helena together a couple hours ago," Bling added. "Drove straight here."

"I'm guessing you're wondering why," Rory said.

"Crossed my mind."

"OK, here's the backstory. Once upon a time, when we were doing some shit for Uncle Sam that good citizens of this country ain't ever supposed to know about, Deke was the man. He ran the unit.

"We were in this hellhole of a country. Locals were wasting one another like there weren't no tomorrow. The four of us and a couple other guys were trapped in this village. It was raining crap – enemy fire from all sides. Ammo was running low. No way were we gonna last the night.

"Another squad got sent to pull us out but they ran into platoon-strength bad guys and couldn't break through. At that point, we figured it was pretty much over. Started making our peace with the world. But in case you haven't figured it out by now, Deke Keats ain't the type to be throwing in the towel. All by his lonesome, he commandeers an enemy assault vehicle and comes racing through that village like some pissed-off superhero."

"You should've seen him," Bling said. "Plowing into the bad guys who don't get out of his way and shooting the rest of them."

"Crazy son of a bitch saved our asses, got us out of there," Toothpick added.

"Genuine Medal of Honor stuff," Rory said. "Only they tend not to give medals for the kind of classified op we were on."

Aiden understood what Ned had meant when he suggested
Keats cash in his chips. Rory, Chef, Toothpick and Bling were
the chips. They were here to make good on a debt no amount of
money could repay.

"What the hell's this?"

Keats stormed toward them flanked by Jessie. Their dark pants
and sweatshirts were caked in mud.

Rory beamed. "Yo, Deke! About time you got here. Hungry?"

"No. And when you're done stuffing your faces you'll be hitting
the road."

"Can't do that."

"I told you back in Virginia, not your fight. You've got families
to think about."

"We could say the same about you."

"Homefront's covered," Toothpick said. "This is a done deal."

"The least we can do for Greg," Bling added.

Keats glowered.

"It's all right, Aiden knows," Rory said. "Ned spilled the beans."

Keats turned his high-beam indignation on Aiden.

"I'm sorry they killed your son," he offered. "And don't blame
Ned. I made him tell me the truth."

Keats looked like he was having trouble swallowing that. He
tried holding onto his anger but it slowly seeped from his face.
Aiden figured he was genuinely moved that his old unit had
showed up in his time of need.

"All right," he said finally. "When you're done, upstairs, Room
206."

He headed off. Jessie grabbed an extra chair and squeezed in
between Toothpick and Bling.

"What's this about his son?" she asked, flagging a waiter and
ordering a Heineken.

The soldiers traded off relating the full story of the railfans'
encounter with Nobe. When they finished, Jessie finally turned to
Rory, who'd been staring at her the whole time.

"What the hell's your problem?" she demanded.

"Icy Ned wasn't kidding about you."

"If that's supposed to mean I'm a smart woman who can take care of herself, I'm all ears. Otherwise, Peg-leg, keep it zipped."

Rory laughed. Jessie, still with fire in her eyes, whipped her gaze to Aiden.

"So what's your story?"

Hello to you too, Mom.

But now wasn't the time to hit her with that particular revelation. He took a swig of beer and settled for a macho-flavored quip.

"Didn't want to miss all the fun."

FORTY-NINE

The seven of them gathered in Room 206 to discuss the next day's assault. Keats commandeered the desk chair, leaving Aiden, Jessie, Toothpick and Bling to sit on the twin beds. Rory hopped up on the dresser. Chef remained standing by the door, a mute sentinel.

Keats revealed that he and Jessie had driven fifty-odd miles east, parked the F-150 and hiked to the bridge where the train presumably would come under attack. In the event Tau Nine-One had roving night patrols or the mercs had sent advance scouts, they'd crawled the last few hundred yards to reach an overlook. The ground being wet from an earlier rain accounted for their muddy clothes.

"The recce didn't reveal much," Keats said. "Hard to say which direction the mercs will be coming from. We'll have to be ready for pretty much anything, even being mistaken for hostiles by those Marines on the train once things go loud."

Aiden listened halfheartedly as the soldiers reviewed tactical scenarios. He should have felt encouraged. Their own force now included five battle-hardened soldiers. But he was more anxious than ever. There were still too many unknowns. They didn't know how the mercs intended to board the train or how many of them they'd be facing.

Keats asked what gear the men had brought.

"We scrounged up surveillance cams, headsets and a few

other toys," Rory said. "And one perimeter intrusion kit. Laptop controller and five remote ground sensors."

"Excellent. Weapons?"

"Since the four of us were flying commercial together, thought it best not to. Four ex-military dudes from different states, all on the same plane, all checking firearms into their baggage? That's TSA bait."

"Besides," Toothpick added, "Ned said you had enough firepower."

Keats described the weaponry they'd procured. "Would've liked to have body armor. But considering the terrain and the length of the hike to reach the target, my hunch is that the mercs will go light too, leave their vests at home. Still, no guarantees it'll play out that way."

He got to his feet, planted hands on hips and regarded the four soldiers sternly. "What's the drill?"

"Expect worst-case scenario," they uttered in unison.

"All righty then!" Rory said, grinning. "Tomorrow we find these assholes and trash their day!"

He hopped off the dresser but his funky prosthetic touched the floor at a bad angle. The mechanical knee made a harsh *click-clack* sound and he stumbled forward. Chef, with surprising speed for a big man, lunged and caught the medic before he fell.

Rory pulled up his pants leg. The lower part of his metal limb was fitted into a running shoe. Mock astonishment filled his face.

"Goddamn! Where the fuck's my foot?"

Bling and Toothpick laughed. Chef managed a grunt. Keats wasn't amused.

"You gonna be this noisy during the op?"

"Nothing pliers and a can of WD-40 won't fix," Rory countered.

A maid knocked and entered, informed them their other rooms were ready. Keats made the assignments. He and Rory would bunk here in 206; Chef, Toothpick and Bling would share the room next door. That left Aiden paired with Jessie in a third room at the end of the hall.

Aiden considered asking someone to switch with him. But that would probably piss off Jessie so he kept his mouth shut. Besides, he hadn't slept at all last night. Even if one of his biological moms made another pass at him, being dead tired should be enough of an excuse to deflect her.

Ten minutes later they were alone in their room. Jessie quizzed him about Ana Cho. He tried to beg off answering her questions until morning but she was adamant.

He told her about the encounter with Cho and Grant. A sixth sense warned him not to reveal anything about Grant manifesting the cleaving and Aiden sticking his hand through it. Such knowledge might give Jessie even more encouragement to go after the quiver.

He saved the big revelation for last. Jessie was appropriately stunned to learn he was White, the anomaly, even more so when he described his miracle birth.

"You just appeared out of thin air?"

"Pretty weird, huh?"

"And the six of us are your genetic parents?"

He nodded.

"Wow."

"Yeah."

"And that's why you didn't want to have sex with me. You see me as your mother?"

"One of them. And it's not something conscious, more of a gut sensation. I just know that it wouldn't have felt natural."

"Not natural," she murmured.

He couldn't read her expression. Sadness maybe? Disappointment to realize that sex with him wasn't going to happen? Or something else, perhaps a renewed acknowledgment of how being a quiver kid had warped her life.

Aiden was too tired for further speculation. He retreated to the bathroom, locked the door and stepped into what could be his last cleansing shower.

FIFTY

Michael retreated to the basement. The long-awaited day was here, Tarantian about to reach fruition. He'd sent Trish on an errand for supplies to get her out of the chateau for a couple hours. Except for one of Nobe's men waiting down at the helipad to pilot the four-seater Maverick and fly him to ground zero, he had the place to himself.

He'd helicoptered back from the cabin near Churchton Summit where the final assault plan had been reviewed with Nobe, Kokay and the full contingent of mercs. By now, the men would have broken into small groups to avoid attention and be headed into the wilderness to take up positions. Michael's only criticism of the plan was that they'd reach ground zero relatively late. But Nobe didn't want to risk arriving too far ahead of the train.

He tugged at the hidden latch behind the furnace. A false wall slid back. He placed his hand on the palm lock of the steel door and leaned in close. The retinal scanner flashed green and the door unlocked with a loud click.

Ceiling lights came on automatically as he entered the windowless lab. Lined up on a bench along the far wall were six medical-grade containment vessels. Three of the transparent cylinders harbored pristine manifestations he'd recently created, the gelatinous brown masses suspended in a nutriment liquid. If the plan went off without a hitch, he'd only need one. But it was best to be prepared.

He selected the endmost vessel, hit the controls and watched the murky liquid drain into a refuse pipe. The door slid open and he reached in. The instant his palm touched the manifestation, he saw and felt the shadow forming beside him.

It began as a blurring of the air. Within seconds, the spectral figure coalesced. Other than an occasional fade into translucence, the apparition poised at his side was a perfect double, down to the clothing Michael wore.

Occasionally, a doppelganger was flawed and unreliable to control. As always, he performed a series of basic tests. In his mind, he imagined lifting his arms and flexing his fingers. His real self, his physical body, remained motionless, but the shadow mimicked his mental commands with robotic precision. Energized purely by his will, it was ready to do his bidding.

Early experiments had limited him to sending a shadow only to destinations he'd already been, places he could clearly visualize. A working familiarity with the target location had been necessary in those days, his sense of vision the sole means of directing a transmission. But then he'd made the discovery that enabled the final pieces of Tarantian to fall into place.

Vision was based on the narrow portion of the electromagnetic spectrum associated with visible light. Michael had access to other parts of the spectrum, specifically the microwave carrier frequencies associated with GPS technology. On the day of the railfan incident, the method had enabled him to lock onto a signal from Nobe's radio and send a shadow to the top of that ravine.

Most times he wore a Halloween mask to prevent any chance of his doppelganger being recognized, especially vital on those occasions when he'd sent a shadow into the headquarters of Krame-Tee competitors, secretly spying on board meetings from adjacent rooms or closets. Had he been caught, escape would have been as easy as dissolving the shadow. But his face was known in segments of the corporate world, hence the masks.

Today's plan called for a more encompassing outfit. He stripped and donned a black body suit. At his side, the shadow mimicked his change of clothing. Sewn into the suit's fabric were strings of tightly spaced red LEDs. Michael flicked a switch in his pocket to turn them on.

The result was impressively creepy, worthy of a state-of-the-art Hollywood special effect. He and his doppelganger now appeared to have blood vessels lining the outside of their bodies. The final touch was donning a custom mask he'd designed himself, a demonic visage with scaly skin, glowing crimson eyes and forehead nodules suggestive of nascent horns. He pulled it over his head, pleased at the shadow's frightful and hideous appearance.

The insider had passed along personnel files of everyone working at Tau. Although a religion was not specified in most cases, analysis via a proprietary Krame-Tee algorithm suggested that an 87 percent majority of the workers and Marines adhered to mainstream Christian faiths, which meant his devilish appearance would have a strong psychological impact.

The next step would depend on the insider, the one aspect Michael had the least control over. But he'd spent months studying and cultivating the woman before he'd felt confident enough to ease her into Tarantian.

He was confident she wouldn't let him down. Five million dollars, half of which already had been transferred to her offshore account as down payment, was enough incentive for anyone to betray their country. But she also had personal reasons for seeing the plan through, reasons that Michael understood and even empathized with. Vengeance, as he knew all too well, was a powerful motivator.

FIFTY-ONE

They'd set out from Jaffeburg in two vehicles, the F-150 borrowed from Ned and a Jeep Wrangler the soldiers had rented. They parked the vehicles off-road amid a cluster of pines some five miles from the bridge. It was a cool and cloudy morning, ideal conditions for a wilderness trek.

Assisted by a GPS navigator, Keats led the way. Should they encounter any civilians, they were just seven hikers on a camping trip. Privately, Aiden doubted such a cover story would hold up. Even though weapons and gear were stashed in equipment bags slung over their shoulders, the soldiers' khaki outfits broadcast infantry.

Keats had selected the most rugged route to the bridge from the southeast, which made for a rougher hike across a series of steep hills and valleys. But based on last night's recon, his best guess was that the route would be avoided by the mercs, who likely would approach over less inhospitable terrain from the west.

"The hills and the foliage should help shield us in case the mercs have portable ground radar," Keats had explained during final prep before leaving Jaffeburg. "I doubt they'll have access to real-time satellite intel, although we could be spotted if they send up drones with thermal imaging. But I can't see any good reason for them to complicate the op with flyovers."

The plan was to arrive at a staging area near the bridge and begin the counterassault just as the mercs hit the train.

"Maximum confusion, maximum advantage," Keats said. "They'll surprise the train crew. We'll surprise them."

It sounded great in theory. But none of Keats' words allayed Aiden's growing sense of foreboding. Still, compared to entering one of Grant's cleavings or going into hiding, it still seemed like the best of his limited options.

Keep telling yourself that.

They walked in a single line. Keats set a vigorous pace. Aiden was breathing hard after less than a mile. He'd always considered himself in pretty good condition from those daily runs. But the soldiers, all of whom were at least a dozen years older, put him to shame. Even Rory with his slight limp and artificial leg – now oiled into silence – moved with effortless speed.

Aiden had made a quick call to Darlene this morning from Keats' encrypted phone. Not surprisingly, the conversation hadn't gone well. He'd tried to assure his sister he was all right and was just following a trail of information about his past. But she sensed he was lying and, being Darlene, probed and cajoled with the intensity of a black site interrogator.

"Send my love to Leah," he'd said, terminating the call before it got ugly. Still, he had a lump in his throat as he hung up. There was a good chance he'd never see them again.

Keats signaled a five-minute break when they were halfway to the bridge. Aiden sat on a log beside Chef. He'd just taken the first bite of his sandwich when Chef lit a malodorous cigar, sending a cloud of smoke wafting into his face.

Aiden coughed and glared. Chef got the message and stood up. Before moving to a spot farther away, he gazed down on Aiden from behind mirrored sunglasses. His voice was deep, his words echoing with profundity.

"Gravity is a compulsion, never a choice. Fall where you stand. The sacred will bestow its essence."

Aiden had no idea what that meant. But it was definitely the most words he'd heard Chef utter in the short time they'd been together.

Rory chuckled at his bewilderment. "You didn't get what he was trying to tell you?"

"Not a clue."

"Join the club. Most times we don't know what the hell he's talking about either."

Rory lit up a joint. Keats scowled but didn't protest. Rory offered Aiden a toke. He declined.

"Sure it's a good idea to get mellow right now?" he asked.

"Weed it when you need it, when you don't, you won't." Grinning, Rory spun toward Chef. "See, I can say weird shit too."

Bling and Toothpick laughed. The faintest of smiles seemed to play across Chef's face, although Aiden might have been imagining it. The soldiers were here to repay a debt to Keats but Aiden sensed other motivations. They missed the camaraderie of their younger days, of being part of something bigger than themselves.

Keats ordered them to get moving again. Half a kilometer farther on, they came upon the remnants of an old trail, probably dating from the era of fur trappers and assorted tradesmen. The path wound through the trees on a slight downhill course, momentarily easing their trek.

Jessie broke ranks and came up beside Aiden. "I think I know how Michael's going to smuggle the quiver out of Tau. He's going to send in one of his shadows."

"How would that help?"

"I don't know, not exactly. But even if he's not there in the flesh, he could help his insider carry out the theft."

"Keep it down," Keats warned. "Voices carry further than you think in these woods."

"Michael is powerful and dangerous," Jessie whispered, a devious smile curling her lips. "But don't forget, so am I."

She fell back into line. A chill went through Aiden. Once the action started he'd really need to keep an eye on her. And if she made a grab for the quiver...

PART 4
THE INSIDER

FIFTY-TWO

Héloise Hoke didn't believe coincidences required mystical interpretation. The fact that two critical events in her life were taking place on the same day represented nothing more than the flakiness of a random universe. Still, she couldn't help but acknowledge the irony, that she was betraying her country on her father's birthday.

Then again, Unit X, who'd orchestrated her treachery and set the date, might have planned it that way. Although she'd never seen his face and had no idea of his identity – she'd assigned the dehumanized moniker early in their dealings – he clearly was a devious bastard. Unit X may have deliberately arranged the birthday-betrayal conjunction to dispel any last-minute doubts and provide added incentive for Héloise to carry out his plan.

If so, he was overthinking it. When he'd first contacted her last year through an intermediary and proposed that she help him steal the quiver stone, the enticements of revenge and financial gain had been more than enough to earn her support.

Besides, there were good reasons for selecting this particular Wednesday for the theft. The elevator leading down to the maximum containment lab area housing the quiver was in the midst of a rebuild, leaving the emergency staircase the only way in or out. Three key researchers, including her supervisor, were in Dallas for a conference, leaving the MCL lightly staffed. And

Colonel Rodriguez, the base commander, was in Bermuda for a long-planned vacation with his family.

The Colonel. His family. The words resonated, evoking darkness. Héloise had been twelve when she'd lost her own father. He too had been in charge of Tau Nine-One.

Colonel Royce Jenkins had been a strict but loving parent, brave and honorable. That hadn't stopped those bastards in DC from crucifying him. She'd never learned the details of why the Pentagon had made him their fall guy, only that some secret experiment involving babies had been the catalyst. Although the brats apparently hadn't been harmed, Daddy had been raked over the coals. Héloise was convinced that the stress of having his career destroyed brought about the cancer that ultimately killed him.

And did his death satisfy them? Not a chance. They made sure he was eternally damned. A dishonorable discharge and loss of his pension left Héloise and her mother impoverished. Mommy had reverted to her maiden name and moved them far from Montana to escape the disgraced Jenkins moniker. She'd been forced into working two crap jobs just to make ends meet. That she too died young was yet another repercussion of what they'd done to her father.

Goddamned bastards.

"Héloise, you OK? You look kind of pissed."

"I'm fine," she said, forcing a smile as she turned to Elias, her research partner. The two of them had been alone in the module down on lab level since morning, their arms mostly inside glove boxes. They were doing what they did nearly every day: biopsying or dissecting baby mice that had been exposed to the quiver stone. Escaping such ass-numbing work was an extra benefit of going through with Unit X's plan.

Her phone vibrated in her pocket. She checked the clock above an equipment cabinet. 16:08. The moment she'd been anticipating for months was finally here.

"Bathroom break," she said, withdrawing her arms from the glove box.

"Shift's almost over," Elias said. "By the time you suit up again it'll nearly be dinnertime."

"Nature calls."

Héloise exited the module before he could lodge further protests. In the adjacent room, she removed and discarded her face mask and grabbed her handbag. She passed through the second door and into the main corridor. At the far end was the out-of-commission elevator up to ground level, thirty feet above. Beside it were two fire doors. One led downward to the small nuclear reactor and its control room buried even deeper in the complex. The other door was the emergency staircase. It was now the only way up to the surface.

She headed the opposite direction and passed through an unsecured door into "Q" corridor. A young Marine sat behind the security desk. Ostensibly, he was observing a console of surveillance cameras. But Héloise knew he spent most of his time playing videogames on his phone.

She approached with a practiced smile. "Hey, Chet. I need a few moments in the vault with Auntie Q."

Nobody called it quiver. The higher-ups preferred official codenames, which they changed every few months. The current one was Oscar Zeta Three-Seven – military gobbledygook and way too clunky for those who actually worked down here. For reasons that preceded Héloise's tenure and remained lost in Tau Nine-One history, Auntie Q had become the preferred shorthand.

She did a digital sign in and left her handbag on the shelf by Chet's station. Scanning her daily pass opened the door behind him. She entered the anteroom, donned a pressure suit with breathing gear and headed for the airlock. Two doors later she was in the vault, the inner sanctum. For someone with Héloise's security clearance, gaining access to Auntie Q was relatively easy. Smuggling it out would be the hard part.

The circular lab didn't look all that impressive. Five narrow doors led to various menageries where the test animals were kept. One curving section of wall contained biocabinets similar to the ones she and Elias worked with. But these glove boxes were heavy-duty, with bulletproof glass and rip-proof gloves. Only the test animals fed into the boxes through flexible chutes were permitted to come into direct contact with Auntie Q.

In the center of the vault was the coffin, so called because it was the quiver stone's resting place when not undergoing experimentation. It looked like an overturned freezer sunk halfway into the floor.

Héloise checked the clock. 16:13. Two minutes to spare. All she had to do now was wait for Unit X's computer virus, the one she'd secretly input into Tau Nine-One's network, to activate.

Would the virus function as Unit X promised? Her confidence level was high. Then again, bad shit happened to people even when they didn't deserve it. If the virus failed, the plan would be DOA and Héloise likely arrested for treason once they traced it back to her terminal. Screw it. She could deal with jail if it came to that. In some ways, she'd been confined to a mental prison ever since Daddy's crucifixion. One with real bars wouldn't be all that much of a change.

But that fate was unlikely. Unit X was monumentally careful. The more likely outcome was she'd get away clean but spend the rest of her days in hiding. On the bright side, she'd have enough money for a comfortable lifestyle off the grid.

The clock reached 16:14. Héloise found herself wondering again why Unit X wanted Auntie Q. Selling it was a likely motivation. No doubt there'd be plenty of bidders for such a treasure. Unit X, obviously already a rich man, might be in a position to dramatically multiply his wealth.

Still, the theft might have nothing to do with money. Maybe he'd learned something about the substance no one else had figured out and had an entirely different use in mind. In any case, they were meant for each other. Unit X and Auntie Q. It sounded like a marriage made in hell.

She counted down the seconds in sync with the digital display. Bottom line, his intention didn't matter. All that was important was that she'd be five million dollars richer and have her revenge on the bastards who'd messed up her life.

The clock reached 16:15. The virus would be racing through the network targeting specific systems, including Security. Surveillance cameras would fail. Locks would open. Héloise would begin her new life.

FIFTY-THREE

At 16:16 pm, Michael envisioned the microwave segment of the electromagnetic spectrum and tuned himself to the three-dimensional GPS coordinates provided by the insider. Instantaneously, his shadow was transmitted into the vault. As always, he could still sense his physical self back at the chateau, a faint presence standing in the basement lab. It would remain there until he completed the mission and terminated the shadow. Only then would full consciousness and complete freedom of movement return to his real body.

His doppelganger took shape six feet from the insider, who stood on the other side of the quiver coffin. Early in his experiments Michael had worried about transmitting a shadow to coordinates already occupied by physical matter, something other than air: a person, for instance. His fear of some kind of weird fusion had proved groundless. A shadow seemingly did not interact with matter.

Even though the insider had been prepared for his devilish features, her eyes widened in alarm at his appearance. Michael was pleased. If he could frighten someone who knew he was coming, the effect should be greater upon those he intended to scare. Héloise Hoke wasn't aware he was a quiver kid with special powers. He'd explained his appearance as a technological breakthrough in holographic transmission, and she hadn't questioned the lie.

Michael had never figured out how to transmit audio or speak through a shadow. He could hear sounds although sometimes they could be low and muddled and challenging to discern. Hand signals would suffice for today. Besides, a silent wraith would have greater impact.

He nodded toward the coffin. Héloise punched in an access code to unlock it and pulled back the heavy door. The quiver rested in the bottom of a spherical canister. It was translucent and only slightly larger than the stone itself, which was the size of a tennis ball. Michael stared in fascination at the glasslike orb within. Even though it was impossible for his spectral form to physically touch anything, he had the urge to try. Years of anticipation filled him with longing.

Héloise carried the canister to the airlock. Michael's shadow followed. They passed through the double portal to the anteroom where she removed the pressure suit and deposited the canister in the front pocket of her loose-fitting pants.

They waited. Any second now...

Emergency alarms on the ceiling activated, flashing yellow. The virus had attacked its first target. Cameras and sensors throughout the lab level would be failing.

The insider pushed a button and the door slid open.

The Marine on duty in the Security vestibule was on his feet, futilely trying to reach the main station on ground level on his landline phone. But the virus had taken out local telecom access as well.

Héloise faked a terrified expression and lunged through the door. Michael heard her panicked screams. It was just as they'd planned.

"Chet, run! It's come alive!"

That was Michael's cue. He slipped through after her. The young Marine took one look at his hazy demonic figure with its glowing blood vessels and dropped the phone. He tore off down the corridor on Héloise's tail.

She reached the far doors, whirled to face him.

"Chet, shoot it!"

The Marine recovered his poise. Whipping out his sidearm, he turned and took aim at the slowly approaching monstrosity.

"Stop or I'll fire!" he warned.

Michael ignored the warning and kept coming.

The Marine fired. Five bullets went through Michael's vaporous chest, ricocheted off the anteroom door behind him.

Chet froze, astonished his gunfire was having no effect. Héloïse took the opportunity to jab the hypodermic needle into the side of his neck.

The anesthetic was fast-acting. Chet didn't even have a chance to make a grab at the needle. He crumbled to the floor, unconscious before he hit.

Héloïse dragged him back to his station and shoved him under the desk. He wouldn't be immediately noticed by anyone passing through this corridor unless they actually walked behind the console. She retrieved her handbag, tucked the quiver canister inside and dashed up the emergency staircase. The door closed behind her.

Michael's work was done here. He could make several jumps with a single shadow within an hour or so of its formation as long as he returned to his point of origin between them. After that, a shadow would lose strength and dissolve. But an hour was more than enough time to induce terror in the nuclear reactor's control room.

FIFTY-FOUR

Héloise ascended to ground level, a curving hallway flanked by maintenance closets and storerooms on the inside wall of the circular core building. The corridor was deserted. Ceiling lights continued to flash yellow, signifying the situation was serious but noncritical.

She walked at a normal pace a third of the way around the circle. By design, the virus hadn't crippled the surveillance cameras up here. A calm demeanor was needed so as not to alert the main Security station. Adhering to protocol for a yellow emergency, she headed to T-wing to await either an all-clear or further instructions.

The first door on the outside accessed the walkway to T-Wing, where the train would be prepping for its scheduled departure at 1700 hours. Unknown to the locomotive crew or anyone else, they'd be leaving a bit earlier.

She glanced at her watch. 16:22. The virus should be attacking its next target.

Héloise heard footsteps behind her. She opened the door to the walkway but paused to allow Elias and a pair of female techs to catch up. Other than the unconscious Chet, they were the only other people who'd been down on lab level this afternoon. The women had been doing experiments in an adjacent module dedicated to metamaterials research.

"Any idea what's happening?" Elias asked.

Héloise shrugged. "I'm guessing some kind of minor glitch."

She held the door open and allowed the three of them to proceed along the walkway ahead of her. They were halfway down the windowless corridor when the yellow lights turned red. Critical emergency klaxons wailed.

Elias froze. "That's the radiation alarm!"

Right on time.

A robovoice accompanied the alert. Considering its message, the gender-neutral tone was surprisingly serene.

"A reactor malfunction has been detected. All personnel must proceed immediately to T-wing. This is not a drill."

The warning repeated on a loop. Elias and the techs sprinted toward the closed door at the far end of the walkway. Héloise followed, knowing the riskiest part of the plan was about to unfold.

FIFTY-FIVE

Michael returned to his basement lab and tuned himself to the second set of coordinates provided by the insider. His shadow was instantly transmitted into Tau's reactor control room, a compact chamber at the deepest level of the complex.

His devilish figure took shape behind three male techs. They occupied wheeled bucket seats facing a wide curving console. The klaxons bellowing throughout Tau Nine-One had been silenced in here; only flashing red beacons signified the ongoing alert. The men were accessing data from their computers while scanning a large widescreen TV on the wall beyond the console. Colorful graphs and morphing data readouts indicated reactor status. An urgent message scrolled across the bottom of the screen.

A reactor malfunction has been detected. This is not a drill.

"Are we absolutely sure it's not a drill?" the tech on the left asked. "How do we know it's not another psych test to trip us up?"

"Not a chance," the tech in the middle said. His name was Tompkins and he was the oldest and most seasoned of the trio, and the one in charge.

"But something's screwy here," the left-seated tech continued, his voice rising in urgency. "Primary annunciators 12B through 17C show coolant leakage and possible exposure of the core. But the aux system registers all-clear."

Tompkins remained calm. "Doesn't matter. The manual says we

treat the worst-case scenario as authentic until evidence proves otherwise."

Michael was no expert on nuclear reactor operations. But he'd educated himself enough to understand the disparity the techs were referring to. Although the multi-target virus implanted by Héloise was incredibly sophisticated – Michael had hired top-tier hackers to design it – it couldn't cripple the auxiliary readouts. Safety protocols rendered them a backup system on a segregated, air-gapped network.

The techs followed a list of emergency procedures. Soon they would perform an emergency reset of the problematic annunciators and realize the entire incident was based on computer error. Michael's task was to drive them out of the control room before they came to that realization.

He moved his shadow closer. He was now only a few feet behind them.

"Anything yet on com?" Tompkins asked.

"Not a goddamn word." It was the tech in the third chair and the tension in his voice was palpable. "Can't reach anybody upstairs, not even with my cell. We're completely cut off."

The third tech's name was Kapolardi. He was Michael's first target. Not only a new addition to the reactor team, he was a devout churchgoer, which the insider had learned through an overheard conversation. Already under stress due to the emergency, his reaction should be the most intense.

Michael moved the shadow forward until he stood right behind Kapolardi. He raised his arms, an effect that made him appear larger and more threatening.

The tech's peripheral vision sensed the shadow's presence. Kapolardi swiveled his head.

Michael couldn't have hoped for a better reaction. Kapolardi took one look at his devilish figure and unleashed a terrifying scream. Lunging from his chair in panic, he crashed into Tompkins, who was also starting to rise.

The two men went down in a heap. The first tech gasped when

he saw what had frightened them and erupted from his seat as well.

The control room manual stated that at least one tech had to be seated at the console at all times. Pressure sensors on the chairs reacted to the sudden noncompliance, triggering another alarm and incessant beeping.

The virus had been crafted to anticipate just such a reaction by the techs. A subroutine of its main program initiated, activating a recording of horrifying guttural noises akin to what the designers felt a rampaging devil might sound like. The noises poured from the room's speakers at max volume.

That was too much for Kapolardi. Scrambling to his feet he raced to the exit. Frantic fingers punched in a code. The door unlocked and he raced through. It automatically locked behind him, which triggered another subroutine, permanently sealing the door. Anyone trying to enter or leave the control room from here on out would require a cutting torch.

Tompkins grabbed the arm of the remaining tech. "Into the bunker!"

Perfect, Michael thought. There was no specific procedure for the appearance of a devilish monster but they reacted as anticipated. He moved toward them but at a snail's pace, making sure they had enough time to enter the bunker, a shielded chamber with radiation suits and other survival gear.

They ran into the chamber. The door slammed shut. They stared wide-eyed at him through the bunker's small window, no doubt wondering what hellish thing had invaded their domain. They'd be trapped in there for a while. As with the exit door, the virus would assure a lockdown.

He checked the wall clock. 16:27. Tarantian was right on schedule, nearly down to the second. His rout of the control room personnel had gone off without a hitch. The false emergency would prompt Tau Nine-One's evacuation.

Michael couldn't resist a final scare. Spinning toward the bunker, he lunged at its door. The techs, glued to the window, backed away so fast they nearly tripped and fell. He permitted himself a grunt of laughter as he dissolved the shadow.

Full consciousness returned to his body in the chateau. He stripped off the scare suit, locked up the lab and headed upstairs. A quick change into regular attire and he was dashing for the helipad. Next stop: ground zero. By the time he arrived, Nobe and his men should have secured the quiver.

FIFTY-SIX

T-wing was packed, and the crowd on edge from the wail of emergency klaxons and looped warnings. Héloise estimated a hundred-plus workers and a dozen Marines on the platform. Anxious muttering filled the air. The process of boarding the four passenger coaches was functioning at a crawl. Guards funneled everyone into a single line to pass through the array of detection gear: holographic imagers, backscatter x-ray scanners, trace portals and more.

Héloise scowled. During a reactor emergency, the gate separating the platform from the train cars was to be opened, freely allowing workers to board, but with the understanding that upon arrival at the Churchton Summit station they would have to pass through similar detectors. But apparently the guards hadn't received a specific order authorizing emergency boarding.

It was a glitch in the plan. Héloise hoped it wouldn't be a fatal one.

The crowd was getting antsier. Angry voices were shouting at the guards, urging them to use common sense and let everyone leave.

"What are you waiting for, a goddamn meltdown?!" one man hollered. His words incited a swelling outcry that rippled up and down the platform. The guards looked sympathetic and equally concerned but followed orders and held their ground.

Héloise casually drifted to the back of her line. No way could she get the quiver in her handbag past the detectors. When she reached them it was all over.

Salvation came. A Marine lieutenant dashed onto the platform and ordered the guards to unlock all the gates and allow unfettered boarding. The workers poured through.

Héloise selected the third car and the last row of seats. In theory it was the safest place to be when the train reached the bridge. Besides that, she could keep her eye on everyone and not worry about being observed from behind. The Marines would be one car back, but Unit X had special plans for them.

On a normal return trip, the front cars disembarked first, giving those up front a slight headstart to the Security exit turnstiles and the parking lot beyond. But with today's evacuation, the Churchton Summit station would go fully active, forcing everyone to pass through the detectors. Because of the emergency situation, the exit screening would be more thorough and take longer, which prompted the evacuees to scramble for seats closest to the front of the train. The first two coaches filled quickly – only half a dozen workers spilling over into Héloise's car. All took seats up front. Several cast curious glances back at her, wondering why she'd chosen isolation. She ignored them.

The engineer blew the first locomotive's air horn, signifying imminent departure. Everyone apparently was onboard except for emergency personnel and two special squads of Marines whose duties required them to go down with the ship.

The gentle tug of forward movement ended the babble of nervous conversations. They were on their way to safety.

The train passed through the exit portal, which was ringed by motion detectors to prevent anyone from slipping through. Héloise gazed out her window as the coach transitioned from T-wing's overhead fluorescent lights to cloudy late-afternoon skies. The curving rails passed through an automatic gate in the outer fence and across a grassy expanse that the maintenance staff kept trimmed to golf course standards. Her mother had told her that when her father was base commander, he used to come out here to practice his swing. The thought brought a swell of bitter memories.

The train reached the track switch that formed the end of the connecting loop. A familiar vibration came through the flooring as the coaches passed over the switch. She turned to the windows on the right side facing the loop and glimpsed the edge of the complex. It would be her final look at Tau Nine-One.

She'd done her part. Now all that remained was to endure the assault and hand over the prize. The next potential crisis would come when she encountered Unit X's men. The possibility of being double-crossed had never been far from her mind.

Tau Nine-One disappeared from view and, with it, most of the daylight. Wilderness enveloped the train, the tree canopy dark and heavy. It felt as if they were gliding through an oppressive tunnel.

PART 5
THE TRAIN

FIFTY-SEVEN

Aiden and Keats lay face down on a summit, hidden behind a cluster of bushes. They'd been at the vantage point for two hours, overlooking staggered rows of hemlocks, just out of sight of where the tracks crossed the bridge. Too close and they risked being spotted by the mercs. But so far there'd been no sign of their quarry.

Visible through the trees to their left was a steep ravine. Keats' attention kept darting that way. Aiden knew it was holy ground, the place where Nobe had murdered his son.

Rory and Chef had taken up flanking positions ten yards away, while Bling and Toothpick served as eyes and ears on the front line. Having donned ghillie suits – cloth netting covered with foliage and burlap strips – the pair had slunk around the target perimeter to plant the ground sensors and cameras. Task accomplished, they'd selected positions with unimpeded sight lines to the bridge and hunkered down, Bling was buried in a mass of shrubbery. Toothpick was fifteen feet up on the thick branch of an oak. Both were armed with the scope-fitted M16 rifles.

They'd likely draw first blood.

Jessie returned from a nature call and crept back into position beside Aiden. He could feel her warmth and smell her aroma, a blend of honeyed cologne and sweat, oddly pleasant in spite of the circumstances.

He studied her profile. She seemed ablaze with excitement,

eager for the action to begin. Aiden wished it was over. Yet a suspicion had been growing that even if he survived this day, it was just an opening salvo. Once again he had the sense of being on a lifelong journey toward some uncharted destiny, a destiny entangled in quiver's true nature… whatever that might be. And as much as he tried not to dwell on it, he suspected that his fate lay on the other side of a cleaving.

Singularity beguiles, transcend the illusion.

The phrase increasingly coursed through him, its meaning still agonizingly cryptic.

Stay focused, he told himself. *Concentrate on not getting killed.*

He turned his attention to Keats' laptop. A split screen displayed views from the two cameras planted by Toothpick and Bling. On the left was a panorama from high in a tree. It showed the railroad track as it approached from the direction of Tau as well as the truss bridge and the S-curve through the rock cuts. On the right, the second camera offered a tighter, low-angled view of the stream and bridge in profile. The cameras occasionally cycled into heat-signature modes, rendering their imagery into multicolored smears ranging from cool violet to hot crimson. But other than the occasional bird or darting squirrel, no interlopers appeared.

At the bottom of the screen, a quintet of green lights indicated the ground sensors were online. They would blink red if substantial movement was detected nearby.

It was closing in on 5pm. Aiden was getting antsy. Could they have made a mistake about the site of the attack?

Another unsettling idea occurred. He turned to Keats.

"The sensors, the cameras, our radios… when the mercs jam the signals from the train, won't they get knocked out of commission too?"

"Doubtful. Wide-range jamming could jeopardize their own comms frequencies as well." Keats shrugged. "But if it does happen we'll just have to play it by ear."

The answer wasn't reassuring. Keats apparently noted Aiden's growing stress and repeated his instructions.

"You and Jessie hang back. We'll call when it's clear."

The soldiers formed a well-oiled combat unit, albeit one out of practice, not having fought together in years. Nevertheless, Keats didn't want a pair of clueless civilians messing up his firefight.

Jessie's expression indicated she wasn't happy about being relegated to a secondary role. Armed with her shotgun and a pistol taken from one of the dead mercs, not to mention her projectile manifestations, she was gung-ho to be in the thick of it.

Keats, Rory and Chef bore three of the H&K submachine guns. Aiden had the fourth one. Keats had given him a quick primer back at the hotel.

"On full automatic it's a room broom," Keats explained. "Sweeps an area clean. I tricked out yours for three-round burst fire only. That way you won't burn through a mag too fast. If you have a clear shot, take it. Keep firing until your man's down. Aim for center mass. If he's in hard body armor you might not get penetration so strafe below the waist. No fancy head shots, they're harder than they look. And know your target before you pull the trigger; there are friendlies on that train. And make goddamn sure you're not shooting at one of us."

"Look," Jessie hissed, pointing at the screen.

One of the ground sensors blinked red. Seconds later, two men in ghillie suits slunk into view on the wide-angle cam. They hid in a cluster of bushes on the far side of the tracks, north of the bridge. One of them carried a rocket-propelled grenade launcher.

Keats donned his headset and activated his mic. "Bling, Toothpick?"

"I see 'em." Bling said. "Too many trees in my way. No clean shot."

"Snakes one and two targeted," Toothpick reported. "Their RPG has a nonstandard warhead. Long and thin, possibly custom made. Not sure what it's for."

"Doesn't matter," Keats said. "We don't let them fire it."

"Roger that."

Another ground sensor went red. A big dark-skinned merc

carrying a large knapsack dashed out of the trees. He ducked under the north bridge pier and disappeared from camera view.

"We've got snake three," Keats said. "It's Kokay. Anyone have a bead on him?"

"Negative," Toothpick and Bling uttered in unison.

Keats stood and hefted his submachine gun. "All right, we're going in."

Rory and Chef affirmed the order and the three of them raced off into the trees. Aiden stared at the screen, riveted. Other mercs must be out there as well. His hunch was confirmed a moment later when a third ground sensor blinked red. The duration of the signal suggested multiple targets. It was impossible to tell how many but he guessed a large group. They were approaching from the west, on the far side of the rail line. The number of mercs Nobe had tasked for the assault was a question Keats and his men had batted around since last night.

Don't think about the odds, just about staying alive, Keats had reminded them.

Jessie froze and grabbed his arm. "Listen!"

Aiden couldn't hear anything. The forest seemed to have gone unnaturally quiet. No chirping birds, no background hum of insects. Maybe the silence was the native denizens sensing that something bad was about to happen.

He finally discerned what her more sensitive ears had picked up. From the north came the distant rumble of approaching locomotives.

"Time to go," Jessie uttered.

She lunged to her feet and strapped the shotgun across her back.

"We should wait," Aiden urged. "Follow Keats' orders."

She ignored him and sprinted away. Aiden muttered a curse at her eagerness and his own lunacy for volunteering for such madness. Then he closed the laptop, tucked it under his arm and scrambled after her.

FIFTY-EIGHT

Héloise's escape plan called for her to hike to her waiting SUV, hidden off-road several miles from ground zero. She'd drive straight through to Seattle and take an early-morning flight to Los Angeles. A wealth of confusion arising from the assault should keep the authorities bewildered for a time, making it doubtful they'd heighten security at such relatively distant airports. As an added precaution she'd booked her flight with a fake ID obtained with the help of one of Unit X's illicit contacts.

From LA she'd board a second flight to Mexico City, where Unit X had arranged for a plastic surgeon. Her facial alterations would be minor but should change her appearance enough to pass through most border gateways. Eventually she intended to make her way to South America.

Her attention was drawn to the left windows. The train was passing a rotting tree that had fallen two winters ago during a storm. It was the first signpost. They were almost at ground zero.

Ten seconds later they reached signpost two, a quartet of soaring pines in a square-ish configuration. The train was now half a mile from the bridge.

Héloise pried the cushion off the empty seat beside her. She pinched it between her knees and the empty seat in front. Popping in a set of ear buds, she checked the radio app on her phone. During these rides, she often listened to a streaming FM station that played Nineties rap.

The station came in loud and clear, the DJ droning on about tickets available for some concert. She waited expectantly. Any second now, the frequency jamming equipment planted by Unit X's men should wipe out the train's satellite-enabled Wi-Fi.

The station went dead. The train was incommunicado.

Héloise lowered her head against the cushion and braced for impact.

FIFTY-NINE

Aiden couldn't believe he'd lost sight of Jessie. She'd been right in front of him, tearing through the bushes with what initially seemed like maniacal speed, although on second thought probably was more indicative of his own excessive caution. He'd come up and over a slight rise and she was gone.

The ground was too hard to leave signs of her passage, at least none he could discern. He had no idea which way she'd headed. The growl of the locomotives grew stronger but the wilderness was playing sonic tricks, disguising the train's location.

He tried her on his headset but whispered appeals brought no response. He guessed she'd angled left and zigzagged through the trees in that direction. A dozen paces later he came to a sudden stop. The tracks were directly ahead, less than thirty feet away. The train sounded perilously close.

I shouldn't be standing in plain view.

He pancaked behind a cluster of bushes, wincing as thorns from hostile foliage scratched his arms and legs. The locomotives burst into view to his left. The earth rumbled beneath him, the vibrations seeming to course through muscle and bone.

Peering through the underbrush, Aiden could just make out the tiny figures of the engineer and conductor in the rounded contours of the lead cab. The train was slowing in anticipation of the bridge and the S-curve beyond. Flashes of late-day sun reflected off the shaded windows of the four passenger cars. He couldn't see inside and hoped he was hidden well enough to avoid being spotted.

The coaches passed his place of concealment. He flipped open the laptop, maximized the view from the panoramic camera as the train approached the bridge. He was startled by Toothpick's voice in his headset.

"Snake one is aiming the RPG. I think they're targeting the last coach."

"Take 'em," Keats ordered.

Two rifle shots rang out.

"Snakes one and two down," Toothpick said.

"First blood." It was Rory's voice. He sounded juiced.

A round of machine-gun fire spilled through the forest. Another burst sounded, this one closer to Aiden.

"I'm taking fire," Toothpick said. "Snakes at my ten o'clock. Can't see 'em."

Aiden's attention was drawn back to the laptop. Kokay raced out from under the bridge pier, his face now hidden by black mask and goggles. He carried a dark object the size and shape of a bowling ball. Climbing the short embankment, he darted across the tracks and rolled the ball toward the oncoming train.

The engineer spotted him, laid on the horn. Bullets pinged at Kokay's feet. One of Keats' men was trying to bring him down. The diesel's screaming chimes nearly muffled the gunfire.

Kokay leaped off the far side of the tracks and vanished from view.

Despite the train's reduced speed there wasn't enough time to brake hundreds of tons of steel. The front coupler and snowplow of the lead diesel passed over the bowling ball.

A burst of luminescence erupted from beneath the locomotive. The blast echoed through the forest.

Gilded flames and a shower of debris shot out from beneath the diesel. The front wheel truck jerked upward and swiveled sideways, momentarily putting inches of air between the undercarriage and the rails. The wheels slammed down an instant later but no longer aligned with the twin ribbons of steel.

Hideous screeching filled the air. The distressed locomotive skidded across the bridge, its snowplow raking the ballasted surface. Waves of gravel cascaded off the deck, pelting the waters below like jet-powered hail.

Before the locomotive could complete the crossing, its coupler and snowplow dug in. A shudder seemed to pass through the entire train.

The diesel splintered the flimsy railing and sailed off the side of the bridge. With a percussive howl, it plowed headfirst into the stream embankment.

Plumes of dirt swirled into the air. The rear coupler snagged a length of broken rail and ripped free, severing the lead locomotive's connection with the second diesel and the coaches. The untracked leviathan, its front end planted deep in the dirt embankment, uttered a defeated groan and rolled onto its side, slamming the shallow waters with a thunderous splash. The rest of the train came to a jerking halt with the remaining locomotive and the first coach centered on the bridge. The train remained railed but would be going no farther. Fifty feet of track in front of it had been buckled by the bomb and the lead unit's wild trek.

Aiden was stunned by the wreck's savagery. They'd envisioned mercs leaping from the trees and onto the coaches like nineteenth century train robbers, not blasting a locomotive off its rails.

The upward-facing cab door of the overturned diesel was pushed open. A crewman struggled to climb from the compartment. He was bleeding from the forehead and clutching a pistol.

Someone lobbed a grenade. It bounced off the crewman's chest and dropped through the open hatch at his feet. Panicked, he struggled to get clear of the cab.

He didn't make it. The grenade exploded, catapulting him twenty feet into the air. His body slammed into the stream.

Rory's voice erupted. "They've got another RPG!"

The unseen merc fired before Rory could call out a position. Aiden watched onscreen as the rocketed grenade ripped through a window in the middle of the last coach. Moments later, a dense cloud of pinkish smoke poured out through the shattered window frame.

Doors were flung open at both ends of the coach, emitting more swirls of pink haze. Marines appeared within it, hands pasted over mouths and noses, trying not to draw breaths.

They seemed to be exiting in slow motion. Two of them, male and female, managed to navigate the steps and reach the ground. But they got no farther and collapsed face down in the dirt. The rest didn't even make it that far. Aiden watched several more fall in the vestibules at both ends of the coach. The warhead must have contained a fast-acting knockout gas. At least he hoped that's what it was and not something more permanent.

He was a good hundred yards behind the afflicted car. The gas was already dispersing but he had no intention of venturing closer.

Hollering and occasional screams emanated from the forward coaches. Presumably there were injured passengers, hurled from their seats when the train was brought to its abrupt stop. No one attempted to exit. The sporadic gunfire was enough to keep them inside.

Aiden stood up. A mistake. Machine-gun fire ripped at the earth in front of him. He couldn't tell where it was coming from.

He dove back into the bushes. On the other side of the tracks, a figure lunged out of the trees. Another merc in black mask and goggles. His weapon looked similar to Aiden's.

The man charged at him, firing short bursts. Aiden tried to raise his own gun. But the twice-be-damned bushes snared the shoulder strap. He couldn't swing the barrel toward the fast-approaching threat.

The merc reached the tracks, took note of Aiden's problem. He stopped, planted his own gun against his shoulder and took careful aim. But suddenly he hesitated and lowered his gaze. His trigger hand was enveloped in a gelatinous brown mass.

One of Jessie's droppers.

The merc started to turn. Jessie burst from the trees behind him, fired her shotgun from three yards away. The blast ripped into the man's flank, flinging him violently sideways.

Aiden untangled himself from the bushes, in the process violently tearing off the headset when the mouthpiece caught a sprig. He checked the merc for a pulse. The man was gone. He wasn't wearing body armor, which meant the others probably weren't as well.

"Thanks," he muttered, fumbling to get the headset back on.

"You… lucky… wasn't close enough… aim was… "

Her words were cutting in and out. His headset may have been damaged.

"Gas… dispersing…"

That was all he got. Either she'd stopped talking or his headset was finished. She turned and dashed toward the train.

"No don't!" Aiden warned. "The gas!"

Either she didn't hear him or didn't care. Her optimism was alarming, more the byproduct of adrenalin than common sense. Aiden grabbed the laptop and hurried after her.

SIXTY

Héloise got up and moved into the aisle. She was unhurt. The six occupants at the front of coach three had been thrown forward against the seat backs. Their injuries seemed limited to minor bruising. They huddled low, checking phones, perplexed that calls and texts weren't getting through. Occasionally, one of them would peek out the bottom of a window to see who was doing the shooting.

She'd expected a bit of gunfire but not this much. It sounded like a war zone out there. Had something gone haywire with Unit X's plan?

Turning to the vestibule's rear door, she smacked the hydraulic actuator. Erring on the side of caution, she covered her mouth and nose with a hankie and strode across the metal plates between cars to enter the last coach. The Marines were strewn around like rag dolls, out of commission from Unit X's fast-dissipating gas. By the time they awoke in a few hours, Héloise and the mercs would be long gone.

As planned, she crouched over the nearest Marine and retrieved his radio. She also drew the brown Sig P320 from his belt holster, which was not part of the plan. Checking to make sure the slide lock was engaged, she popped the magazine out. Seventeen 9mm rounds. She snapped the mag back in and tucked the gun in her handbag.

She was an excellent shot. Whatever all the shooting was about, she'd be ready. But that wasn't her main purpose in securing a weapon. She'd decided early on to arm herself in case Unit X attempted a double-cross.

Keeping low, she made her way back to the third coach. Movement out the right-side windows caught her attention. On the hill above, two of Unit X's men in black masks were chasing and firing their machine guns at a third man running parallel to the train. Their quarry was neither masked nor in uniform.

Héloise was astonished. Their quarry wasn't military. Who the hell was he?

The mercs closed on the man, whose movement revealed an odd gait. Either he'd been shot in the left leg or had some kind of preexisting condition that resulted in a limp.

He ducked behind a tree, spun and returned fire. The two mercs separated, closed in from diverging angles to catch him in a crossfire. In seconds his cover was gone, his flanks exposed. He limped toward a new hiding place behind more distant trees but didn't make it. Amid bursts of gunfire he fell forward and tumbled out of sight over a hill.

A machine gun raked the left side of Héloise's coach. She and the workers at the front dove to the floor as bullets shattered three windows.

She switched the radio's frequency to the one provided by Unit X and punched in the encryption code.

"Miracle to Downspin One!" she whispered, using their code names. "I need a status update."

She plugged in an earpiece to avoid being overheard by the others and waited. No response came. She repeated the message.

This time she was answered by a man with a Scottish accent.

"Is it secure?" he asked.

"Yes. What the hell's going on out there?"

"The situation is being resolved. Hold your position. We'll come to you."

The radio went silent. Héloise wished she had access to the mercs' tactical channel so she'd have some idea of how the battle was going. But that wasn't something Unit X had been willing to provide.

She crouched as low as possible in the rearmost seat with her back to the bulkhead, making herself as small a target as possible. There was nothing to do now but wait and hope no further glitches disrupted the plan.

SIXTY-ONE

Aiden watched Jessie run parallel to the track, heading toward the last coach of the disabled train. But just before reaching it she darted left into the woods. He guessed she'd been spotted by mercs and sought cover. He lost sight of her amid the trees.

The gunfire had relented. He continued on but with extreme caution, hyper-aware of every sound and movement. He squatted behind a large tree and opened the laptop. The panoramic camera view of the train and bridge was eerily devoid of movement. He may as well have been looking at a still shot.

He switched to the tighter, low-angled perspective from the other camera. Prominent in shot was the front end of the overturned locomotive. Its headlight, just beneath the stream's surface, continued to shine, the yellowish beam forming an eerie cone of subterranean light. Camera resolution was good enough to make out small fish darting back and forth in the beam, distressed by the massive intruder into their habitat.

A man in a ghillie suit armed with a submachine gun emerged from under the bridge pier. He waded into the stream, moving along the locomotive's flank in waist-deep water, heading toward the camera. Even in disguise, Aiden recognized Toothpick's skinny frame and oversized glasses.

A second man entered the frame, creeping into view on the edge of the embankment and heading down toward the stream. Although masked, Aiden knew it was Kokay.

They were moving perpendicular, on a collision course. Once they cleared the locomotive's bulk, they'd be within sight of one another.

He whispered urgently into the headset, hoping that at least the mic was still working.

"Toothpick, watch out. There's a merc, at the front of the locomotive."

No response. He tried again. Nothing.

"Keats, Rory, anyone? Can you hear me?"

Frustrated, he ripped off the headset and cast it aside.

Kokay froze at the bottom of the embankment. He must have heard Toothpick splashing toward him through the stream. The merc took three bounding steps and leaped out into the flowing waters.

Toothpick whipped up his gun. He was an instant too late. Kokay machine-gunned him from chest to groin. Toothpick tumbled backward into the stream. Aiden could only watch in horror as Kokay splashed toward the fallen soldier, stood over him and unleashed a short burst at his head.

Branches rustled to Aiden's left. Easing the laptop closed, he raised his gun and aimed it in that direction. Whoever it was they were moving fast and making no effort to disguise their movements. It seemed like a lot of noise for one person.

There was no time to make a run for it. Whoever it was, they were almost on top of him. His heart pounded. His finger tickled the trigger.

The barrel of a gun pressed into the side of his skull. So intent on the approaching threat he'd had no idea someone had snuck up on him.

"Finger off the trigger," the man with the gun ordered.

Aiden was never so happy to comply with a command.

"Keats!"

"Shh. Quiet!"

Keats lowered his machine gun. Moments later, Chef emerged from the trees in front of Aiden. In his hand was a leafy branch.

He'd been using it to rustle the bushes and make enough noise to allow Keats to inch closer. They'd obviously thought he was a merc.

"Bling's dead," Keats said without emotion. "Have you seen the others? Can't reach Toothpick and Rory."

"Toothpick didn't make it," Aiden said.

Keats took the news in his stride. He walked over to Chef to confer privately. Aiden couldn't hear what they were saying.

The whirr of a helicopter reverberated through the forest. It skated into view from the south and hovered almost directly overhead, a scant dozen feet above the dense canopy. A four-seater with civilian markings. No weaponry was visible.

Keats and Chef whipped up their guns but hesitated, unsure whether it contained mercs or friendlies dispatched from Tau.

The passenger door slid open. A small object flew out and fell toward them.

"Grenade!" Keats hollered.

Aiden leaped to the opposite side of the tree and flattened. Just as he hit the ground, an earsplitting roar shook the forest.

SIXTY-TWO

Michael leaned forward in the copilot's seat and gazed down to survey the damage. The two men who'd been standing were both face down and unmoving, their guns scattered nearby. They'd been well within the blast radius of the concussion grenade, whose airborne detonation made for a more extensive impact.

Just prior to the explosion, however, he thought he'd caught a flash of movement. Possibly there'd been a third man.

It didn't matter. He flipped his radio headset to the primary tactical channel and gave Nobe their position. Dead or alive, two men or three, the mercs would finish the job.

A better idea abruptly occurred to him. He called Nobe back.

"If they're still breathing, keep one of them that way."

It would be helpful to know the interlopers' identities and who'd sent them. Michael's best guess was that Green, Magenta and their mysterious friend, the GAO analyst, had either taken part in the assault or arranged for it. In either case, uncovering the truth might head off any future threats. If one of the men below had survived, he'd be flown back to the chateau. There, the necessary information could be extracted at Michael's leisure. Afterward, the body would be taken to the old quarry to provide Maisey Latorsky with eternal companionship.

He checked his watch. They were still within the safe window but had used up more time than anticipated. And there could be more interlopers down there. Hovering in place elevated the risk of the helicopter being targeted.

Michael motioned to the pilot. The merc nodded and banked for their original safe zone a mile to the south. They'd stay there until Nobe signaled all threats had been neutralized.

SIXTY-THREE

Aiden got shakily to his feet, clutching his temples with both hands. The tree had protected him from the blast's direct impact but a painful ringing noise coursed through his head. It felt as if his brain was vibrating in his skull.

He peered around the trunk. The helicopter was gone. Keats and Chef were prone and motionless. Checking to see if they were still alive wasn't something he looked forward to.

Before he could carry out the task, fast-approaching footsteps sounded from the wilderness to his right. This time, the sounds clearly emanated from multiple locations. At least two or three individuals were approaching, possibly more. With Keats and his men dead, wounded or MIA, only Jessie remained unaccounted for. Possibly it was workers who'd gotten off the train. But the greater likelihood was mercs.

Aiden gripped his gun and swung the barrel toward the sounds. Keats and Chef could still be alive. He needed to stay here and protect them. Even if they weren't breathing he'd stay anyway. He'd make a final stand, go out in a blaze of glory.

Think smart. Stay ahead of your troubles.

His father's counsel tuned consciousness to a less fatalistic wavelength. Better to live to fight another day.

Head still pounding, he grabbed the laptop and hustled away with all the stealth he could muster.

SIXTY-FOUR

"Stay on the train. Anyone trying to get off will be shot!"

The warning came from outside. Héloise heard three distinct voices bellowing the words over and over.

At least five minutes had elapsed since the last gunfire had erupted from up ahead at the bridge. Shortly thereafter had come that explosion from somewhere behind the train. It was likely that by now, Unit X's men had dealt with the intruders. Hopefully, the plan was back on track, so to speak.

Agitated murmuring arose from the workers at the front of the coach. One man, a portly administrator who had something to do with payroll, roared to his feet in a panic. He looked ready to ignore the warning and bolt for the nearest vestibule.

Fellow workers grabbed at his arms, urging him to stay calm. He finally relented and dropped back into the aisle, scrunching into a fetal position. One of the women leaned over him, clutched his hand and patted his back reassuringly. He started to sob.

"Downspin One to Miracle."

Héloise was startled by the voice in her earpiece. It was the merc with the Scottish accent.

"I read you," she whispered.

"How many others in your coach?"

"Six."

"Don't move. We're comin' in."

The door at the front opened. Three mercs, faces hidden by

masks and goggles, entered. Two of the men pointed their guns at the workers and gestured for them to move forward into the second coach. The panicked administrator and his female helper were the last to comply. The two mercs followed, leaving Héloise alone with the third man.

"Let's see it," he ordered.

His accent was more conspicuous in person. With machine gun dangling from a chest strap, he sauntered toward her. He looked like someone without a care in the world, out for an afternoon stroll.

Héloise wondered if he was Unit X. She'd never heard her benefactor's real voice. The few times they'd communicated by phone he'd used a vocal distorter.

She removed the canister from her handbag and placed it on the seat in front of her. As unobtrusively as possible, she slipped her hand back into the bag. Gripping the Sig, she disengaged the pistol's slide lock.

His head followed her movements. She had the impression he was smiling beneath the mask.

"You won't be needin' a gun."

"I've taken other precautions," she said, uttering the words she'd rehearsed for weeks. "I've put certain evidence in a safe deposit box that will–"

"Nobody cares, doll," he interrupted.

The merc held his phone close and snapped a picture of the quiver stone through its translucent container.

They waited in silence. Presumably, he'd sent the photo to someone – Unit X? – for confirmation.

"OK, we're good," the merc said, closing the lid and tucking the container in his belt pouch.

"The rest of my money?"

"It'll be transferred into your account within the hour, as promised." He cocked his head in a way that gave her the impression he was amused. "If we were going to double-cross you, it would have happened already. You'd be dead."

Héloise nodded. That was still no guarantee they weren't planning to kill her out in the wilderness. Or maybe a lesser betrayal, not depositing the rest of her compensation. At least she'd accounted for that possibility. She already had Unit X's first two and a half million dollars. If the rest didn't materialize, she'd manage.

The merc turned and headed back down the aisle. Héloise kept her eye on him until he passed through the vestibule and back into the second coach.

She retreated to the last car. Stepping over the unconscious Marines, she proceeded to the far end and warily stuck her head out the rear door.

No one in sight. She jumped to the roadbed, raced down a short embankment and headed into the woods. A swift hike and she'd reach her vehicle, and be well on her way to a new life.

SIXTY-FIVE

Aiden wandered through the wilderness, uncertain what his next move should be. He'd evaded the mercs without being spotted and was pretty sure he was headed in the general direction of the train. His wilderness navigational skills were for shit as he'd quickly learned. And without a radio he was essentially alone. Worse, he felt increasingly guilty for having abandoned Keats and Chef.

No choice. If I'd stayed, I'd be dead too.

The justifications didn't help. He still felt like a coward.

He spotted Jessie up ahead, crouching behind a fallen tree caked in serpentine clusters of vine. She sensed his presence, whirled with the shotgun.

"It's me," he hissed.

She lowered the gun, motioned him to get on the ground and crawl toward her.

"I think we're the last ones," he said.

She shook her head, pointed to the train. The coaches were visible through the foliage twenty yards ahead.

"I saw three mercs dragging Keats into the third car a minute ago. He wasn't moving but he must still be alive. Else, why take him?"

Aiden grimaced. His guilt over the abandonment mushroomed, became a psychic ache that could only be assuaged by action. No more running away.

"All right," he said. "We go get him."

Jessie's eyes flashed agreement. "I think they're holding all the passengers up front in the first two cars. Mercs peek out of those vestibules every so often, looking for more of us. They could've moved Keats there too."

"Maybe. But it would make more sense to keep him isolated from the others in case they want to question him. I'm betting he's still in the third coach."

"If you're right, our best chance is to come in through the back of the last car. The Marines are still out cold. No reason for the mercs to be guarding them, right?"

"Right," Aiden said, layering the word with more assurance than he felt.

They retreated deeper into the woods and made a wide loop back around to the track. Crouching low, they dashed onto the roadbed and scrambled across the wooden ties. They reached the rear of the fourth coach without incident.

Aiden reevaluated their plan. "This won't work," he whispered. "Even if we reach the third car without being seen, we still have to get through two vestibule doors with windows. They'll see and hear us coming."

"You're right."

They stood quietly for a moment, considering options.

"OK," Jessie said. "We need to get creative."

Leaning her shotgun against the coupler, she handed Aiden her pistol. She squirmed out of her jacket and spread it across the ties. It served as a dropcloth to keep the rest of her clothes from getting dirty as she stripped off the items one by one. In seconds she was down to matching bra and underpants, magenta-colored no less.

"Not sure I'm following the logic here," he said, keeping his attention on her face as she removed the final two items of clothing and added them to the pile.

"This'll give us an edge."

"You're going to walk in there bare-ass naked?"

"And without weapons, at least not the kind that have triggers."

"That's one hell of a bad idea."

"Look, they probably already have an idea what I can do with the droppers. I go in there clothed and with weapons, they're probably going to shoot first, ask questions later. But this way I have the element of surprise. Big guns or not, they're still guys with dicks. They'll hesitate. That's when I'll take 'em."

Her plan still sounded dubious.

"You stay outside," she instructed. "Make your way forward. After I do my thing, hop aboard."

There was clearly no stopping her. And maybe it was crazy enough to work.

"Just make sure you aim those droppers better than last time," he said.

"Don't worry. Help me up. I can't reach the door."

He figured she could easily climb up on her own but there was no time to argue.

"Hurry up," she hissed.

Aiden stepped in close. She grinned at his wary expression. "Grab my butt and push."

He tucked the pistol in the back of his pants and lowered his eyes.

She turned, swung a foot up onto the coupler. Once balanced atop the coupler, it was a short hop up to the vestibule. She palmed the hydraulic actuator and the inner door whisked open. Stepping over an unconscious Marine, she headed in. The door closed behind her.

Aiden held his breath, waiting for gunshots. None came. But maybe they just hadn't seen her yet.

Keeping tight against the side of the coach, he crept forward. He glimpsed Jessie through the windows and moved in tandem. Should one of the mercs in the front cars choose this moment to stick his head out, Aiden was screwed.

But none did. He and Jessie reached the end of the last coach together. He slipped around the sprawled body of a Marine and scrambled up the steps to the vestibule. Staying hidden behind the bulkhead, he watched Jessie stride past and hit the actuator to coach three.

"What the fuck?"

The male voice erupted from inside the car. Jessie adopted a meek and vulnerable tone.

"Please, they took my clothes. Please help me."

Aiden sensed that she was advancing into the coach. He gripped the machine gun, ready to lunge around the corner and do whatever was necessary.

"All clear!" Jessie whispered.

He ducked into the car, grasped the scene in an instant. Two mercs were on their knees, writhing in the aisle as they struggled to breathe, their fallen guns beside them. Hands clawed desperately at droppers enveloping their masked faces.

Keats was in a seat toward the front of the coach. He was hunched over and motionless. Someone had cloaked the window of the nearby door to the second coach with a blanket, a stroke of good fortune. The covering was probably meant to prevent the workers confined there from seeing what the mercs might have in store for their special prisoner.

Aiden crouched low in case other mercs roamed outside and raced down the aisle. Keats' wrists and ankles were bound in flex cuffs. He checked for a pulse.

"He's alive."

Aiden scrambled over to the nearest merc. The man's body was spasming, in its final death throes. Aiden drew the serrated blade from the merc's holster, unable to avoid staring at the brown mass enshrouding his face. As with Rosen back in Jessie's living room, the merc had tried tearing away the sticky goo with his hands, causing the dropper to grow its finger-crushing tentacles.

He tore his eyes away from the grisly sight and returned to Keats. Propping the machine gun nearby, he cut through the plastic foot bindings then moved to the wrists.

"Wake up," he whispered, guiding Keats upright in the seat and shaking him. "We need to get out of here."

No reaction. There was a nasty bruise on his forehead but no obvious injuries elsewhere, such as shrapnel impacts. The grenade must have been the concussion type with minimal fragmentation. Hopefully, Keats was only stunned by the blast and would wake up soon.

He started to slice the wrist cuffs. Before he could finish, the front door flashed open. A merc lunged in, his machine gun pointed at Aiden.

"Drop the knife!"

Aiden let the blade slip from his hand. He turned toward Jessie. She was striding toward them, trying to get closer before hitting the merc with a dropper.

"One more step, you die!" the merc warned, shifting his barrel to target her. His gun had a laser sight. Its red dot painted a spot between her breasts.

Jessie stopped and closed her eyes. Before she could form a dropper, another merc rushed into the coach behind her, a big man with dark skin. Even masked, Aiden knew it was Kokay.

"Jessie, look out!"

His warning came too late. She spun and met the butt of Kokay's raised weapon. It cracked her forehead and she collapsed to the floor.

The first merc snatched Aiden's machine gun before he could think to reach for it. The man shoved him violently backward. He fell against Keats.

A thumping noise from outside filled the coach. The helicopter was returning. It skated into view, hovered above them. The floor pulsated as the whirring blades output a cascade of vibrations.

The helicopter descended. The coach roof groaned as the pilot landed crosswise on it. Rotor blades grew sluggish. The worst of the noise abated.

A third merc entered the car behind Kokay. He stared at the unconscious Jessie, who'd landed face down.

"Nice arse. I'm guessin' the front side ain't bad either."

Aiden couldn't squelch escalating panic. The newcomer's accent was terrifyingly familiar.

Kokay gestured to the mercs' bodies. "I think the bitch did that. I say we shoot her in the fucking head before she comes around."

Nobe removed his goggles and mask and stared the length of the car at Aiden. His smirk was as chilling as ever.

"Well now, it's our clever bloke. I'm really curious how you got away from Farlin. But I suppose the fun of finding out will have to wait until–"

He paused and put a hand over his ear, straining to hear someone on the radio above the drone of the helicopter blades.

"Uh-huh, it's still secure… Oh, and you get a bonus, a couple new colors for your collection… Magenta and Green… Yeah, got it."

Nobe faced Kokay. "The Clerk wants 'em both on the chopper. Help me carry Princess. We'll come back for clever boy."

"What about the accountant?" He gestured to Keats.

"Don't need him anymore. I'll do him before we leave."

Nobe and Kokay picked up Jessie and carried her out the rear door. Even through the whine of the rotor blades, Aiden heard them climbing onto the roof and maneuvering Jessie up there.

He couldn't allow himself to be bound by Michael's men a third time. Once they had him cuffed and aboard the helicopter, it was all over.

His only chance was Jessie's pistol, still tucked in the back of his pants. But the remaining merc's weapon remained trained on him. He'd never reach around for the pistol in time.

Footsteps scampered across the roof. Jessie was being put aboard the helicopter. In seconds they'd return. Impossible or not, Aiden had to chance it. He mentally rehearsed the move and steeled himself for the intense pain that surely would follow.

He never got the opportunity. A hand slithered up his back, yanked Jessie's pistol out of his belt.

Keats came alive, shoved Aiden hard. He flew across the aisle, slammed into the opposite seat. A gunshot rang out.

The merc crumbled, a red blemish between his eyes.

Keats grabbed Aiden's machine gun and thrust it into his hands.

"Cover the front door. Shoot anyone who opens it!"

Keats dashed to the rear of the coach and ducked behind the end seat bulkhead.

The front door hissed open. A merc rushed in. Aiden pulled the trigger.

Nothing happened. The merc who'd taken his weapon must have flipped the selector to the safe position.

Bullets whizzed close to Aiden's head but from the other direction. It was Keats. He'd fired at the newcomer. The merc fell.

Kokay swung down from the roof and rushed into the coach. Keats leaped out in front of him. Kokay swept up his machine gun but Keats was quicker. Pressing the barrel of the pistol against Kokay's chest, Keats fired five times. A sixth squeeze of the trigger had no effect. The magazine was empty.

Five shots were more than enough. What didn't make sense was that the fatally wounded merc was flying forward rather than backward from the impact of the bullets.

Kokay plowed into Keats. The pair crashed to the floor, with Keats on the bottom.

The reason for Kokay defying the laws of momentum became clear. Nobe had lunged into the car, pushing Kokay from behind.

Aiden flipped the selector to the firing position, swung the barrel around and squeezed the trigger. His aim was bad. The three-round burst pinged off the right bulkhead behind the last row of seats. Before he could re-target, Nobe's laser sight painted his chest.

At that instant, with death certain, Aiden flashed back to the feeling he'd experienced in the garage with Farlin, and in Jessie's living room with Rosen and Vesely, and minutes ago when she'd shotgunned that merc. Each time, Aiden was sure he was going to die. Each time, someone had saved his life.

That wasn't going to happen here. Nobe pulled the trigger.

The spray of bullets never touched Aiden.

A chunkie formed in front of his chest, instantaneously expanding into one of Grant's giant donuts. The deadly hail from

Nobe's machine gun poured through the transparent center of the cleaving and disappeared into the shroud.

Before Nobe could overcome his surprise and fire again, Keats' boot heel sprang from beneath Kokay's body and smashed Nobe's ankle.

The merc stumbled forward. His barrel jerked upward as he squeezed the trigger. Bullets stitched a jagged line across the roof.

That was enough for the helicopter's pilot. The craft lifted off and headed away. Its departure must have served as a signal to the remaining mercs guarding the passengers. Aiden saw three of them sprinting from the forward coaches and running for the woods.

The cleaving vanished. Aiden whipped his attention back to the aisle.

Keats had scrambled out from beneath Kokay's body. He and Nobe were on their hands and knees, furiously wrestling for control of Nobe's machine gun. Keats yanked hard, managed to rip the weapon out of the merc's hands. But the gun got knocked away from him. It flew through the air, landed on a seat ten feet away.

Keats had the weight advantage but Nobe was wiry and preternaturally fast. Twisting and contorting, the merc got the upper hand. He forced Keats onto his back and head-butted him with brutal force. The base of Keats' skull slammed the floor with a resounding crack.

Aiden raised his gun but hesitated, afraid he'd hit Keats. He moved closer for a better shot.

An explosion startled him. It came from outside. He whirled toward the window.

Something had happened to the retreating helicopter. Black smoke and tongues of flame cascaded off the tail rotor. Its blades were twisted, no longer rotating. The pilot tried to climb but the rear stabilizer fishtailed madly. Losing altitude, the spinning craft disappeared beyond the tree line.

Aiden returned his attention to the combatants. Nobe had drawn a knife. Clutching the hilt with both hands, he was attempting to force the blade down into his opponent's heart. Keats, still on his back, had grabbed the merc's wrists and was trying to wrench the knife away from its target. The faces of both men grimaced with exertion.

Keats twisted the blade to the side, sparing himself a fatal stabbing. But Nobe kept enough pressure to slice the tip across Keats' left shoulder.

Keats grunted in pain. Aiden knelt in the aisle, steadied himself and took careful aim.

Don't miss.

Before he could pull the trigger, Keats drew upon some incredible reserve of strength. Bending at the waist, fighting against the full weight of the merc atop him, he performed an impossible sit-up.

The two men were again face to face. Aiden's shot was blocked.

Blood streamed from Keats' shoulder as he continued to struggle for control of the knife. For a moment it seemed neither man had the upper hand. But then the smoldering intensity Aiden had witnessed in that West Virginia garage returned, a defiant posture that said losing was not in Deke Keats' nature. With a bestial growl equal parts agony and rage, he ripped the knife from Nobe's grip.

The tip of the blade slashed across the merc's neck. Carbon steel tore into a jugular vein. Nobe's hands impulsively clutched the wound. The effort was futile. He couldn't stem the crimson flow.

"That's for my men," Keats said, grabbing Nobe by the chin and pushing his head back.

"This is for my son."

Keats torpedoed the blade deep into Nobe's guts. Astonishment flickered across the merc's face, as if the idea of his own death was implausible. And then those vacant eyes went cold for good.

Keats tried to stand but collapsed in the aisle. Aiden helped him to his feet and supported his weight. They staggered through the rear vestibule and exited.

Outside, Keats sat down with his back to an oily train wheel. The six-inch knife slash across his shoulder looked deep. He'd lost a lot of blood. Aiden eased the knife from Keats' iron grip and used it to cut off a sleeve of his own jacket. Wrapping it tightly around the wound, he placed Keats's hand over the makeshift bandage to hold it in place. There was also the beginnings of a large ugly bruise on the back of the head from where Nobe had slammed him against the floor, and that was bleeding too. Keats looked on the verge of passing out.

Workers were emerging from the forward coaches, milling around in confusion. Several gazed warily at Aiden and his gun.

"It's OK," he yelled. "We're not with the others." He turned back to Keats. "I'm going to see if I can find a doctor or medic."

"No, we need to follow the chopper. Michael must have been aboard."

"There was an explosion. I think it went down. Not sure why."

"I think I know," Keats said, managing a weak smile. He motioned to the trees.

Aiden turned, astonished and pleased to see two men coming toward them. The lower part of Rory's prosthetic leg from the ankle down was gone and he was leaning on Chef for support. The medic's face was badly bruised, his left eye pinched shut. He was holding a blood-soaked cloth to his right side where he'd apparently been shot.

"Through-and-throughs," Rory said, wincing in agony as Chef helped him sit down next to Keats.

"You took out the 'copter," Aiden concluded.

Rory nodded. "Found one of the mercs' RPGs. Chef got off a clean shot."

"Jessie was aboard."

"Sorry. Didn't know."

"Never mind that," Keats said. "We need to get to the wreckage."

He struggled to his feet. But immediately his eyes glazed over. Aiden and Chef guided him back to a seated position. Rory stated the obvious.

"Deke, you and I need to sit out this round."

Keats gave a disappointed nod and turned to Chef. "Up to you."

Chef looked reluctant to leave them.

"Go!" Keats urged.

Aiden knew he had no choice but to follow. Before he could scamper after Chef, Keats grabbed his wrist.

"Finish it."

SIXTY-SIX

Chef led the way, navigating through the occasionally dense foliage with a degree of stealth Aiden couldn't mimic. His own footsteps sounded like the Hulk.

Every so often Chef would pause, glance around and sniff the air. Aiden hadn't the faintest clue what he was doing. Maybe scanning for debris from the damaged helicopter or maybe smelling the sacred Earth so it could bestow its essence. Aiden asked how he'd evaded the mercs after being knocked out by the grenade.

"To abide the trembling you must become part of the wake," Chef replied.

"That explains it," Aiden mumbled.

They came upon the helicopter. It was below them, upright at the base of a small hill, the crumpled front end wedged against a tree. The landing window was shattered and the skids grotesquely bent. There was no sign of the pilot or passengers. But they couldn't see the far side of the craft.

Chef hand-signaled and they approached warily, circling in from opposite sides. Their caution was justified. A man sat with his back to the fuselage. As Aiden poked his machine gun around the edge of the shattered tail section and peered out, the man whipped up a pistol.

"Drop it," Chef ordered, emerging from the trees on the opposite side.

The man swiveled his torso to take aim at the new threat. But his injuries were severe enough that even such a simple movement looked agonizing. Seeing weapons trained on him from two angles, he wisely tossed the gun.

He was thirtyish with a shaved head and an old scar on the side of his neck. Chef leaned over him, laid a hand on his midsection then moved the hand to his left thigh. His touches caused wincing.

"Broken ribs, broken femur," Chef concluded.

"Tell me something I don't know," the man snarled.

"You the pilot?" Aiden asked, retrieving the man's pistol.

He gave a grudging nod.

"Where are the others? Was Michael aboard? Was Jessie still alive?"

His questions were met by a defiant glare.

Chef made a fist and pressed it hard into the broken ribs. The pilot groaned in pain. Aiden gently took hold of Chef's wrist and eased the fist away. His own burns and the memory of how they'd been administered were never far from his thoughts. He wasn't about to stoop to torture.

"No reason for you to suffer any more than you already have," Aiden said, squatting beside the pilot. "It's over. You're hurt pretty bad and obviously not going anywhere. Nobe is dead. So are most of your buddies. And I'm guessing Michael left you here to deal with the aftermath."

The pilot's scowl told Aiden that his last statement was on the money.

"Makes no sense being loyal to him. It'll go easier on you if you cooperate." Aiden paused. "You got family?"

The question touched a nerve. "Wife and kid."

"Then do the right thing. Do it for them."

The pilot's resistance evaporated. "The girl was out cold. Last I saw, the Clerk was dragging her off in that direction." He pointed into the trees. "The Clerk had an ATV stashed nearby, emergency backup to get him to his vehicle. In case things didn't go as planned." A bitter laugh escaped him.

"Where's Michael going?"

"He has a chateau west of Helena." The pilot withdrew a notepad and pen, scribbled directions.

Aiden weighed his options. Tau's Marines and emergency personnel undoubtedly would soon reach the train. Despite Keats urging him to "finish it," the smarter course would be to return, surrender and tell the authorities where to find Michael.

But relating the whole convoluted story to military inquisitors, even if they could be convinced Aiden was on the level, would eat up precious hours. Michael almost certainly had the quiver. Who knew what enhanced abilities a second infusion would bring him? He also had the financial wherewithal to disappear, maybe to some country without extradition treaties.

And then there was Jessie. Under any scenario Aiden could imagine, if she wasn't dead already, she soon would be.

There was only one thing to do. "That Jeep of yours, it's got GPS?"

Chef nodded.

"I need your keys."

"I'll drive."

"No. You should go back to the train. Take the pilot with you. Surrender together."

Chef looked skeptical. Aiden adopted his most persuasive tone.

"Your buddies are in bad shape and might be unconscious by now. No matter what Keats said, you need to be with them. Someone has to tell the authorities the whole story and make sure they're treated right. The rest of this is my fight, not yours. And it's something I need to do alone."

Aiden could hardly believe the words pouring from his mouth. He wasn't trying to be macho. He remained as scared as he'd been at the start of the firefight. But something within him had changed. It was more than just an urge to save Jessie, more than the fact he'd somehow manifested a chunkie that morphed into a cleaving at an opportune moment.

The real impetus was deeper, something fundamental to his very being. Questions about being swept toward an unknown destiny had been flashing through him with ever-greater frequency. No matter the risk, he needed to unveil the answers. What was quiver's purpose? What was the meaning behind his unnatural entry into the world?

Chef seemed to read the intensity of Aiden's commitment and also apparently recognized that staying with Keats and Rory was the right move. He surrendered his key fob and phone, which had a nav app for locating the Jeep. Considering Aiden's lousy navigational prowess, it might come in handy.

The pilot looked worried to be left alone with someone who'd been ready to inflict torture.

"It wouldn't be right," Aiden said to Chef, "for this guy to end up getting hurt any worse than he already is. He needs proper medical treatment."

Chef nodded and stood. He laid an imposing hand across Aiden's shoulder. "Always stand taller than you can fall."

Whether the words were endowed with mystical significance or merely the outpourings of someone who'd smoked too many malodorous cigars or hallucinogenic substances, the advice was as good a sendoff as any. Aiden checked the app, pinpointed the Jeep's location and raced off into the trees.

PART 6

THE ANOMALY

SIXTY-SEVEN

It was well after dark when Michael pulled up in front of the chateau. He remained in the SUV for a moment, contemplating his next move.

The interior lights were out. Trish likely had gone to bed, which meant one less complication to deal with. His original notion for bringing her here, a celebratory seduction, was a nonstarter. Sex was the last thing on his mind at the moment. Tarantian's goal had been achieved. He had the quiver. But too many things had gone wrong with the plan.

Most of the mercs, including Nobe, likely had been killed. They weren't Michael's concern. It was the ones who'd escaped from the train as his helicopter was taking off, moments before the RPG had struck. What should have been a quick and bloodless assault had turned into a raging battle that consumed more time than anticipated, which in turn put the mercs' getaway plans at greater risk. The survivors didn't have as much of a head start as anticipated to reach their hidden vehicles, which increased the likelihood of capture. If even one of them was caught, he'd probably take whatever deal the government offered in exchange for turning on Michael.

That went for the pilot as well. Michael and the unconscious Jessie had been in the back seat and had escaped harm – the flight deck had taken the brunt of the crash. On the spot, Michael had made the decision to kill the injured pilot. But the man had been wary of just such a double-cross and had kept his sidearm handy, robbing Michael of the opportunity. Hopefully, he'd succumb to his injuries before being found. Yet it was equally likely he'd be captured and spill everything.

A sudden rage came over Michael and he smashed his fist against the SUV's dashboard. The authorities might already be looking for him. Even if he eluded capture, he could be forced to leave the country and become a wanted individual, the same fate to which the insider had been consigned.

In Héloise's case, the government eventually could track her down. Nobe had suggested averting the possibility with a bullet to her head but Michael had resisted. Héloise's desire to extract vengeance resonated with him. His main drive was a second infusion, yet in some dark and morbid place deep within, he too sought vengeance against his parents. It was troubling that they remained the focal point of so much anger even though they'd been dead for years.

In retrospect, he probably should have ordered Nobe to kill the insider. Still, right now he had more pressing worries.

He repressed his anger, forced calm. Besides, none of his concerns took into consideration his ace in the hole. In a worst-case scenario, Michael possessed a bargaining chip that provided immense leverage.

He got out of the SUV and opened the back. Jessie, still unconscious, lay nestled beneath a blanket in the cargo area. To prevent her from waking during the ride and smothering him with one of her fascinating psychic weapons, he'd injected her with a version of the drug Nobe had used during the kidnappings of Blue and Green. Even if she came to from that blow to the head, she'd be too unfocused to pose a threat.

Michael picked her up, blanket and all, and threw her over his shoulder. He carried her around to the chateau's side entrance. If Trish happened to wake, she'd be less likely to hear him entering that way.

He made it to the basement lab without incident. Locking the door he laid the naked Jessie on the floor and uncurled the blanket.

Damn, she was beautiful. He'd waited nearly a decade to see Princess like this. He'd have to keep her drugged when they eventually fucked. But he'd done that enough times with women.

He opened the satchel hanging from his belt and removed the canister. Placing it on his desk, he unlatched the spherical halves and peeled back the top. There it was in all its glory.

The quiver stone.

What powers would come to him with a second infusion? Would he be able to transmit his physical self rather than just a shadow? Would the lethal abilities of Princess become part of his repertoire? Perhaps he'd be blessed with both, as well as other incredible faculties yet to be imagined.

His concerns over everything that had gone wrong seemed to melt away. He'd done what he'd set out to do. The prize was his. Now it was time to enjoy the fruits of his success.

How long would an infusion take? What he'd learned from the insider indicated that transference occurred within a mere ten seconds or so of skin contact.

But whereas the infusion itself might be near-instantaneous, the amount of time it would take for the effects to take hold remained a question mark. Would it happen immediately? Or take hours, days or weeks, or perhaps even longer?

Michael smiled. He was pretty sure the powers would come to him relatively fast. They were just waiting for the proper impetus to bring them to life: himself.

It's my destiny.

He picked up the stone and clutched it between his palms. He'd known it was unnaturally light but the absence of solidity still proved surprising. Quiver felt like a balloon that might float away should he release his grip.

He tightened his fingers around the stone and squeezed, imagining a godlike future.

SIXTY-EIGHT

Aiden had plugged the directions provided by the pilot into the Jeep's GPS and had been guided toward the chateau without incident. But it had taken him longer than anticipated hiking the five miles from the downed helicopter back to the Jeep, probably because of being more fatigued than when the day had begun. It was dark by the time he reached his destination.

Half a mile out on the winding private lane, he inched the vehicle up the final section with the headlights off. He had to strain to see much farther than a few feet beyond the Jeep's hood.

The outlines of a rectangular building loomed before him in the darkness: a six-bay garage. Parking behind it, he armed himself with the machine gun and pistol, and a flashlight from the glove compartment.

The night had brought a chill. He tightened the collar of his jacket and peeked around the corner at the stilted structure on the terrace above. An imperious silhouette, it seemed to hover against one of the richest starfields he'd ever seen.

Looking up at those thousands of stellar furnaces induced a sense of awe, momentarily sidetracking him from his purpose. Memories of Dad taking him on a camping trip surfaced. Deep in northern New Hampshire's White Mountains, they'd spent several evenings lying on their backs in a clearing, staring up at skies blessed with a similar plenitude of stars. On subsequent nights, he'd dreamed of rocketing out there to explore that endless void.

He recalled that it was the same trip in which *Blackie Redstone* entered family lore. Dad's subsequent adoption of that phrase to warn him against wild or foolish behavior now invoked a certain irony.

You set me on this path, he longed to tell his father. *Your letter was the catalyst*. The idea brought no bitterness, only a renewed sense of loss that his father was gone.

He refocused concentration and lowered his gaze to the chateau. A lone SUV was parked in front. Presumably it was Michael's. His nemesis had gotten a good headstart and almost certainly would have arrived more than an hour ago. Most likely, he'd already infused himself with the quiver. Would Aiden be facing a man with newfound superpowers?

It didn't matter. His first priority was rescuing Jessie. The bigger questions, the ones fundamental to his existence, would have to wait.

There were no interior or exterior lights on but that didn't mean Aiden hadn't been spotted. Ground sensors and hidden cameras might be covering the area.

Keeping the flashlight off, he dashed along the shadowy lane between chateau and garage and trotted up the wooden staircase onto the lower porch. Flattening himself against the wall between two windows, he froze, alert for any signs he'd been seen or heard. But the chateau maintained its hushed presence.

He checked the front door and curtained windows. Locked. Stickers in the corners of the panes warned that the property was protected by a security system. He couldn't spot any surveillance cameras but that didn't mean they weren't there.

No outside stairs led up to the second-floor balcony. That raised the possibility that whoever installed the security system hadn't bothered protecting the less accessible upstairs windows.

Aiden studied the posts supporting the balcony. They featured decorative indentations matching the style of the railing. Footholds? He slung the machine gun on his back, selected a corner stilt and began climbing. The ascent was trickier than anticipated. Halfway up he missed planting a toe on one of the notches and almost fell. But he recovered, made it to the top and swung himself over the railing.

He was disappointed to realize the second-floor windows were also alarmed. However, the curtains weren't drawn. He shined the flashlight through the first set of quartered panes, revealing an empty bedroom.

The second window also looked into a bedroom. This one was occupied.

The lights were out. A petite woman with curly blond hair sat on the edge of the bed with her back to the window. Her head was lowered and she was tightly clutching a handbag. Aiden had the impression she was preparing to leave.

She suddenly became aware of his flashlight beam on the far wall. Spinning around, she leapt to her feet, her face a mask of terror.

"No, it's OK," he whispered, holding up his hands in a sign of surrender, hoping against hope she could read his lips and his intentions. "I won't hurt you."

She just stood there, staring at him in fear. Was she Michael's lover? If so, at any moment she might shout for him. If she did, Aiden was ready. He'd shoot out the window and storm inside.

Interminable seconds passed as they gazed at one another through the glass. Gradually, her expression changed. Fear morphed into something approximating curiosity.

Aiden was encouraged. *I need your help*, he mouthed, pointing toward the balcony door. *Let me in*.

She nodded and slipped out of the room. Either she'd carry out his request or use the opportunity to get out of the line of sight of his weapon and summon help. He inched toward the door, gripped the machine gun tighter and prepared for the worst.

An LED at the side of the portal blinked from red to green as she disabled the security sensors. The door opened. The woman took a wary step back into a dark hallway.

"It's all right," he whispered, lowering the barrel. "Is Michael here?"

She nodded.

"Is he alone?"

Fear arced across her face. An avalanche of words tumbled out of her.

"I think he went back into the basement. He got here about two hours ago. I was watching from the window and he was carrying a woman wrapped in a blanket, and I couldn't tell whether she was dead or alive, and I heard the door to the basement open, and I'm sure that's where he took her. I should never have come. I should have stayed in LA like my friends told me too but I didn't listen, even after I'd heard the Maisey Latorsky stories, about her never being seen again after he brought her up here. I wanted to call for help but I can't get a signal on my cell phone and you need a special code to use the landline, and he never gave me the code. I wanted to run away but the garage is locked and I was afraid he'd come after me if I was on foot and–"

"Whoa, slow down," Aiden urged. He slipped into the hallway and closed the door behind him. "I'm here to help. What's your name?"

"Trish Belmont."

"Trish, you said Michael went back into the basement? Was he somewhere else first?"

"A few minutes after he first got here he went out again. I saw him walking toward the garage but it was too dark and I lost sight of him. I didn't hear an engine start but he has electric cars and ATVs down there, so he might have driven one of those. He was gone a long time, at least an hour and three-quarters. He just got back maybe ten minutes ago. I was so scared I didn't know what to do. I thought he might come for me next."

"How do you get to the basement?"

"The stairs are at the back, just before you reach the kitchen. First door on the right."

"Is there another way in or out?"

"I don't know. I was never down there."

Aiden was about to instruct her to return to her room and lock herself in when he had second thoughts. If things didn't go well, such advice could sign her death warrant. She didn't look capable of a believable poker face. If Michael suspected she'd let Aiden in...

He dug out the fob and handed it to her. "I'm parked behind the garage. Take the Jeep and get as far away from here as you can."

He motioned for her to follow him down to the first floor. The curving staircase was carpeted and they moved with the stealth of mice. The mahogany railing had golden LEDs inset along its lower edge to function as nightlights. They provided just enough illumination to forego the need for the flashlight.

At the bottom, Trish pointed to the hallway leading to the kitchen. He guided her in the opposite direction to the front door. Inset into the adjacent wall was a control panel for the alarm system.

"He gave me the code," she whispered, reaching for the panel.

"No, wait," Aiden said, grabbing her hand. "I have a better idea. Leave the system armed."

She looked confused. "But it'll go off when I open the door."

"I know. So make sure you run like hell to that Jeep. Drive away as fast as you can."

"Maybe you should come with me." She sounded genuinely concerned for his safety.

"I'll be fine."

"Thank you for doing this," she said, giving him a crushing hug.

The embrace surprised him. He'd spent too many recent days under duress, caught up in derangement and violence. The last time he'd experienced human touch unfettered by hidden agendas was when he'd comforted Leah after her nightmare. That had been nearly a week ago. It seemed like forever.

He found himself hugging Trish back with an almost desperate urgency. It took effort to pull away from her.

"Count to twenty," he instructed. "Then open the door and go."

She nodded. Aiden tiptoed toward the back of the chateau. The door to the basement was closed. He went past it into the kitchen and crouched in an alcove beside the refrigerator. It provided a good view of the door. When Michael appeared, Aiden would have him in his sights... providing he didn't instead use a shadow to scope things out. If that occurred, Aiden would have to adjust his plan. Adjust it *how* he couldn't exactly say.

Even though he was ready, the alarm startled him. The pulsing siren was louder than anticipated. He realized it would drown out any footsteps coming from below.

He waited, finger near the trigger. If Michael bore a weapon he'd have to shoot first, gun him down. He'd done it before with the merc, Vesely.

And my first shot missed.

He quelled such negative thoughts. This time his aim would be perfect.

Half a minute passed. The door remained closed.

Something's wrong.

The alarm stopped. The only sound was a lethargic hum oozing from the fridge.

Aiden couldn't just stay here in the kitchen. He crept from his hiding place, still wary of the door opening and Michael lunging out. Dinner plates visible through a glass-fronted cabinet gave him an idea. He took down a stack of plates and set them on the floor in front of the basement door. Opening it would knock them over and serve as an alert.

Easing past the portal, he froze at the sound of a vehicle heading away from the chateau. It must be Trish. He was relieved she'd gotten away.

He waited until the engine sounds faded before moving again. The fridge compressor shut off. The chateau was again as silent as a tomb.

He reached the main hallway. The front door remained wide open. Someone must have deactivated the alarm, either from these controls or another one. The basement probably had a panel.

But if Michael had silenced the alarm, where was he? Waiting for Aiden to venture down into the basement?

He had no intention of doing that. The more he considered it, the more he doubted Michael would just hide down there. Red was too much of an aggressor. He'd go on the offensive.

The logical conclusion was that the basement had another egress, probably an exterior one. That meant Michael had either come back into the chateau through the open front door and was hiding somewhere inside, or had concealed himself outside, waiting for Aiden to show himself.

There was a variant possibility. He might have taken one of the vehicles and raced off in pursuit of Trish. After all, her abrupt departure would be cause for concern.

Aiden rethought his strategy. If Michael indeed had left the basement, Jessie must still be down there. Rescuing her remained the priority.

He retreated toward the kitchen, sweeping his gaze front and back, alert for the slightest movement. He carefully moved the plates away from the door.

There was an odd whirring noise. It lasted only a few seconds.

As best he could determine, it came from upstairs. He inched his way back to the main staircase. Along with ambient starlight through the open front door and the LEDs in the railing, there was enough illumination to outline the steps. But the landing above remained a puddle of darkness.

Had the sound been accidental, something inconsequential like a thermostat tripping a heater? Or had Michael caused it deliberately in an attempt to lure him up there?

Whatever the case, Aiden was through being cautious. Keats' parting words echoed. *Finish it.*

Treading stealthily, he headed up the steps. Halfway there, he paused. The whirring noise returned, again for only an instant. It sounded vaguely familiar yet didn't last long enough to identify a source. But it definitely came from the second floor.

He continued the climb until he was just below the landing.

Drawing a deep breath, he raced up the final few steps, ready to fire.

The hallway was bathed in shadows but clearly deserted. Doors on both sides were closed. A light switch on the wall beckoned. Aiden decided it was time for proper illumination.

He flicked the switch. Nothing happened. The junction box for the lighting was likely in the basement. Had Michael thrown a circuit breaker to keep them in the dark?

The whirring noise returned. This time it didn't end but grew steadily louder. He identified the sound at the same moment he spotted its source.

A drone, a toy of some kind with a grinning monster head. It leaped up from the shadows at the far end of the hallway and flew straight at him.

He swung the machine gun to bat it away. He missed. The toy and its quartet of spinning plastic blades grazed his shoulder as it flew past. Startled, Aiden lunged sideways.

The move saved his life. A shotgun blast ripped into the ceiling above, showering him with plaster.

The shot came from below. He whirled and fired a three-round burst into the darkness at the bottom of the stairs. He glimpsed a figure ducking into a room off the main hallway.

He rushed down the steps, firing more bursts toward the shadowy doorway. Halfway down, he tripped over the drone, which must have been taken out by the shotgun blast. He tried to regain his balance but failed. Head over heels, Aiden tumbled the rest of the way down the staircase.

SIXTY-NINE

Aiden landed hard on his back. Somehow he'd held onto the machine gun. Rolling onto his side he started to rise.

A boot heel slammed into his guts, knocking the wind out of him and putting him flat on his back again. A hand snatched the weapon from his grasp.

A flashlight beam hit his face, momentarily blinding him. When his eyes adjusted, Michael stood over him. The flashlight was attached to the shotgun. It was pointed at Aiden's midsection.

"Aiden Manchester, quiver kid extraordinaire," his captor hissed, smug amusement playing on his face. "I just can't seem to be rid of you."

Michael took a step backward. Aiden sensed he was getting ready to pull the trigger and didn't want to be hit with backspray, namely Aiden's bloody entrails.

Aiden's only chance was manifesting another cleaving. But what had happened on the train had been subconscious. He had no idea how to create a hole into another universe or dimension by willpower.

Maybe like a guardian angel, a cleaving would magically appear the instant Michael pulled the trigger, the possibility of Aiden's death the impetus for its creation. There didn't seem to be much else to hope for. The pistol was tucked in his jacket pocket. But with the shotgun pointed at him, there was no chance to reach it on the sly.

Michael apparently changed his mind about killing Aiden in the chateau, probably concerned there'd be too much mess to clean up. Stepping back a pace, he motioned for Aiden to stand.

"Outside," Michael ordered, motioning with the shotgun.

Aiden walked ahead. The reprieve provided extra moments to contrive an escape. But he couldn't come up with any good ideas. He'd never draw the pistol in time. And spinning around to make a grab for the shotgun was suicidal.

He stepped through the door, walked to the steps at the edge of the porch and halted. In the short time he'd been inside, cloud cover had moved in, hiding much of the starry heavens. The wind had picked up and the air had grown damp. It felt like a storm was coming.

"Keep moving," Michael ordered.

There was no sense prolonging things. If a cleaving was going to save Aiden, better for it to happen now.

He turned, faced his executioner with as much composure as he could muster. "Where are we going?"

Surprisingly, Michael answered. "Not far. A quarry. An old friend of mine is already there. She'll keep you company."

"You know it's over, don't you? Tau knows all about you by now."

Megalomaniac that he was, Michael couldn't help but respond with a triumphant smile.

"Minor setbacks. Let's just say I have the bargaining chip to end all bargaining chips."

Aiden understood. "The quiver. You gave yourself a second infusion and then hid the stone." That explained why Michael had been gone for almost two hours after depositing Jessie in the basement. "Wherever it is, they'll find it."

"Doubtful. Anyway, I'd love to continue this debate but I do have other chores. So please, let's get moving. Unless you prefer being shot where you stand."

He was about to say, *Go ahead, do it*. But wisdom prevailed. There was no guarantee a manifestation would save him. And however long it took to reach the quarry gave him that many extra minutes to generate an escape plan.

Aiden turned back to the steps to comply but froze, startled to see a cleaving. It hung in the air three feet away. He wasn't sure what was more surprising, the giant donut's appearance itself or its position. Instead of forming between Aiden and the shotgun, the cleaving had taken shape *behind* him. Back there, its bullet-ingesting power would do him no good.

"What is that?" Michael demanded.

Had Aiden's subconscious created it? Or was the cleaving a product of Michael's quiver-enhanced abilities. Whatever the case, he wasn't about to explain.

"You tell me," he said, forcing a shrug.

"Step away from it."

A flash of movement, from behind his captor. Jessie, garbed neck to feet in a bizarre Halloween body suit with luminescent blood vessels, charged through the chateau door.

Michael read Aiden's startled look, whirled with the shotgun. He was too late.

Jessie plowed into him, knocking the weapon from his hands. Aiden had an instant to register the fury on her face before their tumbling bodies knocked him backward off the edge of the porch.

Sailing headfirst through the air, his face upturned toward the shadowed skies, he plunged through the center of the cleaving.

SEVENTY

Everything is wrong.

That was Aiden's overall impression of the realm in which he found himself. If this was indeed the shroud, it existed in defiance of all that was familiar and reassuring.

His senses functioned abnormally, jumbled together into confusing and contradictory arrangements. The air was breathable but every inhalation created a splash of garish orange light, momentarily brightening the murky gray clouds he seemed to be floating within.

He *tasted* drumbeats, their volume and rhythm erratic, as if from a percussionist lacking even the most basic ability of keeping time. Unable to feel his own skin, he ran a hand across his face to make sure it was still there. But instead of reassuring flesh, the touch triggered his sense of smell, bringing an array of scents, from lilies and wintergreen to an overpowering odor of undiluted vinegar.

He recalled there was a condition called synesthesia, where a person saw letters or numbers as colors, or heard sounds that induced the feeling of being touched. But if Aiden was experiencing that syndrome, its effects were amplified to an unprecedented level.

There seemed to be no up or down, no left or right, no forward or backward within the gray clouds. He knew instinctively that what he was experiencing was different from what astronauts described when in space. In his case, the normal three dimensions didn't seem to exist at all. He knew that to be true because although he maintained control of his muscles, turning to the left induced the sensation of being turned upside down and facing backward. Other attempts at movement brought similar jarring deviations from what was expected.

Everything is wrong.

And then the breeze came, just as it had when he'd inserted his arm into Grant's cleaving in those Portland woods. The breeze wafted across his body from head to toes.

It turned icy cold. Fear coursed through him as he recalled that earlier experience and what had happened next.

A bizarre creature lunged toward him out of the gray murk. He had a sense of writhing snake-like appendages, no two alike, attached to some bulbous central mass. Before he could even think to move from its path, one of the appendages lashed his right ankle. The pain was similar to what he'd experienced with his arm in Grant's cleaving, like being rubbed with coarse sandpaper. But it hurt worse, enough to cause him to cry out. But instead of sound came a spray of quivering bubbles.

The creature flashed past. Without thinking, Aiden whipped around to follow it, wary of a second attack. But the swift movement sent him tumbling end over end through the gray murk, out of control.

Amid the gyrations he glimpsed another creature, this one even more bizarre. It was a humanoid-shaped thing covered in leathery fur. Instead of a head, a plume of shimmering ice crystals sprouted from its neck. The creature plowed into him with such force that it knocked the wind out of him. He struggled to suck down air as the hit sent him cartwheeling in a new direction, the gyrations increasingly violent.

He felt pressure on his right forearm. A thing resembling a baby seal but with two heads – one at each end – had wrapped itself around the appendage. The impossible creature squeezed his arm like an organic tourniquet, right over his burns.

The pain was intense. He screamed. Again, no sound emerged.

This time his shrieks transmuted into a sickening smell, like rotting garbage.

He tried wrenching the two-headed seal-thing off his arm. But he couldn't get a grip. The creature didn't seem to be composed of solid matter but of jarring musical notes, non-melodic clusters hijacked from some nightmarish chromatic scale.

The seal-thing finally melted into a puddle of goo that streamed away from Aiden's tumbling body. But other creatures attacked. A bat-like insect attached itself to his face and bit his cheeks. Something with talons raked his lower back. A gigantic shark-like monstrosity opened its yawning mouth, ready to swallow Aiden whole. As he frantically batted his hands to keep it away, it shrank to the size of a goldfish, slithered between his lips and lodged in the back of his throat. He tried spitting it out but ended up swallowing it instead. He *saw* the creature race down his esophagus and into his stomach, where it was consumed by roiling acids.

There was no sanity to what was happening to him, only confusion, agony and heightening vertigo from catapulting out of control through the gray murk. He couldn't take much more without being driven mad.

"Where are you?"

It was a woman's voice. She appeared in front of Aiden, upright and motionless relative to his position, close enough to touch. Either she was acrobatically in tandem with his tumbling – a welcome reference point, an icon of sanity – or neither of them were actually in motion. He had no idea which.

There was a plainness about her, not in the physical sense – she was far from homely – but in a way that somehow gave him the sense of a level-headed and practical individual. Short brown hair framed an elfin face with hazel eyes. Dripping wet bangs and a pale yellow robe suggested she'd just stepped from a shower or bath.

"Where are you?" she repeated, this time more forcefully.

Aiden realized he'd misunderstood the intent of her question. She wasn't trying to determine his location. Instead, she wanted to know if *he* knew where he was.

"I'm in the shroud."

Thankfully, the words leaving his mouth were liberated from sensory chaos. He didn't see or smell or taste the syllables. They flowed in normal fashion.

"Have you been instructed?" the woman asked.

"Instructed?"

"Have you received any dispatches?"

"Dispatches?"

Annoyance compressed her lips. "We don't have much time. Parroting me is counterproductive."

"Are you talking about 'Singularity beguiles, transcend the illusion'?"

"Yes! I like that! Succinct, straight to the point. OK, so your first step is to follow the instructions. The second step is to–"

"But I don't know what those instructions mean."

"Yes, you do."

"No, really. I've been hearing those words as far back as I can remember but I've never been able to figure out–"

"There's nothing to figure out." Her annoyance morphed into anger and she gave him a light smack on the forehead. "Don't overthink it, White. You've got the pieces, let them flow together."

"Who are you? How do you know my color?"

"Never mind all that. Want to live?"

"Of course."

"Then pay attention. I'm holding back a wave but I can't protect you for long. That wave's gonna come crashing down any moment now and pour me back into the world. When that happens, all those nasty things swarming around in here will start kicking your butt again. Trust me, you haven't come close to experiencing the worst they have to offer. You won't survive for long."

"OK, I'm listening."

"Good. Again, first step – follow the instructions. Second step – come up with a system."

"A system?"

"Got any hobbies?"

"Hobbies?"

Her scowl could have frozen sunlight. He answered quickly before she could snap at him again or smack him for repeating her words.

"No, I don't have any hobbies. When I was a kid I liked rocketry. I used to fantasize about piloting a spaceship–"

"That'll work. Try imagining a system that uses the various components needed for a successful rocket flight. So, first step, follow the instructions. Second step, create a system. Third and final step, cross over to the other side."

"The other side of what?"

She glared as if he was being willfully ignorant. "The shroud, of course!"

"What's on the other side?"

"No idea, never been. Don't have the chops for it. I'm like the others, strictly a one-trick pony. But you're different, you're the anomaly. If any of us can make the crossing alone, you can."

Aiden suddenly knew her identity. "You're Cyan."

His deduction earned another smack to the forehead, this one harder. "Jeez, White, get it together! Concentrate! Step one, step two, step three. You don't have time to waste."

Her arrogance was pissing him off. It reminded him of the haughty tone Darlene sometimes adopted.

"Why don't you just tell me what I need to know rather than all this three-step bullshit?"

"You're lucky I'm helping you this much."

"And I'm supposed to be grateful?"

She raised her arm to administer a third smack. This time he grabbed her hand before she could follow through. The instant their palms clasped, the sensation was electric.

He *felt* her, felt her very essence. It was like nothing he'd ever experienced before with another human. An aggregate of emotions washed over him – *her* emotions – who she really was beneath perimeter defenses, caustic guard towers and snarky fortifications that he sensed were common to many individuals. He perceived a woman who was passionate, tender and kind, yet also tough, resourceful and resilient. And he caught glimpses into an even deeper level of her being, a realm where her rawest urges and needs bubbled within a quantum broth of ambiguity.

"Enough of this Peeping Tom crap," she hissed, wrenching free of his grip. "I suggest you get to it, do what needs doing."

Her eyes widened with sudden alarm. "Uh-oh, time's up! The wave's coming for me. Remember the steps. And don't forget to–"

She cartwheeled away from him, disappeared into the murk. The wake of her departure revealed a host of those malignant creatures clustering in the distance, orbiting Aiden's position like carnivorous satellites. All too soon they'd begin round two of sanity-smashing attacks.

SEVENTY-ONE

You've got the pieces, let them flow together.

Aiden struggled to figure out what Cyan meant by that. Then he realized he was doing exactly what she'd warned against.

Don't overthink it.

"Singularity beguiles," he whispered. "Transcend the illusion."

This time he didn't dwell on the words or attempt to decipher their meaning. Instead, he stopped trying to ratchet answers through the machinery of intellect, allowed the words to simply wash over him like they did in his green dreams.

Miraculously, a veil was lifted. The phrase echoed with newfound clarity. It was so obvious he was shocked he'd taken this long to comprehend. Maybe such a lucid perspective was only possible within this strange realm of the shroud.

Throughout his life he'd been deceived – beguiled – into believing that he was one person – a singularity – little different from the billions of other humans on the planet. But that assumption was wrong. At a fundamental level of his being, deep down where he floated within his own quantum broth of ambiguity, he was different from everyone else.

He wasn't one person, he was six.

That was the illusion that required transcending.

His impossible birth – his bizarre arrival into that Tau nursery – had endowed him with more than just a six-pronged genetic heritage. He'd been given something beyond mere DNA. His inheritance encompassed the spectrum of abilities the others possessed.

Aiden wasn't a quiver kid.

He was *quiver kids*.

The malignant creatures tightened their orbits. Time was running out.

Step one – follow the instructions.

He'd done that. He'd transcended the illusion. He knew who and what he was.

Step two – create a system. Cyan's words again echoed.

Try imagining a system that uses the various components needed for a successful rocket flight.

At first glance, the instructions seemed too vague to become a workable plan. But surprisingly, the solution came to Aiden in an instant. It was as if he'd been pumped full of some magical drug that created myriad new synapses and neurons, hypercharging his capacity to interconnect disparate thoughts.

The idea of a system was simply an analogue, a way to elucidate his hexagonal persona.

A rocket needs a launch platform from which to blast off.

Green.

The launch platform corresponded to Grant Cho's ability to create a cleaving and enter the shroud. Aiden also possessed that ability. It was what had brought him here.

The rocket needs a propulsion system to thrust it forward.

Red.

Michael's ability to create a shadow and use it to move from place to place in the real world performed a similar function here.

A gyrostabilizer was necessary to keep the rocket from tumbling out of control.

Cyan.

The woman whose real-world name was Meira Hirshfeld had temporarily held back the shroud's sensory-warping monstrosities, stabilizing Aiden, keeping him from being driven mad.

Those monstrosities orbiting him began to swarm. The attack

was imminent. But now he knew how to fight them off.

The rocket needs shielding to protect it against the dangers of the void.

Magenta.

He envisioned one of Jessie's manifestations, aimed it at the nearest creature, the bulbous mass with writhing appendages that had initially attacked.

His chunkie shot forward, growing larger as it closed on its target. At the moment of interception it was big enough to envelop the creature in a gelatinous brown sac. The monstrosity halted, writhing madly within the suffocating manifestation.

Aiden found himself able to create chunkies with machine-gun speed. He sent them hurtling toward the approaching threats. Yet for every creature he repelled, a dozen more emerged from the murk to join the assault. The very act of combating them seemed to increase their numbers.

He needed a better strategy. The solution was obvious. He willed a shadow into existence. Unlike Red's shadows, which were physically separate from Michael's body, Aiden's was inside him, an internalized dynamo, part of his very being.

Propelled by the shadow, he sailed through the shroud at dizzying speed. The attacking creatures were left floundering in his wake.

The ride was exhilarating, and for a time he flew through the murk without any sense of purpose. But Cyan's third step beckoned.

Cross over to the other side.

Problem was, there was nothing to distinguish one part of the murk from another. Where was the other side, which direction?

The rocket needs an instrument that enables the pilot to navigate.

Gold.

That was Bobbie Pinsey's function, or perhaps the entity that spoke through her, and which had served as a kind of navigator to bring Aiden this far.

He listened for Bobbie's voice, expecting it to offer directions.

Instead of words, however, a sinewy stream of golden light flowed away from Aiden. Mentally adjusting the course of his internalized shadow, he aligned it with the wavering beam and headed in that direction.

Aiden couldn't have said how long he traveled. Minutes, hours, days – time itself became too abstract to measure. Eventually, however, the stream petered out. He halted at the spot where it ceased to exist.

The region he was in offered no distinguishing features. The gray murk was the same here as elsewhere. He pondered the dilemma, concluded that the solution must relate to the abilities of the sixth quiver kid, *Blue*.

Problem was, Rodrick Tyler was the one quiver kid he'd never met. Blue had perished in that London apartment building. Other than what Michael had mentioned about his attempts to penetrate the realm beyond the beasts, Aiden knew nothing about him.

But maybe he knew enough. The realm beyond the beasts had to refer to the monsters in the shroud. He considered the problem through the lens of the rocket-system analogue. There was one component of his theoretical spacecraft not yet accounted for.

A landing system.

A memory surfaced from last week when he'd met with Marsdale at that café near Towson University. Aiden had been asking about the other quiver kids and Marsdale had recalled that as toddlers, Blue and Green tended to scrap, as if they had conflicting personalities.

Aiden realized why those particular babies had fought. In terms of their abilities, Blue and Green were polar opposites. Grant Cho's cleavings were an entryway into the shroud. Rodrick Tyler, even through the haze of his addiction, must have sensed that he too could create a cleaving. But his wouldn't have led into the shroud but *out* of it.

But out of it to where?

Aiden had never consciously created a cleaving. But having it happen twice subliminally while he was awake provided a mental template.

It was easier than anticipated. He brought the cleaving into existence by mere force of will.

It looked exactly like the previous ones, a giant chocolate donut with a hole in the center. Although he feared what awaited him on the other side, he told himself it couldn't be worse than the nightmarish beasts swarming here.

Steeling himself, he dove through the hole. At the moment of passage, he found himself wondering what had happened to Michael and Jessie in those moments after they'd slammed into him and knocked him into the shroud.

And then he crossed over and all such concerns became irrelevant.

SEVENTY-TWO

The first thing Aiden noticed was the gratifying tug of gravity pinning his boots to a luxurious carpet of white sand. He stood on a circular island no wider than the length of a school bus, a featureless clump within a turquoise ocean extending to the horizon. Above, pale golden skies devoid of a sun radiated ethereal light. The illumination evoked those first hazy moments of emerging from a pleasant dream. A fortifying breeze wafted air neither too hot nor too cold across his face, prompting him to breathe in great gulps, heavenly and cleansing.

His arms felt strange. It took a moment to realize that the pain of his burns, never entirely vanquished by Rory's pills, was gone. His other aches and bruises had vanished as well.

"We've short-circuited your discomfort and fabricated agreeable surroundings," Aiden heard himself say. *"Best to limit distractions."*

The words startled him. They came from his own mouth and sounded like his own voice. Problem was, he hadn't uttered them. Someone or something was speaking through him.

"We talk, you listen," the mystery voice continued, shaping Aiden's lips like a ventriloquist controlling a dummy. *"Then you talk, we listen. A fairly straightforward process, wouldn't you say?"*

He clamped his mouth shut, trying to will it to stop. Having his vocal cords and facial muscles manipulated like this was incredibly intrusive and disorienting. But his efforts proved futile.

"We realize how strange it must feel. Perhaps Invasion of the Body

Snatchers *anxieties are percolating in your mind. But rest assured, this is not that."*

"Then what *is* this?" he whispered. The words were his own, or at least he thought they were.

"Simply a form of communication dictated by circumstances. Knock knock."

"What?"

"Knock knock."

Aiden shook his head, refusing to engage further.

"Knock knock," the voice repeated a third time, but with such intensity it felt as if his mouth was being violently wrenched open and snapped shut.

"Stop that, all right! I'll play along. Who's there?"

"First doctor."

"First doctor who?"

"The actor William Hartnell. He played the role from 1963 to 1966."

Aiden felt himself smiling. He was confident the expression was his own.

"Not a gut-buster, we'll admit. But a little humor can often serve to quell distress and induce relaxation."

Aiden indeed felt himself beginning to accept the eccentric mode of conversation. It still felt weird but no longer quite as upsetting. Perhaps knock-knock jokes deserved greater respect.

"You keep saying we," he challenged. "There's more than one of you?"

"I am many people, places and things. Don't worry about trying to figure it out. Einstein and Hawking would lose sleep attempting to deduce the physics."

"How is this happening? How are you inside my head?"

"That's complicated too. We can't read your mind, at least not the direct stream of your forefront awareness. Mostly we pick up background material. Tempo and style of your thought patterns, subconscious tidbits from your memories, that sort of thing."

He experienced a sudden revelation. "You're the voice from my green dreams, the one who spoke through Bobbie Pinsey."

"'Singularity beguiles, transcend the illusion.' Those words served their ultimate purpose. They led you here."

"But why couldn't you have just–"

"I'm sure you have numerous questions. But there's a limit to how long you can remain. Before your time runs out, we need to focus on getting you to understand the big picture."

He nodded, then wondered if they could understand gestures.

"Ages ago, there were two fundamental realms of existence. For simplicity's sake, let's refer to them as Reality – the spacetime you normally occupy – and Elementary, which is our home and the place you are presently situated.

"Back then, intelligent beings on both sides could cross in either direction with relative ease. But then the Corruption appeared, a vile phase of existence that was neither Reality nor Elementary. It imposed itself between our two realms, which meant that anyone making the crossing had to pass through it."

"The shroud," he whispered. "Those grotesque monsters."

"The Corruption made it exceedingly difficult for we of Elementary to cross over to your side, and impossible for you of Reality to reach our side. That was a bad thing. Interaction between Reality and Elementary is necessary to keep both sides healthy and vibrant."

Aiden became aware of something. The island he stood on, originally the diameter of a school bus, was gradually shrinking. It was now closer to the length of a delivery van.

"What's happening?"

"Diminishment has begun. We don't have much time. Bear with me and try not to interrupt."

He nodded.

"Balance needed to be reconstituted, a way found for omnidirectional crossing to be restored. With great effort we managed to send messengers from Elementary into Reality, programming them to seek out worlds where intelligent life existed or was likely to develop. One of these messengers landed on Earth some seventy thousand of your years ago."

"The quiver stone."

"A messenger that comes in contact with nascent intellects engenders

CHRISTOPHER HINZ   345

the manifesting ability, but always in one of six different ways. That deliberate partitioning was done to attempt to inhibit any one individual from becoming too powerful and succumbing to megalomania. A single individual with enhanced capacities or resources too often craves superiority over fellow members of the species. That almost always proves detrimental to civilizations."

"Absolute power corrupts absolutely," Aiden whispered. Considering what Michael had become – a maniac out to conquer the world – such partitioning seemed prudent.

"We hoped that by creating sextets, the six individuals would realize they needed to work together and combine their abilities in order to pass through the Corruption and cross over to our side."

Aiden became aware the island had contracted even further. It was now barely a car length in diameter. He couldn't actually see it shrinking. The contraction seemed to be happening in a way his senses failed to register.

"Unfortunately, no sextet from any intelligent species within Reality has displayed the level of cooperation necessary to reach Elementary. The individuals of every sextet – and there have been many – inevitably end up competing with one another in a bid to become all-powerful."

For the first time, Aiden sensed hesitation creep into the voice.

"That fact may indicate an essential flaw in our understanding of Reality."

The island was now barely the length of a motorcycle and seemed to be shrinking at an alarming rate. What would happen when there was no place left for him to stand?

"But that flaw also may produce an unanticipated solution, a way to restore the proper interaction between Reality and Elementary. The fact is, you, Aiden Manchester, are the first intelligence to make a successful crossing since the Corruption appeared.

"No sextet has ever conceived an immaculate conception such as yourself. For reasons unknown and by methods inexplicable, the sextet on your world brought you into existence. Beyond that, nearly everything about your creation remains a mystery to us. All we know for certain is that you have the potential to become–"

The island disappeared. There was no longer anything beneath Aiden's feet supporting him.

He fell.

SEVENTY-THREE

He could see and hear nothing. It felt as if his body was being squeezed through sets of rollers on some grotesque assembly line, flattened into impossibly thin two-dimensional wafers. Each trip through another set of the rollers elicited outpourings of emotion. He cycled through bouts of mad laughter and helpless weeping, and an array of other feelings resistant to characterization.

Suddenly he was through the rollers and again in freefall, plunging downward. Feet first he dropped, his speed increasing at an alarming rate. Far below, another donut hole took shape. He was heading straight for it.

Through the new cleaving he could see Michael and Jessie from high above. They were at the edge of the chateau porch where he'd left them, clawing and kicking and punching one another, trying to get the upper hand. Had their fight been transpiring during the entire time Aiden had been gone? It seemed unlikely. Time flowed at a different rate within the shroud and within Elementary. Maybe back here only a few moments had elapsed since he'd been hurtled into the cleaving.

He reached the donut hole, plunged through it. He swung his legs to one side to spare Jessie a direct hit and braced for what he sensed would be a violent impact. Entering the cleaving somehow braked his fall. But he was still descending at a good clip when his boots plowed into Michael's chest.

It was a satisfying hit on many levels.

Michael catapulted off the porch. His head cracked the railing and he landed on his back at the bottom of the steps. The collision threw Aiden sideways into Jessie. The two of them slammed the ground in a heap.

Aiden got up. His left side felt a bit tender from the landing but the fall didn't seem to have caused any other injuries. However, the pain from his burns and previous aches and bruises had returned.

He craned his head skyward. The cleaving he'd fallen through was gone. Cloud cover had increased; the air had continued to cool and dampen. Thunder rumbled in the distance. The storm was close.

Jessie scrambled to her feet, wide-eyed with surprise. "Where'd you go? What was that thing, that weird hole?"

"Long story. What's with the Halloween getup?"

"All I could find to put on."

Aiden found it disturbing that, even without a mask, the devilish outfit seemed to suit her.

They checked on Michael. He was alive but out cold. The back of his head was bloody from bouncing off the stair railing.

"I couldn't find the quiver stone anywhere," Jessie said. "I checked the basement but I don't think it's down there."

Aiden explained about Michael having left the chateau for nearly two hours, presumably to hide the quiver after having given himself a second infusion. Jessie didn't take the news well.

"Where is it?" she demanded, grabbing Michael's shoulders and shaking him. "Wake up, you son of a bitch!"

"I don't think he'd tell us even if he was conscious."

"Then I'll beat it out of him!"

Her face contorted and she pounded her fists against Michael's chest. "Tell me, goddammit! Where is it?"

What earlier had been mere yearning for another infusion seemed to have degenerated into desperate craving. Jessie looked like an addict in need of a fix.

Aiden saw no reason to stop her. Attacking an unconscious man might get some of the rage out of her system before he broke the *really* bad news to her. Seeking a second infusion was a fool's errand. Even if she found the quiver stone it would do her no good. She and Michael, and probably Grant as well, were driven by an erroneous belief.

He couldn't have said how he knew that. But he was certain it was true.

The carnage instigated by Michael – the killing of Blue, the Tau Nine-One assault, Aiden's torture, all the rest of it – was for naught. A second infusion would convey no new abilities. The sole purpose of quiver was to give the six of them an opportunity to work together, make the crossing into Elementary as a harmonious sextet. Cooperation, not competition. But in their cases, either consciously or unconsciously, they'd rejected that idea.

Could such rejection, in some fantastic time-warping way, have been the impetus for the original appearance of the Corruption in the distant past? Were Reality-based concepts of the temporal – human concepts – fundamentally flawed?

However intriguing such notions, and as much as he sensed an underlying validity, there were more important concerns at the moment. He returned his attention to Jessie. She continued to pound and shake Michael, as if her fury would somehow awaken him.

Aiden wanted to tell her that she needed to find a way to transcend her anger. But now clearly wasn't the time. She wasn't ready to hear it.

Perhaps she never would be.

SEVENTY-FOUR

Birdsboro was unseasonably cool this third Saturday in August, welcome conditions for Aiden's late afternoon run. Dark clouds were churning to the west, however. A storm was blowing in.

He sprinted along the shoulder of Route 724, went under the railroad bridge and hooked a right to access the Schuylkill River Trail. Heading west, he was soon enveloped by forest. The trees were mainly deciduous, unlike the Montana wilderness with its rich diversity of evergreens. These Pennsylvania forests would be swept into autumn soon, the leaves changing into vivid hues before their fall.

It had been a relatively calm three months since *the week*, Aiden's tag for those seven momentous days, from the Thursday morning when he'd learned of his father's hidden safe to the following Wednesday evening at Michael's chateau when he and Jessie had been arrested.

The interrogations that followed had been intense: good cop/ bad cop encounters with DOD and Homeland Security agents in unadorned rooms at several locations. Aiden had remained steadfast throughout the grillings, giving the interrogators an honest account of the week's events, at least up to a point. His major digression from the truth – flat-out lies, actually – involved the manifestations and the supernatural-type events he'd witnessed or experienced.

The interrogators apparently had learned about chunkies from questioning Jessie and the others. He suspected that Maurice Pinsey had been the most talkative. But Aiden had admitted only to being a quiver kid, and denied possessing any extraordinary abilities.

That hadn't gone over well with the grim-faced men and women in those rooms, always on the other side of a table from him, on occasion looking like they wanted to leap across the gap and beat the crap out of him. But, other than the occasional mild slap or shove, they'd curbed their most aggressive instincts. No waterboarding, no truth serums. Most of their threats had been verbal and centered on Aiden being sent to prison for a very long time if he didn't come clean. But considering everything he'd experienced over the course of *the week*, he'd been unafraid and hadn't allowed them to intimidate him. And he'd eventually learned to counter their threats with a subtle one of his own.

"I just want to put this entire incident behind me. The last thing any of us wants is a media circus."

None of the interrogators admitted it, but Aiden could tell they were uneasy whenever he uttered those words, the implication being that he'd go public if pushed. Officials at the highest levels of the government still considered quiver, with its cryptic properties and unknown potential, off limits. And although the experiment with the babies was far enough in the past so that political blowback wouldn't unseat the current administration – per political expediency, predecessors would be blamed – public uproar about the experiment was not something any president, legislator, or Pentagon or Homeland Security official wanted to face.

Of course, the government could elect to go full-blown nasty and make Aiden and others who knew too much disappear. He didn't think they'd go that far, but to dissuade them from the notion he'd hinted that the whole story would automatically be released to the media should anything happen to him. His fearless attitude helped sell the bluff, and on the third day, release orders came down from on high, pending his signature on a top-secret nondisclosure agreement that swore him to secrecy about the attack and anything related to quiver. Since he had no intention of talking about those things anyway, the price of freedom had been bearable.

As for the train attack, too many individuals had been involved to keep it under wraps. The government sprang leaks and the "Battle in Montana" was featured for several news cycles, putting Tau Nine-One under the spotlight. But the spin-doctors ultimately triumphed, and the government's cover story held: the attack had been planned by a Tau employee with a grudge. Whether by nefarious behind-the-scenes action or simply Washington's good fortune, blaming Héloise Hoke, the daughter of disgraced Colonel Jenkins, had been a winning move.

So far she hadn't been found and therefore couldn't be questioned. Agents had traced her as far as Mexico City before the trail went cold. Supposedly.

The interrogators wanted very badly to question Michael de Clerkin. But he hadn't regained consciousness from slamming his head into that railing. The last Aiden had heard, he was being kept alive through a medically induced coma.

Despite weeks of extensive searching over hundreds of thousands of wilderness acres, using high-tech tools ranging from drone and satellite scans to overflights with lidar and ground-penetrating radar, no clues to the location of the missing quiver had yet been unearthed. The storm that had pounded the area shortly after Aiden's return from Elementary had wiped away tire tracks, footprints and other forensic evidence of where Michael might have hidden it.

Perhaps that was just as well. Considering the trouble quiver had caused, Aiden figured it might not be such a bad thing if the stone remained lost. Maybe someone would uncover it again in another seventy thousand years.

The searchers did find the gravesite of a woman who'd gone missing a while back. If and when Michael awoke, he could be charged with her death. Then again, it was unlikely the government would allow him within a thousand miles of a courthouse.

Aiden was prohibited from contacting Keats, Rory and Chef. He had no intention of pushing the envelope and seeing just how serious the government was about putting him behind bars for violating the nondisclosure agreement. Besides, he had a hunch that everyone involved in the Battle in Montana would be under surveillance, their phones and computers tapped.

Word of their fate reached him anyway. Two weeks ago, an innocuous spam email from an unknown address had arrived at the same time as a prepaid phone was mysteriously left at Darlene's back door. The phone came loaded with the app Keats had used to access Icy Ned's information about Maurice Pinsey. Aiden used the app to unveil the email's encrypted data.

It was a letter from Keats. Among other things, that was how Aiden learned of the fruitless search for the quiver.

Keats had recovered from his injuries and was back working at the GAO. He, Rory and Chef also had endured long interrogations. But since the three of them were decorated ex-soldiers whose actions at the bridge had disrupted Michael's plan, they'd been released too after signing nondisclosure agreements. Although the government wasn't about to give them medals for taking down a band of vicious mercs, they did provide Rory with a new prosthetic limb. According to Keats, he'd promptly modified it.

The helicopter pilot and the other surviving mercs had been caught but let go as well, their continuing silence bought with the promise of no jail time.

Keats' letter concluded with the latest on Jessie. After her release she'd returned to Nebraska, where she'd been scrapping with insurance adjusters trying to deny paying the policy on her burned home. Although government agents had swooped in and removed all traces of the slain mercs and her basement experiments, the insurance company was claiming that the fire was arson, with Jessie the likely culprit.

Aiden wished her well.

The wind picked up. A pile of fallen leaves swirled into a vortex on the trail before him. The air dampened. Soon the rain would come.

He kept running.

Thankfully, he was no longer plagued by subconsciously created chunkies, or by the green dream and its signature phrase. But some nights when he was drifting off, in those twilight moments between awareness and slumber, those last words from Elementary washed over him.

All we know for certain is that you have the potential to become...

Become what? Did the rest of that truncated sentence contain a more profound message? Was there still some unknown destiny he was slated to fulfill? It seemed likely. After all, he was the anomaly.

But he was no longer a plurality as he'd been within the shroud and within Elementary, cognizant of his unique six-part consciousness. Passage through that last donut hole into Reality had refracted him back into a singularity – sort of the reverse of how white light through a prism dispersed into a rainbow of colors.

Whenever he considered the analogy he was reminded of Cyan, whose intercession had enabled him to survive the shroud, the Corruption. In retrospect, the rumor he'd heard from Grant, that she'd become some kind of monk, seemed to make sense. That brief, tantalizing glimpse he'd been afforded into Meira Hirshfeld's deepest self suggested that a monastic life of spirituality and enlightenment would prove attractive to her. Someday, he hoped to encounter her in the flesh here in the real world.

Of all the quiver kids, he sensed they had the most in common.

Naturally, there was a way for Aiden to possibly learn more about her, as well as answer many of the other questions still haunting him. He could create another cleaving, dive back into the Corruption and cross over into Elementary.

Not today.

He'd been mumbling that rejoinder frequently over these past months, whenever he found himself seriously considering a return. Eventually, he might indeed do it. But for now, the reassuring solidity of a normal life here on planet Earth with Darlene and Leah was all he desired.

That life incorporated some major changes. He'd been in freefall for way too many years. Since coming back, he'd stopped drinking, other than an occasional beer or a glass of wine. He'd also gained the confidence to talk himself into a new job, one with more responsibility and greater promise. Beyond that, he was seriously considering a return to college to get a degree. Maybe in philosophy. Maybe physics.

"Character building," Darlene called the change she saw in him. She sensed his reluctance to talk about what had happened during his time away and hadn't pressed him, even though she obviously suspected he'd been involved in what had transpired at Tau Nine-One. But for now she was satisfied that whatever her adoptive sibling had undergone, it served as a healing experience.

The skies unleashed. Waves of droplets splattered Aiden's cheeks. He raised the hood of his sweatshirt, turned his back on the storm and sprinted for home.

ACKNOWLEDGMENTS

A hearty shout-out to the dedicated editorial nucleus of Angry Robot Books, Eleanor, Gemma and Sam, whose efforts qualitatively improved this novel. As always, a huge thanks to Etan, publisher, entrepreneur and maestro of mind sports, and to Mark at Trident Media Group, whose resolute efforts ensure smooth sailing.

CHAPTER 1

The assignor had a hunch the meeting would be unpleasant. He wondered if the young woman entering his office already knew the outcome.

LeaMarsa de Host wore a black skirt and sweater that looked woven from rags, clothing surely lacking even basic hygiene nanos. Whether she was making some sort of anti-Corporeal statement or whether she always dressed like a drug-addled misfit from the Helio Age was not apparent from her file.

The assignor smiled and rose to shake her hand. She ignored the courtesy. He sat and motioned her to the chair across from his desk.

"Welcome to Pannis Corp, LeaMarsa."

"Thrilled to be here."

Her words bled sarcasm. No surprise. She registered highly alienated on the Ogden Tripartite Thought Ordination. Most members of the bizarre minority to which she belonged were outliers on the OTTO scale.

"Would you like something to drink?" he asked, motioning to his Starbucks 880, a conglomeration of tubes and spouts. The dispenser was vintage twenty-first-century, a gift from the assignor's wife for his thirtieth birthday. "Five hundred and one varieties, hot or cold."

"I'll have a juggernaut cocktail with Europa cryospice. Hold the cinnamon."

"I'm sorry, that one's not in the menu."

She grimaced with disappointment, which of course was the

whole point of requesting such a ridiculously exotic drink.

He unflexed his wafer to max screen size and toggled through her file. An analysis of her test results appeared.

"The Pannis researchers at Jamal Labs were most impressed with your talents. You are indeed a gifted psionic."

She flopped into the chair and leaned back. An erratic thumping reverberated through the office. It took the assignor a moment to realize she was kicking the underside of his desk with the toe of her flats.

He contained his annoyance. Someday, he hoped to have enough seniority to avoid working with her type. And this young woman in particular...

She was thin, with long dark hair hanging to her shoulders, grossly uncouth. His preadolescent daughter still wore her hair that long, but who beyond the teen years allowed such draping strands, and LeaMarsa de Host was twenty three. Her skin was as pale as the froth of a milkshake and her eyes hard blue gems, constantly probing. She smelled of natural body scents. He didn't care for the odor.

"Let's cut to the chase," she said. "Do I get a starship?"

"At this time, Pannis Corp feels that such an assignment would not be in the best interests of all involved."

"What's the matter? Afraid?"

He'd been trained to ignore such a response. "Pannis has concluded that your particular range of abilities would not be conducive to the self-contained existence of stellar voyaging."

"What the hell does that mean?"

"It boils down to a matter of cooperation."

"Haven't I cooperated with your tests? I took two months out of my life. I practically lived in those hideous Jamal Labs of yours."

"And we're certainly pleased by your sacrifice. But when I'm speaking of cooperation, I'm referring to factors of which you may not even be conscious. Psionic abilities exist primarily in strata beneath the level of daily awareness."

"Really? Never would have guessed."

He paved over the snark. "You may wish to behave cooperatively but find your subconscious acting in contrary ways. And trust me, a year or more in a starship is a far cry from what you underwent in our labs."

"You're speaking from experience?"

"Actually, no. I've never been farther out than Luna."

"Then you don't know what you're talking about."

She stared at him so intently that he worried she was trying to read his mind. The fear was irrational. Still, like most of the population, he was categorized as a psionic receptor, susceptible to psychic forces, albeit mildly.

He forced attention back to the wafer.

"Pannis is willing to offer you a choice of more than a dozen positions, all with good salary ranges. And the benefits of working for a mega are remarkable."

"What's the most exciting position?"

"Exciting? Why, I don't know." He tapped the wafer, scanned pages. "Ah yes, here's one that sounds quite exciting. Archeological assistant, digging up nineteenth century frontier cultures in the American southwest in search of lost caches of gold and silver."

"Blizzards?"

He looked up from the wafer. "Pardon?"

"Do you have anything with blizzards? I like storms."

Storms? Dear god, these people were a trial, and more trouble than they were worth. Still, he understood the economics behind the current frenzy among Pannis and the other megas to employ them.

Only last week the latest discovery attributed to one of LeaMarsa's kind had been announced, a metallic compound found in the swamps of the dwarf planet Buick Skylark. The mega funding that expedition, Koch-Fox, was touting the compound as key ingredient for a new construction material impervious to the effects of sunlight.

He scanned more pages on the wafer. "Yes, here's a position where storms factor in. The south polar regions, an industrial classification. You would utilize your abilities to locate ultra-deep mineral deposits."

"While freezing my butt off? No thanks. Anyway, no need to read further. I've made my decision."

"Excellent."

"I choose a starship."

The assignor couldn't hide his disappointment. "Again, you must understand that a starship is not in the best interests of…"

He trailed off as the door slid open. An immaculately dressed man with dark hair and a weightlifter's build strolled in. He wore a gray business suit with matching headband. A pewter-colored vest rose to his chin and a dwarf lion perched on his shoulder, a male judging by its thick mane. The cat couldn't have weighed more than two pounds. A genejob that small cost more than the assignor earned in a year.

The man was a high-ranking Pannis official, the InterGlobal Security VP, a rank rarely seen on this floor of the Manhattan office complex. His name was Renfro Zoobondi and he was hardcore, an up-and-comer known and feared throughout the corporation. The fact that Zoobondi was here filled the assignor with dread.

A black mark, he thought bitterly. *I'm not handling this situation correctly and my file will soon reflect that.*

Zoobondi must have been monitoring their conversation, which suggested that LeaMarsa was even more important than her dazzling psionic ratings indicated. The VP was here to rectify the assignor's failure.

He won't come right out and criticize me. That's not the Pannis way. He'll say I've done a fair job under difficult circumstances and then see to it I'm given a black mark.

Zoobondi sat on the edge of the assignor's desk and faced LeaMarsa. The diminutive lion emitted a tinny growl.

"You are being uncooperative, Mizz de Host." The VP's voice was deep and commanding.

She shrugged. He regarded her for a long moment then turned to the assignor.

"Access vessel departures. Look for a minor mission, something leaving within the next few weeks."

The assignor did as asked while cloaking surprise. Is he actually considering such an unstable individual for a starship?

Zoobondi wagged a finger at LeaMarsa. "Understand me, young lady, you will not be given a major assignment. But Pannis is prepared to gratify."

The assignor called up the file. He scanned the lengthy list, narrowed down the possibilities.

"The *Bolero Grand*, two-year science project, galactic archaeology research. Crew of sixty-eight, including two lytics—"

"Perhaps something smaller," Zoobondi suggested, favoring her with a smile. "We want Mizz de Host to enjoy the special bonding that can develop aboard vessels with a minimal number of shipmates."

"Yes, of course. How about the *Regis*, crew of six? Fourteen-month mission to Pepsi One in the HD 40307 system. They're laying the groundwork for new colonies and request a psionic to help select the best geographic locations on the semi-liquid surface."

"Perfect. Does that work for you, LeaMarsa?"

"No. Sounds boring."

"It does, doesn't it," Zoobondi said with a smile. "I'd certainly get bored traipsing across a world of bubbling swamps looking for seismic stability."

The assignor was confused. Something was going on here that he didn't understand. If Zoobondi wanted her to accept the *Regis* mission, he would have made it sound more attractive.

"Any other possibilities?" the VP asked.

"Yes. Starship *Alchemon*, eighteen-month mission to the Lalande 21185 system. Investigation of an anomalous biosignature discovered by an unmanned probe. Crew of eight, including a lytic."

Zoobondi shook his head. "I don't think so."

"Why not?" LeaMarsa demanded.

He hesitated, as if working on a rebuttal. The assignor understood.

He wants her to accept this mission. He's leading her along. The assignor had been with Pannis long enough to recognize applied reverse psychology, which meant that this meeting with LeaMarsa was part of a high-level setup.

It was possible he wouldn't get a black mark after all. "Departing lunar orbit in seven days," he continued, following the VP's lead. "They'll be landing on the fifth planet, Sycamore, where the probe found evidence of bacterial life. It's a violently unstable world, locked in perpetual storms."

He glanced up at LeaMarsa, expecting the presence of storms to produce a reaction. He wasn't disappointed.

"Sounds perfect. I want it."

The VP adopted a thoughtful look, as if pretending to consider her demand. The dwarf lion rubbed its mane against his ear, seeking attention. Zoobondi ignored the animal.

"Where do I sign?" LeaMarsa pressed.

"Would you please wait in the lobby."

She strode out with that stiffly upright gait that seemed to characterize so many psionics. Renfro Zoobondi held his tongue until the door whisked shut behind her.

"You'll take care of the details, make sure she's aboard?"

It wasn't really a question.

"Yes sir. But I do have some concerns."

The assignor hesitated, unsure how forthright he should be. This was obviously a setup. For reasons above his security clearance, Pannis wanted LeaMarsa on that ship. But dropping a powerful and moody psionic into such a lengthy mission fell outside the guidelines of standard policy, not to mention being enticing bait to some Corporeal prosecuting attorney looking to make a name. He didn't want to be the Pannis fall guy if things went wrong.

"Sir, I feel obligated to point out that LeaMarsa de Host is no ordinary psionic. The Jamal Labs report classifies her in the upper one-ten-thousandth of one percent for humans with such abilities."

"Your point?"

"There are a number of red flags. And the OTTO classifies her as–"

"Most psionics have issues. A long voyage might do her good. Bring her out of her shell."

"She suffers from the occasional loss of consciousness while wide awake, a condition the Jamal researchers term 'psychic blackouts.' Even more disturbing, she's been known to inflict bodily harm on herself through self-flagellation or other means. Presumably, she does this as an analgesic against some unknown emotional torment originating in childhood."

The VP looked bored. He stroked the lion's back. The animal hissed.

The assignor tabbed open another part of LeaMarsa's file and made a final stab at getting his concerns across. "Sir, to quote the Jamal analysts, 'LeaMarsa de Host is a disturbing jumble of contradictory emotions. It is imperative that careful consideration be given to placement in order to prevent–'"

"The *Alchemon* is one of the newer ships, isn't it? Full security package?"

"Yes sir, the works. Anti-chronojacker system with warrior pups. And of course, a Level Zero Sentinel."

"A very safe vessel. I don't believe she'll cause any problems that the ship and crew can't handle."

The assignor knew he had to take a stand. "Sir, putting someone like her aboard that ship could create serious issues. And wouldn't it make more sense for her vast talents to be utilized on a mission here on Earth, something with the potential for a more lucrative payoff?"

"Better for her to be first given a less critical assignment to gauge how she handles team interaction."

"Yes sir, that makes sense, but–"

Zoobondi held up a hand for silence. He slid off the edge of the desk and removed a safepad from his pocket, stuck the slim disk to the wall. A faint, low-pitched hum filled the office as the safepad scrambled localized surveillance, rendering their conversation impervious to eavesdropping. The lion squirmed on the VP's shoulder, bothered by the sound.

"We're entering a gray area here," Zoobondi said. "Trust me when I say it's best you don't pursue this subject."

The assignor could only nod. If things indeed went bad, he likely would be the one to take the fall. And there was nothing he could do about it.

Zoobondi smiled and threw him a bone. "I believe you're due for a promotional review next month."

"Yes sir."

"Everything I've read suggests you're doing a fine job. Keep up the good work and I'm certain that your promotion will come through."

The VP deactivated and pocketed the safepad and strolled out the door. The assignor was relieved he was gone. There were dark tales murmured about Renfro Zoobondi. He was ruthlessness personified, supposedly having arranged for the career sabotage of g men and women standing in the path of his climb up the corporate ladder. There was even a rumor that for no other reason than the twisted joy of it, he'd killed a man in armor-suit combat.

The assignor returned to the file on the *Alchemon* expedition. Reading between the lines, he wondered whether researching a primordial lifeform was really the mission's primary purpose. Could Pannis have a different agenda, a hidden one?

He closed the file. If that was the case, there was little to be done. He was midlevel management, an undistinguished position within a massive interstellar corporation. Going against the wishes of a man like Renfro Zoobondi was career suicide. The assignor had a wife and young daughter to consider. What would happen to them if he lost his job and possibly fell into the ranks of the "needful majority," those billions who were impoverished and struggling? It wasn't so farfetched, had happened to a good friend only last month.

That night, the assignor slept fitfully. In the morning he awoke covered in sweat. He'd been in the clutches of a terrifying nightmare.

Thankfully, he couldn't recall any details.

Get your Science Fiction, Fantasy and WTF
kicks, all from Angry Robot!

Check out our website to find out more
angryrobotbooks.com

Science Fiction, Fantasy and WTF?!

@angryrobotbooks

We are Angry Robot

angryrobotbooks.com